Wicked Words 9
A Black Lace Short-Story Collection

Other Black Lace short-story collections:

Wicked Words 9
A Black Lace Short-Story Collection
Edited by Kerri Sharp

BLACKLACE

Black Lace books contain sexual fantasies.
In real life, always practise safe sex.

This edition published in 2004 by
Black Lace
Thames Wharf Studios
Rainville Road
London W6 9HA

Design by Smith & Gilmour, London
Printed and bound by Mackays of Chatham PLC

ISBN 0 352 33860 1

Contents

Introduction and Newsletter

I'm often asked 'what makes an ideal *Wicked Words* story?' I think good characterisation is the most important factor in the mix, as this is what hooks the reader and sets the scene for convincing and arousing sex scenes. Women tend to require their erotic fiction characters to be more believable than the pneumatic nymphets of men's mags. A little depth and a lot of attitude goes a long way. Great popular fiction characters should jump off the page as recognisable personalities. There are many characters in this ninth collection of *Wicked Words* who do just that – whose dialogue is sharp and sassy, even though their motivations may not always be honourable.

We kick off with great piece of pulp noir Americana featuring a dangerous babe that James M Cain would've been proud of. We then hop from the Californian desert to the lingerie department of a very British department store – where a certain Mr Fosdyke, the store manager, is about to have his authority undermined by a very saucy minx making off with a lacy little something. Then it's off to Dorset to indulge in the exquisitely crafted rustic shenanigans of *The Woodlanders*. This is one of my favourite *Wicked Words* stories of all time. The subtle combination of malevolence and humour is a delight, and really proves the 'less is more' rule by eschewing anatomical detail and concentrating on the transgressive element that is essential to good erotic writing. Actually, this is *great* erotic writing.

However, *Wicked Words* is a broad church in terms of style and content – and after we leave the mannered and cultured lifestyle of Miss Charmond, we plunge into a world populated by a dazzling array of characters and sexualities. There's some wonderful foot fetishism explored in *Bootblack* and then again in *Foot on the Line*, which has to be our first Canadian lesbian tennis-girl/jock story – and very saucy and liberating it is too. We have a wonderful pagan witchcraft setting for *Wytchfinder*, which is evocative of Piers Haggard's marvellous movie, *Blood on Satan's Claw*, and features a fantastic scene of repressed religious lusts. It gets better and better with every swish of the cane in *Six of the Best*, and there's a real treat for those of you who have always wondered what 'dogging' is in *Man's Best Friend*, where a 'normal' woman becomes a naughty little doggie called Rover. You have to read it to believe it! *Wheels on Fire* is an example of the best and bravest of contemporary writing anywhere to deal with the complex and controversial issue of sex and people with disabilities. There's also the best of down-to-earth raw sex in *Charlotte Meets her Match* – one for the Rugby fans among you – and in *Signal Failure*, a horny story of sex on the railways that features characters who grab you instantly and who are no strangers to a bit of dirty humour. Before I go, mention must be made of *Beverley's Pastime*. If anyone knows of a worse bitch than Beverley (apart from the Black Lace editor of course), then my commiserations go out to you! She may be nasty, but boy, you can't help reading just how nasty she's going to be next. And getting a sneaky peak inside the head of someone very different from yourself is exactly what good characterisation is all about.

* * *

That's all for now. There is never space to mention all the stories but I'd like to say a big thanks to everyone who has contributed to this volume. *Wicked Words 10* will be a celebration of the best of *Wicked Words* so far: an editor's choice of the hottest, best-written and most imaginative stories, and after that we will be putting together themed collections, the first of which will be 'sex in the office' or 'sex at work'. I'll be looking for surprises, great dialogue and, of course, engaging characters!

Salute!
Kerri Sharp
October 2003

We are always looking for talented new writers who know how to entertain and arouse their readers. If you think you could write for Black Lace please get hold of our guidelines by sending a large SAE to

Black Lace Guidelines
Virgin Books
Thames Wharf Studios
Rainville Road
London W6 9HA

If you are sending mail from the United States please bear in mind that only British stamps can be used for return postage. Alternatively you can read the guidelines at www.blacklace-books.co.uk

Desert Fever Karina Moore

Kirsty Mae Blade had been born with guile. Just as well, she always thought, because she hadn't been born with a whole hell of a lot else. Born into the wrong life on the wrong side of town to the wrong do-gooder parents, guile had been her ticket out of many a tricky childhood situation. Then her teenage years yielded more riches – no adolescent angst or pimples for Kirsty Mae, no sir, just delicious pert breasts, long colt-like legs, fresh smooth skin, and eyes as big and blue as a summer sky. And her twenties brought along the final weapons in her arsenal: colt-like became sleek, fresh became luminous, cheekbones emerged from her baby-doll face, and a knowing sensuality danced in her big blue eyes. She discovered the self-serving merits of charm. And as always there was guile. What it all mounted up to was one lethal package. Self-absorbed, artful, enchanting dynamite!

All of these attributes had stood her in amazingly good stead as she worked with commitment towards the life she craved, and now here she was, at age 29, rich, secure, living the right life on the right side of town. Married to citrus millionaire Nathan Blade, her home was a swanky mansion in Riverside, California, and she had date palms to look onto from her bedroom window, where it used to be stinky backyards.

Nathan had been the coup de grâce in her life plan. Handsome for a man of 55, fit, athletic, successful enough to make her blink dollar signs, Nathan was categorically The One, and she'd homed in on him with marksman-like precision. She shone. She sparkled. She enthralled. Nathan Blade hadn't stood a chance. His middle-aged wife had stood even less, and was speedily dispatched to make way for lovely Kirsty Mae.

So here she was, at age 29, rich, secure, living in a swanky mansion, married to Nathan Blade ... and bored. Bored beyond reason.

Enter one Joe Marks. Who was as far from boring as any man could be. Who was the reason she was jeopardising everything she'd worked so damn hard to achieve and had her speeding over to meet him faster than a fire chasing gasoline. If the idea were not so ridiculous, Kirsty Mae thought she might even be in love.

She pondered that preposterous thought as she pressed her foot down hard on the gas, and hit a burning trail from town into desert land, heading with a zing for the Coachella Valley and the Pioneer Hotel. Mid-afternoon, and the parking lot in front of the hotel was almost empty, which suited Kirsty Mae just fine. Adultery was best left unseen, especially with so much to lose. She glided to a halt, stepped from her car and made her way to Room 105. Her heels clicked daintily on the outside timber decking while her heart knocked a good deal less daintily against the inside of her ribcage.

As always the door was unlocked. She pushed against it and stepped inside, onto a deep champagne-coloured carpet. It was spotless and expensive. So was the rest of the room – Kirsty Mae was way past slumming. Her gaze washed with satisfaction over the king-side bed towards the double French doors and their sunbaked desert outlook. Behind her she heard the door click quietly shut, and the subtle turn of the key. She felt his touch on her shoulder and his breath warm on the back of her neck as he leaned to her ear and murmured, 'You're late.'

'Nathan took forever to go out,' she murmured back.

'Nathan should be more considerate,' he said, trailing his fingers down her bare upper arm.

'You'd think so,' she smiled, as she let herself slowly be turned around. On the first occasion she'd met him, her stomach had literally cartwheeled. Then, it had been a novel and surprising sensation for Kirsty Mae. Not any more. It had happened every time she saw him thereafter, and now was no exception. Joe Marks had the ability to move her, like no one had ever been able to move her before.

He leaned back casually, one heavy-booted foot pressed against the wall, his gaze trailing openly down the length of her body. Kirsty Mae returned the compliment, lingering a moment on his soft dark hair, taking in the angles of his mesmerising face, dropping to the T-shirted perfection of his chest, then down the long muscled lines of his thighs. Again her belly flipped, and for the thousandth time she wondered how someone who looked like he did could be found working construction on the Simpson Estate.

He eased off from the wall, smiled and moved close. She knew he knew his effect upon her but that did nothing at all to lessen the appeal. 'Let's not waste any more time,' she said, her voice a little quick, a little slurry.

'Whatever the lady says,' he said, dipping to the side of her neck and trailing the tip of his tongue down to her shoulder. She tilted back her head as he moved his tongue up the column of her throat and a little frisson of pleasure shook her. She felt his smile on her skin. 'Did you miss me?' he asked softly.

She chuckled. 'It's only been a day.'

'Yeah, but did you miss me?'

'No,' she lied.

'The hell you didn't.' He smiled, kissing her suddenly

on the lips, forcing the lie back down her throat. When he broke the kiss, his black eyes were flashing, fiery with lust. He took her by the hand and led her to the centre of the room. Then he sat on the edge of the bed, his knees apart, his forearms on his knees. Kirsty Mae stood in front of him, waiting, anticipatory flutters going on deep down inside.

'Take them off,' he said, looking at her spike-heeled ankle boots.

She toed off each boot, kicking them gaily away, then curled her bare toes into the carpet. Cocking a hip, she hooked her thumbs through the belt loops of her low hipster jeans and gazed confidently into his eyes. Silent, equally confident, he gazed back before gesturing at her jeans. Slowly, slowly, teasing herself almost as much as him, she toyed for a moment with the button, then nudged down the zip with the knuckle of her forefinger, exposing the fine lace of her white string panties. Finally she peeled the denim down each thigh and stepped clear, standing barefoot and barelegged, her white gypsy top cropped at her waist and her tiny panties snug on her hips.

'Good girl,' muttered Joe, moving in front of her. He was five inches taller than her, and she had to tilt up her chin to meet his level. Gently, he tucked her short blonde hair behind her ears, touched the white diamonds sparkling in her earlobes, then ran his hands down her shoulders and arms. 'Now pull down your panties,' he purred.

A knock of excitement fluttered in her stomach and she obliged, easing down the scrap of lace, her face still tilted up to his. Neither one of them looked down, but the rude delicious exposure brought a flush to her cool, sophisticated cheekbones. He held her at the waist a long moment, then skimmed the smooth skin of her tummy and moved to the sides of her hips. Down her thighs a little. Stroking. Caressing. On her hips again, then her stomach, then lower. She held her breath, taut with excitement, and couldn't stop a gasp when she felt his touch stray to her pussy hair. He curled his fingertip round a silken coil, subtly rubbing her mound through her trim nest. His other hand reached behind, drifting across the surface of her bare bottom, a feather-like touch, scarcely there at all. Still they maintained eye contact.

He moved his finger lower, slipping it between her legs. 'Beautiful,' he murmured, tracing the closed seam of her nude sex, delicately trailing back and forth. She wanted to step wider but was constricted by her pulled-down panties, and she savoured the delicious ache this gave rise to in her thighs. But the faint friction on her clitoris was so exquisite that soon the ache became unbearable, spreading to her breasts and bottom, and hurriedly she took off her gypsy top, shrugged out of her bra and wriggled her panties to the floor. Entirely naked now, warmth flaring in her abdomen, she defied him not to look at her, and finally his eyes left her face and settled on her breasts, gazing so raptly at her small pretty globes that Kirsty Mae felt them swell from the attention. Easing back her shoulders, she pushed out her chest, revelling now in his open admiration. Looking down at herself, she smoothed her open palms up over the butter-gold plane of her flat stomach, up her slender ribcage, letting her thumbs rest momentarily in the undercrease of her bust, and then closed her hands over each perfect breast, cupping and squeezing her own firm flesh. Her nipples responded instantly and, when she took her hands away, stood out hard and proud. 'Look, Joe,' she teased, framing her breasts in the open curve of her hands.

'Touch them,' he ordered, his voice hoarse and low.

Light as a spring breeze, she flicked her fingertips

over her nipples and, when that became too much, pressed her rosy little tips between each thumb and forefinger, pinching them gently, rolling them round, delighting in the thrills darting through her body. Joe watched intently, his fiery black eyes belying his casual demeanour. Her nipples began to feel overly tight, too sensitised to continue the gentle teasing, and with a moan of frustration she snatched at Joe's T-shirt, wresting it upwards and pressing her tingling tips to his hot hard chest. After a moment of gratifying contact, Joe stepped back, tugging his T-shirt over his head, exposing the tough masculine beauty of his body. Flawless skin, tanned the colour of Mexican pine. Lean honed muscle, hard as granite. Kirsty Mae wet her lower lip and smiled. 'Looking good, Joe,' she whispered, reaching up on tiptoe for his mouth, nudging her tongue along the join of his lips then sliding it hungrily inside. The hot fresh taste of his mouth left her reeling, and she ran her hand feverishly down over his groin, feeling his erection, wanting him right there and then. Without breaking their kiss, she tugged at the buttons of his fly, popping them open with luck and sheer force.

'Not so fast,' said Joe, spinning her around suddenly and leaning her over the edge of the bed. Supporting herself on her arms, she twisted her head back at him, her eyes shining with surprise and arousal. Casually, Joe ran a knuckle down the sculpted length of her spine. 'Arch your back,' he said, as she trembled with pleasure.

She arched a little, tipping back her neck.

'More,' he said.

She curved her back as much as she could, pushing out her bottom, and he laid his hand at the base of her spine. 'You were late,' he recalled softly.

Kirsty Mae didn't answer, tense with excitement.

'I don't like to be kept waiting, Kirsty Mae.'

She nodded, her mouth dry, her body burning.

'So,' he murmured, 'here's what you get for making me wait,' and he lifted his hand and smacked her hard on her behind. The sudden stinging shock of it thrilled her.

'I was very late,' she whispered, bracing herself.

Joe nodded, spanking her again, and she closed her eyes in delight at the sparks of pleasure on her bare tender flesh. 'Do it again, Joe,' she urged, craning round to watch as he brought his hand down sharply on her bottom, her firm rounded cheeks quivering on impact. 'It's so good!' she gasped, wriggling her hips, bucking back to meet his next series of slaps. He spanked her rhythmically, each smack loud and crisp and blending with her mews of anticipation and delight. Fascinated, she watched Joe's taut stomach muscles flicker as he delivered each stroke, and saw her own golden derrière turn a vibrant pink, while the smarting pleasure diffused through her abdomen.

Flushed and lightheaded, she turned to face forwards, so aroused that her legs felt weak and her mind was dizzy, and the next time she felt Joe's clap on her tingling bottom, she pressed her cheeks urgently against his open palm.

'OK, sweetheart,' he said grasping her long thighs and roughly lifting them apart. Then he cupped her soft wet sex from behind.

'Oh God,' sighed Kirsty Mae as Joe fondled her excited pussy and murmured appreciative endearments to her all the while. 'How's that, baby?' he whispered, rotating his hand on her succulent sex. The strength drained from her legs and the coherence from her mind as all feeling seemed to centre on the hot, pulsing desperation between her thighs.

He flipped her over, lifting her easily onto the bed. Feverishly she sat up, wrenching down his jeans and shorts, letting his cock spring free and, seemingly with one fluid movement, he kicked off his boots and shed his own clothes. Without a pause, she grabbed his hips and pulled him down to her, opening her legs wide, readying herself for him. As he entered her, she froze with the joy of it, savouring every inch of him until he was fully inside. She lay outstretched, her arms flung wide, Joe kneeling between her thighs, filling her completely. Holding her hips, he started to move, long, slow, expert strokes, and Kirsty Mae lost her breath at the indescribable pleasure within.

She looped her arms back through the headrest as each gliding stroke rippled magically up her body. When he began to move faster she lifted up her head, studying his handsome face, glazed now with passion, then turned her attention to the muscles in his arms as he held her hips steady, and the sheen of sweat on his tightly ridged stomach as he thrust his hips smoothly. And as she studied him, the glorious thrills between her legs tightened and intensified. She started to rock her hips in rhythm with his, straining up against him, sweating, breathless, close to the edge. He leaned forwards, half-twisting his body and resting on one forearm, while he lifted her left leg high over his other shoulder and electrified her with short, fast, magnificent thrusts. She came on a rushing, tumbling ride of sensation, her mind dripping and spinning, her insides dancing rapturously, propelling Joe to orgasm too, making him groan in ecstasy along with her.

They lay side by side, naked and beautiful, glowing with sweat and heaving for breath. After a time, Kirsty Mae turned on her side, propped her head up on her elbow and slowly traced Joe's left eyebrow with a finger. 'I'll say this, you know how to please a girl, Joe Marks.'

He gazed up at the ceiling with a complacent smile. 'Well, ma'am, I aim to please me too.'

She chuckled. 'You're an alley cat, Joe. It's why we're so good together – we like to please ourselves, you and I. We're two of a kind.'

He flicked her a sideways glance. 'Yeah, maybe.'

'No maybe about it,' she said, circling her finger on his chest. 'It's the truth.'

He reached over and ran his hand possessively down the side of her damp body, following the sensuous line of her hip. 'Afternoons were meant to be spent this way,' he said quietly. 'How in hell am I going to be able to give them up?'

'Who's talking about giving them up?' she asked, stretching, lazy and feline beneath his caressing hand.

His hand stopped. 'I am.'

She laughed a fluttery, incredulous laugh. 'What're you talking about? You're *ending* it?'

'Not here, now now. But the work at Simpsons'll be done in a week.' He shrugged. 'Then I got to move on, sweetheart. Find another paycheck.'

'And another girl to while away an afternoon with,' she sniped, tight as whipcord.

His black eyes danced with amusement. 'Would that be a little of the green-eyed monster talking?'

'I don't do jealous,' she snapped, her guile all but deserting her.

'Shame,' he said, smiling, 'because it tears me up inside to think of Nathan touching you, and I wouldn't mind some reciprocal feeling going on.'

'OK,' she purred, altogether more relaxed, 'I can do possessive. As in, another woman so much as looks in your direction and I'll rip her hair out.'

'Sounds a lot like jealousy to me.'

She didn't answer, dropping her head on his chest, silent and contemplative.

'And it'll do just fine,' he said, stroking the damp tendrils of her hair at the nape of her neck.

The words were out before she could swallow them, openly beseeching. 'Don't go, Joe.'

'Crew's moving on,' he muttered. 'I got to move on too.'

She lifted her head, searching his face. 'You could be anything. Stay here, and be anything. Why'd you have to go and work lousy construction for a living?'

'A man's got to eat.' He winked. 'Besides, how else could I get to cut loose for afternoons, and still have the guys cover my ass?'

The little stab of hurt she felt at his flippancy was another entirely new sensation. She shrugged it off and affected nonchalance. 'Don't say I didn't ask.'

'Of course, there's always another option,' he said softly.

'Oh yeah, and what would that be?' she muttered.

'You could always come with me.'

Give up everything and go with him!

Give up her lifestyle, the mansion, the money, the insouciant luxury of being Nathan's wife. Or give up Joe.

Both options wrenched at her gut, and she felt physically sick as she arrived home that evening, the car tyres crunching the gravel of the courtyard, the large mansion lighting up the night. Hell, she had so much to lose, she thought, as she wandered distractedly into the house.

Nathan's voice startled her and she whipped her head up to see him looking down at her from the galleried landing. 'Where've you been, Kirsty Mae?' he was asking.

She reacted instantly, calling her perfectly honed technique into play. Back straight, eyes wide and innocent, a big, big smile for her bigwig husband. 'Out with the girls,' she said, suitably unflustered. She mussed up her short hair carelessly and began climbing the stairs towards him. 'A too-long night altogether,' she sighed, pressing her lips to his cologne-scented cheek. 'I missed you, baby.'

'So why stay out so long?' he said, circling her waist affectionately. 'I've been home three hours.'

'For once,' she quipped, tapping the end of his nose and whirling away. He caught her as she moved, and whirled her back into his arms, holding her firm in an iron embrace. 'Now, where've you really been?' he said quietly.

'I told you,' she said, 'out with Mimi and Zara. The cinema and coffee afterwards.'

He nodded, relaxing his hold, and she stepped away, displaying an exact measure of righteousness. 'You wouldn't be not trusting me, would you, Nathan?'

'No,' he answered. 'You said where you were and naturally I believe you.'

'Good,' she said, smooching against him.

He held her tenderly again, gently cradling her head on his shoulder. 'Because,' he whispered, 'naturally you wouldn't lie to me.'

'You know I wouldn't,' she said, smooth as syrup.

'Or betray me,' he went on.

She tensed just a little beneath his cradling hand.

'Because that would be foolish, and I know you're no fool, Kirsty Mae. I know you'd never be fool enough to betray me and force me to throw you out without a dime to call your own.'

She left the shock in her eyes, added a little hurt, and made herself look up at him. 'You know I wouldn't,' she whispered. 'How can you say these things?'

He cupped her chin, his features set and humourless. 'I'm telling you I believe you, is all.'

She dropped her head back on his shoulder, her cheating heart rapping a choppy rhythm. Nathan kissed her hair softly. 'I must have made a mistake tonight,' he murmured.

'A mistake?' she repeated, her heart rap-rapping.

'When I thought I saw Zara dining with a companion at Alfredo's. It must have been somone else.'

'It must,' said Kirsty Mae, forcing out a tinkle of laughter. 'Zara was with me the whole evening.'

'As I said, my mistake,' crooned Nathan. And Kirsty Mae, mistress of guile and deceit, caught the falseness of his words as though she'd uttered them herself, and couldn't slow her rapid pulse as she realised the truth.

He knew.

Today was different; today Kirsty Mae arrived early. She sat calmly in Room 105 of the Pioneer Hotel and waited for Joe. It had been two days since she'd seen him, two days of guarded cat-and-mouse with Nathan, two days of deciding her next move.

Joe turned up, looking cool and laidback. If he was surprised to see her there before him, he didn't show it. He kicked the door shut, a flicker of a smile on his swarthily handsome face, and Kirsty Mae felt her insides burn up. She went straight to him, and they began to kiss – deep, passionate, urgent kisses. So far neither one of them had spoken. Between and even during their kisses, they pulled and tugged at each other's clothes until, naked and entangled, they tumbled to the carpet. Joe pushed her on her back, cupped together her small breasts and kissed her nipples, sucking each rosy tip in turn, making her arch her spine with the pleasure of it. He kissed his way down her stomach, her satin skin quivering to gooseflesh with each touch, and when he reached her small mound he stopped his kisses, nudged her thighs open and dipped his head in between, sucking lightly on her pretty clitoris, flicking, licking, till she felt herself swell. 'My

God, Joe,' she groaned ecstatically, her first words uttered.

'Mmm?' he murmured, making magic, expertly stimulating, teasing and toying with her bud until relief swept up her body in a deep, delicious shudder. Weak and serene, lost in ebbs of pleasure, she felt him ease her over onto her hands and knees. She leaned forwards onto her forearms, lifted her bottom high and moved her legs apart, letting him see all of her, and Joe's groan of appreciation made her dizzy with excitement. After an exquisitely strained time without contact he touched her, drawing his finger slowly along her velvet crack. Up and down he trailed, and she felt the residual tingles in her sex prickle upwards between her cheeks. She closed her eyes, swaying her hips slightly in the air, savouring the heat as it began to build once again. Joe moved to her side and, still teasing her rear, reached beneath her and began to play with her breasts, letting them fall into his hands, brushing his palms lightly across her nipples. The pleasure was almost agonising and, when she couldn't stand any more, she twisted round to him. 'Lay back, Joe,' she panted, pushing him down, running her hands frantically over his chest as she knelt astride his hips and sank down on him.

She leant forwards slightly, resting her hands on his chest as she began to move, sliding up and down his gloriously hard cock. Joe threw his arms back, giving her free rein. She tried to slow things down, to prolong the moment, rising up on her knees with just the tip of him inside her.

'Jesus,' groaned Joe.

'I know,' she gasped, teasing them both, hardly able to sustain it as she gazed down at him. He looked entirely too good, too sexy, his eyes hot with passion, his dark hair ruffled, his tan hard muscles tensed with excitement. With a yelp of frustration she dropped down, letting him fill her, sensing his relief. She locked her arms to the sides and bobbed energetically, riding his cock in a frenzy of sensation. Her small breasts jiggled deliciously as her belly danced inside and jitters of pleasure fanned outwards from her core. He half-leaned forwards, grasped her waist, and began to nudge his hips up and down in perfect harmony with her own.

Perfect harmony, she thought gleefully. Two of a kind.

And there wasn't a shred of doubt in her mind as to her next move.

Joe blew out a long line of smoke, deep in thought. Kirsty Mae watched it creep towards the ceiling and vanish. 'So, you think Nathan knows about us,' he said calmly.

'He suspects something,' she said.

'You took a helluva chance coming here today, then?'

She shrugged dismissively. 'No point locking the barn door after the horse has bolted.'

Joe shook his head, chuckling lightly.

'Besides,' she said, smiling, 'he's gone away for two days.'

'Ah,' he nodded. 'And when he gets back?'

'It'll be over,' she said dispassionately. 'He's going to ditch me, I know it. And he'll do it so's I don't get a dime.'

Joe pulled on his cigarette. 'So, you'll be coming with me?'

'Uh, uh.' She shook her head.

He flicked his eyes to her. She smiled serenely. 'That is, not yet.'

'Say again?' he said, raising one eyebrow.

She leaned across, brushing his lips with hers. 'Nathan would never sit back and let us run off and live happily together. You have no idea how connected he is. He'd make sure you never worked in this state again.'

'That a fact,' Joe muttered.

'And besides,' she added, 'I'm not cut out for being poor, there's no way I'm going back to being that.'

''Scuse me, sweetheart, for being a little addled here, but what exactly are you telling me?'

Her voice was as soft as a baby's breath. 'I'm telling you that Nathan's going to cease to exist.'

'You're shittin' me,' laughed Joe.

She didn't laugh back, but held his gaze. 'Two days from now, he's going to return from his trip, take his gun from his gun closet, put it to his temple and end his misery. He was a little depressed, is all, but no one, especially his young wife, will ever really know why he did it.'

Joe stared at her in silence.

'More to the point,' she whispered, 'no one will ever know *who* really did it.'

'And who would that be?' said Joe.

Kirsty Mae kissed his neck lightly, breathing out the answer. 'You, baby. You.'

'It's perfect,' she explained. 'No one knows about you and me. Nathan suspects something but he doesn't yet know what. There's no connection to you at all and, soon as it's done, you move on with the crew anyway. Clean as a whistle.'

Joe smoked his cigarette lazily. 'And exactly why would I be doing it?'

'We want to be together, don't we? Together and rich. If we do it, we'll be both. Nathan won't have time to scout you out, won't have time to get the proof that he needs to ditch me openly, and,' she exhaled sharply, 'most importantly, won't have time to change his will.'

'Leaving everything to you?'

'Mmm,' she murmured. 'All of it.'

'You sure about that?'

'Totally,' she said. 'He made a new will when he married me. He paid his ex-wife off with a clean settlement when he divorced her – far too generous a settlement, if you ask me.'

'Kids?' asked Joe.

'One son, a wild kid, Nathan doesn't talk to, doesn't see.'

'But the kid would have a claim?'

'Uh, uh, Nathan thought of that, and left him precisely five hundred dollars. To show his intention and invalidate any claim on his estate.'

'Hmmm,' said Joe, leaning across her to the ashtray on the bedside table to stub out his cigarette. He lay back, silent, reflective, his fingers tapping idly on his taut flat belly. Kirsty Mae watched him patiently, intuitively knowing to wait him out. Eventually, he stopped tapping and met her patient gaze. 'How would we do it?' he said quietly.

'I'll make sure I'm out, with people. I'll give you a plan of the house, with a marked door unlocked. I'll also leave the gun closet unlocked. Nathan gets back around eight. He'll go straight to his den. All you have to do is wait behind the curtain which is directly behind his desk. And when he sits down . . .' she let her words trail off.

Joe's face was inscrutable. 'And . . .?' he said.

'And afterwards,' she murmured, 'you put the gun in his hand, and then you disappear. I'll get someone to drop me home later. I'll come in, discover the body. And you'll be long gone, baby. No one to touch you.'

'Except you,' said Joe, narrowing his fine eyes.

She pressed her hand to his cheek and kissed his lips

tenderly. For once in her life, she spoke the truth, 'Think about it. I could never hurt you without hurting myself,' she whispered. 'I've planned this for us. You and me. For us.'

Joe looked at her hard, searching her lovely face.

'D'you love me, Joe?' she asked softly.

He nodded.

'Then do it for us both, baby,' she urged.

He was still for a long, long while. Then, finally, he nodded again.

On a hot silent night, two days later, Kirsty Mae made herself highly visible. She wore a white linen dress, snug against her curves. She wore four-inch heels, highlighting her slender calves. She tousled her bleached-blonde hair into a short, mussed-up halo. She made up her face to a vision of loveliness. And she made sure everyone noticed her.

By seven p.m., she'd met up with friends in a downtown bar. She drank a little too much, and never checked her watch once, but instinctively knew when the clock struck eleven. Blaming the alcohol, she asked a specific friend, Lennie, to drive her back home. Lennie, a lovestruck young lawyer, obliged without question.

She tried not to think of what awaited her at home, filling the car with tipsy, vacuous chit-chat instead, and when Lennie pulled up to the gravel entrance a short time later, she whimsically suggested he come in for a nightcap. 'Say hi to Nathan,' she said, utterly smooth in her treachery.

'I'll have to pass, Kirsty Mae,' Lennie replied. 'Got an early call in the morning.'

Shit, thought Kirsty Mae, having to blink several times to hide a sudden stab of anxiety. Lennie was her rock-solid alibi, Lennie was supposed to be with her when she 'discovered' the body, Lennie *never* said no to her, Lennie *never* refused a nightcap. 'Oh, c'mon,' she coaxed playfully, 'one little drinky.'

'Really, no,' smiled Lennie, infuriatingly resolute.

'Sure?' pouted Kirsty Mae.

'Sure,' insisted Lennie.

To press him too hard would look strange, she realised. 'OK,' she quipped, sounding carefree. Goddammit, she thought inwardly, as she got out of the car.

Ever the gentleman, Lennie waited till she'd opened the front door and stepped inside, before waving merrily and driving off into the night. 'Stupid dope,' muttered Kirsty Mae, seeing her designated witness disappear. She'd banked on Lennie being with her, as much for company as for her more calculated reasons, and now, alone in the huge hallway, irritation gave way to a few more flutterings of anxiety.

She hesitated a moment but, knowing she had no other choice than to continue alone, she spun on her heel and immediately noticed Nathan's bags at the bottom of the staircase. Clearly he'd returned from his trip as scheduled. At least that had gone to plan. 'Nathan?' she called out tentatively.

No reply.

'Nathan?' she called louder.

Still no reply.

Reassured a little by the silence, she wandered past the bags and through the large hallway, turning the corner towards Nathan's den. She hadn't turned on the light in this part of the hall, and the long passageway before her was dim but for a strip of soft yellow light escaping from beneath the den door. She felt an unprecedented chill snake down her spine, but her resolve was strong, and she moved purposefully towards the door. A simple loud knock met with no response.

With a pit-pat of nerves cavorting in her belly, she

curled her fingers round the handle and quietly opened the door. The room was bathed in the cosy yellow light which softened the look of the heavy masculine furnishings. She dropped her eyes to the crimson carpet, trailed her gaze slowly towards the dark oak desk and finally, bracing herself, looked up.

Nathan was seated behind his desk, his head and upper body slumped forwards across the desktop.

Kirsty Mae exhaled a short hard breath. She remained for several seconds in the doorway, taking in the scene. The curtains behind Nathan were closed, hanging in perfect even folds. No sign that Joe had lain in wait behind them. No sign, in fact, Joe had ever been there. All looked undisturbed.

Perfect, mused Kirsty Mae, taking a first small step into the room. Each tiny step drew her closer to Nathan, until she found herself standing by the side of the desk, staring down at her dead husband. Her nerves seemed to have calmed, but there was a feeling inside she couldn't quite gauge. It wasn't regret, she decided as she looked down at Nathan, but it might have been a tinge of sadness. He looked so restful, she thought. Could've been asleep. The right side of his head was pressed to the desk, concealing the tiny bullet wound, and his right hand was closed around the gun, just as she'd envisaged. Joe had committed the crime perfectly and she felt a sweep of pride at her lover's competence.

Now her thoughts turned to the importance of the time line. She reached forwards for the telephone, lifted the receiver, and made ready to blub hysterically down the line. It took several seconds before she realised the phone was dead. The second blip in her careful plan. She dropped the phone carelessly, striding determinedly from the room, making for the phone in the hall. She was halfway across the room when she heard it.

'Not a single tear for your dead husband, Kirsty Mae?'

She stopped on the spot, an army of blood cells charging at her chest. Slowly, she turned.

Nathan was sitting upright. His hair was ruffled on the right side of his head but he was otherwise unbloodied, unmarked. 'Hello, my darling,' he whispered.

She opened her mouth to speak but words wouldn't come, so she closed her eyes tight and flashed them back open, hoping against hope it was her mind playing tricks. It wasn't. Nathan still sat there, motionless but alive. He stared at her steadily, then suddenly switched his gaze to a point behind her, and a sardonic smile began to dance at the corners of his mouth. She twisted her head to follow his line of vision.

Joe was leaning casually in the doorway. Kirsty Mae whipped her head round to Nathan then back to Joe once again. She raised her eyebrows to Joe in total confusion and he made a little nonchalant shrug in response. 'I may be wild,' he said lazily, 'and it surely was a pleasure baggin' his new young wife, but even I draw the line at shooting the old man's brains out.'

Kirsty Mae took in Joe's words sluggishly before returning her gaze to Nathan. She narrowed her eyes, mentally darkening the many strands of silver in Nathan's full head of hair, knocking the life lines from his face, and suddenly she could see it quite clearly: the fine black eyes, the dark handsome features. So similar in looks, so different in age.

'I believe you know my son,' remarked Nathan quietly.

And Kirsty Mae Blade, mistress of guile and deceit, realised that for the very first time in her charmed life, she'd been well and truly had.

Caught You! Primula Bond

I was halfway through Ladies Separates before he caught me. A few yards away I could see the escalators sliding lazily up and down in the dazzling glass atrium. Up meant Evening Wear and the canteen. Down meant freedom.

'Caught you.'

There was a sharp tap on my shoulder just as the automatic doors were opening to release me. I stopped, sighed, crossed my arms across the turquoise shirt we all had to wear and looked surly.

'Mr Fosdyke.'

'There is another 35 minutes until we sign off for the day. You are two and a half departments away from your workstation. Where do you think you're going?'

I glanced over my shoulder at the escalators and gave up the fight. No point telling him I was doing a runner. That he could stuff his dreary job where the sun don't shine.

'My watch must be wrong, Mr Fosdyke.'

He picked up my wrist. I was so stunned by the gesture that I let him lift it right up to his face.

'It's perfectly correct, Sonia. You're heading for a caution, you know.'

'You can go one better than that, if you like,' I said, my voice muffled by the dark pink carpets and the murmur of shoppers. 'You can sack me.'

He didn't drop my wrist at such rudeness, but lowered it, still holding it, until our joined hands rested against my stomach. I hoped he couldn't smell the expensive scent I'd sprayed on earlier when I was skiving in the Perfume Parlour on the ground floor.

'Could you please go back, Sonia, and finish your shift. There are customers that need assistance. Please.'

I stood my ground for as long as I dared. Five seconds or so. I'd never stood close enough to see what colour his eyes were. Now I could see that they were a kind of yellowy hazel, like a lion's, with ridiculously thick lashes. And he was much bigger than I realised. When I watched him on the shop floor running his hands along the clothes rails, advising dithering customers on the garment that would most flatter them and operating the till like a musical instrument, he almost merged his maleness into the silky, lacy female environment. Perhaps it was those eyelashes that did it.

But here, standing in Ladies Separates, he towered over me, blocking out the glaring lights and the bustle all around us. We could have been alone in the enormous store, just us and rows and rows of shirts and skirts. His authority was suddenly, breathtakingly sexy. I looked him carefully all over as if I'd never seen him before. I was tempted either to lick him or to stick my tongue out at him.

I could see a dent in his shadowed chin, a wide mouth, and broad shoulders that would look quite at home on a rugby pitch. His fingers were tight round my wrist, pulling me in to his pin-striped waistcoat, and shaking, I presumed, with indignation. His body felt rock hard, as if any moment it would burst out of the restraints of his sober suit. And he smelt delicious.

'Whatever you say, Mr Fosdyke.'

I marched ahead of him through the store like a prisoner being returned to jail, aware of him watching the way I walked, and he kept right behind me until I got back to our department, back to my little stool just inside the fitting room.

'Your buttons, Sonia.' He tapped me again, making me turn, and yanked my ill-fitting shirt about, practically lifting me off my feet as if he were dressing me for school. I had undone the damn thing when I'd made my bid for escape. When they'd hired me three weeks earlier they had squeezed me into the last remaining uniform. I couldn't bear the tight collar round my throat, and the darts were too high under my arms and forced my tits together. He pulled the material across my bulging cleavage and there was a little ripping sound. 'We should get you fitted properly, you know. Inside and out. This *is* Lingerie, after all.'

We both looked down. In lingerie departments what we were looking at is known as a bust, but to me they're my tits, and they respond to the slightest attention. As if confirming what he'd just said, my nipples were demonstrating how easy it was to poke through the cheap material of my too-small bra as well as show through the synthetic blouse for all, especially Mr Fosdyke, to see. The middle button was still undone.

'Excuse me. May I try these on?'

A big blonde girl shoved past us into one of the cubicles. We must have looked pretty cosy, Mr Fosdyke and I, him doing up my buttons and both of us staring down at my tits. Without waiting for me to hand her a plastic pass, she had dived behind the curtain and we could hear bags and shoes dropping to the floor as she undressed.

'I'll let you off just this once,' Mr Fosdyke said to me, his thumbs brushing over the front of my shirt as he fastened that last button, before finally returning to the lapels of his jacket, where they were happiest. 'But I'll be watching you.'

I slumped back onto my stool but this time I didn't go into my normal trance. My blouse felt tighter than before. I had expected to be repelled by the tyrannical

Mr Fosdyke's touch, but instead I was excited. I glanced onto the shop floor. He was holding up two bustier sets, one black, one virginal white, in front of a harassed woman with twin toddlers in tow. She was probably trying to celebrate a wedding anniversary. She would trust Mr Fosdyke to discuss her underwear, because he'd gone back into camp mode, which made the customers think he was gay and therefore safe.

'Excuse me,' the girl in the cubicle called through. 'Could you please get me a size 14 in this?'

A fuschia-pink bra and knicker set came flying over the curtain.

'I'm not normally meant to leave my post,' I mumbled, trying to twist them back on to their plastic hanger. The harassed customer outside was smiling now as she playfully snatched the black basque from Mr Fosdyke. Positively batting her eyelashes, in fact.

'But just this once,' I added, and got up to find another set. I went close up behind Mr Fosdyke. I was looking at him through new eyes. I remembered how hard and strong his body had felt, up close and angry. I couldn't help looking at his hands, which had slowly buttoned up my blouse a few minutes ago. Maybe I'd reconsider trying to get myself sacked.

The curtain in the cubicle had fluttered open. I was about to hand the customer the size 14 when I caught a glimpse of her in the long mirror. She was raising her arms to pile her blonde hair up, Brigitte Bardot-style, and she was wearing a gorgeous lilac corset which laced down the front, with the frilled knickers that matched. Her breasts were bigger than mine, pushed tightly together in the rigid whalebone, the tanned swell wobbling sensuously over the bodice as she turned sideways to admire herself.

Over her reflected shoulder I suddenly saw Mr Fosdyke. He was quite a distance away, but he could see her, like I could, through the curtain. His gold eyes gleamed as tendrils of the girl's long hair fell into the crack of her cleavage. His tongue slicked across his lower lip as she tossed her head playfully backwards as if posing for a camera, arching her spine invitingly.

I pulled my stomach in and thrust my tits out, unconsciously aping her movements in the mirror hanging behind my stool, but how sexy could you look in turquoise nylon? Surely I had only imagined that Mr Fosdyke's fingers were lingering over my contours. I didn't really want him to touch me intimately, did I? And if I did, it was only a moment of mad lust to try to liven up my dull day and hasten the minutes until five o'clock.

I frowned jealously back at the girl's reflection. She was lucky, free to leave whenever she liked. She was just dropping her tight purple T-shirt over her head to get dressed. She was still wearing the lilac corset. Her own knickers and bra were on the floor, kicked under the bench seat. She zipped up her denim miniskirt and flung back the curtain.

'Er, madam?' I said, using the fuschia size 14 as a kind of shield. I'd never had to do this before. 'I don't think you've paid for the lilac.'

'So catch me!' she taunted, sprinting past me, knocking over the under-supervisor, Dora, who was coming to tell me to start clearing people out. The girl disappeared behind a rail of see-through negligees being wheeled out of the stock-room.

'Shoplifter!' I screeched, dashing after her.

'You can't use language like that to customers, Sonia. Sonia?' Mr Fosdyke's voice wheeled past me as the rail of negligees went rattling off to one side. One of the girl's bags was on the floor. I jumped over it and looked about. There was no sign of her. Customers and staff were beginning to throng towards the escalators and exits to go home. No one was going to help me.

The stock room door, invisible to the untutored eye, was still ajar. A cashmere sweater, still with its label on, was lying just inside. That didn't come from this department. Woollens was on the floor below.

Through this door was a series of dingy storerooms and corridors filled with rails and boxes of old and new stock. Compared with the plush, scented public face of the shop, the stock-room, staff loos and canteen behind the scenes were like something out of a prison. The door banged to behind me, shutting out the piped music and distant roar of traffic.

I was alone with mountains of lingerie and a possibly violent criminal. I'd never been in here before. Probably because they couldn't trust *me* not to nick anything. There were creamy satin knickers, midnight-blue camisoles, burgundy bras with delicate detachable straps, basques of all colours and sheer pink stockings. Standing just ahead of me on their pedestals, their heads hidden in the shadows of the dusty ceiling, were three mannequins standing with their false arms outstretched and still dressed in display underwear. One wore whorish suspenders and stockings. The second wore a cutesy babydoll nightie in sky blue. The third wore a lilac corset with matching frilly knickers.

Now was my chance to try on the outfit for myself. I went up to the dummy, and felt round its back to see if the label had my size on it. Suddenly an arm went round my neck, pressing my face in to its stomach.

'Caught you,' the mannequin whispered. 'And now I have you just where I want you.'

'You're the thief, not me!' I tried to pull away, but the blonde girl was very strong. She jumped down so that we were face to face, and smiled. Her lips were very full, and shiny with gloss.

'Why don't you try something on? You know you want to,' she said, walking me over to a rail of slinky bodies. 'No one will see us, will they? The shop has closed.'

I glanced over my shoulder. A couple of bare bulbs illuminated the storeroom, but otherwise it was dark. And I couldn't even remember the way back to the department.

'My bag. My clothes –'

'Oh, take them off. They're ghastly, anyway.' She pulled at my sleeve, and it started to rip at the shoulder.

'I meant my home clothes.'

'I know! I've seen those as well. Make you look horribly dumpy, when really – well, you're quite luscious after all!' Her throaty laugh clanged against the concrete walls, and I laughed as well. This was a kind of freedom. Hiding all night in the storeroom while Fosdyke, Dora and the others all clocked off, locked up and went to their dinky homes.

The girl pulled my other sleeve, and that ripped right off, taking half the shirt with it. The air in there was cool on my skin, and I shivered, but she just took the rest of it off me and started unhooking my old white bra.

'What are you doing?' I tried to cover my breasts.

'We're going to dress you up. This will do beautifully.'

I was still holding the fuschia size 14. With my back to her I took my skirt and knickers off, and started to put the new ones on. The girl swivelled me round.

'It does up at the front.'

While she hooked the new bra over my shoulders, I gazed at her – Or, rather, at her soft, lace-covered breasts, which were pushing against mine. I slid my hands hesitantly onto the girl's hips, expecting her to push me off. But instead she leaned closer, allowing me to press the flesh under the corset. The tips of my fingers were wandering over the swell of her buttocks, aware of the warm dark crack between her cheeks. Her pussy was pushed against mine. Our bodies were the same.

She was just about to fasten the bra at the front when she stopped. My breasts were ready to try their new home. They were bare and white, the nipples shrinking into taut points in the cool air. The girl took my breasts into her hands, moulding them in her palms, pressing them together as each forefinger circled a raspberry nipple.

'We shouldn't be here,' I croaked, but my hands couldn't help moving over the lilac satin to the girl's honey-coloured breasts. As she rubbed my nipples roughly between her fingers, it seemed totally natural to want to do the same to her. I tugged the lilac lace away to reveal the full roundness of her breasts and her own reddening nipples awaiting arousal. The heaviness of the other woman's breasts filled my hands and a fresh new desire surged down me, seizing me with a crazy urge to crush my mouth against the girl's smiling lips.

She did up the fuschia bra but, although it fitted, it lifted and presented my breasts like cakes on a dish, and it felt sexier than if they were dangling free. Still we were pressed against each other. Her eyes half closed and her lips opened as she answered my silent urge. Her mouth was warm, her tongue slippery, and I sucked hesitantly on the tip as it flicked behind my teeth and tickled towards my throat. Then we were kissing greedily, her tongue pushing in like a probing penis, our hands roving over each other's bodies, my head light and dizzy with the novelty of it as I ached for more.

I dug my fingers into her buttocks as we kissed and pressed our breasts against each other, and felt her hands plunging down to my pussy, which was already moistening the fuschia knickers. Instinctively I parted my thighs to invite her fingers in, even though my legs were shaking. The girl touched my sex lips and they started to throb, flurries of pleasure radiating up me as she stroked across the tender skin.

Now I was grinding myself against her and trying to bring my hands round from her buttocks to the front, where I wanted to uncover her silk-covered pussy, but she pushed my hand away and jammed her fingers roughly up inside my cunt, expertly targeting my clit and making me gasp as her fingers crawled up higher inside me.

I bent my knees to open myself up more, and spread her buttocks beneath my hands. We were almost dancing now, swaying round and round as our hands directed each other, still kissing. But I was breathless, and pulled briefly away from kissing her, then opened my eyes and froze, my fingers probing inside her butt cheeks, hers burrowing deeper still inside my pussy.

'Hey, don't stop,' she said, nuzzling her mouth round to kiss me again.

'Caught you,' the man's voice boomed into the secret storeroom.

'Mr Fosdyke!' I yelped, leaping away from the shop-lifter as if I'd been scalded.

'Oh, Mr Fosdyke!' she echoed mockingly, letting me go and sashaying across the dusty floor towards him. 'Do you like what you see?'

I felt a mixture of horror at his finding us like that, and fury that she'd dropped me at the sight of the real thing. A man.

She went right up to him, grabbed his turquoise tie and used it to pull him towards her. His face was still stony and inscrutable, but his eyes blazed with undeniable lust, and I was surprised by my white-hot jealousy at seeing her touching him so brazenly.

'I've got security waiting outside,' he said in a rough voice, pushing her away and coming towards me. 'We deal extremely harshly with criminals, I'm warning you.'

'Security, eh?' she smiled, coming up behind him, so that he was now sandwiched between the two of us. 'Well, bring them in, Mr Fosdyke. The more the merrier.'

'But in here,' I said, infected and intoxicated by her insolence as she pushed him right against me, so that the front of his trousers pressed on my belly, 'no one can hear you scream.'

The girl had his jacket off in seconds and her hands snaked round to undo his belt. 'In that case, let's make him scream.'

'Those are stolen goods,' he said, biting his lip as she unzipped his trousers and reached inside them. My breasts were heaving up and down against his shirt, the friction rubbing my nipples into red-hot impatience.

'So are these!' She laughed loudly, drawing out his cock and his soft balls. My laugh caught halfway up my throat. His cock was already hard. Presumably he'd seen us kissing, dressed up in our stolen finery, and it had turned him on. The gay pretence of my supervisor was destroyed for good, and I was eager to know just what he was like under those pin-stripes.

Mr Fosdyke didn't struggle, but let her hand slide up and down the swollen shaft until the dark knob was swollen and ready. I watched her fondling him, unable to take my eyes off the slim fingers wrapped around his exposed cock. I grabbed his hands and planted them on my breasts. They rested there for a minute, and then he started to knead the fuschia-pink silk, pushing my breasts hard together while the girl tugged harder on his cock.

'Stop,' I said to her. 'Don't waste it.'

'OK,' she said, winking at me from behind him. 'You go first then, girl.'

I was quivering with excitement and nerves. This shoplifter gave me the balls to do anything, even to Mr Fosdyke. But she seemed to have the power to make him do whatever she wanted, too. She let go of his prick so that it sprang out of her hands and jabbed into my stomach, just above the triangle of my bush. I raised myself up on tiptoe and hooked one knee round his hip.

At last he came out of his trance. The girl had his trousers down to his knees, now, and was caressing his legs and his buttocks, winding her own leg round him and rubbing herself up and down his back. He shoved me harder against the bare wall, still squeezing my breasts, and with a little jump I lifted my other leg to hook it round him while the girl kept him steady from behind.

I reached down and took the pulsating prick, almost creaming myself just to feel it. Mr Fosdyke's eyes had changed colour. They were dark now, almost hazel, and narrowed as they looked straight in to mine. I flushed, from my toes upwards, and closed my eyes. The girl was behind him, her hands still roving up and down his sides and his legs. She was beginning to gasp as her crotch caught on his bottom, and as she gyrated against him she shoved him further forwards so that my back scraped on the brickwork.

I gripped him round the hips and pulled the leg of my knickers sideways to ease his prick up towards my pussy. Already it was damp, already I could slide his knob easily through the tight curls and up between my tender sex lips. These made little wet sounds as I parted them, rotating his cock to tickle inside them, teasing myself to enjoy every second of his slow entrance. Ripples of forgotten ecstasy were already lapping at me, and I wondered when he was going to stop me. I kept my eyes shut tight and wriggled myself down the length of his shaft, my legs and knees quaking with the effort of keeping hold of him. I wasn't sure I could make it last, and the worry that I was going to lose my grip, along with the reality of what I was doing, started to distract me.

I opened my eyes and a fresh leap of energy surged through me. His eyes were closed, now, but he was biting his lip to contain his own growing excitement. The girl was in her own world, too, almost as if I weren't there. His cock was inside me, but it was going to slip out any minute if I didn't do something.

I glanced behind me. His hands grappled at me to keep me there, but all at once I dropped my legs, my knees knocking wildly, and half staggered, half fell onto an enormous cardboard box which was open, with all kinds of lace and silk spilling out. I saw annoyance on the girl's face, but I was past caring now. I wanted to do it, and I wanted to do it comfortably.

Mr Fosdyke fell on top of me. I stayed just as I'd landed, flat on my back with my arms and legs splayed in the tangle of underwear, my little stolen outfit still in place. He reared over me for a moment, his face still stern. But he couldn't frighten me now. He'd caught me trying to run away. He'd caught me stealing the goods. He'd even caught me snogging a shoplifter. What else could he catch me doing?

'Discipline, that's what you need, Sonia,' he said, 'if you won't obey the rules.'

The girl came and squatted over me, tying my wrists

together with a bra she'd found in the box. She quickly whipped her lilac knickers off and then knelt so that her knees were pinning my shoulders. Then Mr Fosdyke settled himself behind her so that his knees were pinning my thighs. I felt his prick bump over my legs. Then the two of them started moving in unison. While he dragged his prick over my bush and then rammed it hard inside my fuschia briefs, back into my cunt, she lowered herself until her soft pubic hair tickled my face. Her hot, sweet scent filled my nostrils. I couldn't move. I didn't want to move. He was moving back and forth, increasing his rhythm, pushing me violently up and down across the massive box so that we all three rocked with the motion.

She groaned quietly, hooking her fingers inside herself to spread her labia so that the blood red details peeped out and spread across my upper lip. Automatically I flicked my tongue out. I was stunned by the salty, fragrant taste of the other woman, and started to lick frantically at her hot slit.

'She's good, Mr Fosdyke,' the girl groaned. As I licked her, Mr Fosdyke banged himself into me, his cock moving like my tongue. The girl arched her spine, just as she had in the changing room. The two of them were heavy on me, but I felt intoxicated, still light-headed but now burning with the shafts of pleasure shooting all through me.

He slammed into me harder and harder. I stretched my legs wider and wider apart to savour every last tingle, and suddenly the combination of his urgent fucking and my own urgent licking of the girl overpowered me, and the explosion was so violent that I must have nipped the girl, because she tensed up, her own moans turned to screams of climax, and Mr Fosdyke suddenly roared as he came.

At first I couldn't see the pair of them, as my vision

was blocked by the girl's fanny, but they must have gripped onto one another because they rolled off the box and onto the hard floor as one, groaning and then laughing. My hands were tied, but only loosely. I could wriggle free if I wanted to, but I lay where I was, tangled up with fragments of expensive lingerie and wanting to do it again.

'We should go.' The girl was the first to speak, crawling across the floor to grab her T-shirt and skirt.

'I'll stay here, and lock up,' I said bullishly. I could feel there was some kind of tussle going on here. 'Why don't you just let her go, Mr Fosdyke? Surely we don't have to report her this time?'

Mr Fosdyke pulled me to my feet. Although he still had his shirt and tie on like a true store supervisor, from the waist down he was pure shagging sex god. His normally immaculate hair was a mess.

'I said, we should go,' the girl repeated, not thanking me for the idea of letting her off. But Mr Fosdyke was still looking at me. Sonia, the bored assistant he hired three weeks ago. What did he think of me now?

He still had his back to her. She couldn't see that his cock had not yet subsided. He ran his tongue across his lip slowly, and winked at me. I couldn't believe it. My pussy twitched in response.

'You can go. I'll leave here when I'm good and ready,' Mr Fosdyke said to her, reaching out to unfasten my little pink bra. I tensed, nipples smarting with renewed excitement. His voice discovered its authority again. He flicked his fingers at the girl, as he did when one of his staff had made a useless suggestion. 'I'll see you at home, Mrs Fosdyke.'

The Woodlanders (with apologies to the late Mr Thomas Hardy)

Siân Lacey Taylder

It is, I suspect, a symptom of the depths to which modern urban life has sunk that we dream of some rural idyll where the splendid prospect of isolation and a simpler means of existence acts in stark contradiction to our busy, cluttered lives. That is, whenever we have time to dream, for in these days of corporate identity even these private acts of rebellion have been seized upon by a ubiquitous mediocrity. Still, as the approach to the recent Christmas holidays proved ever more intolerable, I decided it was time to indulge myself in a short dose of much-needed fantasy. We booked a small cottage in the village of Little Hintock, a place so far from civilisation that to its inhabitants electricity might be a recent innovation. Little did I know how close was that guess to the truth.

I say 'we' for initially there were four of us – two couples – intending to spend our New Year in the middle of nowhere instead of amongst the debris of civilisation that is London. However, our cosy little foursome was ruptured by an 'incident' at the office party, the exact events of which are lost in a drunken haze. I vaguely recall that myself and Emma – my female counterpart in our 'cosy little foursome' – had stormed out of the party and found ourselves in the heart of Soho. In our inebriated state, I suppose that visiting a women's bar was little more than a touch of ladette bravado but, whereas our intention had been to indulge in a touch of heterosexual superiority, I'm afraid we simply joined in the fun. Emma's partner had come in search of us but was refused entry to the establishment, which was just as well. When we arrived back at Emma's flat he was, unbeknown to us, fast asleep in her bedroom, and emerged just as we were locked in an embrace that even the closest of girlfriends would be hard pressed to excuse as anything other than sexual.

Emma and I laughed, and slept together, but our drunken stupor put paid to any further outrages. I woke before her, kissed her softly on the cheek and said goodbye, then staggered home before the sunrise. I was not the only woman in crumpled gladrags and smudged make-up abroad at that time of a Saturday morning, but I felt slightly elated in being a little 'different'. However, guilt rapidly set in and vastly outweighed the confusion that now described my sexuality.

It was with some relief that I set out for Little Hintock the morning after Boxing Day. I suppose I was secretly hoping for a bit of rough and ready rural romance to convince me that I really wasn't, well, you know what. As I left, the rain began to blow in on a stiff east wind, but by the time I'd left the motorway, as per my instructions, snow was beginning to settle and it was not without some difficulty that I eventually reached my destination just as night was falling. I collected the key to the cottage, unpacked, bathed and fell fast asleep before I even had time to open the large bottle of gin I had brought with me.

I opened my curtains to fields of virgin snow stretching up to the woods on one side and down to the village on the other. It lay thick and crisp and even except where blown against the wall in shallow drifts. Quickly I showered, wrapped myself up and hurried outside lest the spell should suddenly break. The sun, low in the east, illuminated the scene with perfect precision and, for the most fleeting of moments, I was a child again, jumping into the drifts and throwing snowballs into the huge oaks that overlooked the cottage. Then, equally suddenly, I became acutely aware of my isolation, that there was no one to throw snowballs at, and melancholia overcame me.

I dashed back inside, stoked up the log fire, then submerged myself in a deep hot bath. It was at least an opportunity to use up all the cheap and tacky Christmas gifts my 'boyfriend' had bought me. I'd been given a much more expensive set by Emma (prior to our little assignation) and it was these I doused myself in before dressing for dinner.

Feeling in a suitably gothic temperament I put on a long black skirt, boots and a silk top and, with half a mind on reinventing myself as a demon in disguise, I plucked up the courage to wear the black cloak I'd found in a nearby antiques shop. I pulled the heavy hood over my long blonde hair then set off down the High Street, a dark silhouette against the crisp, untouched snow. Although I felt rather conspicuous and more than a little nervous, there was nevertheless an unmistakable frisson within me, a heady mix of anticipation and excitement, as if what I was indulging in were slightly forbidden and even possessed an element of danger. In this twilight world of shadows and half-truths, I decided that my role as a mere urban functionary represented all that was dull and mundane, and so began to reinvent myself as an entirely exotic creature as befitted these seductive surroundings.

Much to my surprise, I was greeted at the inn with a warm welcome and quickly ushered to a table by the fire. Indeed, no one seemed at all perturbed by the sudden appearance of a single woman dining alone. I was served by Marty, a woman of much the same age and appearance as myself – a little plain and unexciting – but such was my heightened sense of awareness that I immediately sensed a knowing look passing between us. Sure enough, she waited upon me like a maidservant, and every time she passed by she would sit down and indulge in pleasantly trivial conversation. Presently, a small crowd had gathered around my table but, despite the fact that we were crammed close together, the table next to us remained vacant. I was just about to suggest we commandeer it when a plush car pulled up outside and a party of five marched in as if they owned the place. Silently, and with an air of authority that was as impressive as it was offensive, they occupied the adjacent table and, before they could even click their fingers, Marty was at their beck and call, transformed from an ebullient flirt into an obsequious and submissive sycophant. Within a moment the evening had lost its pleasure and I became aware that I had run into an encounter with one of the less pleasant aspects of rural life – unreconstructed feudalism.

I really should have left there and then in silent protest but I ordered myself one last drink and sat down to observe my neighbours, who possessed a strange but repugnant fascination. There were two couples, mid-twenties, dressed in taffeta and tie and tails, all somewhat the worse for wear and behaving rather childishly. Typical, I thought, how the rich and the privileged find it hard to behave with the dignity of the poor – but then they don't have to, of course. The fifth member of the party, however, sat apart from her companions and brought them to task whenever their behaviour became intolerable. Perfectly groomed and well spoken, she sipped her gin and tonic with a disdainful elegance that suggested she was only there out of a sense of duty. From behind a fringe of flame-red hair that flowed in waves down to her shoulders gazed a pair of bright, almond eyes from a ripe, handsome face that demanded attention and respect. She was dressed, like myself, from head to toe in black, and I sensed a hint of antipathy in her demeanour. She glowered at me and I, in turn, returned her contempt, disgusted as I was by the deference shown to her by the entire clientele of the inn, who never ceased to bow and scrape before her, although her companions were merely tolerated. More to the point, she had usurped from me the undivided attention of Marty and was relishing it.

I decided to round off the evening with a coffee and signalled to Marty, who was about to come to my service until my adversary loudly clicked her fingers and immediately took precedence. In a fit of egalitarian pique I suggested aloud that it was I who had first requested Marty's attention. To my intense surprise, the pub fell silent and I was the object of a dozen dirty looks, including one from Marty, before she turned her attention to the woman in black. As a murmur of conversation returned I was carefully reminded by one of my neighbours that I'd 'find the ways of country folk a little queer', and was about to smile knowingly when he quickly added, in a voice I thought quite menacing, 'but you'll soon learn not to cross the likes of Miss Charmond'.

I eventually got my coffee, but it was only lukewarm and was not served by Marty. I began to feel excluded and lonely, and that my attempt to break the spell that enveloped them had reaffirmed my status as an outsider. I yawned deliberately, rambled on about how

tiring was the country air then visited the bathroom
before making ready to leave. The only cubicle was
engaged so I gazed lovingly at myself in the mirror
whilst waiting. Just as the previous incumbent
emerged, the woman in black burst into the toilet and
placed her hand upon the door. Accustomed to such
boorish, metropolitan behaviour, my natural instinct
was to obstruct her and elbow my way into the cubicle;
I was quite prepared to resort to physical force and the
fact that I had already formed an intensely unfavour-
able opinion of my adversary made me all the more
determined. Indeed, a minor scuffle was about to erupt
between us until the shuffle of feet reminded my friend
that decorum was required from a woman of her breed-
ing, especially in dealing with an upstart such as
myself. Feeling rather proud of my rebellious streak
and act of defiance, I was in no mood to hurry and
made sure my toilet was a leisurely one. I flushed the
lavatory and waited a further five minutes before I
emerged. My nemesis was still waiting and had apparently swelled in size and stature such that even I, a
taller than average woman, felt dwarfed by her presence. Her wide eyes were burning fire and looked
daggers at mine, though she remained absolutely,
uneasily silent. In such encounters I would normally
posses the wit to deliver the quick put-down I am
notorious for but for once I was struck dumb, my
mouth left hanging agape and voiceless like a simple
fool. Sensing the moral high ground she relaxed her
stare into an icy, antagonistic half smile before turning
away. For a split second I was rooted to the spot and,
when I came to my senses, was overcome with such a
profound sense of unease and apprehension that I left
quickly by the side door.

Whereas my previous night's sleep had been peaceful, relaxed and visited by the sweetest of dreams, I

now found myself tossing and turning in a troubled torpor, despite the substantial amount of alcohol I'd consumed. Although the temperature outside had dropped well below freezing, I lay sweating, naked, under a heavy winter duvet. When sleep eventually came it was accompanied by nightmares in which Miss Felice Charmond featured prominently. I slept late and woke feeling unrefreshed and still tired.

It had snowed again in the night, quite heavily, and was only beginning to ease off as I finished my breakfast. Within the hour the cloud had cleared and by lunchtime bright sun was dancing off the crystals of ice and flickering through the laden boughs, so I decided to take a walk into the estate and get some much-needed fresh air. Such was my lethargy, however, that it was mid-afternoon before I eventually passed by the gatehouse that marked the entrance to the long, tree-lined drive that led straight to the imposing porch of Melbury Bubb.

The air was still and calm, and the sun reflected from the snow felt warm and dreamlike and lulled me into a false sense of security. I was conjuring up images of nymphs, satyrs and demon lovers that tempted me off the well-trodden track and deep into the woods, and, before I knew it, darkness was rapidly descending around me. I came upon an unanticipated junction, examined the map and, without much conviction, took the fork that sloped gently downhill. After an hour's increasingly frantic walking it became clear that I had taken the wrong turning and, if not quite lost, was at least temporarily unsure of my exact location. Yet I was certain I was heading in the direction of the House and would eventually come upon one of the paved roads that dissected the estate which would, in turn, take me back to the village. Despite my confidence, the silence and darkness, relieved only by the flickering stars and lights of the distant Melbury Bubb, put me on edge, and the woodland creatures I had previously sought as mythical lovers now pursued my every stride. However, it soon became apparent that this was no mere figment of the imagination; the soft footsteps in the snow behind me were very real. Terrified, I turned to see what beast was following me; a hand seized my shoulder in its powerful grip and spun me around so that I almost fell. I'm not sure whether it was with relief or disappointment that I realised that I had been accosted by an estate worker, but for some reason I suddenly felt unthreatened. True, he accused me in a deep and gruff voice of trespassing, but there was a complete absence of threat or malevolence. It was not his duty to be judge or jury, merely to fulfil his function in the overall scheme of things. He had no responsibility, merely a role. I protested, loudly at first, but when it became apparent that no one could hear and I was in no immediate danger, I fell silent and acquiesced.

I had not been lost, after all, for we were at the House within five minutes. Typically, I was taken to the rear, the tradesman's entrance, but was at least reassured that after a swift ticking off – which I would vehemently protest – and a reminder of how different rules apply in the countryside and us city folk shouldn't forget it, I would be only a half hour's walk from my cottage.

My captor pulled on a long bell and, within less than a minute, the door was opened by a young woman dressed in a maid's uniform. I have to say that this barely surprised me as I was already growing accustomed to the retrogressive practices of rural Dorset. She was Latin in appearance and I immediately assumed that the poor girl had fled some despotic regime only to become part of another. Whatever, she was clearly aware of the delicate hierarchy in which she existed, for she was polite but short with the henchman who still had my shoulder firmly in his grip.

'I caught this trollop wandering in the grounds,' he murmured, without a hint of malice. 'I thought the mistress ought to know. You know how Miss Charmond feels about such things'.

By now I had convinced myself I'd be left to follow the estate road back to the village. I couldn't imagine that the lady of the house would be bothered with a lost rambler, certainly not in the middle of the festive season, and it hadn't registered with me that the incumbent was the same woman I had crossed swords with the night before. Even so, what could she do? In the wider scheme of the twentieth century I had little to fear from the remnants of the aristocracy, whatever ambivalent feelings she aroused within me.

The maid departed and, on returning, informed my apprehender that his mistress thanked him for his diligence but would deal with the 'miscreant' herself. She placed a coin in his palm then summarily dismissed him, as a queen would her subject, although his grip on my shoulder remained. Then she turned to me, saying in a strained and stilted English accent that belied her background, 'The young lady is to come with me as the mistress wishes to interview her.'

It was at that moment that a distant notion that had been growing at the back of my mind suddenly manifested itself as an unfortunate reality. The owner of Melbury Bubb and its estate, if not the entire village as well, was none other than my adversary of the previous night – the lady in black herself, Miss Felice Charmond. Why this aroused such distress within me I couldn't be sure, only I was vaguely aware that in trespassing into her domain I had entered a realm whose rules and traditions were very different to those

I was accustomed to – that here they were decreed and implemented by this aristocratic dictator. Feebly I began to protest that I had to get back to the cottage to dine with friends who would be waiting for me, but my escort would have none of it. He gripped me tighter still and gently pushed me inside. Behind me the door was slammed shut and bolted. The maid led me through a maze of dark or dimly lit corridors that were – and still are – the servants' quarters. When we reached the more stately rooms she stopped and, quite matter-of-factly, ordered me to strip down to my underwear as I could proceed no further in my muddy clothes. Quite naturally I refused, genuinely concerned that more depraved motives were afoot for which I, as an obviously single and therefore vulnerable woman, was an ideal target. However, the maid simply shrugged her shoulders and turned away.

'It doesn't matter to me,' she murmured nonchalantly. 'I've got all weekend.'

She smiled thinly, stoked up the fire then disappeared. The minute she was out of sight I attempted to make a run for it but before I could even reach the door the tall, elegant figure of Miss Charmond had placed herself between myself and freedom. The maid looked on with a self-satisfied smile; I had dug myself deep into their trap.

'And where do you think you're going, young lady?' demanded Miss Charmond in a firm and authoritative voice.

My natural instinct was to ignore her and, if necessary, resort to violence. Indeed, when Miss Charmond refused to withdraw I raised my hands to push her away, but the moment she took my wrists in her hand my resistance suddenly faltered and I withered before her with little more than a glare of defiance. For a minute or more we existed in a period of tense, strained silence, as if we were both trying to measure each other up and evaluate the situation. It was I, however, who conceded, and I lowered my head and my eyes as if in a gesture of surrender.

'I'm s-s-sorry,' I stammered. 'I'm afraid I became lost in the woods ... when it got dark I panicked and looked for the quickest route back to the village ...'

Miss Charmond snorted and tossed back her flowing mane of red hair. She was, perhaps, two or three years my senior, certainly no more, but unlike me she was immaculately attired, and had poise, style and grace. I stood before her in muddied boots and leggings and an old, shapeless jumper and suddenly felt quite inferior to this exotic and elegant creature.

'Please, madam,' I whispered pathetically, 'I would like to get home, I promise I'll keep to the paths in future.'

'I am afraid, my child, that your apologies will not suffice; they contain neither sincerity nor conviction. We have met before, have we not, and I seem to recall a similar display of insubordination. I vowed there and then to wipe that smug smile off your face, and I see fate has delivered me that opportunity sooner that I could have hoped for. Patience is a virtue one should learn to appreciate but occasionally it has to be taught to those of a less sophisticated disposition. Now, Miss Samantha, I believe that Grace, my maid, politely asked you to strip down to your underwear; perhaps you will do her the honour of complying with this instruction.'

Grace had returned to see what all the fuss was about and a victorious smirk crossed her face when her mistress reinforced her direction.

Utterly confused and emotionally disorientated, I remained immobile until my procrastination roused within Miss Charmond an anger I had never previously had the misfortune to witness, for it was neither harsh nor hysterical. On the contrary, both the tone and volume of Miss Charmond's voice were lowered, and she articulated each vowel and consonant with greater care and precision. She remained calm and aloof and yet the force of her personality enveloped every inch of the hall and caused Grace to flee to her quarters.

'Miss Samantha,' she continued, as if addressing an insolent and insignificant little child, 'despite appearances to the contrary I am a busy woman and I have a function to attend later this evening. I certainly do not have time to waste on the likes of you, and neither am I in the habit of issuing commands for the sake of pleasure –' and here a contemptuous smile passed over her lips as she whispered '– well, not in this case, anyway.' Orders are there to be obeyed whether they come from Grace or myself. Do you understand?'

I stood silent and motionless.

'I said, do you understand?' repeated Miss Charmond, and such was her authority that my instinctive response was a weak and wretchedly whispered 'yes'.

Then, as if completely overpowered by the hypnotic authority of Miss Felice Charmond, I meekly acquiesced. Standing in front of the roaring fire I unzipped my jacket and placed it in her outstretched hands. My boots she placed on the grate along with the watery socks. I paused now, and looked up at my adversary.

'I said down to your underwear,' she hissed, beginning to sound impatient. With great trepidation I tugged off my muddy leggings, my jumper and then, finally, a thin T-shirt, and stood before Miss Charmond in only my knickers and bra.

Her orders adhered to, Miss Charmond finally let out a sigh of relief and called for Grace to take care of my clothes. 'Come with me,' she ordered, and when I failed to obey instantly she took hold of my ear and attempted to pull me along behind her. Instinctively I hit out, but Miss Charmond caught my hopelessly flailing arm and, like a trained fighter, twisted it behind my back. I was so astonished by this display of strength that I yielded and silently followed Miss Charmond through to the main sitting room, where a huge fire was burning. She let go and told me to stand before it.

Miss Charmond calmly sat down on the luxurious sofa and poured herself a drink, making no attempt to hide the pleasure of her triumph. She sipped demurely then attempted to engage me in eye contact but, knowing I was defeated, I stared only at the floor, trying to make some sort of sense of the conflicting emotions rushing through both my mind and my body. For, try as I might, I could not suppress a faint sense of delicious anticipation through the anger and the shame and the sense of injustice. I genuinely hated Miss Felice Charmond and all that she stood for and yet, if I had really wanted to, I could have created a scene and made an escape. To a certain extent, then, I was here of my own accord, in pursuit of a dangerous unknown I had never before experienced in the dull and mundane meritocracy I inhabited. As the ominous silence persisted, however, curiosity gave way to fear and I became both irritated and anxious as a result of Miss Charmond's inactivity.

'I think you've made your point, now, Miss Charmond. I know full well that you do things differently down here and I've played along with your perverted concept of justice and retribution. I think I've been humiliated enough now, so perhaps you'd be so good as to return my clothes so I can go home. Otherwise I shall have no alternative but to . . .'

Miss Charmond's ears pricked and she rose instantly to meet my thinly veiled threat.

'No alternative but to what, my child? I don't take kindly to threats, especially ones of a veiled nature, and especially when they are issued without any substance. As far as I'm concerned, Miss Samantha, there is no such thing as an "alternative" and there is nothing at all "perverted" about the manner in which we live our lives outwith the sway of your metropolitan Pandemonium. Rules are not made to be broken, they exist for very good reasons. They have been created to serve order and harmony.

'Besides which, what authorities do you propose to petition against me? You fail to realise, Miss Samantha, that as far as this part of the world is concerned, democracy and liberalism are mistrusted as modern concepts that have never really caught on in the popular imagination. On the contrary, people trust and respect authority, they like rules; they know where they are, where they stand in the scheme of things. I think you will find that any attempt to subvert my jurisdiction will be met with contempt and disbelief. Think about it: which of us has the greater honour and integrity? As far as everyone here is concerned, Miss Samantha, I am democracy.'

And so saying she turned her back on me and rang the bell. Whilst I stood there, semi-naked, trembling with indignation and wondering how it might be possible to restore some rationality to the proceedings, Grace knocked on the door and, on entering, curtseyed before Miss Charmond, who issued a deliberately inaudible instruction. Grace could barely conceal the huge smile that momentarily passed across her face as she disappeared. She returned a couple of minutes later carrying with her a thin whippy cane.

'Thank you, Grace. That will be all.'

The maid curtseyed once more then took her leave, but not before giving me another of her smug smiles. It was only later that I remembered that I never heard the door click behind her.

As Miss Charmond advanced towards me with an undoubted sense of conviction and justice I was so captivated by the beauty of her brooding menace that it never occurred to me that she would actually go beyond the boundaries of conventional behaviour and strike me. That is to say, there came a point when her intentions became quite clear and for the first time the pleasure of anticipation was overrun by an acknowledgement of brutal reality. When I looked into Miss Charmond's hard, unforgiving eyes all sense of aesthetic indulgence rapidly evaporated and terror took hold. Certainly, pain and pleasure would be part of the complex equation that Miss Charmond has been referring to, but they were not synonymous. The pleasure was to be hers and hers alone; the pain, if I acquiesced, would be mine. But acquiesce is what I did, and for a woman who considered herself to be 'feminine but feisty', the manner in which I crumbled before her surprised me, even if she seemed to find it quite routine.

She led me, gently now, round to the side of a long sofa draped in a black silk throw. I knew what was coming, of course, and, by some mysterious force of osmosis, understood my role and how I was to behave in the ritual. It was an ageless scene, one that had been acted out time and time again within this very room since its construction and would be repeated again in the not too distant future. In a sense I was comforted by this knowledge, that I was part of a sea unseen, that somehow I was sacrificing myself for the greater good. And, as an individual driven by a blinkered desire for self-advancement at the expense of all else, to relinquish autonomy and responsibility and invest my trust in this powerful woman was something of a therapeutic act.

Miss Charmond placed her hand in the small of my

back and eased me over the arm of the sofa until I lay there, bent over, with my hands on the cushion and my backside high in the air. I winced and shivered briefly when she reached for my briefs and eased them down, but her confidence and authority had put me strangely at ease. Miss Charmond lay the cane lightly on my buttocks then raised it high. The whistle of its arc sweeping gracefully through the air gave me sufficient forewarning but did not prepare me for the stinging pain that ripped through my body. I screamed, somewhat extravagantly, then gulped for air as I recoiled from the shock. The next stroke followed swiftly, reiterating the impact of the previous blow and causing involuntary spasms in an equal and opposite reaction. There was a brief pause before a third stroke cut into the top of my thighs and a fourth, the coup de grâce, was delivered with heartfelt force and venom. It was at this moment that my howls gave way to tears welling in my eyes and, expecting another blow of even greater severity, my body shook with terrible anticipation. Miss Charmond must have sensed this, and realised that her punishment had served its purpose and broken any vestige of resistance that might have remained within my soul.

'Relax, Miss Samantha, please,' she whispered. 'Two more strokes and then we are through. The worst is over now.'

The worst was indeed over, but the ritual had to be completed; the carefully woven spell could not be rudely interrupted. The remainder of the punishment was meted out with enthusiasm and vigour but the friction between us was gone: harmony had been restored. I lay prone on the settee, sobbing uncontrollably from pain, shock and humiliation.

It was a well-measured chastisement, carried out with meticulous care and attention and, despite our previous hostility, I could not detect a hint of spite or malice in her actions. From somewhere deep inside the innermost recesses of my psyche came the words 'thank you', to which Miss Charmond smiled, taken aback by the effectiveness of her actions. It later occurred to me that she wasn't quite prepared for the swiftness of my capitulation, nor the intensity of my submission, but so total was my surrender that I would have remained where I was indefinitely had she not asked me to stand up. Feeling faint and feeble, I almost collapsed, and Miss Charmond had to hold me still. For a moment she was so close that I could feel her breath on my neck, sweet with a tinge of gin and tonic. She turned away to hang the cane over the back of a chair and, as I watched her do so, I felt a very strange and not at all unpleasant frisson shudder through my body.

My tormentor's tone had completely changed; the ice queen had thawed and a gentle warmth now oozed out of her every pore. She sat down on the sofa and, much to my consternation, asked me to drape myself over her lap. I did so unquestioningly but this time, instead of a repeat of the pain I had expected, she began to rub into my bruised flesh a thick, cold cream that initially stung but soon brought a warm, tingling sensation to my buttocks and, as her fingers wandered to the top of my thighs, began to stir tremors between my legs.

There was a knock on the door and Miss Charmond, slightly flustered, ushered me to my feet and wrapped a silk dressing-gown around me. 'Come in,' she barked, her voice reverting to its authoritarian tone. Grace entered and informed her mistress that the car was ready for her. She carried with her my clothes, freshly washed and somehow dried and ironed. The servant was abruptly dismissed, and whilst checking her countenance in the mirror – her efforts had barely put a hair out of place – Miss Charmond kept an eye on me as I dressed. She was about to leave when, almost as an afterthought, she turned to me.

'Miss Samantha,' she snapped, remembering my presence, 'I would hate you to come to the conclusion that I am a cruel woman; perhaps you will come to see that before you leave. As you have just learned, duty carries with it rights and responsibilities on both our parts, and sometimes we have difficulty in understanding those complex relationships. As a gesture of reconciliation on my part, please allow me to give you a lift back to your cottage; it will save you a walk on a cold, dark night – not that you'll come to any harm round here, I see to that.'

That she was aware of where I was staying came as no surprise to me. I was convinced that she was somehow involved in the circumstances that had brought me to her tonight, for she seemed more than adequately prepared. I nodded my acceptance of her offer and we made the short journey to the village in silence. When the car pulled up in the snow that had accumulated at the cottage gate, I reached for the handle to open the door only to feel Miss Charmond's hand on mine refraining me from so doing. Instead, the smartly liveried chauffeur got out, walked round the back of the limousine and, before opening my door, cleared some of the snow from my path. As he was doing this Miss Charmond bid me a rather formal goodnight but then added, with a hint of mischief, 'and remember, Miss Samantha, you are quite free to walk my estate if you wish. You only had to ask.'

I returned to my cottage in a trance-like state. In the short space of an afternoon my world had been turned on its head and my body pulsed to a plethora of conflicting emotions charging each other head-on. To complicate matters even further, from somewhere deep within me welled up an incessant sexual energy that would, at some point over the next few days, have to be discharged.

I had arranged to call in at the pub and have a drink with Marty on her night off, but found myself only in the mood for isolation and reflection. I ran myself a deep, hot bath and, before luxuriating in the sweet, herbally infused waters, I stripped off and wandered naked around the twee little cottage. When I caught a glimpse of my body in the mirror, curiosity got the better of me and I decided to examine the state of my posterior. Six angry red stripes, perfectly spaced, stood out from the pale, untouched flesh. I lay in the bath, reliving the events of the evening and etching them deep into my memory. I dried myself by the fire then dived naked under the duvet where I was soon enveloped by deep and delicious sleep, the like of which I had not experienced since I was a child. Next morning I was woken, refreshed and invigorated, by turning on a damp patch on the sheet. For a moment I wondered what had happened until I realised that I was dripping wet. I turned on to my back and explored myself again.

Bootblack Tulsa Brown

'A good living,' I said, 'shining shoes?'

'A damned good living,' Mona said. 'Or it can be. It's up to you, Craig.'

I hesitated, still grappling. 'But why me?'

Mona arched one of her thin, dark eyebrows, her eyes twinkling at me just a bit. 'Because I think you're the right man for the job.'

I needed one of those, quite desperately, but I wasn't sure why Mona had sought me out. We'd shared a few classes in university, passed a word or two together in the crowded clubs, but we'd never danced. I would have liked to. Mona was small and shapely, with pert breasts that swung freely under her T-shirts and blouses, the points of her nipples drawing my helpless gaze every time she moved. Her dark hair was razored short everywhere but the front, where spiky bangs tumbled over her forehead and often into her eyes. I longed to brush them aside, and didn't dare.

There was something about Mona that unnerved me, and maybe everyone else. No one I knew had dated her. She was two years older and seemed light years ahead of me, thoughts flashing behind her blue eyes that I couldn't even guess at. And sometimes she looked at me with a crumpled little smile, her head tilted, as if she were looking through my clothes, right through my skin, into a silent and secret place.

To find what? I thought irritably. There's nothing. It's nothing.

'All right,' I told Mona.

'Good. You start tomorrow. Wear this.' She pulled a skimpy black muscle shirt out of her oversized handbag and tossed it at me. 'And tighter pants. You've got a great ass.'

I grinned like a fool. 'Thanks. You, too.'

Her smile was amused, beaming down at me from a lofty place.

'You've been working out,' she said. 'I noticed.'

I couldn't stop my chest from puffing. 'I try to stay with it.'

'If you need motivation, I'll come along and count for you.' The words were playful but there was a sizzle under them, and a snap. I had a sudden vision of being laid out on the weight bench, sweating under the bar while Mona counted my lifts mercilessly, cool and dark above me. The image was strange and unsettling. I turned away from it, mumbling my goodbyes, but only got a few paces.

'I can't wear this!' I'd finally noticed the white letters that blazed across the scanty black shirt: *the boy*.

Mona's pretty face hardened, and her hand went to her hip.

'Why not? I wear one that says *the girl*. It's how people remember me – the girl shining shoes.'

My face prickled. 'It's ... demeaning.'

'Is it? Well, Craig, let me enlighten you. There are two other shine stands in the airport and I have more business than both of them. Why? Because when a customer climbs up into that chair and I bend over at his feet, his shoes become the whole world.' Her voice lowered. 'There's nothing demeaning about service.'

Strong sensations were running through me, like the fascination of a cliff edge. Mona was looking through my clothes again.

'All right. See you tomorrow,' I said.

'Don't forget your push-ups,' she called mischievously after me, loud enough that people looked.

Bitch, I thought, but the taunt in her voice stroked down my back like a hand.

I was at the airport the next morning at eight. The big complex was already humming with people hurrying or dawdling, depending on their flights. Mona's stand was against a wide pillar, well out from the other shops, and directly in the flow of foot traffic. I realised it was probably good for business but it still struck me as exposed.

Mona had not only opened up but was already at work on a customer, devoting herself to the cowboy boots of a Western-styled businessman. He had a newspaper in his hand but he wasn't reading it. His eyes were riveted on her.

So were mine. She was sitting on her haunches, her thighs spread wide and her knees not touching the ground. It was a precarious position and her back was arched to help her hold it, thrusting her breasts out still further, like an offering. The black T-shirt with spaghetti straps seemed painted over her curvy shape, *the girl* leaping out at me like white neon. It was a sharp contrast to the dark, masculine fuzz of hair on the back of her head, and her tightly muscled arms. She was well-equipped to deliver the hand-rubbed shine her sign promised.

I wanted to see it from the front. There were three chairs on top of the platform, and stairs at either end. I climbed up and sat down, leaving an empty seat between myself and the cowboy, and was immediately hooked.

The spandex clung to her upturned breasts, tension tugging a line between the two nipples and leaving the inner curves a mystery. They swung lightly, saucily, as she buffed, and it took me a moment to notice anything else. When I did, her movements became mesmerising. She wasn't slavish or fawning, but her complete attention was centred on those boots. She rubbed every curve with deliberate, sensual strength, often bending low to inspect her work. It emphasised the distance between them, his rugged body towering over hers.

I felt drugged, excitement like a warm fist in my belly. Just then Mona leaned down again, lifted the pointed toe close to her mouth, and exhaled a soft 'hah' of moist breath on the leather. It was as intimate and shocking as a kiss, and it sent a welt of heat down to my balls. My tight pants were getting tighter.

But she was done now. The cowboy climbed down from the platform, grinning at her as if in a languid dream, and tipped her the entire price of the shine. He walked away unsteadily, looking back more than once.

Mona squeezed the money into her back pocket and whipped around, glaring up at me.

'Get your ass out of that chair.'

The snap in her voice woke me. The bitch was back.

'OK, OK. I just wanted to see.'

'Your job,' she emphasised the word, 'is down here. Don't forget it. Now take your jacket off.'

Reluctantly I did as I was told. In the privacy of my apartment, I'd been pleased with the sharp contours of my muscled arms, the way my chest stretched the little scrap of a shirt, and how my thighs strained against the faded denim. But under the bright, institutional lights of the airport I felt suddenly naked, as obvious as a whore among the stream of suits and ties. *The boy.* The label on my back seemed to burn me.

'My, my,' Mona said, circling me a with gleam, 'aren't you a number. They'll be lining up for you, once I get you trained.'

The innuendo made me prickle. A corner of my mind

was demanding that I go, but I felt helpless in her gaze, stroked by it. Whether crouched at a man's feet or inspecting me like a piece of livestock, Mona was exciting. It was all ... exciting.

'How sweet,' Mona said. 'He blushes, too. Well, let's get started.'

She showed me the polishes and the applicator, which was battery-run. The buffing, though, all had to be done by hand.

'It takes practice to bring up a good shine,' Mona insisted. 'You can start with these.'

She opened a door under the stand and tugged out a box. It was filled with women's shoes: spikes and platforms, flats and pointed boots, some studded with brass rivets. The colours were dazzling – black, brown, red, pink – and the scent of leather wafted up, lush and mysterious.

'Do we get many women customers?' I asked.

'About twenty per cent,' Mona said. 'These are all mine.'

I was reeling with the intimacy of it, the idea of taking her little shoes into my hand, when she plunked another pair of boots down beside me. They were men's boots, made of black leather, square-toed and heavy-soled, with thick bands across the heel and around the ankle joined by a brass ring. They were kick-ass boots, top of the food chain, creased with the weight and wear of a big man.

'Yours, too?' I tried to tease, but there was a catch in my throat.

'They belong to a friend of mine. When you've finished all the others and can do a decent job, I'll let you try these. It's something to work up to.'

Was he fucking her? I wondered bitterly. Did she bend over at his feet, ass in the air, breasts swaying? Yet even in the wave of my jealousy there was another ripple: I'd be servicing the boots that Mona serviced. The thought cupped me between the legs like a stranger's hand, a jolt of pleasure and alarm. I mentally stepped away from it, but it seemed to trail me, an animal that had my scent.

I spent most of the day on my knees, polishing Mona's shoes. Despite the indignity, I found myself becoming enthralled with them: the soft, smooth texture of the leather, the graceful arch of the soles. They were hardly more than the length of my hand and yet there was a danger to them, with their pointed toes and spiked heels. When I imagined Mona slipping her foot into one, I couldn't stop the shiver.

I stole glances at her often. If she wasn't serving a customer she sat on the only stool, stretch jeans hugging her shapely thighs, her face as cool and distant as an icon. Occasionally she came over to check my progress, to correct or instruct, but I got the feeling she was watching me more closely than that, and I revelled in it.

At the end of the day I was working on her 'friend's' boots when Mona leaned over me, a hand on my naked shoulder.

'I have a customer for *the boy*,' she said.

It woke me with a double-edged wallop, the startling heat of her touch and the humiliation of that name. I'd almost forgotten it was on my back. I got up and stretched my stiff limbs, my stomach flipping with trepidation.

I'll never forget that first time, the embarrassment of squatting at a stranger's feet, the sensation of being spread and on display in my whore's clothes. Never mind what Mona had said, I felt subservient, and I couldn't understand the tingles that licked me up the legs. To make it worse, the other man's boots were still vivid in my mind and I was churning with a disturbing blend of lust and resentment. I hated Mona's friend and yet I kept imagining him fucking her, even here in the airport, even while I polished his boots.

Heat on my neck, her hand again.

'That's it, show him how good you can be,' she purred against my ear. Her other hand slipped surreptitiously under my chest and squeezed one of my nipples, hard. I caught my breath, surging against my zip.

Mona was pleased, glowing with pride, even, as she took the money from my first customer. She separated out the tip and sauntered over to me, close enough for me to see the faint gleam of sweat in her cleavage.

'Nice work, Craig. You take direction *very* well, and I know he enjoyed the scenery.' She tucked the bills into my front pocket, a teasing tug on the front of my pants.

I was hot and bold. 'You want to go for a beer?'

She tilted her head at me, smiling a crumpled little smirk. 'Let's just wait until I get you trained.'

That word again, forcing itself into my mind the way a bit and bridle are forced into a horse's mouth. Yet there was a shimmering pleasure in the pain of it – she was excited.

You like that bit, her heavy-lidded eyes seemed to say. *And I like that you like it.*

I was burning, ready. In my mind's eye I backed her against a pillar and lifted her onto my throbbing, engorged cock with the whole airport watching.

'Don't forget your push-ups,' she whispered, turning away.

I went to the washroom before I left, splashed my face and leaned on the sink.

Where are you, Craig? I wondered. Who are you? I couldn't remember another day like this, smouldering with sex one minute, stinging with shame the next. Now it felt as if I'd come to the edge of a vast pool, the silent, dark place in the centre of my own belly. I was frightened, but Mona was waiting on the other side and I wanted her. I wanted it all.

I let Mona train me. Day after day I let her direct my body and my attention, learned to enjoy the warm fatigue in my muscles and the delicious, hungry ache that pulsed between my thighs. I never got used to the bold stares from passing strangers, yet I endured them because I knew Mona was also watching me. I lived for her hard glare or teasing flutter, and the rare steady gaze that said she knew how to open me.

I was opening her, too. When I dropped into a low, uncomfortable crouch at a man's feet, it hooked her. If she wasn't at work herself she would climb up into a chair, cross one leg over the other and swing her foot lightly as she watched me. I was certain she was pulling the seam tight against her sex, rubbing it, and it pushed me down lower over my customer's feet. It became a single, stroking arousal, those leather boots by my face and Mona's wet excitement above me.

Then came the day I grew bold. I was working on a young woman in a short skirt and knee-high platforms, who chatted on her cell phone without looking at me. On a whim I lifted the thick sole of the boot to my chest, letting it press my pecs like a conqueror's foot as I buffed away. Above me, Mona leaned forwards in her chair.

I knew I was holding her. Heart thumping, I bent my head forwards and opened my mouth on the leather toe, a small wet kiss. I felt a sudden throb between my legs and the dark space inside me quivered, rippling outwards in a wave. Mona closed her eyes.

The phone rang late that night.

'Did I wake you, Craig?' Her voice was a low, sensual growl against my ear. 'Are you ready to do those push-ups for me?'

The question lifted me out of blurry half-sleep, bringing me to my knees on the bed.

'I'm ready,' I said.

'Then there's someone I want you to meet. We'll go to his place.' Her voice licked my ear in a tease. 'Are you up for it?'

The heavy black boots with the brass rings suddenly filled my entire mind with a shock of alarm and bitterness. At the same time the welt of desire smacked me with the hard, certain stroke of a whip.

'Craig?' Mona prompted.

'Should ... should I dress for work?'

'No. In fact, don't wear a shirt at all under your jacket. Now, move your ass. I'm waiting downstairs.'

My ass was hers to move. In three minutes I was washed and brushed and down in the street with her, naked under my jacket and trousers.

Mona wasn't dressed for work either. She wore a long black trench-coat that glimmered under the streetlights and had a surprising fluff of feathers at the collar, like a stripper's boa. The front was unbuttoned and through the narrow gap I glimpsed her clingy black top, thigh-high leather mini, and the long, svelte shock of her bare legs.

And new boots. They were breathtaking, black anklets with stiletto heels and a shiny gold cap on each pointed, menacing toe. The ankle and heel were bound by leather straps that joined with a brass ring, a miniature version of the boots that I'd polished – her friend's boots. The sight of them was like a kick in the back of my knees.

'We'll take the subway,' Mona said.

I followed her obediently, awake to every new thrill: my bare nipples chafing under my jacket, the sharp clicking of her heels on the pavement. Still, apprehension gusted through me in waves. Had this been his idea, or hers? What would I have to do, and would I have a choice?

Mona led me into an apartment block that was like any other: glass and concrete, an elevator. Riding up, she astonished me by taking my hand.

'You're trembling. That's so sweet. Are you afraid?'

'Yes,' I whispered.

'Craig, I want you to know two things. First, I think you're very special. Second, you wouldn't be here if I didn't think you were ready.'

I was still back at 'special', soaring with hope. Mona leaned in and cupped my crotch in a squeeze that made me gasp, and opened every blood vessel I had.

'Make me proud,' she murmured. I stumbled out of the elevator after her in a daze.

The man wasn't what I expected. He was big enough to fill those boots, but he wasn't the hulking biker of my imagination. Instead, he was like his apartment: masculine, smooth and calm. About fifty and solid, he had neatly barbered salt-and-pepper hair, expensive khakis and a gaze that ran right through me.

I stood in the living room, bare chested and shoeless, my fingers interlocked behind my head. He kicked my feet wider apart like an experienced street cop, then squeezed my nipple so hard I winced.

'Very nice, Mona. Healthy and strong. Is he well hung?'

'I'm not sure. You said not to . . .'

His smile was almost benevolent. 'Well, you'd better check, then.'

Mona reached around me from behind. I felt the press of her tits against my back as she fumbled for my zip, and was helpless in the rush of need. I closed my eyes, not wanting him to see it.

His hand gripped my chin roughly and I blinked

open again, startled. Steel-coloured eyes drilled into mine.

'Your mistress wishes to display you for her pleasure. That is *your* pleasure.'

He continued to hold my burning face, forcing me to look into his implacable gaze while Mona released my growing hard-on. She measured the thickening length by touch, and it pulled a low moan out of my throat, past gritted teeth.

'Oooh, he's a two-hander,' Mona laughed, undulating her leather hips against me.

'Discipline, Mona,' the man cautioned, glancing over my shoulder at her. 'He hasn't earned it yet and neither have you.' His eyes focused back into mine. 'Do you hate me?'

My guts flared. 'Yes.'

'Good. It will be a better test.' The man let go abruptly and stepped back. 'You may begin, Mona.'

'Get down, Craig. Give me forty push-ups.'

The giggling schoolgirl had transformed into a grave-yard angel, eyeliner and lipstick on stone. Make me proud, she'd said. I re-buttoned the top of my jeans, leaving the zip open to accommodate my erection, and dropped into position, ignited and determined.

'. . . thirteen, fourteen . . .' Mona chanted.

'The trapezius and deltoids are nicely defined, but he could put some effort into the lats. Make him work on that. You'll also need a good cock ring to get any stamina out of him. He looked ready to shoot the second you took him out.'

I burned beneath them, my muscles crying and sweat trickling from my temples. So this is a test, asshole? We'll see who comes out on top.

I made it to forty, and nearly collapsed. With supreme effort I forced myself back onto my heels, panting, rubbery, my veins pumped and throbbing with animal triumph.

He was sitting in a deep leather chair, one leg crossed casually over the other, purposefully unimpressed.

Mona was standing like a goddess, bare arms twined under her breasts, her legs spread and her black heels like daggers in the carpet. Even from the floor I could feel the smoky heat of her eyes, and could almost smell the lush female moisture gathering beneath the leather skirt. If we'd been alone I would have crawled to her on my knees.

'Good boy, Craig. That was very nice.' Her voice was low and intent, huskier than I'd ever heard it. 'Now there's just one more thing. Polish this gentleman's boots.'

Whiplash of fear. 'I can't. There isn't . . .'

'You have everything you need,' Mona said.

Oh God. I knew what she wanted. My face flamed in passing waves as I hesitated, my cock beginning to pulse against my will.

'Should I get his coat, Mona?'

'No! He'll do it. I know he can do this.' The stone angel's bottom lip quivered the tiniest bit, and I knew. This wasn't my test, it was hers.

And I loved her terribly, helplessly, loved her like a hero and a slave. I got up and walked over to the man I hated, knelt down at his boots and began to lap at the dark pool of my own dread.

Electric shocks of pleasure ran from my mouth down to my balls. As I licked at my rival's boots I lost myself in the hypnotic sensation, shame and lust twisting into a powerful coil around me. I wasn't just obedient, I was utterly conquered, and that stoked the steel piston straining between my legs. My cock was nearly bursting with its own life, forcing itself out of my trousers, huge and obvious. There was nowhere to hide. They could both see that I wanted this, needed it.

The man lifted his other boot and laid it on my shoulder, a footstool. I moaned at the sudden, satisfying weight of it.

'My God, he's so beautiful,' Mona said, her voice hushed.

'Do you see now how bewitching you were?' The words were touched by wistfulness.

'I want him. I want him *now*.'

The man removed his foot from my shoulder and used it to nudge me upright on my knees. I swayed dizzily, the wet skin around my mouth like an open wound, and fumbled with the last restraints of my trousers. Mona dropped down beside me, yanking up her clingy top to release her quivering breasts.

'No – make him come to you!'

It was too late. She gripped my thick ramrod and pulled me to her. Our mouths locked together, lipstick and leather-stained saliva smearing as she struggled to get the condom over me, while I squeezed her luscious tits and tugged up her skirt. Oh, glorious God – no underwear. My stone angel was plump, pulsing flesh and wet heat.

She melted onto her back and I followed, moaning as she guided my cock home. I plunged into the sweet, tight embrace, feeling her legs clamp around my back. It didn't matter that the man was watching – we were animals rutting on his living-room carpet. I'd already bared my naked need at his feet, and the memory of it lashed at my ass like a whip, driving me harder.

Mona let out a cry and I let myself go, jetting, shuddering, split open by waves of hot pleasure. And the aftershock of shame that followed squeezed another burst from me, so raw it was almost painful. I came and came, then finally held still in Mona's strong arms, trembling and empty and infinitely well.

'I guess you'll both have to work on restraint,' the man said wryly above us.

I got my clothes on without looking at him, but their murmuring voices in another corner of the room finally made me turn. Mona was dressed, proud and elegant in her heels and coat, the feathery collar like a sovereign's ruff. But when he held out a piece of paper, she clasped his hand in both of hers, and bent forwards to kiss it.

It was a knife in my slave's belly. I knew I would die hundreds of times like this, if she kept me. But whatever the test had been, it seemed as if she'd passed, and I was relieved and glad.

At the doorway he grabbed my chin again to make me look at him. The tears in his grey eyes were a shock.

'Serve her well,' he said. The gust of emotion undid me, cutting through my shame and loathing to a deeper place. I dropped to the floor and kissed the pointed gold toes on each of her boots. And then his.

Outside, it was almost dawn. The stars had faded, blackness giving way to the first deep blush of blue. Mona was thoughtfully silent and I trailed after her, my mind running.

She knew where.

'It was my freedom,' she said at last, reaching into her pocket. 'I'm my own boss now.'

She handed me the paper and I paused under a streetlight to read it. It was a bill of sale for the shine stand – paid in full.

The revelation opened up inside me. Mona hadn't owned the business; she'd just been the right woman for the job.

'It was a good life for a long time,' she said softly, 'but we both knew it wasn't forever. He always promised that when I was ready to go, I wouldn't leave empty-handed.'

'And I was proof that you were ready?' I blurted.

She tilted her head at me, half-shut eyes blurred with melted mascara.

'Ready to begin, yes. Don't think you're fully trained, Craig. There's *lots* you have to learn, and I had a superb instructor.'

'I'll always hate the men who want you.'

'But you'll serve them to please me,' Mona finished. The words rippled that dark pool again, exhilarating, terrifying, because now I knew how deep it was.

'Yes.'

'My little bootblack,' she said, taking my hand. 'Right now, breakfast pleases me. Come on, you can learn how I like it.'

Wytchfinder Lois Phoenix

Rosa-May holds tight to her sister's hand as the small band of girls race across the clearing. Her chest is so tight with fear and excitement she can hardly breathe. Once under the giant oak the girls droop against the trunk, weak with the thrill of escaping the village.

Rosa-May's face looks small and pale in the moonlight. 'I'm not sure I want to come now, Clara,' she whispers.

'Too late now,' Clara hisses back. 'You should have been asleep like you were supposed to be.'

'But this is wrong, isn't it?' the youngster asks, unsure whether to be delighted or terrified.

'If the elders won't allow us any fun, we shall have to make our own. I'm tired of being put to bed like a baby every night. I'm old enough for a walk in the woods, unchaperoned.'

Sarah giggles and clutches her nightgown closer around her bare legs. 'Aunt Rachel told me that greenwood marriages were still allowed when she was young.'

The girls gather around, clutching her arms and suppressing the urge to screech with excitement.

'Tell us again, Sarah!'

'Well, boys and girls of a certain age were allowed to spend the whole night together in the woods at Beltane.' Sarah's eyebrows rise dramatically. 'The whole night!'

'Can you believe it?' Clara whispers. 'Now we aren't allowed to show our hair or even think about boys.' She shakes her dark hair vigorously. 'But tonight we claim our lost rites. Have you brought the branches?'

Every girl holds up a small bough, one from each of the nine sacred trees, each collected and hidden in utmost secrecy.

'Excellent. Then we shall make a Bel-fire and conjure ourselves a lover.'

'A lover!' Rosa-May is giggling fit to bust.

'Not in your case. Stop screeching, Rosa-May, or you'll have the entire village out here. Now, while the moon is high we'll gather flowers in the bottom meadow for our garlands. And when we enter the woods I don't want anyone screaming.'

Deftly the girls gather armfuls of mugwort, mint and rosehip before passing through the veil of trees along the meadow edge and slipping into the wood. They walk in silence, feeling their way with bare feet over damp, springy moss.

'Here,' Clara whispers. 'This is the copse I was telling you about.'

A ring of flowering hawthorn shines like embroidered beads around them in the moonlight. At once the spring night feels milder and safer.

Stamping down a patch of fern Sarah sits down, clutching her flowers. Her toes curl into the fronds beneath her. How wonderful to be free of the constraints of Puritan dress. Her body feels curiously alive, as though a small bird were fluttering low down in her belly.

Clara is eager to begin. 'Pass the boughs into the middle, here. Helena, you help me light the fire. The rest of you, start to weave your flower crowns.'

They do not take long. Their fingers, used to embroidery and weaving, soon entwine the fragrant blossoms and leaves around fern stems.

'Yours is better.'

'No, yours.'

The girls giggle and weave until a small tongue of golden fire flickers amongst the kindling. Their laughter sinks into sighs as they are drawn towards it.

Clara's face reflects the flickering light as the flames consume her small bunches of dried lavender and heather. The scent is sublime. The girls stand transfixed and watch as the flames lick over the boughs of alder, maple, elm and birch.

'Rosa-May, pass me the rowan sprig,' commands Clara. Twisting it into a loop, she holds it aloft. 'Through this loop I shall see the man who loves me.' She takes a deep excited breath. 'Let us begin.'

Slowly, Clara slips her nightshift from her shoulders and turns for Helena to place a garland on her head.

'Do we have to go sky-clad too?' Rosa-May asks.

'Better than explaining burnt nightclothes,' Sarah whispers.

With hushed laughter, the girls step out of their cotton shifts and place a flower crown on each other's heads. Their eyes are full of dancing flames.

'Now let's show the church elders that they cannot stop us from conjuring up handsome young men!'

Whooping and laughing the girls follow Clara around the fire, elegantly dancing towards the warm flames, then pulling back towards the dark whispering woods – around and around until their skin glistens. When the flames start to die and the embers glow deep red, they take it in turns to jump over them. Clara first, of course, her long pale limbs easily clearing the fire.

'Queen of the May,' she calls out, 'bring me a lover to . . .'

A cracking of branches brings the girls to a halt. Their breath beats hot and fast but their flesh is suddenly doused with chill fear. They have not been alone in the forest; someone else has been here with them. Clara's eyes strain to make out a fleeting shape in the darkness. Not a deer. She catches a glimpse of white shift and dark hair. A girl, then, but who from the village would dare to join them?

Then her heart leaps to her throat. Through the leaves, she can just make out two hats of the church elders pushing their way through the laurel bushes. Clara drops like a felled partridge and her friends fall too. They scurry into the bushes and clutch each other in the darkness, bare skin against bare skin, flower crowns crushed as they press together in terror. Rosa-May bites her fist to stop herself from crying.

Through the fern fronds, Clara can just make out two pairs of boots as the elders step into the clearing.

'Did you see her?' Church Elder Smithson booms. 'Fleeing through the wood like a familiar?'

Clara's mouth feels dry with fear. Surely they have seen them also?

'I didn't recognise her. This seems like trickery to me. It will be a matter for the Wytchfinder General,' the other elder snaps. 'My cow in the top field lost her calf today.'

Clara's head swivels to glance at Sarah's white face. She recognises the girl's uncle.

'Woe betide any one who is foolish enough to be caught up in this witchery.' Two pairs of boots kick earth into the flames and the girls are left in darkness.

When they have left, Sarah chokes back a sob. 'What am I going to do, Clara? My father will turn me out.'

'No he won't. They haven't seen us. Anyway, it would be a disgrace on your uncle also, and he wouldn't give up his position as church elder for anything.' Clara scrambles out of the ferns. 'Come on, get dressed. We'll be back in our own beds by sunrise and no one will know where we've been.'

Nine garlands are dropped reluctantly into the ashes of the Bel-fire. They smoulder and the scent of fresias is overwhelming.

Clara looks down at her sister's face, still transfixed by the dying flames. 'No one, Rosa-May, I mean it.' She turns away to gaze at the last of the burning petals. 'You don't want to find out what they do to wytches.'

I have found the perfect cottage, a small step away from the village, secluded and solitary. The soil is heavy with clay but I manage to plant a small herb garden. The brambles and overgrown roses at the gate I leave; it gives the impression that no one lives here. All is peaceful. The cats doze on the porch and the stream tinkles over fat brown stones at the bottom of the garden. Warm May days drift by, and I wonder how long it will take for them to find me.

It takes longer than I thought. Springtime has already begun to bring the valley alive with fresh green, and young ferns are unfurling in the bright sunshine when the first villager comes. I am collecting water from the well, lost in the images shimmering on the black surface, when I hear the hooves and brace myself. A large grey mare rounds the corner and whinnies, jolting her rider. I look up and see a young man watching me. I bite my lip and take in his shape, thick thighs spread across the horse's back, thin shirt stretched across his broad chest. His voice is low and stern as he commands the mare to stand, but she is unhappy and turns in circles before he allows her to walk on.

It only last a few seconds but I see how he sees me.

Alone in the cottage these last weeks I have lost the trappings of polite dress. My bodice is low and tatty, my breasts blushed by the spring sunshine. My hair is loose and blows about my face, catching small leaves and burrs in its dark curls. My lips are sore and red from the outdoors. I feel the burn of his arousal in my own belly. Drops of water splash onto the porch steps as I re-enter the cottage. I ladle the water into my cooking pot and stir; my hand shakes with the knowledge that others will soon follow.

I am not wrong. Two young girls from the village arrive later in the week. They stand on the front step, all smiles and scrubbed cheeks, bearing a pie wrapped in muslin and a pot of preserve. Despite their starched white caps, I recognise them from the fire-jumping but I am careful not to show it. Their cheeriness soon wavers as they follow me in and notice my slatternly housekeeping: saucers of milk on the rugs and potato peeling in the grate. I offer them camomile tea from greasy pewter mugs and they perch, nervous as birds, on the settle, as the cats weave between their slender, stockinged ankles. My calmness makes them chatter with embarrasment and I sense their eagerness to get away and gossip about me in the village.

Then the elders pay me a visit. I see them coming in the flames and I am ready. I clean the cottage, my hair is combed, my dress buttoned. The questions are polite but suspicion glitters behind their eyes. Where is my husband? My children? How do I support myself? Among them is the man who rides the grey mare. He rotates his cup between his big rough hands and glances at me when he thinks I am not looking. His jaw is clean-shaven and he smells of Lyle soap. I sense he is a good man. He shouldn't come here.

But come he does, later – offering to chop wood and repair the front step. I have been sitting by the fire, watching deep in the flames, looking for tomorrow, when he knocks on the door. He looks startled at my appearance; my hair is loose and my bodice undone.

My face is warm from the fire. I call him in. The day is cloudy and dull, I have no wish to see it.

He stands looking and saying nothing until I notice the drops of blood staining his boot. He has caught his fingers with his axe. The cut is deep. I seat him by the fire and fetch a bowl of water and some clean rags. I mix a poultice to prevent poisoning of the blood. He is starting to sweat and I tell him to remove his coat while I brew some tea. He is broad, dwarfing my settle. I kneel between his thighs. He tries not to stare at my nipples grazing the lace at the opening of my bodice. His discomfort excites me and I stand close as I clean the cut. Bending to dip my rag into the bowl, I feel his breath warm against my hair.

The gash is deep across three fingers and, as I wash it, he winces in pain. I clean deeper than is strictly necessary, feeling a pulse begin to quicken deep in my gut. The flesh is tender. I press myself close to his legs, aware of my nipples hardening. His face has paled, and a thin layer of perspiration forms on his upper lip. My fingers wander to the wiry hair on his wrist. He is perfectly still, his eyes lowered, waiting.

I think of his rough, hairy thighs between mine. I can see the sheets of my bed tangled around him, the warmth of his huge body on me, the wetness of his tongue inside me . . .

The cat spits and hisses. He jumps and pulls his hand away, wincing at the pain. The fire has fallen and the room feels chill. I tell him to go and he does.

That night I lie in bed surrounded by flickering candles and think of him. My nipples tighten and chafe against my nightdress. My hand dips between my legs and I imagine him there but the satisfaction will not come.

In the morning I prowl, aroused and restless. I brew

tea laced with woodruff, watch the flames and gather some berries, but all day the feeling churns inside me. When he comes in the late afternoon, it is to tell me there is talk of wytchcraft in the village. Some of the silly young women have been playing games in the woods at night. Arousing each other, and afraid of being found out, they are pointing the finger away from themselves. Away from the village – a small step away.

Silly girls and their girlish urges.

I'm burning applewood in the grate, and the room is full of smoke. He leans towards me but I sense the Wytchfinder coming, hooves thundering and black mane flying. My throat is dry and my hands shake. The village will turn against me and the good man shouldn't be here.

I am collecting logs when the Wytchfinder comes. His black eyes brood with menace under the brim of his hat. His stallion snorts at the gate, its breath clouding the sharp morning air. I barely have time to throw on my cloak before I am dragged down the steps of the cottage. The villagers have gathered to gloat over my fate, thankful it isn't them. I see the village girls watching from a safe distance. They look small under the canopy of the ancient rowan, their faces pale like mistletoe berries. My faithful cats defend me by howling and spitting on the porch. I hope they have the sense to disappear into the forest.

The Wytchfinder towers over me then takes a length of rope from his well-polished saddle and fastens it around my wrists. His eyes hold mine for a moment as his cruel mouth twitches into a half-smile. Holding the other end of the rope he pulls himself effortlessly back into the saddle. I am jerked forwards as he rides towards the village. Arms outstretched, I struggle to keep up, and my feet are soon aching and raw. My flesh is chill under my thin cloak.

At the meeting hall, the stallion is tethered and my wrists released, then a strong hand pushes me up the wooden steps. The Wytchfinder throws me through the doors and I struggle to catch my breath, hiding behind my curtain of hair. The villagers crowd into the warmth of the meeting hall. The elders have a table at the back of the hall. Perched like vultures, their beady eyes glitter when they see that it is a young woman they are testing and not some dried-up old crone.

The Wytchfinder has a good sense of the dramatic. His voice rolls across the hall like the threat of a summer storm, condemning the evil that has gripped the young girls in the village. He tells of the spells that have been cast to bring out carnal lusts in their young, budding bodies. The girls of the village squirm in their seats, craving his hard mouth, his dark eyes, his long legs as he strides to and fro, his broad hands as he grips the table in his anger.

'Harlot!' he hisses and the girls cringe, blushing with shame.

'Here she is!' He grabs my long, thick hair and pulls me forwards to where all can see.

My face is smeared with dirt, my hair wild and my dress torn. I must confess that I have the true look of a wytch about me, wanton and wild.

'This is the wytch who stirs up trouble in her well. Casting spells to ignite us all to join her filthy lusts.' He rips away my cloak and I feel vulnerable and exposed in my thin cotton bodice and skirt. Pulling back my head, he reveals a bruise on my neck, dark blue. 'See the mark of her coupling with the devil.'

A murmur ripples through the crowd. Standing behind me, the Wytchfinder pulls the bodice low over

my shoulders to reveal another bruise below the collarbone. He is standing close enough for me to feel his
excitement at my humiliation. The eyes of the whole
village are on me. I should be terrified, begging for
mercy, but my skin is hot and tight. The Wytchfinder
has my head pulled back and my bodice low and tight,
so that my hard, excited nipples are pushing towards
the crowd. From under my lowered lashes I can see the
young girls chewing their lips till they are sore and
surreptitiously grinding themselves onto the hard
wooden seats.

'The marks of the devil,' The Wytchfinder rumbles,
his big hands burning through the cotton of my bodice.
'Were we to strip this wytch naked I am sure we would
find more.'

My heart hammers and my breathing quickens. The
atmosphere in the room has changed. The men are
gloating, leaning forwards in their eagerness to see
more of the dirty whore in front of them; to see more
evidence of her lusts. The Wytchfinder's fingers are
toying with the laces of my bodice. From behind them
the elders clear their throats. The Wytchfinder turns her
slowly to face them.

'What say you gentlemen? Shall we see the marks?'

Their lust is evident – their faces florid, their eyes
bright. Years of frustration and puritanical living are
being brought simmering to the surface in this village
and it is all being blamed on me.

One of the elders is cleverer than I thought. Clearing
his throat, he takes charge. 'Wytchfinder. I think I speak
for the other elders when I say that these marks are
evidence indeed. The village has been gripped by
strange and ungodly happenings since this woman has
appeared on the edge of our village. Judging by the
effect that this woman has had on the younger females
in our midst, I think that this meeting hall should be

cleared and the matter of judgment now be taken up by the elders.'

An audible groan from the men of the village runs around the room. My heart beats faster and I feel slippery between my thighs with anticipation and fear. Clever, very clever. The elders will be free to inspect the wytch in detail without the whole village looking on. No risk of criticism later. Better that the elders have me all to themselves.

The Wytchfinder pulls me up tight to him and his rod digs hard against my buttocks.

'I think you are right to say so,' he agrees. 'Her powers are potent. I think it best we shield the others from them.'

The men of the village don't want to be shielded at all. There is much grumbling and black looks as they leave. But they are careful not to dissent too much. After all, this is a wytch trial and all are aware how quickly the tide can turn. There is always someone ready to point the finger and condemn. So they shuffle out, aroused and frustrated.

Eventually the meeting hall has emptied except for the long table of elders, one of whom bolts the heavy wooden door and shuffles back.

'Bring her forwards,' the chief elder barks. 'Let us see those marks.'

The Wytchfinder releases his grip on my hair and pushes me towards the table. My neck aches and I shake my head to soothe it so that my hair tumbles over my shoulders.

'A pretty little wytch indeed, but your charms are wasted on me. Step up to the table where I can see you.'

I step up and eye him defiantly. He lies about my charms. I know I excite him. He leans across the table and prods at my bruises as if I were a heifer at market.

'I'm not convinced. It's not much to condemn such a pretty young thing on.' The others murmur their assent; more proof would probably be prudent.

'Oh, I am sure that there are more marks of devilry, gentlemen.' The Wytchfinder's fingers are in my hair, scooping it back to reveal the proud arch of my throat. They drop to the fastening of my bodice and a pulse hammers in my groin. I can hardly breathe. He seems to take a lifetime to release my breasts. They are sore from the chafing of the bodice and it is sweet release when they are bared. The Wytchfinder pulls the cotton down to my ribcage, allowing his rough fingers to snag my nipples. 'See the nubs, gentleman? The wytch has no shame. Even now she revels in her power as lust-maker.'

I can feel the breath of the elders panting on my bare flesh. My nipples pucker even more. The Wytchfinder's hard finger digs a line down my spine and I arch my back, pushing my breasts even closer to the elders.

'And here, gentlemen, is the third nipple, where the devil sucks.' His finger rotates the dark-brown mole on my ribcage. Any fool can see it isn't a nipple, but the elders shift excitedly in their seats.

'Not convinced? Here, feel its likeness to the other two.'

I swallow a gasp as the Wytchfinder pushes me hard against the table. The chief elder licks his thin dry lips and squeezes the mole between forefinger and thumb.

The Wytchfinder's breath is hot on my ear. 'Compare,' he urges.

And he does, squeezing each aroused nipple in turn so that my chest becomes so tight I start to whimper. My eyes slide shut as I am moved down the table and one by one the elders fondle first my mole and then my nipples till they are sore with handling and burning with arousal. Tweaked and pulled and rotated between hard fingers, over and over as the elders of the village convince themselves that the wytch has a nipple to suckle the devil.

One elder takes forever to decide, mumbling under his breath as he traces my puckered areolæ and finds the mole wanting. My knees are weak. I would collapse if I weren't lodged between Wytchfinder and table.

'I am not convinced, Wytchfinder. Not convinced that this is a wytch's third teat. I have heard tell that a wytch's nipples taste of sulphur. I see no evidence of it here.'

'Surely a wytch has the sense to disguise the smell with rosewater?' the Chief elder asks.

'Still,' the elder ponders, flicking a thin tongue over my nipples. 'I'm not convinced.'

I am glad that I am pressed up against the table. I swallow another whimper. I fear I will faint from arousal before this examination is over. The elders are panting with lust, eager for the next degradation.

'If you are still not convinced, gentlemen, then I must show you the wytch's most secret place, where it has been penetrated by the devil.'

The elders gasp and murmur, afraid to move out of their seats lest their own lust becomes evident. The Wytchfinder releases me and moves to find a chair. He pulls me from the table and turns me round before bending me over the back of it. I am weak and compliant with arousal. I bend from the waist and surreptitiously rub my tortured nubs on the rough wood. The Wytchfinder is rolling up my skirt, exposing my bare legs to the elders and finally pushing the cotton up over my waist so that my backside is exposed. His fingers trace the cleft of my buttocks before his strong, warm hands push my legs apart, wider, until my wet secret place is in plain view. The elders' silence speaks volumes. Their desire is heavy and potent in the air.

'Witness the pink, aroused sex, gentlemen. What woman save a wytch would be aroused by the humiliation she has received at our hands today?' His fingers are fluttering over the sex lips, separating them and dipping into the lushness there. I stifle a moan and push myself back onto his fingers. He allows me a brief moment of fulfilment before withdrawing them from my moist sex.

The sound of shifting and buttons popping fills the silence. I glance around and upside down I can make out several of the elders undoing their trousers under the table and fumble for their overexcited genitals.

'Look, gentlemen. There can be no further proof. This wytch has allowed the devil inside her most private entrance and still she writhes and drips with lust. There is no end to this woman's lewdness. I will put her in gaol overnight and tomorrow she takes the ducking stool. What say you?'

A few murmured assents but the elders of the village are masturbating as one, slack-jawed, eyes locked on the wytch's splayed legs.

'Up, wytch, and prepare for your punishment.'

My skirt drops and I am stood upright. The Wytchfinder pulls my bodice up and roughly tightens the laces. We leave silently through the back door as the elders of the village jerk themselves to guilty climaxes. The air is cold on my hot, fevered flesh.

The horse again, and my swollen sex rubs greedily on the saddle. The hooves spark on the village streets as they pick up speed. We are out of sight before the dazed villagers realise that their lustful wytch has been stolen from under their noses.

The Wytchfinder puts a good distance between ourselves and the village before he reins the stallion in. We are on the edge of the woods. A river gushes nearby and the floor is soft with pine needles. He pulls me into the quiet darkness, where the sunlight doesn't penetrate the canopy and throws me to the ground. His eyes are dark and menacing under the brim of his hat.

'I thought you were never coming,' I murmur.

The hat is removed and thrown to the ground. 'How could you think I wouldn't find my wytch?' he grins and drops to his knees. 'I always do, my sweet. Although come the morning she could be gone.' He leaves the inevitable unsaid and I know our ultimate pleasure will be for just this once more. Tomorrow I will make for the west – where the old faith, I've heard, is safer from the interrogations of the pious.

I spread my legs like the whore he wants me to be and he pushes up my skirt. 'You have the charm of the devil himself,' I groan.

'It's my golden tongue,' he whispers back and buries it deep inside me.

Six of the Best Fiona Locke

'Yes *what*?'

We all have our trigger words and hot buttons; our little turn-ons. I think for me the seed was planted at the age of sixteen by Mr Sheridan, my eleventh-grade English teacher. He was the only Brit in my Boston high school and he was accustomed to more discipline than American students are used to. He had the most exacting standards and was merciless with his grades. Everyone hated him.

He was old-fashioned and out of place, but he was also still relatively young and devastatingly handsome. It was his first year of teaching in the States. We all thought he'd have to learn to lighten up to survive, but he never showed any sign of wavering.

He delighted in telling us about the superior disciplinary regime in English schools of the past – uniforms and six of the best. A good dose of the cane, he claimed, would cure us all of our incorrigible behaviour. As if.

They used the paddle in American schools, but Mr Sheridan would never have deigned to touch it. Instead he tortured us with diabolical assignments in detention, like copying out entire pages of the OED or writing interminable lines.

I am the quintessential product of the American school system. I never had to wear a uniform; I had no clue how to tie a tie. With the exception of Mr Sheridan, I never called my teachers 'sir' or 'miss'. The very idea would have been archaic and offensive. I wore whatever I wanted – usually something carefully devised to shock, alienate and offend parents and teachers alike. I was used to doing my own thing, making my own rules and pretty much running the show.

But one day Mr Sheridan kept me after class, just the two of us, to accuse me of handing in work that was 'beneath my abilities'. Beneath my priorities, maybe; I had more important things going on in my teenage life. I told him so.

He shook his head and called me a spoilt ex-colonial – his favourite term. Well, I just couldn't keep my big mouth shut. Americans hate formality. We hate titles and class consciousness and etiquette and all the pretension that has made English culture the butt of so many jokes. We don't like being told what to do. Hence the American Revolution. I told him that too. Then I told him where he could stick his split infinitives.

It was my first real act of teen rebellion and it felt so good I didn't want the moment to end. I was terrified and I knew I'd regret it, but for those few exhilarating seconds I was the leader of my own little revolution. It felt *so* good.

Mr Sheridan was unperturbed, and my elation didn't last long. I remember the dressing-down that followed like it was yesterday.

'You have a good deal to learn about respect, young lady,' he said in his clipped British accent. 'And your attitude needs smartening up.'

I lifted my chin, trying not to let my fear show.

He narrowed his eyes, meeting my stubborn glare. And when he spoke his voice was low and chillingly calm. 'What you deserve, Jenny, is a caning. Six parallel lines. Right where you sit. It would be a lesson you'd never forget.'

His words conjured up images in my mind, memories of films I'd seen and stories I'd read. Images of strict English schoolmasters brandishing swishy canes and terrified schoolboys touching their toes. Was that how it really was? Were English girls subject to the same treatment?

I just stood there, blinking. My courage had evaporated.

He looked so serious, so resolute, that when he turned and opened his desk drawer I flinched, expecting him to take out the cane. No doubt that was exactly what he wanted me to think, because the corners of his mouth turned up slightly.

But all he took out was a form and he sat down at the desk to fill it out. Detention every afternoon for a week. I groaned.

He handed me the slip of paper and his expression was unreadable. 'I have high standards for you,' he said. 'And I expect you to live up to your potential.'

'Uh-huh,' I mumbled, still a little startled. 'I mean yes.'

'Yes *what*?'

'Yes, sir.'

My first revolutionary act. And over so soon.

I spent my week of detention writing lines: *I will learn to apply myself and live up to my potential. I will not submit work that is beneath my abilities.* Five hundred times. And each time I paused to shake the cramps out of my hand I stole a glance at Mr Sheridan. I couldn't get his words out of my head. *Six parallel lines. Right where you sit.* And I couldn't keep from wondering . . .

Five years later, a strange twist of fate led me across the Atlantic, to take the third year of my English literature degree at the University of Durham. It was like something straight out of the period novels I loved. The dark, majestic cathedral was breathtaking: ominously beautiful, with the kind of ancient formality you never find in the States. But the university had a musty, intimidating air that made me feel like an impostor. A slacker among the scholars, I didn't quite fit in.

Oh, I was diligent at first, but it wasn't long before my old habits began to return. I was bored. Restless. Craving adventure. Besides, once the initial charm wore off, I was finding England cold and dismal. It got dark obscenely early and it never seemed to stop raining.

My love life was just as dismal and, after one particularly catastrophic date, I just couldn't face doing any work. So I skipped my first tutorial in Victorian literature, only to discover afterwards that the tutor had assigned an essay. It was the next week before I found out about it. That meant I had to go and see him with some excuse for not being there. I wasn't looking forward to that, but I noted with a chuckle that his name was Sheridan as I read the timetable to find his office room number.

It was early and the halls were deserted, making my footsteps echo unpleasantly. It was as though the university itself were scolding me for my indolence.

When I reached his office I knocked and a voice told me to enter. After I closed the door behind me, I turned back to face him and froze. It was my old tormentor!

The years had distinguished him. He sat behind the desk, a darkly handsome older man with a somewhat gloomy countenance, like Jeremy Irons. He was also wearing glasses, something I've always found appealing.

I must have been gaping because he raised his eyebrows and asked me if something was wrong.

'Oh,' I began, not sure what to say. I stood there stupidly for a small eternity, but he made no attempt to help me. When the awkwardness became too much I finally blurted out, 'Do you remember me?'

He just peered at me over the rims of his glasses, inscrutable. 'Should I?'

I giggled like the nervous schoolgirl I'd reverted to. Of course he wouldn't remember me. He had only aged a few years; I had grown up.

'It's Jenny,' I said with a flirtatious smile.

But whatever he'd been doing since I last saw him hadn't shaken his imperturbable nature. I had thought to embarrass him and make him feel uncomfortable for forgetting someone he ought to know.

My smile faded. 'Jenny Adams?'

Still no reaction.

Then he glanced down at a sheet of paper on his vast expanse of a desk. 'Ah, yes,' he said at last, apparently finding my name there. 'You were absent from your first tutorial.'

He hadn't placed me at all.

'I assume you've come to ask me for an extension on the essay, but if you can't be bothered to come to tutorials, I'm afraid I don't grant extensions. Now, if you'll excuse me . . .'

I stood there, stunned. Here I was, taking the trouble to come to him so I could do what he'd told me I should do all those years ago – apply myself. Hell, he'd made me promise five hundred times that I would – in writing. I was offended.

'No,' I said.

He looked up. 'I beg your pardon?'

'No, I won't excuse you.' I crossed my arms over my chest, appalled at his arrogance. 'I may be a spoilt ex-colonial, but I'm not the only one whose attitude needs "smartening up".'

There was a flicker of curiosity, then of recognition. He peered at me as though through a microscope. At last he smiled.

'Little Jenny Adams,' he said, leaning back in his chair. 'Yes, I remember you now.'

He laughed and got up, shaking off his Professor Snape persona. To my surprise, he hugged me instead of shaking my hand and a little thrill ran through my limbs as I recalled all the times I'd heard his voice inside my head and fantasised about even more intimate contact with him.

The years had been kind to him and I instantly felt my body responding the way it always did to attractive guys. I wanted him: I was lonely, bored, depressed, frustrated and starved for attention. England wasn't the paradise I'd envisioned. University was harder than I'd expected. And the solitude I thought would be freedom was merely isolation. Here was my fantasy come to life. It was not an opportunity I would let slip away.

I held him as tightly as I dared, not wanting to be too subtle. The English boys I'd dated were so different from Americans. They were slow to warm up and I had been frustrated more than once by their inability to pick up my hints. Then again, maybe they were just being 'gentlemanly'. Brits could be so charmingly clueless.

But Mr Sheridan wasn't clueless. He had no trouble reading my body language, as he returned my tighter embrace.

I closed my eyes and pictured him pushing me down on his desk, reaching under my skirt and ripping my panties away; pinning me down with one arm while he wrestled himself free of his trousers and penetrated me, rough and nasty, telling me what a dirty little girl I was. I melted under the image.

I had never actually seduced a teacher before, though I'd certainly fantasised about it. Here was the classic scenario right in front of me. The cheesiest cliché.

Please, Professor, I'll do absolutely anything for that A! I giggled again, relishing my teen memories.

'About this essay,' I purred, classic coquette. I pressed my pelvis into his, rotating my hips ever so gently.

He pushed me out at arm's length. 'You are incorrigible,' he said, but he was laughing.

'You had your chance to fix that,' I reminded him. 'Now it's too late.'

A serious look crossed his features. 'Oh?'

'Perhaps we can work something out,' I said.

There was a gleam in his eyes, sinister and sexy all at once. 'Perhaps we can.'

I was ready to strip off then and there. I had never wanted a man so much.

But instead he calmly looked at his watch. 'Come back tonight,' he said, shocking me into silence. 'At seven.'

I must have looked stung or spurned because he gave me a reassuring pat on the backside.

'Now, now, none of that, my girl.' His tone was affectionately patronising. 'You suggested "working something out" and that's exactly what we're going to do. But you're not going to get out of doing your assignment, you know.'

I closed my eyes and his words took me right back. It was the old Mr Sheridan speaking to me now, the English disciplinarian who had so terrorised us at school. I felt my crotch begin to pulse, practically screaming for him to touch me.

'Do you remember what my detentions were like?'

Did I ever. 'Yes.'

'Yes *what*?'

I thought I would wet my panties. It had been five years since I last said that word and this was the man I last said it to. It came back to me like a forgotten foreign tongue, making my legs feel like rubber. 'Yes, sir.'

'I told you once that you were squandering your potential, that an English school would get more effort from you than you gave in America.'

I remembered that tone well. I used to imagine him kidnapping me and spiriting me away to England, imprisoning me in some gloomy manor and giving me private lessons like Eliza Doolittle.

'I still think you would benefit from some traditional English discipline. If you accept it, you will be allowed to submit your essay. But you're free to decline. The choice is yours.'

My face was scarlet and I couldn't look him in the eye. I stared at the floor, squeezing my legs together. I could never resist a challenge, but this was beyond any I'd ever been given. He was going to cane me. I knew it. After all the years of wondering and fantasising, it was actually going to happen. And my pride wouldn't let me back out. I'd show this Brit what American girls were made of.

I raised my head and it took everything I had to keep my voice steady. 'I'll be here.'

The smile that spread across his face was slow and deliberate, like the almost sensual way a snake has of coiling around its prey. 'Good. Then let me tell you what will happen. We will structure this as the punishment detention you deserved all those years ago. I'm sure you can find something suitable to wear as a school uniform. And I think the orthodox "six of the best" should make a salutary impression on you.'

This wasn't going to be easy. I'd thought all I had to do was come on to him and he'd fall prey to my feminine charms. He'd screw me and I'd get my way. But no, this promised to transcend my adolescent fantasies. I dropped my gaze to the floor, but he wasn't finished.

'Then you will have one hour to write your essay.

You will remember that work produced in detention periods is judged by much higher standards than ordinary homework, and it will not be easy to satisfy me.'

How many times had he spoken to me like that in the past? In high school it seemed fitting; now it was surreal. It was also presumptuous, inappropriate and unbearably erotic. I silently prayed he would just throw me down on the desk and ravish me.

He was looking at me expectantly and I managed to squeak out another 'Yes, sir.'

'Good. I shall see you at seven, then.'

It took me an hour to decide what to wear, but I was happy with the final product. It was the closest thing I could find to a school uniform – short green tartan skirt and white midriff blouse. The blouse had a wide, splayed collar and those sassy French-style cuffs that turn back. I unbuttoned it enough to show a hint of cleavage, then winked at the saucy tart in the mirror and set off.

Of course I had no problem getting a taxi, but the traffic wasn't so obliging. I was fifteen minutes late and it wasn't my fault, but I knew that would make no difference to the implacable Mr Sheridan.

The cathedral bells were ringing out a peal as I raced through the cobblestone streets to Hallgarth House. They seemed to be delighting in my lateness. I could easily think the change-ringers were in on the game with Mr Sheridan – wanting to see me dig myself an even deeper hole. But that was silly. Paranoid. I had no one to blame but myself. After all, he'd said it himself; this was a pattern with me.

I knocked and he made me wait, then looked up as I came in. 'Ah. Adams,' he said with a thin smile. 'Nice of you to turn up.'

I was startled to be addressed by my last name. Was

that what they called you at school in this country? I offered him a sheepish apology, surprised by the teen-age tremble in my voice.

'Your tardiness will be addressed in due course,' he said, looking me up and down. 'After you dress.'

'Huh? But you said –'

'I said you were to report to me in school uniform.'

'Yeah, and I worked hard to find something uniform-like.'

Again that sinister smile. 'Yes, but in my school you wear a *uniform*, not provocative adult clothes that are "uniform-like".'

Silly me. 'But I don't have –'

'I do.'

I was starting to catch on.

Warmth was spreading through my limbs. I was stepping straight into a fantasy, into another world. I opened my mouth to say something, but nothing came out.

'Now, young lady. I realise you were accustomed to a different way of life in Boston. American girls tend to be spoilt, taking for granted the privileges that English girls are expected to earn. I also know that you have never been required to wear a school uniform before, but I am not prepared to be lax on that account.'

I was mesmerised by his little speech.

He reached down behind the desk and retrieved a shopping bag. 'You may change next door, in Mr Wilson's office. You have ten minutes.'

Was he serious? I knew Wilson. A bookish man who taught Romantic poetry. What if he came back and found me there? But unless I wanted to forfeit this little game, I knew I had to do it.

I took the bag from Mr Sheridan and left his office in a daze.

Once there I emptied the bag and grimaced at the

uniform. It was hideous! I'd expected a cute tartan skirt at least. This one was plain navy blue with starchy pleats. There was a simple white shirt and blue striped tie. White cotton knee socks. White cotton panties. And a navy-blue blazer with a large patch on the left breast pocket. It said something in Latin. I never took Latin.

This was not frivolous. This was the Real Thing.

I managed everything easily but the tie. I knew what it was supposed to look like, but I couldn't figure out how to do it. And after four attempts I saw that I only had one minute left. My fingers trembled as I undid it and tried again. It still wasn't right, but it would have to do. Besides, I was terrified that Mr Wilson would appear at any moment. That idea was mortifying, but it was also hot as hell.

I looked at the schoolgirl in the mirror. The uniform was a unique sort of bondage. I felt restricted and uncomfortable. It stripped me of my sexual power. All my assets were under tight control and I couldn't use them to get my way. The vulnerability was overwhelming.

I had never been so turned on in my life.

Mr Sheridan stood right in front of me, assessing my uniform.

He didn't have to tell me he expected me to stand straight and still, but I just couldn't. The bells had no doubt stopped ringing long ago, but only now did I notice the heavy silence. It hung in the air like the early dark and I shuddered in the cloying absence of sound. I shifted my feet and smoothed down my skirt with my hands.

'Do you think *this*,' he asked, lifting my tie with disdain, 'is adequate?'

'I tried, sir. Really. But I've never worn a tie before and –'

'Disgraceful.'

With that, he untied my tie and did it up properly himself, pulling it snug beneath my collar. He also fastened the top button, which I had deliberately left undone. I felt like a child being dressed for school. It was intensely humbling.

'Right, young lady. Let's get on with this, shall we?' With that, he strode to the closet behind his desk and took out the dreaded cane.

I was surprised. It looked pretty harmless – just a thin, whippy length of polished rattan about three feet long, with a crooked handle. After all the build-up, I couldn't believe this was it.

Then he sliced it through the air and the sound alone told me what it was capable of. I paled and took a step back.

My heart was pounding in my ears and a delicious thrill of fear raced through me as I realised I was truly at the point of no return. The roller-coaster's big plunge.

He flexed the cane in his hands. 'Discipline,' he began, his voice low and measured, 'is essential to education. And I am a firm believer in the efficacy of corporal punishment.'

I flushed and wrapped my arms around myself, eyeing the cane with dread.

'Hands at your sides, Adams,' he said sharply.

I obeyed.

But then he laid the cane on the desk and took a straight-backed chair from behind it. He set it in front of me and sat down.

'Before I cane you, I shall address your tardiness. As I recall, you were often late to my classes in Boston. And after all these years, you haven't changed. But now I can deal with the matter. Remove your blazer and hang it up.'

My feet were glued to the floor, but Mr Sheridan eyed me sternly until I finally forced myself to move.

There was a coat hook on the back of the door and the blazer just covered the little window, a perfect curtain.

'Now come here.'

At last I stood beside him, fidgeting and trembling.

'Tardiness,' he said, 'shows a childish disregard for rules. As such it warrants a childish punishment. A spanking.' He patted his lap. 'Over my knee.'

I thought I would faint. My legs were incapable of holding me up and I felt like a limp rag as I stretched myself across his lap.

'Naughty girls must be punished,' he said, placing his left hand in the small of my back to hold me in place. 'And nothing teaches a girl a lesson better than a good, sound spanking. Skirt up. Knickers down. Right on her bare bottom.'

I hadn't known it was possible to blush so deeply. The throbbing between my legs was nothing short of agony, my body screaming for release. I pressed my hands against the floor as he lifted my pleated skirt and tucked my shirt-tail high up over my back. Then his fingers were in the waistband of my white cotton school knickers and he took his time pulling them down to expose my bottom. He rested his hand on my back and I shivered with fear and delight.

He scolded me in a soft voice and I felt like a little girl again. My face was so flushed I felt feverish and my ears burned with each word. I had no idea embarrassment could be so exquisite. He cupped my cheeks as he spoke and I thought I would drown in the anticipation. His touch held both authority and affection, claiming and caressing.

Then his hand fell, sharp and purposeful, and the sting made me gasp. I couldn't believe this was actually happening. It was intoxicating.

I jumped each time I felt his heavy palm, trying not to yelp but unable to help it. He lectured me the whole time, emphasising each trigger word with a well-placed smack. Bad girl. Naughty. Punishment. It was excruciatingly erotic and I could feel myself writhing shamelessly in spite of myself.

It was no play-spanking, either. He laid each smack on with a will and my cries and whimpers were genuine. I could feel my flesh reddening under his palm and the pain only intensified the hot, throbbing girlish longing.

Mr Sheridan paused and rested his hand on my bottom, stroking the tender flesh, teasing me. My body was willing him to plunge his hand between my legs and end the torture, but that wasn't part of his plan. Not yet.

After a short pause he began again, spanking me even harder. Now the stinging smacks made me kick and struggle and when I couldn't take any more I reached behind to deflect his hand. He simply caught my wrist and pinned it in the small of my back, not breaking his rhythm for an instant.

'No, young lady,' he chided. 'This is long overdue and you're going to take what's coming to you.'

With a shudder I reminded myself that I still had the caning to look forward to. I knew he'd stop if I really insisted. But those two deadly sins, pride and lust, wouldn't allow me to consider it. I resolved to see it through to the reward at the end.

His hand rose and fell tirelessly, smacking me again and again, harder and harder. I wriggled and squirmed, but couldn't escape the stinging smacks. I couldn't keep silent, either, and I was yelping loudly. What if someone heard? But Mr Sheridan didn't seem worried. I pictured Mr Wilson returning to his office, cocking his head at the sounds coming from next door. Perhaps he was used to this? Mr Sheridan's very lack of concern was exciting and I sank even further into submission.

Finally, sensing my surrender, he stopped. He had to help me to my feet. I was panting and my face was almost as flushed as my backside. I desperately wanted to rub the stinging flesh, but I still had too much pride to make such a display of myself. My knickers were down around my ankles and I knew better than to replace them. This was only a warm-up, after all. The worst was yet to come.

'Now then, Adams.' He was all business. 'I know that you have considerable ability and are capable of good work. But you need a little incentive. And a lot of discipline.'

He retrieved the cane from his desk and the sense of dread I felt as he cleaved the empty air with it took me right back to the classroom in Boston. I gasped and took a step back, and had to bite my lower lip to keep my traitorous tongue from pleading with him to spare me.

He turned the chair around and tapped the back of it with the end of the cane. 'Over the chair,' he directed. 'Raise your skirt.'

It was as though the chair had invisible tendrils that reached out and pulled me to it. I bent down over its high back, mortified at the way it raised my bottom up so invitingly, then lifted my skirt up over my back as he had done earlier. It was awful to have to do it myself and I lowered my head in shame, putting my hands on the seat of the chair. It was warm from where he'd been sitting.

Mr Sheridan was behind me and he seemed in no hurry. He adjusted my shirt-tail, smoothing it over my skirt to hold it in place, then ran a hand over my sore backside.

I shivered and let out a little moan.

'You will learn to apply yourself in my class. I put a great deal of work into teaching you, and I will tolerate nothing less than your best effort in return. Don't you think that is fair?'

With that he tapped the cane against my backside. I flinched and tensed my bottom in anticipation. This was it. After five years, I was finally going to be caned.

'I think I'd better ask you that again, Adams. Do you think it is fair?'

I'd thought it was a rhetorical question. 'Yes, sir,' I mumbled, drowning in the delicious misery of the moment. I had never felt so completely controlled by a man before. I didn't want it to end.

'Six strokes,' he said. 'You will count them aloud for me. Say "Thank you, sir" after each one.'

My God.

I felt the cane touch my bottom gently, then glide down over it and up again. It tapped, announcing exactly where it would strike, then rose. I felt rather than saw his arm lift behind me, then there was the unmistakable *swoosh-thwack!* as it met my tender bottom at last.

For a moment I felt nothing, but a split second later the pain began to bloom in a thin stripe that burned so intensely it felt like ice. It swelled and swelled until it became unendurable and I cried out and leaped up, clutching my backside to soothe away the astonishing sting.

'Back in position, girl,' said Mr Sheridan impassively. 'Next time you do that, it will earn you an extra stroke.'

I stared at him for a moment, horrified. Then I obeyed, gritting my teeth as I waited. The silence was stifling and I suddenly remembered.

'One,' I said, my voice a moan of shame. 'Thank you, sir.'

'Very good.'

Tapping again, and then the same *swoosh-thwack!*

The second stroke was even harder, but I forced myself to stay down. The white-hot sting eclipsed all other thoughts and I yelped and squirmed over the chair.

I had to take a deep breath before I could count. 'Two. Thank you, s-sir.' Oh, this was torture!

The third stroke fell precisely between the first two. His aim was unerring, and again the sensation was unbelievable. I cried out and gripped the edge of the chair to keep my hands in place. If I had been drunk on the intimate erotic power of the spanking, the cane had sobered me completely.

'Three,' I made myself say, loathing the tremor in my voice and the humiliation of the words. 'Thank you, sir.'

I gritted my teeth and braced myself for the fourth stroke, which literally took my breath away. I nearly screamed as it seared another parallel stripe across my burning cheeks. I locked my knees and rose on my toes so I could lower my forehead to the seat of the chair. My breath fast and shallow, I told myself I had only two more to go. Just two.

Just?

I resumed the position and counted dutifully. I was already learning that Mr Sheridan was not a man to be trifled with. Oh, yes, this would have made an impression on me as a teenager.

The fifth stroke brought tears to my eyes and I could barely keep from grabbing my poor backside. But the terror of even one extra stroke was enough to keep me in place. The revolutionary in me wanted to rebel, but the price was just too high. I bounced up and down on my heels, trying to overcome the agony, but it only made the fire burn even deeper.

I heard my voice counting and it sounded like someone far away.

He delivered the sixth stroke, right in the crease between my bottom and my thighs. And I couldn't help it – my hands left the seat of the chair and before I knew it I was dancing in place, clutching my poor, punished backside and pleading for mercy. This time he got his display.

He shook his head sadly. 'Back in position, Adams,' he said. 'And you were doing so well.'

My precious dignity was gone. 'Oh, no, please, sir,' I babbled. 'Please, I can't take any more!'

Mr Sheridan merely looked at me, indifferent to my suffering.

I had come so far. I had already taken six of the best. I had invested too much in this little powerplay to back out now.

With great reluctance and dread, I bent back over the chair. He took his time readjusting my skirt and shirt-tail before laying the cane against my bottom again, tapping it against the burning flesh.

'Come on, girl,' he said. 'It's nearly over. Make me proud.'

The words of encouragement were unexpected and they made me lift my head. I took hold of the chair seat and stared straight ahead.

At last he gave me the final stroke. It was harder than any of the original six, but I refused to cry out. I crossed my legs, bending at the knees, relishing the heady blend of pleasure and pain as I reconnected with the insistent warmth between my thighs.

'Six,' I panted at last. 'Thank you, sir.'

His hand cupped my aching backside, just near the panty-line, where the worst stroke had fallen. The air around me resonated with electricity. I waited.

Then, moving like a dream spider, his hand crept closer inside. I arched my back slightly, inviting him with my silence. Another fraction of an inch. My skin prickled. I was trembling. Then I felt his touch. His fingertips grazed the silky dampness and I gasped.

I felt like a rippling reflection of myself, and needed the chair for support.

His voice was a distant echo, but there was another unmistakable sound: his zip. He gently parted my thighs and I relaxed in his grip as he took hold of me from behind.

'You see, even the most rebellious girls will surrender in the end,' he murmured.

Oh, yes.

I went limp as he entered me, my head hanging down to the seat of the chair. I could see my knickers pooled on the floor beside my left foot. I shuddered with each thrust and uttered soft little squeaks and whimpers as his pelvis slapped against the punished skin of my bottom.

Mr Sheridan entwined a hand in my hair and pulled me up until my back was parallel with the floor. I could just make out our silhouettes reflected in the steel filing cabinet against the wall, a dark blur behind a white one. I tried to visualise us: the schoolmaster and his errant schoolgirl, her tie properly knotted, her knickers discarded, her bottom on fire. This was a painful lesson, but one I could see myself learning again. And again.

He pounded into me over and over until the pleasure overtook the pain and he clutched me tightly as he came. But my teacher wasn't going to leave me unsatisfied. He drew his hands down the front of my body, spreading my legs and my sex with skilled fingers.

'Have you learned your lesson, naughty girl?'

My body was ready to explode. 'Oh, yes,' I breathed, oblivious to everything but the storm of passion in my tingling flesh.

'Yes *what*?'

He touched my clit and I gasped. That was all it took. The wave broke over me and I surrendered to the pulsing, throbbing orgasm as he held me up. Without his support I would have slipped to the floor.

When the euphoria at last began to fade he turned me around. I stood before him in a daze, my eyes unfocused and dreamy.

He was smiling.

'You see, you *can* learn to apply yourself.' He patted my bottom and I winced, drawing a hissing breath through my teeth.

Too embarrassed to meet his eyes, I could do nothing but stand there and squirm.

His eyes glinted. 'I think the American girl is finally learning that she can't get her way in an English school.'

I had to admit defeat there; I couldn't argue with the effectiveness of his methods. 'You know, you're the only man in the world I've ever called "sir".' I shook my head, still marvelling that he had humbled me so completely.

'How typically American,' he said, amused but not surprised.

'I know, I know, I'm a spoilt ex-colonial.' And I couldn't resist adding, 'But we did defeat you and escape your stifling rule, if you recall.'

'Ah, that,' he said with a grin. 'That was just a tantrum by a rebellious daughter colony. But she knows where to turn for guidance when she's overstepped the mark. And there are still times when her excesses need to be curbed.'

I blushed and looked down at the floor, savouring the thought.

'Right,' he said. 'Now about that essay . . .'

Man's Best Friend Fiona Wilkin

They had been driving towards the sun for an hour. The tarmac drummed through the tyres, sending shivers up Sarah's tired legs. The motorway stretched over the horizon, but the journey was almost over. The sun was low and Ewan reached for his sunglasses. On any other day, Sarah would have handed them to him, even placed them on the bridge of his nose, but this wasn't any other day. Today she wore a black silk blouse with no bra, and her hands were bound behind her back with soft leather. Her legs were constricted from her ankles to her knees, the bindings stopping just below her leather skirt. Ewan had wound the window down to see her nipples harden in the cool air, laughing as he did so.

Ewan was older than her by ten years but still very attractive for a man in his late thirties. He was a dirty blond, not overly muscular but endowed with a heavy frame and broad shoulders. When they first started dating, he had laughed when she called him her Viking. She had never said it since, but the thought remained with her long into their marriage.

'Not long now,' Ewan said.

He took the next exit and the scenery changed quickly into deserted country roads. Sarah began to get excited as she recognised the familiar sights, such as the old twisted tree split down the centre by lightning and the lake that locals swam in when summer came. Then she saw the derelict windmill swing into view and knew they were about five minutes from the car park.

They had made this journey many times, but it was in these remaining moments that she got most nervous. Anything could happen once she'd been dropped off. And anyone could show up. Sarah knew Ewan wouldn't be far away, though, and the sight of him would scare any real lunatics away, but her apprehension remained and wouldn't leave until they were driving home again. Perhaps that's why she did it. She must be hooked on the adrenaline rush.

They drove along a track with potholes so deep they bounced Sarah off her seat. Ewan braced his arm across her chest, securing her as they took a particularly winding turn along the track. Then they pulled into the car park and Ewan turned off the engine.

'Are you ready, honey?'

Sarah smiled back at him.

'Ready for anything,' she said.

'You'll need to be. Now, close your eyes.'

Sarah did as she was told. She heard him get out of the car and open the boot. Her nervousness was replaced by a longing to be outside – a longing that came from between her legs. She could feel her breath coming quicker and her heart beating a little faster. What did he have in store this time?

Fresh air rushed in at her as Ewan opened the door. She wanted desperately to look, but held her eyes closed for those last vital seconds. Sarah felt Ewan's arms wrap around her, lifting her from the car and onto something soft he had laid on the ground. A breeze ran over her body, the air finding its way up her skirt and cooling her thighs. She felt exposed and open – on display to the world and vulnerable to anyone who might chance to pass their way.

Ewan loosened the bindings on her legs and arms and the blood rushed back to her limbs, sending a tingling sensation through her skin. She was free at last and sat up, waiting for permission to open her eyes.

'Just a minute,' warned Ewan.

There was the sound of something heavy being dragged from the car. An object had been in the boot the whole journey, covered with the blanket that she presumed she was now sitting on. She had been forbidden to peek at it since they had set out. Naturally that had only made her want to look even more, but the feeling of denial was too delicious to ignore and heightened her excitement. Ewan set the object down a few yards ahead of her. She could hear his footsteps returning and her heart shuddered with each step.

'Now.'

Sarah opened her eyes and looked around. At first the light blinded her, but it only took a second for everything to swim back into focus. The car park was empty. She looked up at Ewan, who smiled down at her.

'What do you think?' he asked.

In front of her was a dog kennel. It looked like a miniature gingerbread house, with a slanted roof and windows painted on the side. There was a bowl outside and a sign over the entrance that read: 'My name is Rover and I fuck for free.'

'You want me to go in there?' she asked incredulously.

Ewan kept smiling.

'You want me to go in there and wait for someone to come along?'

'You said you wanted a surprise.'

Surprise wasn't the word she was looking for. This was the furthest they had taken their little games. She had been with strangers in front of Ewan before, and had played lesbian games with her best friend Marisa while Ewan had pleasured himself in the corner, but this was a lot to take in. Sarah wasn't sure if she was ready to go so far. She looked up at her husband and he read the uncertainty in her face.

'Listen,' he said. 'I'm going to be around the corner. Nothing's going to happen that you don't want. OK?'

Sarah felt safer knowing Ewan was aware that she felt nervous. He was always extra careful and, if there were any problems, woe betide the person who got caught by him.

'OK,' she said. 'I'll do it.'

Sarah walked over to the kennel and crouched down to get inside. A wave of humiliation washed over her as she tried awkwardly to turn inside and face outwards. She saw Ewan smiling to himself as he got in the car and drove away, leaving her to an unknown fate. She was alone in a car park that was renowned for perverts and odd goings-on. And, what's more, she was housed in a kennel with a sign over it that was bound to provoke all manner of kinky behaviour! Sarah had had many pleasurable experiences in this car park, letting visiting swingers watch her and Ewan having sex, but that was normal in comparison to this game. Today everything felt new. She breathed deeply and waited.

Sarah didn't have a watch. She waited and waited, the only sounds those of the wind rustling the nearby trees and the occasional dog barking in the distance. She didn't know how much time had passed before a car pulled up but she guessed it was about twenty minutes, as the car park was rather remote and did not have a steady stream of traffic. You didn't even have to 'pay and display'. Sarah peeked out of her kennel. It was a Jaguar that had arrived, pillar-box red and gleaming in the sun. She saw the driver regard the kennel curiously from his seat, peeling his driving gloves from his hands. He said something over his shoulder and a

Labrador jumped up from the back. It looked excited, yelping and wagging its tail. Sarah hung her head, shrinking back into the kennel. She wondered where Ewan was. The car door opened and footsteps stopped close by. Sarah cringed inside, feeling flushed with shame.

'What's going on here?' said a deep voice.

She looked up to find a man dressed in a Barbour jacket and beige corduroy trousers, looking every inch the country gent out for a stroll. He had a healthy look that defied his years but he must have been about 65, she thought. He loomed over her, an imperious gaze in his eyes. Sarah knew no one came out here unless they were looking for something very specific. She tried to answer, but found the words stuck in the back of her throat.

'I said, what's going on?'

He spoke in perfect English with a strict, no-nonsense tone. She was suddenly tongue-tied and felt pitiful and stupid. She looked up to him with pleading eyes, wanting to ask for his patience but knowing she could not.

'Can't speak? Perhaps you need some water.'

He nudged the water bowl toward her with his foot.

'Go on. Take a drink.'

Sarah felt the shame burn deeper, but was swept along by his commanding voice. She poked her head out of the kennel and lowered it to the bowl, then began lapping at the water. It spilled down her chin and the man tutted at her clumsiness. He knelt down on one knee and lifted her head with a finger, then ran it over her chin, wiping away the drops. She saw his face up close now. He had a strong jaw line and brown, enquiring eyes, and she could smell the distinct odour of pipe tobacco on his breath as he leaned in towards her.

'What's your name, doggy?'

'My name is Rover.'

The words, finally free, were timid and quiet.

'You know I own a Labrador . . . a beautiful beast like you. Very obedient. I think if it ever spoke, it wouldn't sound like that. Try again.'

Sarah knew immediately from his measured tone that he understood the game and, as a heavy silence filled the air between them, she knew she had no choice but to see it through. She cleared her throat and tried again.

'My name is Rover,' she repeated, but this time in a deep, growling voice. The old man erupted into laughter, ruffling her hair affectionately. Sarah was startled by his reaction; she was genuinely pleased to have made him happy.

'Rover, eh?' he asked. 'And I suppose you're out here to fuck for free?'

Sarah nodded, her heart racing. She felt a glow from her insides. She also felt embarrassed, but she could no longer deny the humiliation was turning her on.

'Come out from your kennel, Rover, and lift up your skirt.'

Sarah followed his command. After wriggling out of the narrow kennel door, she presented herself to the man then lay on her side on the tarmac of the car park and hitched up her skirt. She stared up at him and felt his eyes move over her body. It was an intrusion she was powerless to stop. She wondered what was going through his mind as he looked up her skirt and over her breasts.

'You're a good doggy, aren't you? Aren't you? Now, you come here for your treat.'

Sarah looked up at him. He was standing some distance away, his hands on his hips. She got to her knees and crawled over to him until her head was nuzzled into his leg. It was reassuring to feel his physical presence, and she began rubbing her cheek against the fabric of his trousers. He smiled down at her and she raised her head up to his crotch. Sarah pressed herself into him and felt his hardness growing. She reached up to unzip him, only to find her hand brushed away.

'That's not the treat I have for you.'

He reached into his pocket and pulled out a bag of dog's chocolate drops. Sarah felt a rush of embarrassment and dropped back down on all fours. She could not bear to look in his eyes.

'Come on, girl. Up. Up.'

He held out the chocolate drop for her. Sarah realised he was waiting for her to beg for it. The only dignity she had left was that of a loyal pet. Slowly she raised herself up, dangling her hands in front of her like paws. He looked happy at her response, but denied her the chocolate. Sarah waited, feeling a deeper humiliation than before. A sense of frustration and longing seemed to fill her body. She wanted his acceptance. Before she realised she was doing it, Sarah found herself panting like a puppy, her tongue hanging out of her mouth. Out of the corner of her eye, she could see his real Labrador doing exactly the same. She knew if Ewan was watching, he'd be pissing himself with laughter at her predicament.

'Good dog,' he said, feeding her the chocolate.

Sarah greedily lapped the treat from his hand. It had a peculiar waxy taste, but she did not care; it was his happy smile she was after. He dropped to his knees, a sudden serious look on his face. Sarah panicked that she may have done something wrong, but he began stroking her head, as if distracted by a deeper thought. Sarah tried to placate him by nudging closer and resting her head on his shoulder. His strokes grew longer, starting at her head and reaching down to the small of her back. She shuddered inside. His touch was firm and full, his warm hands moving ever closer to her arse. Her excitement grew. She wanted to be dominated by him. She wanted him to take her, to grab her and knead her flesh with his fingers. She could feel his body tense against her, as if fighting his urge to tear at her clothes.

He stood slowly to his feet, master of his impulses and of her. Sarah resisted crawling after him, but only just. She was ready for him, wet and waiting. She almost began panting again out of sheer frustration. His eyes bored into her and she could sense bizarre fantasies of discipline flashing behind them.

'I think you'd like a game of fetch, wouldn't you?'

Sarah smiled.

'Wag your tail if you want to play.'

Without thinking, Sarah shimmied her behind, hungry for his attention.

The old man walked away and turned to face her. With one hand on his hip, he pulled down the zip of his trousers. Sarah's heart leapt, finally feeling close to fulfilment. He looked proud to be unveiling his manhood, and when Sarah saw it she realised why. He pushed out his thick, long cock so that it stood magnificently in the cool air, then waved it at her, a smile creeping on his face. Sarah could not resist any longer, charging at him on her hands and knees. She jumped up at him and pawed at his clothes, getting fully into her role. He staggered back under her weight, laughing and pushing her back down, but she was insistent. Sarah leapt back up, pushing her face into his crotch and lapping at him with her tongue.

'OK, OK. Be a good doggy.'

He offered her his cock and she sprang upon it, taking him in her mouth. He stood still as she fed upon him. She wanted to use her hands, but knew that would destroy the fantasy, and tried to feel him through her mouth and tongue. He patted her gently on the head and moaned. The need to satisfy him surprised her. She wanted her own climax, but she would have to wait. Now was his time. Her master needed her and Sarah, so consumed by her role as pet and servant, desired only to please. She moved her hand between her legs, her index finger edging under the material of her knickers. She wanted to moan, but held back. She didn't want him to know how much his cock was making her wet.

'I'm going to come on you, doggy,' he said.

Just then another car screeched into the car park. Sarah froze and looked up at her master, his member still hard in her mouth. The car jerked to a halt. Inside were three teenage boys with shaven heads staring back at them. The gent carefully pulled his cock from her mouth and pushed it back into his trousers. He scratched her fondly behind one of her ears and left, walking quickly towards his car.

Sarah watched him go, feeling abandoned. She took her hand out of her knickers. The swift bond she had built up with the older man felt unreal, but she trusted him. Her master was gone and she longed for Ewan to take her away. God knows what these boys would do with her. She was beyond embarrassment or shame and she wanted to escape. The only place to go was back into the kennel and she scrambled inside, half-running and half-crawling, hoping foolishly the young men would just leave.

She waited there, trembling. She couldn't explain what she was doing there; she had been caught in broad daylight with a stranger's cock in her mouth. A stranger old enough to be her father. More than that, she had been caught wanting to take him and pleasure him better than any other woman could. The boys must know the car park's reputation, and would know what she was there for. Maybe they would use her for anything they wanted. Footsteps closed in around her kennel and her heartbeat quickened.

'Get her out, Burnsy,' came a rough voice.

Sarah backed further into the kennel, pushing her head into her knees. A head appeared at the opening, but she could not look.

'Come on, darling. We only want to look.'

Sarah looked out and saw the face of a lad no more than eighteen. He had dark skin and a face that suggested he was no stranger to a Saturday-night fight.

'Come out, love. We're not gonna hurt you.'

Burnsy backed away, leaving enough room for Sarah to poke her head out. She looked up from her hands and knees at the three boys standing over her. They were all of the same age as Burnsy. They were slim and toned, the way most teenagers' bodies are. Two of them were drinking beer.

'What you doing with that old fucker, eh?' Burnsy asked.

One of them noticed the sign on her kennel.

'She was fucking him for free.'

They laughed, and Sarah felt a fresh feeling of shame. She desperately wanted Ewan to take her away, but she knew he wouldn't. He'd be watching carefully from a hiding place and rubbing himself, no doubt. She waited while the laughter died and braced herself for another insult, but no one spoke. They looked at each other, each fully aware that their afternoon drinking session had just taken an unexpected turn.

'What do you reckon?' one of them said.

Another boy regarded her thoughtfully as he took a long drink of beer. Finally, he finished and crushed the can with one hand before throwing it away.

'OK, boys, she's a little nervous,' said the older man. 'Why don't you try and coax her out?'

He was back. Her master was back! Sarah heard the boys laughing and imagined them nudging each other with knowing smiles. Now the older man was back Sarah felt she could really let go.

'Come out, love. Let's have a look at you.'

If it had not been for the older man, she would have stayed securely inside her kennel, but she felt safe in his presence. Hesitantly, she crawled into the sunshine, her head bowed, not daring to look into their eyes.

'Beautiful, isn't she? A real pedigree,' said her master.

The teenagers suddenly became quiet and uncertain. Sarah could tell this was a new experience for them. Their nervousness made her bolder and she looked up at them, a shy smile on her face. There were three of them, all dressed in T-shirts and jeans. Two of them had intricate tattoos snaked around their biceps. The other seemed younger still, a man with baby-soft skin that was lightly tanned. A woman of blatant sexuality could control these boys, she realised. Her apprehensions gave way to excitement. She moved closer to the older man, nuzzling into his inner thigh and looking over her shoulder at the teenagers as she did so.

'What are you going to do with her, mate?' asked one of the tattooed boys.

Her master smiled and ruffled her hair. For the first time, Sarah noticed he was holding a collar and chain. He had obviously brought them from the car while she had been hiding in the kennel. He knelt down and fixed the collar around her neck, then clipped the lead to it.

'I'm going to give her some exercise,' he replied. 'You can watch how well trained she is.'

He took a step back and pulled on the chain. Sarah was reluctant. That small flame of power was extinguished, replaced now with a fresh sense of humiliation. The boys smiled and waited.

'Heel!' her master commanded.

His firm tone was all she needed to comply, and she crawled to his side. She could feel her cheeks burning with a mixture of shame and excitement. The old man patted her behind as he would any other dog when rewarding its obedience. He began to lead her in a circle around the group of boys, who turned to watch her. Their eyes roamed freely over her body, leering at her swinging breasts and waddling backside. She was in awe of how this made her feel. In the bondage of her role she felt freer than she had ever been, because all her decisions were being made for her. It felt safe and natural to be paraded around like this. It gave rise to a feeling of abandonment, fuelling her wantonness.

Sarah looked up at each of the boys in turn and growled seductively. She strained at the lead, trying to get at them. She expected to be yanked back by her master, but he seemed happy to let her play. He had power over her, but she had power over them.

'What's the matter with her?' one of the boys asked the master.

'Oh, she just wants you to pet her, that's all. It's OK. Go ahead.'

Sarah was thrilled at the idea of having six pairs of hands stroking her at once. She stopped growling and adopted the playful look of a puppy, lowering her head to the ground and raising her behind. The boys looked anxious.

The old man pulled at the lead to get her attention.

'Show them you won't bite, doggy.'

At first, Sarah didn't understand his command. How could she invite them to touch her without speaking? But then she had an idea. She began to whimper, trying to incite their sympathy, making her lower lip tremble in mock subservience.

One of the teenagers stepped forwards and tentatively stroked her head. His touch was gentle and gratefully received. She gave a yelp of excitement that encouraged the others, who then placed their hands all over her body, brushing her long hair and caressing her back. They slid their hands over her arse, the back of her legs and down to her calves. Hands manipulated her breasts and found the place between her thighs. The sensation was enough to halt her breath. She did not dare move, wanting to savour each contact. She could see the satisfaction on the master's face. He looked like the proud owner of a pet that instantly pleases a crowd. But then he backed away.

'Go on, lads. You can play with her for a while. I'll be watching from over there –' he pointed to a cluster of bushes that formed the perimeter of the car park '– so no real rough stuff, OK?'

He began walking away, and the minute he was out of earshot they reverted to normal. One boy placed a hand on her head, patting her gently, and the other on her arse. He slapped one of her cheeks and the group erupted into a fresh bout of laughter.

'Enough of that poncing about,' said the one called Burnsy. 'Pull her skirt up, Wazzo, so we can see her arse.'

Wazzo turned and yanked up her skirt. The boys moved behind her to get a better view.

'Imagine sticking your cock in that, lads.'

He slapped her arse again, but this time no one laughed. Sarah felt the mood change from amusement to something more primitive. They were all admiring her, which caused Sarah to flush with pride. A familiar, foolish daredevil feeling arose within her and she wanted to go further.

She lowered her face to the ground and pushed her rump into the air. She wasn't sure what she was doing, but thought it best to do what they wanted. She noticed an urgency building within her, her cunt throbbing from all the humiliation. She heard hushed whispering from behind her and Wazzo appeared by her side.

'Coleman was wondering if you'd let him have a toss over you.'

'Shut up, you prick,' Coleman shouted.

'What do you think, love? Will you let him?'

The thought of a teenage boy wanking over her face excited her more than ever. Better me than a crusty old magazine he stole from his Dad's drawer, she thought. Suddenly, she found herself worrying about their age. They were just boys, so it would probably be over too soon. She realised to her own shame that she would probably need all three of them to satisfy her. What kind of a slut am I? she thought to herself. She looked to Wazzo with a smile and decided she was going to speak – a silent doggy no longer.

'They can do what they want if you take off your clothes,' she said.

Wazzo seemed shocked. He looked to his mates, who cheered back at him. There was no ceremony, no seductive strip. He was here to get laid. He quickly pulled his shirt over his head, almost as if he were getting ready to take a shower. He was slim, with soft-looking unblemished skin. Sarah watched as his nipples stiffened in the air. He yanked down his trousers, revealing muscular but hairless legs. He hesitated before pulling down his boxer shorts, but then, as his boys cheered him on, he pulled them down to his ankles. Sarah could see he had a thin, teenage cock and tattoo of a cartoon devil nestled among his pubes.

Wazzo looked down at her, a challenging look on his face. Sarah kneeled before him and took his soft penis in her hand. She looked over her shoulder at the boys and smiled, turned back to Wazzo and slipped his stiffening cock into her mouth. Impatient, like the youngster he was, he grabbed the back of her head and pushed into her. She felt the warm head press against the roof of her mouth. He wasn't big enough to make her gag, so she let him thrust into her mouth as she held onto his firm, young arse.

Rough hands from behind her fell upon her body, rubbing the flesh of her cheeks, pulling them apart and kneading them together. She felt a shudder run through her, something they must have seen.

'She loves it, lads,' Wazzo said. 'Give her one.'

Her underwear was pulled down to her knees and an unknown finger thrust into her. They were rough, seemingly prodding her out of curiosity rather than any attempt to arouse her. She began to feel like their experiment, a plaything they had found in the car park and intended to use for their pleasure.

Burnsy approached her from the side, his dick in his hand. Wazzo pulled out and let his mate take his turn, patting him on the back as he stepped back to watch. Burnsy began rubbing his balls over her face, smothering her with his genitals. She lifted up his cock and lapped at his sac, tasting his sweat and wiry pubes against her tongue. Wazzo straddled her. He reached underneath her and squeezed her breasts, pinching the nipples through the material of her blouse.

'Hey, Burnsy. She's got a great rack.'

The sensation of six rough hands doing what they pleased was ecstatic. She could feel that familiar warmth growing between her legs. It began to build as hands crushed and played with her breasts, a cock pushed into her mouth and finger slipped in and out of her pussy. Her desires were strengthening and Sarah wanted more. She was being used by three teenage boys. She hoped that Ewan was watching this. They'd really come up trumps today.

'Hey, Coleman,' Sarah shouted brazenly over her shoulder. 'Stop fucking around with your finger and put your cock in me.'

She could see the surprise in his face, even fear, but he undid his jeans and pulled out his penis, already thick and hard. She felt it rest briefly on the crack of her arse before being guided downwards into her pussy. Coleman rubbed the head between her folds as she gasped and fed Burnsy's cock into her mouth, wanting to feel totally full at both ends. Wazzo began tearing her blouse from her, and threw it to one side. She could feel his naked cheeks warm against the skin on her back. She couldn't see him, but she thought she could feel him playing with himself. Coleman eased himself into her, burying his cock as far as it would go. Sarah moaned over the flesh in her mouth, and Coleman began pumping into her with a novice's rhythm. He was quick, with no technique, and reminded her of her first boyfriend. Suddenly she thought Coleman might be a virgin, which gave her a guilty thrill, and she sucked deeper on Burnsy, making him moan.

Coleman was thrusting with a frantic pace. She ground down upon him as much as she could, but he was unstoppable. She let him fuck her as fast as he could, enjoying the feeling of being used. Burnsy began thrusting into her mouth and she could taste his come on the way. Spit ran down her chin and his cock made obscene slapping sounds as it slid in and out of her.

Wazzo stood in front of her, nudging Burnsy's penis away with his own. They fought to put their cocks inside her mouth as Coleman pumped away from behind. A dizzying sensation fell over her, one matched by a growing orgasm. She closed her eyes and felt them all at once, pushing into her, wanting her and needing her. They were thrusting and filling her. Wiping their cocks over her face. Orgasm building. Pumping and fucking. It was sudden, rushing at her like a wrecking ball. She howled out her ecstasy, Burnsy's and Wazzo's cocks inches from her mouth. It swept over her, swimming through her body and swamping every nerve. She tensed and relaxed as it slowly ebbed away, leaving her sated and happy. She opened her eyes and saw Burnsy and Wazzo staring at her, in awe of seeing a woman coming. Coleman, too, had stopped his insane fucking, and watched as she caught her breath.

She looked at each of them.

'You!' Sarah pointed at Wazzo. 'On your back.'

Without hesitation, Wazzo lay on the ground, his hard cock swaying in the air like a flagpole. He laughed nervously at Coleman, whose face was a picture of frustration. Sarah stripped off her remaining clothes and straddled Wazzo's cock, wet with saliva and shining in the sunlight. She guided him in and felt her juices squeeze out of her.

Burnsy quickly whipped off his jeans. He stood above Wazzo, his cock in his hand, waiting to put it in her mouth again, but Coleman had other ideas. He picked up her panties and tied them around her mouth. The material was dry and pressed tightly into the sides of her mouth. She could smell herself on her knickers.

'What you playing at, you little fucker?' Burnsy barked.

'Don't worry, mate. You can have her arse after I'm done.'

Coleman pulled open her cheeks and rubbed a moistened finger over her arsehole. Sarah could feel the spit cooling on her anus before he pushed his fingertip into the hole. He worked his knuckle through the ring and pushed deep inside her. The material of her knickers grew moist with her breath as she began to pant. He twisted his finger and circled it inside, stretching her ring and preparing it for his young cock. She moved slowly up and down Wazzo's cock. The sensation was unbelievable, and she found herself wanting Coleman's cock in her dirty hole. She took Burnsy's penis in her hand and rubbed it over her face. It was wet and left a trail of pre-come over her skin.

Sarah felt the soft head of Coleman's cock pushing at her backside. She bit down on her knickers as he forced his way in. At first, only his head would fit, but on the second thrust his full shaft followed. She could feel Wazzo's cock and Coleman's rub together through the thin wall of her sex. Together, they found a rhythm. As she pushed down on Wazzo, Coleman withdrew from her arse and she gave two or three strokes to Burnsy's cock. Coleman thrust into her as she lifted off Wazzo, and stretched her arsehole until she could feel his pubes on her butt-cheeks. They moved faster, sweat building on their bodies and cooling in the air. Her hand moved faster and Burnsy tensed. With an animal growl, he came, sending jets of warm jizz over her face. Wazzo winced as it dripped from her chin onto his face, but he was too busy with his cock to care.

Behind her, Coleman moaned and withdrew from her arsehole, which was stretched and tingling. With a few strokes, he shot his sperm over her back. She could feel it running down her spine, like a fingertip playing with her skin.

The lads stood back and watched her grinding on their friend. He gripped her cheeks and fucked her with a quickening pace. It was all she could do to keep up. She panted and grunted like an animal.

'That's it, doggy. Take it.'

Wazzo arched his back and came inside her. The warm sperm oozed in her canal, making sucking sounds as Wazzo made his final thrusts. Coleman and

Burnsy started clapping and cheering. Sarah laughed and clapped with them. She was wet and slippery, exhausted and relaxed. She had been filled with three cocks and her body ached happily.

She climbed off Wazzo and lay next to him, allowing the breeze to dry her naked body. She wondered if Ewan and the older man had come too. And anyone else who had been watching them fuck.

'Bloody hell, love,' Burnsy said. 'You're an animal!'

Sarah looked at him, catching sight of the kennel behind him.

'I could say the same about you,' she said and laughed.

Sarah couldn't tell how long it took her to raise her head. She was lost in that mellow world that always follows a great orgasm, but when she did, the boys were gone. She could not remember them leaving or the sound of their car when they left. She looked up to find the old man looking down at her with a smile and Ewan standing by his side. For a moment she felt disorientated, as if reality and her doggy life had come crashing together.

'Ewan?'

Ewan looked extremely pleased. He smiled at the old man and they seemed to share a moment of congratulation.

'What's going on?' she asked.

Ewan knelt down and undid the collar and lead. Sarah had forgotten she was even wearing it, and left him to undo the bindings while she got her bearings.

'Did you enjoy that, honey?'

'Yes,' said Sarah, smiling. She was certain of that.

'Good,' said Ewan. 'I'd like you to meet Mr Rickman. He's a carpenter.'

'What?'

'Sorry, dear,' said the old man. 'I'm not the lord of the manor you took me for. Just a humble craftsman and friend of your husband. I hope you like the kennel I made for you.'

Sarah stumbled to her feet, the doggy fantasy slipping away from her like an evening gown after a long night of celebration. Ewan gave her a hug and thanked Mr Rickman before leading her away. She looked back at the old man, who leaned on the kennel and waved. To her, he had no name. He wasn't a carpenter or even the country gent she had mistaken him for. He was the master who had unlocked her secrets.

She got in the car and they left the car park, but Sarah knew they would be back soon. She had a feeling that Ewan and Mr Rickman would be planning other adventures for their favourite pet very soon.

Wheels on Fire
Mathilde Madden

I first noticed her in the library. I noticed the way sunlight from a high dusty window bounced off her hair. I noticed the dress she wore: a tight, fitted white cotton dress with a print of red cherries on it. She was a little prim looking, like a school teacher; just a nice-looking woman standing next to me, as I reached for a book on a high shelf, stretching in my wheelchair.

The book I wanted was almost out of reach, but I got a fumbling grip on the spine and pulled, and at that same moment she leaned over quickly and whisked it from my tentative grip, no doubt in an attempt to help me out.

That annoyed me. 'I can manage,' I growled through my teeth.

She ignored my complaint and turned the book over in her hands. 'Jackie Collins,' she noted in a stage whisper.

I realised I was staring at her lips; they were the same colour as the cherries on her dress.

'It's for my mum, OK.' I kept my voice low.

'Well of course it is. A beautiful man like you wouldn't need to read about it.' Her tongue flicked over her lips, turning the matt to gloss. She bent down slowly, so her eyes were level with mine and I could see straight down the top of her dress. Her voice dropped even lower. 'You'd be surprised, though, just how dirty these books can be. I think it's quite amazing that you can find the filthiest things right here in the public library.'

I felt my face redden as she suddenly dropped the book into my lap and walked away without another word.

I sat there for several moments, my heart beating fast and my mouth dry, but I didn't move. Six months ago I wouldn't have even questioned such a blatant come-on. I would have followed her and given as good as I had got, shown her just where such deliberate prick-teasing could lead. But not now. After all, I was in a wheelchair these days. Pretty girls like her didn't come on to pathetic cripples like me.

So it couldn't have been a come-on; I must have been mistaken. No doubt she just felt sorry for me and thought she'd talk to me for a few moments. Brighten up the day of the poor boy whose legs didn't work any more.

Pushing the girl out of my mind, I leisurely found the other books I wanted and checked them out. Then, balancing them in my lap, I wheeled my way carefully down to street level by way of the substandard ramp outside, a new addition to this ancient building.

As I zigzagged I saw her again. On the low wall at the bottom of the steps sat the girl in the cherry-print dress. She was eating an ice cream, a 99, and didn't seem to have noticed me. I was planning to wheel straight past her, but as I did so she said, 'Hey.' So, not wanting to be rude, I stopped my chair right in front of her.

'Oh, hi.'

'Come to the park with me.' She winked and jerked her head towards the iron gates over the road.

'I can't,' I muttered, turning my head to look at her. 'I'm in a hurry.'

She stretched her leg out and stuck the chunky high heel of her brown shoe into the spokes of my wheel. 'Go on,' she said, pulling the ice-cream-smeared chocolate bar slowly out of her 99. 'I'll let you have my flake.'

I didn't reply, but just looked down at the chunky heel jammed in my spokes, trapping me. What could I do? I looked at her cherry-print dress and her cherry-red lips. I met her eyes and something in her expression seemed to captivate me. Silently I nodded my head.

As she leaned forwards and slid the chocolate bar into my mouth I felt as if I were falling under her spell. I had no choice but to obey when she whispered hoarsely, 'Don't bite it now.'

I watched her expression as she inched almost the entire thing into my mouth, a fraction at a time, and then slowly began to pull it out again. Then in it went again, then out, gradually picking up speed. My breathing quickened. I hadn't had so much as a chaste kiss from a girl in months and now, suddenly, I was fellating a chocolate bar for this one, outside the public library.

And I couldn't remember the last time I was this turned on.

All the time we stared at each other. I was trying to will her on with my gaze, begging for more, wanting nothing in the world except to let her fuck my mouth, to her satisfaction, with this makeshift phallus.

But then she sighed and must have shifted position, because I heard her heel click against my spokes and the sound broke the spell. I remembered in a rush why things like this didn't happen to me any more. I remembered that I was sitting outside a library in a wheelchair. I remembered what was wrong with this picture. I bit down through the flake and pulled my head away.

I chewed the chocolate, licking more of it from my lips and wiping the spills away with the back of my hand.

'Thank you,' I said coldly, when my mouth was almost empty.

She seemed unconcerned by my sudden change of heart, and just smiled seductively at me. 'Well, that's my part of the bargain over with; now it's your turn.'

'What?'

'The deal was, I'd give you my flake if you came to the park with me, so, off we go.'

She hopped down from the wall and, making no attempt to push me, I noted, started across the road.

I followed her through the Victorian wrought-iron gates, my wheels crunching on the gravel as I trailed her around the rose garden.

She didn't say much as we followed path after path, just pausing to point out the certain blooms or, once, a squirrel. Most of the time she just let her eyes slide over me, looking down as if she couldn't bear to tear herself away. I felt self-conscious under her gaze, finding myself bowing my head and hunching my shoulders. But deep down inside me, I liked that feeling. There was something between us, something in the air, and it scared me, but I knew I couldn't resist it. Maybe that was what scared me the most of all.

At one point she leaned over and plucked the petal from a very dark red rose.

'Look at this one,' she said, her eyes glowing. 'It's exactly the colour of blood, but it feels so soft.'

She rubbed the petal briefly on her cheek, before leaning forwards and trailing it slowly across mine. Her face was inches away from mine, and I felt sure she was about to kiss me, but she didn't; she just said, 'Let's go to the pavilion and get some tea.'

And we did, settling ourselves at a sticky table and making perfunctory conversation about nothing. She picked up my library books from the table and looked through them.

'So,' she said, 'are all these books for your mother?'

'No, just the Jackie Collins, like I told you.'

'You need to drop it off today?'

'No, I'll do it tomorrow, on my way back from physio.'

'Right.' She drained her teacup and placed it carefully in the saucer. 'Let's go to your place.'

'Why?' I used the last part of my resolve to try and resist her, reminding myself that whatever she said it was just pity. Just an offer of a pity fuck for a poor cripple. And I didn't need her pity.

She looked hard at me, her face completely matter-of-fact. 'Because every time I look at you, I want to get on my knees and run my tongue along your footplate, until you're desperate for me, rock hard and writhing in that chair like an animal in heat.'

I stared, thoughts of refusing her 'pity fuck' suddenly drained away. I couldn't speak.

She smiled. 'And I'd rather not do that right here.'

I don't remember how we got there, but it hardly took any time at all.

I hurriedly showed her around my flat, which she surveyed with a polite lack of interest until we reached the bedroom.

We both stared at my unmade bed. For minutes.

'You can get into bed without any help, right?' she whispered eventually, as if not wanting to disturb the charged atmosphere our mutual heavy breathing had cast in the small room.

'Sure.'

'Well, go on then.'

And within moments, we were in the bed, both naked, and her mouth was clamped on mine. She was rough, driving her way inside and sucking brutally on my lower lip.

Her skin against mine felt so good. It was all I could do not to come just from the sound of her rapid heartbeat and the feel of her heat.

She moved from my mouth, nipping her way across my cheek until she reached my ear. 'I want to fuck you with my mouth,' she hissed.

I laughed. 'Don't you mean you want me to fuck your mouth?'

'No.'

She rolled me onto my stomach, with an impassioned sigh. Once I was positioned the way she wanted she straddled my legs and bent down to flicker her tongue across my exposed buttocks.

I flinched, uneasy, not sure if this was something I wanted, but somehow I couldn't find the words to tell her to stop. So I quivered there beneath her, as she let her tongue dart everywhere. Absolutely everywhere.

I gasped when she nudged at my hidden little hole, at the same time splaying me, with one hand, so that I was open and wanton for her. And then I found myself moaning as she teasingly let her tongue lap over that hot little mouth, again and again, until it was so hungry, so wanting, that I was thrusting my hips up to meet her every caress. Aching. Aching for something. Anything. More.

Responding to my desperate thrusting, she pushed

the very tip of her tongue gently inside me. I was so needy and desperate for her by that point that I bucked like an animal, half begging and half sobbing, my face buried in the pillows while my desperate erection ground against the mattress.

Thankfully my frustration didn't last long. One of her hands snaked underneath me, forming a lubricated fist around my aching cock. I thrust into the warm soft well gratefully. Seconds later her tongue, which was starting to feel hopelessly small inside me, was replaced by a finger, then two, and the most amazing sensation, as she stroked her way inside me with her other hand, fucking me decisively. I'd never felt anything like it.

And in moments, with her hands manipulating me from every direction, I was spasming for her, soaking the sheets beneath me, half screaming, half blacking out.

She held me for a long while after that, brushing my hair away from my face, waiting until I had recovered. Eventually I found I could speak again. 'If that was a pity fuck,' I breathed, 'then I think I do need your pity.'

She propped herself up on her elbow and looked down at me. 'It's only a pity if we don't do that again,' she said, emphasising her point with a brief kiss before clambering from the bed and walking naked into the kitchen of my tiny, specially adapted flat. I heard the ancient pipes squeal and then she returned with a glass of water, and slipped back into the bed so we could share sips in silence.

'I need to go to the loo,' I said, when the glass was drained.

'Do you need any help?'

'No, I can manage.'

I manouvered myself from the bed to the chair and wheeled myself into my bathroom. When I returned she was sitting up in bed, grinning. 'Stay in the chair,' she said distantly, as I parked up next to the bed.

'Why?'

'You look so beautiful, naked in your chair – please, I want to see you come in your wheelchair.' She flipped back the bedclothes and crawled across the bed in a couple of quick movements, stopping to kneel up right next to me.

'Are you going to make me come again? I asked in disbelief.

'More than that.' She licked her lips. 'I will suck your cock every time I see you naked in that chair and that's a fucking promise.' My sudden erection twitched.

And then with one final hungry look she buried her head in my lap, sucking greedily, almost before I had time to engage the brake.

Her tongue swirled around the head of my cock, coaxing and teasing me to my second orgasm.

I barely had time to question whether I would be able to climax again so soon before I exploded in her mouth. I felt my fingers tightening against the rubber tread of the tyres, nails digging in so hard I was surprised I didn't end up with a puncture.

She lifted her head, wiping the spills from her chin and smearing them down my chest. As I went to wipe them away she snapped, 'Don't move.' I froze obediently, again feeling I had no choice but to obey.

She flopped down on her back, watching me through lust-lidded eyes. Hitching up her knees, she let them fall apart, exposing herself blatantly to me. I felt my breath catch as I saw how pink and wet and ripe she was. She held my gaze as she let one of her hands trail between her legs.

She smelt so delicious I could almost taste her, but I understood her game by now. I knew she wanted to direct the action.

'I bet you'd like to fuck me,' she murmured as she let her hand glide over her dark, shiny pubic hair.

'Yes,' I moaned, helplessly. 'Oh God, yes.'

'Mmm,' she cooed, 'but I'm afraid I can't let you right now. I'm torn but, if you come and fuck me, I won't be able to look at you. And you look so beautiful, naked in your chair, sated, with your come smeared over you. Tell me you don't mind waiting.'

There was that hypnotic tone to her voice again. I could hardly bear it. But I swallowed hard, trying not to shake with frustration. 'I don't ... I don't mind.'

I could scarcely believe it was possible after coming twice in quick succession, but my cock stirred as I watched her movements become more vigorous.

'Have you ever come in your chair before?'

'No, never.'

'Really?' She was panting so hard now she could barely get the words out.

'Really, I've never. I haven't done anything like this since – since I've been like this.'

'You never ... you never even made yourself come, though? You never played with yourself while you were sitting in the chair?'

I shook my head. 'No. I only do that in bed.'

'You should.' She was bucking against her hand now, squirming hard on the bed. 'I'd like to see that. I'd like to see you touch yourself. Do it now, just so I can see what you do.'

'I can't.' I hated to deny her, but there was no way I was going to get anything further out of my cock at this moment.

She smiled. 'Just touch it. Play-act for me.'

I reached down and took my very tender cock in my hand, stroking it lightly, doing what I hoped would put on a good show for her.

I'd never thought of myself as an exhibitionist before, but soon I was throwing my head back, moaning and biting my lip, acting the slut, just because I wanted to make her come harder.

And she did, as I writhed and moaned for her; she did the same for real, arching up into her own hand, and screaming something about me being the most beautiful thing she had ever seen.

Much later, in the middle of the night, I woke to find her rubbing herself against my leg, sliding, wet and needy, against my unfeeling thigh. When she realised I was awake she began kissing me roughly and, every time her mouth was free, asking me to tell her, again and again, that I couldn't move, that I couldn't feel her wetness coating my useless, broken legs, that I couldn't walk.

'Again.'

'I can't walk.'

'Again.'

'I can't walk.'

'Again.'

'I. Can't. Walk.'

And she came, screaming, twisting both my nipples hard, so I screamed too.

I don't know what kind of effect she had had on me, but the very next day at my physio session the therapist asked me if something had happened to change the way I felt about myself. I couldn't help it. I ended up telling him all about her.

Well, not all about her. In fact not even half of it. I simply told him I had met the most wonderful girl and was happier than I had ever been. He suggested I ask her if she wanted to come to some of my sessions, see how I was getting on.

But she never did. We had other things to do.

Like find new ways for her to play with me in my chair. One evening she wheeled me into the kitchen and stripped me, then painted my body with warm, shiny chocolate. She wrote the word 'slut' and 'cripple' across my chest while I moaned for her, and I writhed when hot splatters dripped from her fingers and landed on my stomach.

Painfully aroused, I pleaded and begged, but there was nothing I could do to relieve my frustration. She had ordered me to keep my hands on my tyres and I did so. I was always powerless to disobey her orders. So I kept my hands in position, even when she leaned forwards to lick me clean and drew one nipple, hard, into her mouth, nibbling and teasing until I was a frantic squirming mess.

And then she was licking me clean of come as well as chocolate.

She did indeed, one night, get on her knees and lick my footplate. And it was one of the most erotic things I had ever seen. She moaned softly as she ran her tongue along the bright metal and caressed the tread of my tyres with her hands.

I was frantic for that mouth to be on my cock, long before she had done all she wanted.

She asked me things no one else had ever asked. Breathless, late-night conversations that scared me and made me want her even more: 'If you weren't in your chair, how would you move?'

'What do you mean?' I rolled over so I could rub against her, pressing close in the dark.

'I mean, well, would you crawl around? What could you do?'

'I couldn't really crawl; I could pull myself along. My arms are pretty strong.' I felt her shiver against me.

She swallowed slowly, then said, 'So, sort of on your belly?'

'Yes, just like that.'

'I'd like to see you doing that.'

'Why?' I asked with a teasing smile.

'I just would. Show me.'

So I did. Suddenly the lights were on and I was in my chair, wheeling myself into the living room where there was most floor space. I let her gently tip me onto the carpet and watch me drag myself across the floor on my stomach, as best I could, naked and utterly vulnerable.

'Tell me why you're doing that,' she said, her voice so ragged it was barely recognisable.

'For you.'

'No, no, tell me why you have to move like that.'

I changed my path and started to drag myself towards her, meeting her eyes from way down on the floor. 'Because I can't get up.'

I could tell how much this was turning her on and it aroused me to see her almost frozen to the spot with desire. My cock was painfully hard against the carpet as I continued towards her.

She stared at me in silence after that, until I reached her and ran a passionate, wanting hand up her bare leg, trying desperately to reach her cunt. As my hand grazed her upper thigh she took half a step backwards, pulling deliciously just out of my reach. And I whimpered. Begging. Helpless. Everything she loved.

Then she growled and flipped me over roughly, and we fucked until I felt sure she had worn away the carpet beneath me.

So I never actually asked her to come to my physio sessions, and she never showed any interest anyway. When the taxi came to pick me up she would just snuggle down deeper in the sex-stained sheets and I would drag myself away, reluctant to miss even a second of her beautiful half-hidden curves.

It was two weeks after we had first met that we had our first and only conversation about my physio-therapy. That night she straddled my already bucking, needy body and tied my wrists to the bed frame. I struggled a little, gazing up at her handiwork. 'Is that really necessary?' I asked, laughing. 'I'm not going to run away, you know.'

'I know.' She grazed the pad of her thumb down the sensitive side of my forearm. 'But the less you can move, the more I like it.'

'Would you like it if I couldn't move my arms at all? If they were like my legs?'

'Yes,' she said huskily, rocking her hips against my erection.

Encouraged and relishing the pressure I went on. 'What about if I couldn't move any part of my body? If all I could do was blink?'

She leaned forwards and licked my temple. 'If all you could do was blink, I'd blindfold you and then fuck you through the mattress with an enormous strap-on.'

I moaned greedily as she kissed me on the lips. 'But I wouldn't be able to feel it,' I muttered into her mouth, as she pulled away.

'Well, I'd have to describe it to you, wouldn't I?' She scooted back down my bound body as she spoke, drop-ping kisses onto my chest between words. 'Blow by blow.' And her lips closed languorously around my cock.

'So when I can walk again, is this what you'll do to me? Tie me down every night?'

She slid her lips from my cock with a pop and sat back on her heels, frowning. 'What do you mean?'

'I mean, to keep me helpless. The way you like it.'

She frowned at me. 'No, no,' she said slowly, shaking her head. 'What do you mean: when you can walk again?'

I stared at her and she stared right back, her mouth open.

There was a moment's pause before I spoke. All I could say was, 'Oh my God.'

'I thought you knew,' she said quietly.

But I hadn't known. I hadn't known until that moment. I spoke slowly. 'I thought you liked to make me helpless. I thought you liked having power over me. I thought that was your thing. But that's not it, is it? It's all about the chair. It's all about the fact I can't walk. That's it, isn't it?'

'Did your physio say you'd get better?'

'He said I might. Actually I've been improving since...' My voice trailed off, strangely soft. 'I even thought you'd be pleased.'

But now I realised that that wouldn't please her at all.

I realised, with a sickening, creeping dread, that the thing I wanted most in the world was the one single thing she didn't want. And she didn't care about me; hadn't chosen me for her power games because of who I was. Just what I was.

It was as if a strange sexual spell had suddenly broken; as if suddenly, after almost two weeks of continuous fucking, I felt ashamed to be naked in front of her.

I didn't need to say it out loud. Without speaking she slipped off the bed and picked her dress up from the floor.

'I'm sorry,' she said, fastening the buttons so fast she fumbled over most of them and ended up taking twice as long. 'I should go.'

'Yes,' I said, glancing up at my still-bound wrists. 'Would you mind untying me first?'

In reply she picked her way across the room and set me free with a few deft moves. I pulled myself upright.

'I'd better go,' she said again.

'Yes,' I said. 'I think you'd better.'

And she left. It was the first time I'd slept alone in two weeks. My erection wouldn't go down all night. But I couldn't bear to touch it in case I thought of her.

The next morning I found a note had been slipped under my door, asking me to meet her back at the park, in the tearoom.

When I arrived she was sitting there, sipping her tea. She was wearing a blue dress. It was the first time I'd seen her in a different outfit. That cherry-print dress seemed to have been crumpled on my bedroom floor for the whole two weeks we were together. A black coffee, the drink I had ordered in this same tearoom with her two weeks ago, sat across from her on the table.

I wheeled myself over.

'I'm sorry,' she said. 'I shouldn't have reacted like that. It was just such a shock. I'd assumed it was permanent.'

'Really. Well, they don't really know.' I took the dripping filter contraption off the top of the cup, placing it messily on the table, and took a sip of the too-hot liquid underneath.

'Yes, of course. I mean they don't know for sure if you're going to get better or not, do they? And even if you do, well, I'm sure it could be OK.'

'Could it?'

'Yes. Maybe.'

I fixed her with a stare. 'Well, forgive me if I don't

see how, because it's not me, is it, with you. It's just the chair.'

'No. It's not that simple.' She ran her tongue over her lips. Suddenly my mouth felt very dry, but I knew the coffee would still be too hot. 'The chair is part of you. I want every part of you.'

'Yes, especially the parts that don't work.' I saw her swallow hard, but ignored it and went on. 'Admit it – that was what attracted you, wasn't it? If I could walk you wouldn't be interested.'

'Well, so what? You can't. So what does it matter?'

'So what! So what if you're not interested in me for me, just because of some sick fetish?'

'Why is it sick? We have a good time, don't we? I have a fetish for wheelchairs, you're in a wheelchair. What's the problem?'

'I want you to want me for me. That's the fucking problem.'

'I do. And that includes all the things about you that make you different from other people, including the fact you can't walk. So can't you want me for all the things that are different about me, including the fact that you not being able to walk turns me on?'

I looked at my lap for a long time. 'No,' I said eventually, not looking up. 'No, I can't.'

I kept my head bowed and heard her chair scrape against the tiled floor. I listened to her chunky-heeled footsteps walk away, before I looked up. So I don't know if she cried. And I don't think she knows I did.

Sometimes, when I go to the library I see her there. Standing in shafts of dirty sunlight, running her finger along a high shelf, clunky brown shoes clip-clopping on the old parquet flooring. We never speak. I wouldn't know what to say.

But if I do see her, I always end up touching myself when I get home. There's no point in resisting her if I want to sleep at all. It's the only way to get her out of my head.

And I do it naked, in the chair.

Foot on the Line
Heather Towne

I was sitting in the college library, supposedly studying for one of my summer school courses, when I gazed out of the window at the tennis courts in the distance. It was hot outside, and the asphalt playgrounds seemed to shimmer in the scorching sun; or maybe it was just that my eyes were as fuzzy as my brain – glazed over with erotic thoughts of my tennis partner, Madison.

I'd met Madison a month earlier when she had joined the tennis club I belonged to, and we'd hit it off right away. She was my age – eighteen – but whereas I'm tall and lean and kind of pale with shoulder-length black hair, sky-blue eyes, a tight squeezable butt and firm medium-sized boobs, Madison is short and sun-tanned with long blonde hair normally twisted into a ponytail, brown eyes, a big bouncy butt, large, heavy-looking hooters and supple sculpted legs. She looks awesome in the short, tight ass-wrap and form-fitting tube top that she usually wears when she plays tennis, and even better when she's wearing nothing but her personality in the hot, steamy shower room after the game.

Unfortunately, I couldn't spend as much time with this gorgeous honey as I wanted to, because I was always stuck in class, or studying. But I could conjure the little tennis vamp up in my mind any time I wanted, and that's just what I was doing as I stared, unseeing, out of the library window. Madison and I were swatting the furry ball around on the grass centre court of our home club, and I had just nailed a blistering backhand down the line ...

'Match point, Madison!' I yelped gleefully. I ran up to the net to shake hands and she jogged over to meet me, her big boobs bouncing beneath the sweat-soaked, stretched-tight aquamarine top she was barely wearing. Her toned, tanned legs flashed, smooth and inviting, under the hot sun, her short, short, oh-so-tight skirt straining to cover her taut bum and white panties.

She grabbed my hand and squeezed it, breathing hard. 'You sure were lucky that last set,' she said laughing.

'Gotta be good to get lucky ... I mean, be lucky.' The heat and her body had muddled my mind. It was mid-afternoon on a weekday, and the secluded club was all but deserted. 'Got the legs for another spanking, sweetie?'

She skipped over to the water bottle leaning against the net post, scooped it up and squirted some cool refreshment into her open, pink mouth. Some of the liquid spilled down her chin, onto her glistening, heaving chest. 'Maybe,' she gasped. 'Want a drink?'

I nodded, and was about to take the bottle from her when the playful hottie squirted a stream of water right into my face. 'Hey!' I yelled, scampering backwards. 'Sore loser, huh, girl!?'

She flashed her gleaming white teeth and beckoned me forwards with a finger, the water bottle cocked in her right hand. I took a few tentative steps closer, and the leggy young miss squirted me again then burst out giggling. I retreated again, but this time I plucked a couple of tennis balls off the court and whipped them at her – not hard enough to bruise her delicious body, of course. She shrieked and ducked behind the net, the balls missing her by a mile; I could paint the lines of a tennis court with yellow fuzz when I had a racquet in my hand, but I still threw a ball like . . . well, like a girl.

'Getting thirsty, Heather?' Madison teased from her crouched position behind the mesh. She waggled the water bottle and giggled some more.

I couldn't help but laugh at her antics, but then something even more stimulating tickled my fancy – the awesome sight of Madison's deep-brown cleavage busting out of her straining, nipple-indented top, her round, tight bum protruding from under her hiked-up skirt. I dropped the ball I'd been fondling and strolled over to the net, daring the tennis brat to hit me with her best shot. She jumped to her feet, grabbed me around the shoulders and squeezed the water jug so that it spat another stream of liquid out into my face. I didn't even try to break free of her tight, warm embrace, defiantly standing there and letting her douse my face with the cool water, and her mischievous smile soon drained away as she realised that I wasn't playing a game any more.

She lowered the bottle until it was splashing water down onto my cleavage, soaking my tight white Lycra top and turning it almost see-through. As she held me and sprayed me, we both watched as my nipples flowered to incredible hardness in silent, sexual awe. She squirted first one breast and then the other, waving the water bottle slowly back and forth, my drenched, tingling nipples outlined rigidly against the thin fabric of my top, my body shivering with something other than cold.

'Did that cool you off?' she asked softly, halting her tit-dousing. She stared at me, her eyes sparkling, her arm still encircling my bare shoulders.

I swallowed hard, lost in her deep, warm eyes, my nipples and pussy electrified with fevered anticipation. 'That only made me hotter,' I said huskily.

She smiled a wicked smile, then dropped the water jug and pulled me closer. She ran her fingers through my hair, then gently traced the oval shape of my face. The outside world became a forgotten thing as Madison slowly and exquisitely brushed her index finger across my parted lips, then slid it into my mouth. I instantly began sucking on the provocative teen's slender finger, my soft, wet tongue cushioning and licking it.

She watched me perform my sensual finger-fellatio for a minute, and then withdrew her glistening digit and replaced it with her lips, kissing me. She held me in her arms, and I held her, our heated bodies pressing hard together against the net, our inner passion bursting into open, flaming desire. I painted her pouty lips with my slick, pink tongue, and then we mashed our mouths together greedily and devoured each other under the broiling sun, in the middle of the blazing, empty tennis court.

Her lips were soft and full and relentless, and my head grew dizzy as we savaged each other's mouths. She darted her tongue inside my mouth, exploring the interior with her slippery pink spear. I tightened my grip on her, and met her probing tongue with mine, until we were frenching each other ferociously, slapping our tongues against one another with reckless urgency. Her hands slid down to my ass, then reached under my skirt and cupped my butt cheeks.

'Mmmm,' I groaned into her mouth, as she kneaded and fondled my bottom. I clutched at her tightly bound golden hair, and savaged her mouth with mine. Then I told her to stick out her tongue, which she did, and I latched my lips onto it and started bobbing my head up and down, sucking on her kitten-pink tongue. She stuck it as far out as she could, imploring me to suck it like a slut sucking a stiff, pink cock.

I sucked on her tongue for a good long while, before

she finally pulled it out of my mouth and then tried to push up my soaking wet top and bra, struggling to rid me of my drenched clothes. I helped her, and we rolled up my top and broke open my bra till my slick breasts were bare for the taking. She cupped them and a shiver of delight raced through my body. She squeezed and kneaded my super-sensitive breasts and tickled my tingling nipples, feeling me up like only a loving girl can feel up another girl. Then she moved her head closer, and flicked her tongue under and over my engorged nipples.

'Yes, Madison,' I breathed, watching through lust-misted eyes as the star of so many of my masturbatory fantasies licked at my nipples.

She teased my buds even harder with her talented, swirling tongue, and then took one of my nipples into her mouth and sucked on it. I swear I saw stars in the clear blue sky as the petite blonde bombshell tugged on my nips. She hungrily suckled my breasts, first one, then the other, before swallowing as much of my right boob as she could – which was most of it – and pulling on it. My body was aflame, my pussy smouldering, my clit a pulsating hair-trigger to orgasmic explosion.

Madison disgorged one saliva-soaked breast and attacked the other with her mouth, and slid a hand into my shorts and panties then started stroking my swollen clit.

'God almighty!' I screamed, getting all religious as a result of her righteous breast worship and sinful clit-rubbing. My body quivered as the blessed babe set me off like a fireworks display, fiery ecstasy blazing up from my pussy and consuming me.

She kept her wanton mouth locked onto my tit, her tongue sliding back and forth against the underside of my boob, as she buffed my clit and brought me off with her blistering forehand. I bit my lip and whimpered with joy as orgasmic spasms buffeted my sun- and sweat-drenched body, leaving me dazed and exhilarated.

Eventually, after I'd gone totally limp, she slid her lips off my breast and took her hand out of my shorts, then let me lick my juices off her fingertips. Then I stared into her eyes and blurted, 'I want to make love to your feet!' surprising both of us. My fetish for female feet was something I didn't normally discuss with a lover until well into a relationship. But I thought Madison could handle anything I could volley her way – and I was right.

'You like my legs and feet, don't you, baby?' she asked rhetorically, her brown eyes burning with want, her hot little hands still fondling my bare breasts.

'Let me show you just how much,' I murmured.

She grinned and broke away from me, then bent down and untied and pulled off her shoes. She was about to tug her cute little socks off too, but I told her not to. So she stood there and watched as I stripped away my skirt and top, bra and panties, until I was standing before her in nothing more than my tennis shoes, the sun beating down on my naked body, the hot, wind-whipped air caressing my damp, glistening nudity. I cupped and squeezed my boobs, and then rolled my long, hard, damp nipples between my fingers.

'Game, set, and we're a match!' Madison enthused, peeling off her own togs till she was as naked as me, clad only in her tennis socks. Her lush body was bronzed all over, her mocha nipples inflamed to an incredible length and thickness and her stunning legs smooth and slender and lightly muscled.

'Put your right foot up on the net,' I said, and she quickly obeyed. She gripped the post for better balance as I laced the fingers of one hand around her slim ankle and started massaging her socked foot with the other.

She kneaded her tits and moaned as I plied her delicate, sensual foot, running my fingers up and down the length of the arched appendage and rubbing and squeezing her toes.

I played with the fluffy pink ball that decorated the back of her white sock for a moment, then slowly and gently tugged the soft garment off her foot. I draped the sexy footwear over the net, picked up the water bottle and doused her feminine ped, her wriggling toes, with water. She gasped when the cool liquid hit her hot, sun-kissed foot. I bathed it with a steady stream of water, and then dropped the bottle and went to work on it with my loving hands.

I squeezed and rubbed and massaged her bare, sparkling foot, worshipping it with my warm, sure hands, and she closed her eyes and moaned and threw back her head, abandoning the quivering sole and instep to my needful ministrations. Her ripe, sweat-sheened body shimmered under the glaring sun, her long pony-tail dangling down her arched back until it just about touched the grass, as I rubbed and rubbed and then bent down to kiss her dazzling foot.

Her eyes shot open and she stared at me, fully comprehending now just how deep my foot lust ran. 'Suck my toes, Heather!' she urged, quickly getting into what I had been into for a long, long time.

I dropped to my knees in front of her golden foot, holding it in my hands only inches away from my face. I gazed at its splendid, curved beauty for a long, covetous moment, and then licked it from heel to toe in one slow, continuous tongue-stroke.

'Fuck, yes!' Madison shrieked, her knuckles turning white on the post, her leg shaking violently as I joyously lapped at the sensitive underside of her ped.

I licked and licked as Madison squirmed, pressing my tongue flat and running it hard along her sole, from heel to toe, coating her delicate flesh with my hot, hot saliva, over and over and over again. I tongued and tongued the underside of her exquisite foot, until she screamed out that she couldn't take it any more, her sweet, agonised wailing shattering the hushed silence of the sunbaked surroundings.

I stopped tongue-lashing her sole and let her quieten down, then started attacking her toes. I teased her slender, silver-tipped digits with my tongue, then squeezed it in between them as they wiggled and stretched out, snaking it back and forth and all around. I slathered her toes with spit, before popping them, one at a time, into my mouth and sucking on them. I sucked wildly on each of her smaller toes, then swallowed her big toe into my wanton mouth and tugged long and hard on it, painting it with my tongue.

'God, that feels fantastic,' Madison groaned, her body and the net that supported her luscious leg quivering uncontrollably. She let go of her tits and frantically plunged two fingers into her dripping pussy, finger-fucking herself desperately as I pulled on her toes with my mouth – all of them at once now.

'I'm gonna come, Heather!' she screamed, my reverential foot-worship overpowering her battered senses and firing her buffed body into raging flame.

I bobbed my head up and down on her foot, all of her toes crammed into my warm mouth. I sucked her toes relentlessly, frenziedly as she hammered away at her pussy, and she ...

A book slammed down on the floor, shocking me back to reality. I opened my eyes, closed my mouth and gave my head a shake, then hastily pulled my hand out of my panties, took my other hand off my tits and peered around the half-wall of the study carrel into the stunned eyes of a guy staring back at me. I guess my unconscious moaning had tipped him off to the fact that I wasn't doing much learning. Thankfully, our cubicles were buried way in the back of the library, behind stacks and stacks of books, otherwise the whole dry, dusty place would've been in on my very wet fantasy.

I smiled shakily at my fellow student, quickly gathered up my unopened books and papers, and exited the building – taking up where I'd left off in the privacy of my own dorm room.

A week later, after Madison and I had finished off a couple of gruelling sets of night tennis at our club, she suggested that we take a soak in the outdoor hot tub. It sounded like a good idea to me, so we hightailed it back to the locker room, stripped off our sweat-soaked duds and scooted into the shower room.

I soaked up as much of the gorgeous girl's curvy, sun-kissed body as I could get away with while we lathered and rinsed in the open-air, six-head shower. I polished my nipples extra-hard and rubbed thoroughly in between my legs as she swirled her hands all over her wet-dream bod, as the hot water caressed her like I wished I was caressing her. It took a monumental effort on my part not to succumb to temptation and lay loving hands on the sultry tennis vixen right then and there, when we were both nude and lubed, but somehow I managed to restrain myself, and we finished showering and towelling and sauntered back into the locker room. We slipped on our itsy-bitsy bikinis in preparation for some hot-tubbing, my blood already well past the boiling point.

She caught me staring at her succulent legs as she was shimmying into her tiny yellow bikini bottom. 'And just what are you looking at?' she asked petulantly, pulling up the skimpy thong until it barely covered her pussy, securely wedged between her big round butt cheeks.

'Huh? Oh, I was just ... I mean, um ... nice swim-suit!' My face was redder than an overripe tomato.

She laughed at my embarrassment, then yelled, 'Race you to the tub!' and took off with me in hot, and getting hotter, pursuit.

She beat me to the cedar-lined, six-person bucket of bubbling water, and we climbed in. The hot tub was located between the clubhouse and the tennis courts, on an open-air patio. It was about nine o'clock, so there wasn't anyone around the patio, but we could hear the puk-puk of balls being slapped back and forth on the tennis courts. Fortunately, the fifteen-foot high chain-link fence surrounding the courts was covered with thin, green sheets of fibreglass, so the players couldn't see us in the tub.

Madison splashed water in my face. 'Hey, Heather, like, I wanna know! Why are you always staring at my body?'

'Huh? I just, you know, think you look good – take good care of yourself. That's all.' We were both up to our nipples in the foamy-wash, and I was blatantly staring at her big, shiny, sun-burnished boobs. I could clearly see her thick brown nips outlined against the wet material of her clinging top.

'Thanks. I think you're pretty, too,' she said, return-ing my weak volley with some authority. Then she splashed more water into my face and added, 'You don't have a crush on me or something, do you, girlfriend?'

I splashed back, avoided her eyes.

'Heather loves Madison! Heather loves Madison!' the saucy tennis teen started yelling, as we flung water back and forth.

'C'mon, quit fooling around, Madison!' I hissed, glancing around. Then, when she wouldn't quit chirp-ing, I stood up and waded over to her, intent on shutting her up before the whole tennis club came out to investigate what was going on.

She gave the frothy chop a solid backhand that almost drowned me, but I managed to grab her, pull her up, and clamp a hand over her sassy mouth. We stood there for a while, staring good-naturedly at each other, my left arm coiled around her dripping, semi-nude body, pulling her hard and hot against my own, the steam rising and the water boiling. Then she licked my hand, and I pulled it away. We separated, and sat back down in our previous places.

'I don't mind that you have a crush on me,' Madison said quietly. 'And just out of curiosity, what part of me do you happen to like the best?'

I gazed longingly into her liquid eyes and was about to answer when...

'I think you like my legs the best,' she said, her full-bodied lips breaking into a knowing smile.

'Well, I –'

'Or my feet?' she interrupted again. 'How 'bout my feet?' She slid further down into the heated water and lifted her right leg up so that it floated on the bubbling surface. Her sexy, glistening foot was only a few inches away from my mouth, her wiggling, outstretched toes waving at me. 'Wanna suck my toes, Heather?' she breathed.

I answered her erotically charged question by seizing her drifting, golden-brown leg about the ankle and calf and pulling her foot to my lips. She squealed with delight and slid even further into the water, almost going under. I brushed her slender, silver-painted toes against my glossy, cushiony lips, kissed them, then let her penetrate my lips with her toes until they were inside my mouth and I was sucking on them.

'Yes,' she murmured, anxiously gripping the sides of the roaring hot tub and staring up at the star-studded night sky, her whole beautiful body floating near the surface of the churning water as I tongued and sucked her toes.

I crammed all of her slippery digits into my mouth and sucked hard on them, my hands rubbing and stroking her slim ankle, her fleshy calf, the soft, vulnerable back of her knee. Her smooth bronze leg shone under the lights, under the stars, under the loving caresses of my hands. I popped her toes out of my mouth and grabbed onto her other ankle, so that I held both of her succulent legs as she clung to the edge of the hot tub.

I moved closer, placing her feet on my shoulders, and used her feet to push down the straps of my bikini top until they slid off my shoulders and my breasts shone nude and lewd in the hot evening air, my cherry-red nipples engorged to one inch lengths. Madison's sun-kissed feet fondled and rubbed my nips and boobs. Her wriggling toes tweaked and rolled my inflamed nipples, like fingers would, sending electric shockwaves crashing through my arching body and setting my pussy ablaze.

'Feel me up with your feet, Madison,' I groaned, and let go of her ankles.

She cupped and squeezed and kneaded my breasts with her daring, dripping feet, holding first one tit between them and then the other, rubbing them, playing with them, buffing and pulling my nipples with her toes. Her heavenly feet clambered all over my heaving upper body, fondling my nipples and tits, caressing my neck. I caught her splashing, dancing feet in my hands again and rubbed my face with them, polished my cheeks with the soles of her feet, and then lapped at the smooth soles with my tongue.

I licked and kissed and bit the underside of her peds, and then her toes, until she cried out with uncontrollable sexual pleasure. It was time to consummate our lust with orgasm. I submerged her legs in the foamy water and pulled off my thong, then spread my legs apart and jammed her right foot, toe-first, into my aching pussy. 'Foot-fuck me, Madison!' I implored.

'You too!' she gasped, and I pressed my foot against her pussy. She quickly pulled her thong aside so that my searching toes could part her puffy lips and dive inside.

The water grew more and more choppy as we frantically fucked each other with our toes, pounding our feet into one another's pussy. I grimly gripped Madison's ankle and helped her piston her foot back and forth, her big toe plunging in and out of my burning snatch, her smaller toes bumping and grinding my electrified clit. She pumped her toes faster and faster into my flaming pussy as I did the same to her, over and over and over, frenziedly foot-fucking each other until we cried out in unabashed ecstasy, orgasms thunder through our thrashing, toe-joined bodies.

Finally, after the longest sustained period of white-hot joy I had ever experienced with a girl, I calmed down sufficiently to pull Madison's sweet toes out of my smouldering pussy and bring her spectacular foot back up to my mouth. I kissed and licked her toes, tasting my own simmering juices as I sucked on her pussy-pleasing big toe.

She closed her eyes and said, 'I could walk all over you and you'd love it, wouldn't you, baby?'

I could only nod my agreement, as my mouth was crammed full of glorious foot.

Birthday Suit Florence Hoard

He checked into the resort at Mystic Beach just as the chaises began getting scarce, about 9.00 a.m. The sun already asserted itself on the horizon, warning the bronzed bodies what was in store for them.

Nude beaches were not new to him. His family had spent their summers at Cap d'Agde, where he had matured among naked bodies of all shapes, sizes, ages and muscle tones. He was grateful for the early exposure, for it enabled him to grow up with no inhibitions about his own body and no fears about women's.

He slipped out of his clothing quickly and headed for the bright expanse of sand. Even at fifty, his six-foot frame and seven inch penis turned heads. He kept himself firm and tanned, and knew that his lustrous, full head of dark brown hair didn't hurt either.

He took the first available lounger, nodding to the man next to him. '*Bonjour*,' he said politely.

'Hi, there,' his older neighbour said. 'I'm Frank.'

'Jacques,' he replied, leaning towards the man to extend his hand. '*Enchante.*'

The older man's pubic hair had been shaved, revealing a smooth groin and sleek balls. His cock was an average size and certainly seemed to loll happily in the warm sunshine. The French would have called Frank *sympathique*. Basically, a nice guy.

Jacques settled into his lounger, enjoying the warmth from the sky as it soothed his grateful body. He wore darker sunglasses than Frank – no eye contact was made between the men but an easy silence filled the air as

Jacques stretched his long legs out before him. He felt Frank's eyes assess his soft but sizeable package and smiled to himself. Men never ceased to find the comparison of their genitals a highly engaging activity.

He let him look, completely unthreatened by the man's gaze. He was accustomed to being watched but spent little time watching others. Why watch when there was so much to do?

'You're here with French Telecom, I guess,' Frank ventured.

'Yes. French Telecom. Just for today,' Jacques replied without turning to his neighbour.

'Good, good. What studio are you in?'

Americans. So inquisitive. 'Fourteen,' he said.

'Oh! Here comes my wife.'

Jacques glanced in the same direction as Frank and one eyebrow shot up involuntarily. Since Jacques' adolescence, his eyebrows usually went up just before his cock did. He sometimes wondered if they didn't actually cue it somehow.

The woman appeared to be considerably younger than her husband; Jacques guessed around 50. Her body, a study in controlled voluptuousness, instantly triggered the circuitry between his legs. Her skin dripped with salt water and glowed with health.

'The water is fantastic!' She exclaimed, eyes ablaze with life. Her breasts were full and remarkably high, with pretty pink nipples that revelled in their freedom. She looked ripe and succulent, as if she'd ooze sweetness if he bit into her. And he did want to bite into her.

'You look very refreshed,' he heard himself say.

His words forced her to look at him and as she did, Frank stepped in with introductions.

'Lillian, this is Jacques. He's with French Telecom, working on that project near the aqueduct. Jacques, my wife, Lillian.'

Now her eyes danced. She did not hesitate to take his outstretched hand, and her grip communicated as much as her eyes. This was not a shy woman.

'Hello,' she said. 'And yes, I am refreshed.' A sly smile crept across her face. No matter what this woman said, it would sound sexual – and he liked that very much.

A subtle breeze swirled itself around his stirring cock, as if to announce his imminent erection. His sense of decorum would not allow him to get hard for a woman in front of her husband, so he abruptly but politely got to his feet.

'I think I'll enjoy some of that refreshment myself,' he explained, and headed quickly toward the sparkling waves.

He'd seen her gaze linger on his swelling cock. She probably knew that his escape to the ocean was an excuse to hide his arousal, but what of it? If there was one thing he'd learned about women, they liked a long, slow flirtation. She had seen what he had. Now he had to make her wait for it.

As he floated in the cool water, he imagined how her eager pussy had already begun to cream with anticipation. She'd be talking to Frank right now, but her cunt would be thinking about being fed by this mysterious, foreign stranger. He had to confess that he liked the waiting, too: the delayed gratification that resulted in rock hard cock and drenched pussy, the prolonged explosion of fantasy into reality. With the right woman, the process was unforgettable. Older women knew how to pace themselves without holding back passion. As he swam, his penis thickened with every stroke. When he was ready to come out, he forced himself to wait a little longer, secure in the knowledge that the more time he took to return to his lounge chair, the hungrier she'd be. Few things turned him on more than a hungry woman.

Finally he emerged from the sea with his semi-erection leading the way. As he walked towards the couple his rod swayed, lightly slapping one thigh and then the other. The subtle friction merely served to harden him further. By the time he was close enough to Frank and Lillian for them to recognize him, his seven inches of manhood had puffed up to eight.

Lillian didn't even pretend to look anywhere but his crotch. Frank looked on with bemusement and a thinly veiled awe. Jacques found himself developing a certain manly respect for the guy. There weren't many husbands, especially American ones, who would be secure enough in their masculinity to allow their wives to enjoy the sight of another man's goods, let alone what those goods could deliver.

Jacques prepared himself for some awkwardness. He was clearly hot for Lillian and Lillian hardly seemed opposed to the idea of him, but there was the complication of her husband. Jacques decided to let Frank determine the course of the action.

'Welcome back, Jacques. I see the water is fine. Think I'll jump in for a bit myself.' And with that he ambled away towards the shore.

'Your husband is a brave man,' Jacques commented from behind his dark glasses as he made himself comfortable in his lounge chair.

'Brave? Why? Are there sharks in the water?' She chuckled at her own wit.

'No, but there are a few here on the sand.' He would have winked if it hadn't been for the glasses.

'Is that supposed to scare me?' Her smile was constant now. Their sexual swords had been drawn and the battle of innuendo begun.

He laughed. 'When was the last time you were scared? I cannot picture it.'

'It's rare,' she confessed. While he'd been swimming,

she had repositioned her lounger so it sat at an angle, half facing the water, half facing him. As she opened her legs ever so slightly, he understood her motivation for the new arrangement. Like her husband's, her privates were completely free of hair. Even without the gap that now existed between her thighs, the folds of her labia and the curves of her mons were obvious and more than a little beckoning. With her knees apart, the smaller pink and pinched folds were also on display. He looked but did not linger long enough to be accused of ogling, even though that was clearly what she wanted him to do.

'Are you and your husband here for a while?'

'We spend a few weekends here every summer, and we also try to squeeze in a full week or more as time allows. How long are you here?' The question had none of the coy pseudo-innocence it might have had from a younger woman's lips. Her directness captivated him.

'I fly back to France tomorrow.'

She grinned. 'So much to do, so little time.'

'*C'est vrai.*' He grinned back, still under cover of his Polaroid lenses. He watched her search his face for clues that only his eyes could give.

'And yet you picked a good day to be here.'

'Oh? I think any day seeing you would be a good day.'

An uncertain breeze tousled Lillian's light-brown hair slightly. The ocean was reflected in her eyes as she smiled with the right side of her mouth. She drew her knees up to her chin and hugged them, still keeping her smooth pussy lips in clear view – in better view, in fact, now that they were framed by her thighs.

'You know, most women say they don't trust charming men, but personally, I think they're fun. What I meant about this being a good day was that it's my birthday.'

'*Mais non!*'

'*Mais oui!*' She laughed. 'Frank has promised me that anything goes today. Whatever I want.' Her eyes penetrated him without wavering.

'And have you decided what you want?' He was hard now and let his erection speak for itself. It rose to signal her but she'd long ago established communication with it. Now she assessed it as if she knew that she was responsible for its growth.

'Yes, I think I have.'

'Will your husband let you have it?'

'He said anything goes,' she repeated.

The juice between her legs sparkled on her swollen cunt. He knew she was close to dripping on her lounge chair and considered just reaching over to that moist little furnace to sample her. Instead, he stayed inscrutable behind his sunglasses. To what lengths might he get her to go by playing hard to get?

The spectre of Frank, ghost-like moments ago, now became a more tangible threat as he walked towards them from the water. His slightly shrunken penis bobbed happily with every step and his eyes sparkled nearly as much as Lillian's.

'I think there's something special in the water here,' he grinned as he towelled off the seawater from his body.

'I was just telling Jacques that today is my birthday,' Lillian said, smiling.

'Indeed it is!' Frank agreed as he dropped into his lounge chair.

'And I was also telling him that you said I could have anything I wanted today.'

'As you can year round, my dear,' he said, taking his wife's hand and giving it a squeeze.

'See? I told you.' Lillian winked at Jacques.

'I never doubted you.' Jacques chuckled. 'I believe

you also said you knew what you wanted.' If she was going to flirt, he'd give her a challenge.

'Yes. I want Frank to oil me up, right here and now.'

Sly woman.

'Well, that can be arranged,' Frank said, getting up from his chair in search of the suntan oil. Meanwhile, Lillian lowered the back of her lounger and gracefully flipped over onto her front. Her beautiful ass curved deliciously upwards, full and wantonly exposed for both men to view.

Frank stood over her now, looking mischievously from his wife to the Frenchman. He winked at Jacques conspiratorially. 'You know you *really* want your front oiled, Lillian. I know you.'

As she laughed, the muscles in her back contracted and relaxed with an ease Jacques found compelling. 'Humour me. Start with my back and we'll work our way to the front.'

Frank held the bottle several inches from the middle of her shoulder-blades and carefully poured a thin stream of oil along her spine. The liquid snaked along her skin like an eager tongue, lingering in some spots and gliding over others, happy to be everywhere. She groaned when Frank's hands touched her skin.

'Oh, that's good,' she moaned. She had turned her face away from Jacques so he couldn't see it.

What a fascinating connection she and Frank clearly had. As his hands massaged oil in and worked tension out, a brief silence fell that felt like theirs and theirs alone. Jacques dared not speak as Frank's palms communicated with Lillian's skin. The air around the three of them thickened with mystical overtones. Then he looked down and realised that the only real thickness was between his legs. He was hard now, harder than he'd been in weeks, so hard he could think of nothing pithy to say to break the awkward moment.

She turned her face towards Jacques but kept her eyes closed. 'Frank, honey, my gluteus maximus is aching. Work a little magic on me, would you? You know what to do.'

Frank positioned his hands where cheek melded with thigh and pushed upwards with slow, sensual stealth. Her fleshy mounds yielded only slightly to his touch, staying firm but pliant enough for Jacques to wish passionately that he could trade places with Frank.

Lillian separated her legs slightly and opened her eyes. Looking directly at Jacques, she spoke to her husband. 'Some oil has snuck in between my legs. I've always heard that oil and feminine juices don't mix well. You should probably lick it up,' she advised, smiling.

Jacques stared as Frank bent to place his face between her ass cheeks. Dutifully, he licked.

Jacques looked around, to be sure that nobody objected to their little display. In France, this would have been no problem, but he knew Americans were not known for their sexual tolerance. Fucking was great for them but sinful for others. At the moment, none of the other guests seemed to notice.

'I hope you don't mind,' Lillian teased. She'd drawn up her arms so they framed her face, exposing the sides of her ample titties. 'We've tried using towels but nothing seems to clean like Frank's tongue,' she said giggling.

'I don't mind at all,' Jacques commented. 'I'm a little concerned for your neighbours, though. They may want to join in!'

'But I only have eyes for you.' She winked.

Frank continued to lap away at her butt cleavage, while Jacques waited to see what she'd do next.

'What do you think, Jacques? Am I done on this side?'

'Only you know your own body, *madame*.'

'I know my body quite well, *monsieur*. I've gotten to know it intimately over the years, in fact. Frank knows my body pretty well, too, but that doesn't mean someone new couldn't teach me a few new things about it.' She turned over on her back as Frank watched, grinning. The oil greased her movements.

'I'm harder to handle when I'm slippery,' she added. The delight on her face at catching a glimpse of Jacques' erection was obvious. 'And I see you're just harder when I'm slippery.' Smiling at her husband, she directed her next comments to him. 'Work my front, honey pie. Show the man how it's done.'

Frank was at full tilt as well, Jacques noted as the man repositioned himself to fulfil his wife's latest request. The man's smooth balls gleamed from being so taut as well as being covered with oil. Jacques had been so enthralled with watching Lillian that he hadn't noticed that Frank had indulged himself in a bit of the oil too. He bent over his wife now, cock and balls hovering near her face as he leaned forwards to focus attention on her breasts. Jacques said nothing as he watched Lillian's beautifully tanned and firm breasts being manhandled by Frank: squeezed, kneaded, grabbed and manhandled by Frank. Jacques made a conscious effort not to touch himself.

The oil gleamed seductively on her soft curves, beckoning to him. Frank had moved his ministrations to her shapely hips now. He stroked her lovingly from her thighs to her beautiful bald sex and the couple seemed unaware of anyone but each other. Could Lillian so easily bounce between flirting with him and enjoying her husband? Of course she could – that's what made her so appealing.

As Frank massaged her toes and the mood lightened

enough to allow conversation again, Frank announced he was going to Pedro's to pick up some ribs for lunch.

'All right, sweetheart. I think I'll just go back to the studio and shower off some of this sand. You'll keep me company, won't you, Jacques?' She sat up in her lounge now, glistening with oil, her feet on the beach sand and her legs together. If he didn't know better, he'd say she looked downright demure. 'I'll open a bottle of wine if you stay here.'

Jacques looked to Frank cautiously to discern the correct course of action. One had to tread so delicately in these matters ... But Frank nodded enthusiastically, eyebrows raised as if to add an exclamation point to his encouragement. Leaving his wife alone with the Frenchman seemed part of his plan.

And so Jacques followed the voluptuous beauty as she led the way to the studio. She swung her ample hips with the carefree, lascivious air of a woman who knows she's transferred a man's brain directly into his penis. Her firm ass cheeks had become so much a part of his fantasies now that he could almost taste them.

She sauntered up to the outside shower at the back of the studio, and wordlessly began her shower. He removed his sunglasses and set them down on the small table, then turned to watch her. Running her hands along the slopes of her waist, her eyes met his in sexual challenge. She did not invite him to join her with words but her gaze lured him with unstoppable determination.

'May I join you?' he asked, mostly to be polite. His cock was doing the thinking for him now, so no matter what her response, he would have proceeded into the refreshing spray until he was close enough to touch her, just as he did now.

The cool water did nothing to squelch the sizzle

between them. Her nipples, hard and pink under his wandering fingers, acted as barometers of her lust. When he kissed her mouth, her soft lips kissed him back. Suddenly, though, she stepped away from the shower, leaving him standing there alone.

'I just needed to rinse the sand off. I'll go get the wine now.'

Her eyes sparkled and his erection bobbed with frustration. Rather than watch her distracting curves sashay into the studio, he shut his eyes and tried to get the water as cold as possible. There was no adjustment, though, and so he remained under a steady cascade of tepid water. He would play her game but he didn't like the idea that they only had as much time as it would take Frank to go to Pedro's. He wanted to enjoy Lillian now, rather than later, and wasn't sure whether Frank would take kindly to seeing his wife reamed by a visiting Frenchman. He did his best to summon up his Parisian *laissez-faire* attitude, vowing to leave things to fate, which had always served him well in the past.

The shower had no discernible effect on his raging hard-on, so he sat at the small round table near the shower and waited. Stroking himself as an interim measure occurred to him but he dismissed it as amateur, unsophisticated behaviour. When his cock got friction, it would be from that beautiful woman's wet pussy.

'Here we are,' sang Lillian as she emerged from the studio. A bottle of wine and two glasses sat on the small tray she carried. 'I've been saving this bottle for a special occasion.'

'I'm flattered you feel this is it.' He smiled.

'I think my birthday qualifies as a special occasion, don't you?' She stared at him, eyes ignited with mischief. 'What shall we drink to?' she asked as she poured the wine. Normally, he would have intervened – a woman should never pour when a man is there to do it for her – but she seemed to have things well under control. Her control.

'Well, *madame*, we could toast to Mystic Beach, birthdays, French Telecom, or the beauty of the feminine form. I have fond feelings for all of them.'

'I'd like to drink to handsome men with incredibly large cocks. How do you say that in French?'

'Like this,' he said, leaning forwards and making contact with her mouth before she could protest. She was warm, soft, fiery in spirit.

Her free hand wandered downwards between his legs, seeking out the smooth heat of his shaft. She looped her index finger around his girth and brought her thumb around to close the gap. And then she stroked – long, slow, perfectly timed sweeps upwards then down, stopping short of his mushroom head on the way up and travelling all the way down to his dark brown pubes. His body trembled.

He couldn't reach her pussy amidst the jumble of arms and wine glasses, so he put his glass down as he continued to gently tongue-wrestle with her. She emanated more heat when he tickled her shaved mons, and by the time he burrowed between her thighs to access her moist sweetness their tongues were practically down each other's throats.

She broke free of the kiss first, not abruptly, but firmly nonetheless. 'You know, in this country, a woman with a birthday gets to make requests all day.'

'Is that true?'

'Oh yes,' she whispered, smiling a crooked smile. 'I ask you now to step inside so that you may ravish me.'

He laughed in spite of himself. 'Why do I get the distinct impression that *I'm* the one who will be ravished?'

'Scared?'

'Is this the erection of a frightened man?' he asked, directing both their attentions to the rock-hard enormity in his lap.

She stood, took him by the hand and led him into the studio through the sliding glass doors. The bed loomed, a wide expanse of white among small, simple wooden furniture. Though the room looked much like his own, its appeal was double – no triple – that of his.

Was it she who guided him on top of her or had he placed himself into that dominant position? Regardless, he now looked down on her as she laid on her back, expectant and ready.

His cock had a purpose, a driving purpose, in fact, but his mind wanted to explore Lillian more slowly. He wanted to play this woman as a musician plays an instrument, caressing her body for optimum performance, coaxing heights of excellence from it that only pure appreciation could evoke.

He put his lips to one large nipple and licked reverently while he listened to her gasp. Her sounds encouraged him to slip his other hand into her steamy folds, fondling and stroking until her cream coated his fingers.

'Luscious, luscious woman,' he mumbled between laps at her breast. He squeezed her gently, enjoying the fullness in his hands.

Her fire was unrestrained now and her coquettish side had disappeared. Only her womanly essence was with him in the room at this moment, surrendering to her desires and stoking his. She spread her legs wide for him and he immediately slipped one, then two, then three fingers into her dripping wet hole. As he slid his digits in and out of her, he frigged her clit with his thumb. He was surprised by how large it became at his touch, and how sensitive it was. She writhed with happiness and rocked her hips in tandem with his thrusts to send him deeper inside her.

Her hands were not idle. They'd found his pulsing cock and pumped it in exactly the right rhythm. He could always tell when a woman went through the motions of playing with cock, as opposed to thoroughly enjoying doing so. Lillian was of the latter variety, as obsessed with stroking him as he was with stroking her. Her enjoyment of his equipment turned him on even more. He could actually feel her swelling under his fingers and gushing into his hand.

'I have another request,' she whispered.

'*Oui, madame. Quoi que vous voulez.*'

'What?'

'Whatever you want.' He grinned. He was so lost in the moment, he'd retreated to his native language.

'I want you to fuck me. Slide that beautiful piece of meat inside me. I haven't been able to think about anything else since I saw you this morning.'

'I'm afraid I cannot do that, *madame.*'

Her eyes opened wide in guileless wonder. 'Why not?'

'Because my desire to eat you is greater than your desire to be fucked.'

Her worried face relaxed into a knowing smile. 'Well, then, by all means, eat my pussy.'

He kissed his way down her body, from breastbone to navel, then slowed his pace as he approached her hairless mound. Her hands went to his head, where she grabbed handfuls of his hair. Her scent hardened him more and made him slightly dizzy. He couldn't recall ever wanting a woman so badly.

She tasted of salt air and fresh breezes but also of rich, spicy femininity. As his tongue played at her engorged clit, her juices dripped into his mouth and he closed his eyes to keep from swooning. She spread herself wide for him and, as she did, her labia parted to expose every glistening pink part of her. Her clit grew still larger as he licked it.

Her entire body stiffened and arched as she pulled more urgently at his hair. When she came, her shouts filled the room. She undulated and bucked as he continued to lick her, pushing her over the edge of whatever precipice she called pleasure.

'Now!' she cried. 'Fuck me now!'

His only thought now was to please her. With his cock past the point of containment anyway, he mounted her and gasped at the heat that suddenly surrounded his steely rod. Not only was Lillian the juiciest woman he'd ever experienced, she was also the steamiest. Any hotter and he might have felt pain.

He could not postpone his release as he could with other women. Looking at her now, with her pretty face in a kind of possessed state of transcendence, and feeling her tight cunt pull and squeeze his cock as if to milk the come right out of him, he surrendered to her, shouting nearly as loudly as she had as he filled her with thick, gooey fluid.

A slight movement in the corner of the room made him turn his head, and at the sight of Frank standing there, mouth agape, he froze. Lillian, however, seemed undisturbed by his sudden and unannounced arrival.

'Hi, there.' She smiled at her husband.

'Hi, yourself. You just couldn't wait, could you?'

Jacques did not, could not, breathe. In his elevated state of arousal, perhaps he had used bad judgement. Perhaps he should have waited to see what Frank preferred. He'd tried to read him but maybe his lust had clouded his judgement. He waited for Frank's next move, ready to apologise or flee, whichever seemed most expedient.

'No, baby, I couldn't wait. You saw the member on Jacques. Did you think I wouldn't want it as soon as I could get it?'

Frank smirked. 'No, I knew you'd do this. It's what I hoped you'd do,' he said, placing the bag of ribs on the coffee table. 'Why would I get you a birthday present you wouldn't enjoy?'

Lillian looked from Frank to Jacques and back again. Jacques was relieved to have the plan exposed but wasn't sure how Lillian would react, now that she knew he'd been hired to please her.

'You mean you're a gigolo?'

'Well, not technically. A gigolo is more of a full-time job.'

'Are you French, at least?'

'*Oui, madame. Je suis Français.*' He smiled. 'But I am something else, as well.'

'And what's that?'

'Very, very hot for you. You are an incredibly sexy woman. When Frank hired me, he said I should only do what felt right. Once I saw you, there was no question about what was going to feel right.' He moved his hand to her still gushing pussy and stroked her swollen lips. She kissed his forehead.

Frank approached the bed, sturdy erection in hand. 'I'd love to see Jacques fuck you from behind,' he suggested.

'Mmmm, good idea,' Lillian agreed. 'And I can suck your cock while he rams me.'

And so they assumed their positions. Lillian's cunt, carrying a heady blend of scents from then and now, accepted Jacques' cock easily. The fact that he remained hard even after his orgasm of just minutes before was testament to his rampant hunger for her. As he pumped her, he watched the provocative jiggling of her womanly ass cheeks with fascination. She even pushed up against him in time to his thrusts to force him deeper into her pussy. He found he could hold himself back somewhat more easily now that his first eruption had passed, so he watched her suck off her husband.

What a gift she had for knowing what a penis needed! As he followed the movements of her tongue around Frank's grateful cock, that cock became his own. He imagined his own meat stuffed far down her throat as her tongue swirled around it, tickling the underside of his knob and stroking the sensitive patch right near his come hole. The longer he watched, the harder he got.

Just as he was ready to let another load go inside her hot cunt, the walls of her pussy tightened around him. Frank's cock muffled her shouts but she didn't let that impair her enjoyment. She ground her ass wildly up and back towards Jacques and made Frank's cock completely disappear down her throat.

Frank signalled to Jacques to pull out. Confused but mindful of his role, Jacques obeyed. Frank held his tumescent, nearly purple member in one hand and Jacques did the same.

'Roll over, Lillian. We want to give you something,' Frank instructed.

Lillian turned over onto her back and, the moment she did, both men sprayed her face and torso with thick ropes of jizz. She looked like an x-rated Jackson Pollock painting.

'Mmmm,' she said, rubbing the streams of come into her skin. 'That was fantastic. I may never bathe again,' she said, laughing. Jacques couldn't resist helping her massage the orgasmic fluid into her supple skin.

'Good sex always gives me an appetite,' Frank commented. 'Ribs, anyone?'

Charlotte Meets Her Match
Jill Bannalec

Charlotte Bingham had become all that her teachers had said she should strive to be. Now, as a qualified accountant, always smart, always punctual, and a pillar of the bank, she watched her colleagues sit in front of their PCs and, like her, wonder when the nightmare would end.

What a complete cock up! Another thirty years will mince my brain, she thought despairingly, staring at the screen and feeling like an inmate in an institution. Her conscientious, head-down, no distractions approach to studying had rewarded her with a healthy income and the trappings to go with it – fine clothes, a luxury flat and a sports coupé – but she had missed the student parties, had no real friends, and her sex life was non-existent. She longed for someone to share her troubles with, to get reassurance from, to talk about 'girly things' with, and even have a laugh with. Most of all, though, ever since a brief, passionate fling at university, she missed sex. She often felt as horny as hell, with a nagging itch that her self-imposed lifestyle prevented her from scratching. She had frightened off her male colleagues with her reserved abruptness, and was so rusty at relationships that she had become too scared to give the wheel of destiny a gentle push. Things were about to change.

Depending on your point of view, the various reps visiting the bank could be either a pain or a pleasure, although they were usually the former. It had always been Charlotte's practice to dismiss them as unnecessary distractions, but her unsatisfied libido eventually made even one particular 'white van man' look attractive. His name was Simon Armitage, and every month he called to exchange the chilled mineral water bottles. He was a big man, not too tall but solidly built and quite good looking, treating the heavy refills as if they were empties. Charlotte had, true to form, rejected his original advances – he was only a delivery-man, after all. In so doing, she had dented his considerable ego more than she realised. Simon's reputation amongst his friends was as someone who 'kissed the girls and made them cry'. She would be just another notch on his bedpost. However, she had an Achilles heel – a secret passion for the game of rugby union, or rather the players.

Charlotte's collection of videos included a comprehensive library of international matches, from the flamboyant, cavalier but undisciplined French to the rugged, dour Welsh, and she often fantasised over their powerful bodies, and how she would surrender herself to a strapping lock forward. She had heard that it was a game played by men with funny shaped balls and was still hoping, one day, to find out. When someone let slip that Simon was a keen player, she began to see him in a different light, wondering what he looked like with his firm meaty arse clad in those skintight shorts that the broad-shouldered forwards always seemed to be ready to burst out of.

One day she returned to her office to find a PC-generated sign on the door. It read 'Welcome to the Ice Queen's Palace – Abandon hope all ye who enter her'. The wording and deliberate misspelling were designed to hurt her, and they did, even though she suspected it was one of the clerks getting at her for reporting their lateness a couple of weeks ago. Charlotte recognised more than a grain of truth in the cutting message, and it became the last straw that convinced her that she had something to prove, to herself as well as others, and that Simon was the one to help her.

On his next scheduled visit she engineered a situation to get them both in the stockroom at the same time, and gave him the eye. He responded as she had hoped, cornering her behind the photocopier, and she enjoyed the rare warmth of arousal as he pressed his surprised but obviously excited body against hers, dismissing his confusion at her sudden flirtatiousness after months of aloofness bordering on hostility. Charlotte knew he was thinking that she might be a stuck-up boring accountant, but she was a stuck-up boring accountant with a great body and a sports car, and she knew he couldn't resist getting inside her conservative suit and having a stab at the goods. Unknown to him, she merely wanted to dispel the rumour that she was, like the literary Ice Queen, destined to remain a perennial virgin. A public demonstration of her power over poor, gullible Simon – only a delivery-man, for goodness sake – was all she intended. Unfortunately, as far as Simon was concerned, she would just be another notch on his bedpost.

Charlotte quickly made it known that she was to see him play in a match the following weekend, prior to a few drinks in the clubhouse. He played every Sunday lunchtime, and the idea of watching him and 29 hunky, sweaty guys grappling in the mud appealed to her baser instincts. She had a particular thing about the way the players in the scrum placed their arms between the legs of the one in front and grabbed their team-mates' shirts to hold the pack together. I wouldn't mind a go at that myself, she thought, imagining herself bent over, moulded around the straining body of the guy in front, her arm between his legs, her hand pumping his swollen cock. The guy behind would be pumping her ... She took a deep breath and reassembled her composure. Anyway, as a fall-back, if she found she didn't fancy Simon after all she would have the pick of the rest. She congratulated herself on a good plan.

Simon's team were playing away from home, and she agreed to meet him before the kick-off at noon. Unfortunately, although she had a good idea where the ground was, she was late, having spent far too long getting ready, and it was 12.15 when she parked her pristine two-seater in the car park next to the clubhouse. She checked her hair and make up, having dressed to impress in a new cream two-piece suit, with matching sling backs and sheer stockings. Underneath, lace-trimmed silk lingerie was waiting for him, if she ever let him get that far. Since the weather was threatening she also wore a raincoat and broad-brimmed hat, with an umbrella for extra insurance. It was a good move, she told herself, as the rain fell steadily as it had all month.

As she swivelled on the red leather seat and swung her shapely legs out of the car, she revealed a glimpse of stocking top under the short skirt, and the brief kiss of the cool breeze on her naked inner thighs seemed to awaken her dormant arousal. She stood up and opened the umbrella, looking towards the pitch to see the match already in progress. An assortment of wives, girlfriends and children, more appropriately clad than Charlotte in Wellington boots and anoraks, were holding aloft an assortment of brightly coloured golfing umbrellas and cheering every move their team made. The wet winter and spring had ruined the pitch, and the little grass that remained was only evident along the touchline. The rest of the pitch was a quagmire and, even after only twenty minutes' play, it was becoming difficult to distinguish which team was which, as more and more of the steaming players became covered in a sheen of glossy mud. Charlotte's mind immediately began to wander, imagining that she was the referee, able to make them do exactly as she wished . . .

She felt a more pronounced glow between her thighs, smiled to herself, then glanced up at the leaden sky and started to walk towards the touchline. She picked her way across the turf, and quickly realised why the other less fashion-conscious women wore rubber boots, as she suddenly felt one foot go very cold. She looked down to see that it was completely immersed in a puddle of brown water. 'Shit!' she muttered to herself, anxiously looking around for drier ground. There wasn't any. She attempted to retrace her steps but found only soft mud (at least she hoped it was mud) with her other foot. She angrily abandoned all thoughts of watching the match from the touchline and returned to the car, shaking her feet as she danced from puddle to puddle like a kitten walking on snow.

Once there, she grabbed a handful of the tissues she always kept in the glove box and removed the shoes from her wet feet. As she stuffed them with tissues she saw that her once sheer stockings were stained pale brown as far as her ankles. 'Shit and more shit,' she whispered to herself, as she attempted to wipe the mud from her shoes, but she soon realised that the soft kid leather had already absorbed the pigmentation, and would never be the same attractive shade of cream again. 'Bugger!' she exclaimed, but then, surprising herself, she felt compelled to smile for the first time in a long time at her uncharacteristic brush with the elements.

She sat in the car for a few minutes, listening to the

radio as the windows steamed up. It was still not half-time, and she toyed with the idea of going home, but after noticing the lights come on in the clubhouse bar she decided to have a drink and watch the rest of the match from there. She spent a minute or two refreshing her make-up and brushing her hair, then grabbed her coat, locked the car and, ignoring the rain and puddles, ran towards the clubhouse. She looked around for assistance, but the place seemed deserted. She knew that the bar was on the first floor, with the changing rooms and toilets directly underneath, and warily walked in to find that she was the only one there, apart from an elderly man busy behind the bar.

Charlotte approached him cautiously, feeling slightly incongruous in her designer trenchcoat and hat. He smiled a welcome, and she ordered a G & T, feeling that he seemed over-interested in her appearance, apparently standing on tiptoes to peer over the bar at her.

He said little, speaking in a broad accent that she struggled to understand. She half expected him to offer her a Scotch egg or pickled onion from the 'extensive à la carte menu' written in chalk on the wall behind the bar. She paid for her drink, noticing it cost half of what she paid in the bar near the bank and seemed a larger measure, then went and sat, still wearing her raincoat, next to a large window overlooking the pitch. She peered through the rain-streaked glass, without a clue what the score was, which was Simon's team or even which player he was. She prayed that the match would finish sooner rather than later.

A dozen or so miles away, Sharon Stevenson, professional name 'Dolly Part'em', was getting ready for work. She was a strippergram of some experience. When she boasted she'd 'been there, done that', she really meant it. She was always prepared to bend over backwards, literally, and go the extra mile, which meant, in her job, about six inches. She had a passion for her work fuelled by an unparalleled need for sex and money, after her husband had traded her in for a new model, and even with the CSA in full Rambo mode, bringing up her kids had demanded full use of her occasionally hidden but more often displayed 'talents'.

Today's job would net her £150, performing at the final game of one Simon Armitage, who was retiring from the field of play having reached the grand old age of forty. She knew what entertaining fifteen drunken rugby players in the privacy of their own dressing-room could entail. She was taking no chances. Just in case of accidents, she selected her oldest gear, although she would charge any replacements against tax as if they were new. Into her small vanity case went the baby oil, an aerosol of squirty cream and a couple of dildos. Then she pulled on a black PVC cupless bra, which she covered with a black lace one, then a sheer black blouse, two pairs of knickers – one to rip off and one to get ripped off – her red lace suspender belt and black fishnet stockings, and a short crimson PVC skirt that left nothing to the imagination. When she bent over, she knew the faithful would see the promised land. Finally, she put on black knee-length boots and a long raincoat and, after finishing packing with a complete set of 'normal' clothes, climbed into her twelve-year-old Maestro and left for the club.

Charlotte drank another two cheap G & Ts, the second a double, before the match finished, each time retreating to the window seat after ordering to avoid the lecherous gaze of the barman, who was making a very poor job of disguising his unhealthy interest in what she was wearing under the coat. The rain continued to pour down, and even if she had wanted to, it would have been impossible to follow the match from her vantage point, since by now every player seemed to be playing for the All Blacks. The alcohol was the only redeeming feature of a miserable afternoon, and she was feeling quite tipsy, not having eaten since muesli at breakfast. She sat and wondered if it was all worthwhile.

After what seemed ages, the referee blew for time, just as the rain stopped and the sun came out. The teams trudged wearily off, each making a tunnel for the opposition and clapping each other off, and disappeared into the dressing rooms directly under where Charlotte sat, steam still rising from their weary bodies as they passed below her. She looked in vain for Simon. They all looked more or less the same – muddy and knackered. By now she was becoming desperate for a pee and would eventually reluctantly have to ask her friend behind the bar where the loos were. Down below, unseen by Charlotte, her Simon made his way into the away dressing room, and Sharon's Simon gratefully dragged his painful joints towards the home one.

Ten miles away, however, Sharon's Maestro was stopped in a lay-by, steam and water escaping from a split radiator hose. Without a mobile phone and with few buses on the weekend, she had no option but to wait for the engine to cool down, and then slowly drive the three miles home, rather than attempt the rest of the journey to the ground. She sat inside watching the rain fall, and cursed her bad luck. She would not get paid, and Simon would never know what he had missed. She was only half right.

Charlotte's Simon felt he had performed rather well, and couldn't wait to join her in the bar to receive her praises and claim his reward. As he soaped himself in the showers his mind wandered and he felt his pride and joy begin to stiffen as he pictured her waiting only a few feet above his head, no doubt fantasising about him naked below. He casually moved his thoughts elsewhere and rinsed the soap off his thickening cock. Charlotte was indeed still sitting in the bar, but her thoughts were on more immediate needs; she'd had her legs firmly crossed, hoping to avoid the need to talk to the barman, but eventually her bulging bladder gave her no option. She carefully stood up, and gingerly approached the bar.

'Dutch courage?' he grunted. His remark puzzled her.

'Ladies?' she enquired, quietly but pleadingly. He studied her for a few seconds.

'Next door to the Gents,' he boomed embarrassingly. 'But watch it, there's no "Ladies" sign on the door. We don't get many ladies in here.'

'Can't think why,' Charlotte thought, and painfully and slowly made her way downstairs to find herself in a long whitewashed corridor with several doorways leading off it.

Simon the elder, a veteran of 23 seasons, had the trophies to show for it – missing teeth, a nose that had been squashed across his face, cauliflower ears and gammy knees. He had staggered into the dressing-room full of nostalgic memories of tries scored and forwards thumped, but was secretly glad it was all over. He suspected the lads had something special planned to mark the occasion, and would be disappointed if they hadn't. A few yards away, Simon Armitage the younger was climbing out of the communal bath, recovering quickly, and looking forward to his after-match escapades with the lovely Charlotte.

* * *

Charlotte slowly began to walk along the long corridor, gingerly picking her way through the mud and clods of grass deposited by the boots of the two teams as they left the pitch. She glanced down at her once pristine shoes and cursed her uncontrollable – and fast becoming seriously unsatisfied – lust for rugby players. Just then, however, a player appeared at the end of the corridor and, as he walked towards her, dirty, breathless, his steel-studded boots clicking on the stone floor, she was reminded, quite vividly, of why she found them such a turn-on.

She tried and failed to avoid staring at his bulging shorts, noticing his coiled cock bundled around inside. He grinned a welcome, as if he were half expecting her. His friendly smile was unexpected and disconcerting, a flash of piercing blue eyes under his bedraggled, once blond hair, and she felt herself returning it with interest, intense arousal suddenly pervading her body. As he passed she flattened herself against the wall to avoid his muddy, powerful thighs brushing against her. Although she stood nearly six feet in her high heels, he towered above her. She felt a loss of control at being so close to him, feeling his body heat, smelling the aroma of liniment, earth and sweat, and looking openly at his powerful mud-caked thighs and his bulging packet. Her organised brain switched off as her hormones switched on and, for the first time in ages, she had to fight to control the urge to place both hands around his waist and nuzzle her face against his crotch. It felt rather too pleasant to be true.

As they passed, her bottom pressed against the cool wall as she just managed to avoid him brushing against her pristine skirt.

'Are you Simon's, er, sorry about the pun, "Dolly bird"?' he suddenly asked, his unexpected question making her jump. 'I'm his mate, you know, Lee.' She was confused, but nodded, all the time unable to take her gaze off his lunchbox, a few inches from her midriff. He smiled broadly. 'He'll be well pleased, which is more than I can say for Charlie.' A look of concern formed on his face as he noticed her bottom still pressed against the wall. 'You better make your peace with him before you leave.'

'Who's Charlie?' Charlotte asked, losing all sense of the conversation and struggling to keep a clear head after her four G & Ts.

'Our groundsman. He whitewashed that wall this morning and it won't be dry yet.'

A look of realisation then horror appeared on her face, and her frantic hands gingerly touched her bottom. Sure enough, when she inspected her fingers they were covered in white paint. Charlotte gasped and stifled a cry of anguish. Seeing her obvious distress, Lee tried to reassure her.

'It comes off easily. Don't you worry. Just get some water on it. Besides, you can always claim it against expenses. You'd better come in here now. Follow me.' He winked and beckoned her in, holding the door open. She hesitated for a second, then remembered the need to get some water on the stain and stepped inside. As she did so, she was suddenly conscious of how much warmer it had suddenly become, her designer spectacles steaming up in an instant. She started to clean them with her handkerchief, not noticing the door being fastened and locked behind her.

She put them on and looked around her. The effect that one player had had on her in the corridor was suddenly magnified by at least a dozen. Charlotte gazed around the noisy, humid changing room and registered the smiling faces attached to muscular, naked, or near-naked male torsos. Some were standing under showers, while others peered at her over the edge of a vast, steaming, white-tiled bath. A few balanced on one leg as they removed the last vestiges of their strip. It suddenly went very quiet as the men realised she had arrived, but then the brief silence was punctured by a shout from the back of the room. 'Get Simon. The stripper's arrived!'

The predicament in which she found herself was suddenly all too apparent. Her immersion in a mixture of alcohol, unfulfilled fantasy and arousal reached a new level, and she became aware of an out-of-control feeling of melting liquidity between her legs. She tried to hide it as she stared in disbelief at the rest of the team, some of whom were still muddy, the only pink bits being the parts originally clothed. Her arousal, though, was intensifying by the second, a tingling heat between her thighs building by the second. She felt like she had gone to sleep and woken up in heaven. It was also becoming all too obvious how pleased to see her several of the men were, and she allowed the final vestiges of self-control to slip away. 'Oh, my goodness,' she thought, as a voice inside her told her to turn and run. A louder one still spoke directly to her aching need, and she found herself breaking into a broad smile and quickly removing her spectacles. She slid them into their case, then placed her hands challengingly on her hips. 'Hello, boys', she said. 'Now where's my Simon?'

She slowly slid her coat off, one shoulder at a time, and offered it to Lee. A spontaneous cheer echoed around the crowded room as he took it from her. Seconds later shouts of 'Simon, Simon' echoed around the room, and he was pushed towards her through the throng, clad only in a jockstrap. After a brief moment of shock as she realised that this wasn't the man she'd expected, Charlotte smiled at him, her eyes settling on the bulging material between his legs. 'You must be

Simon,' she said. 'I'm pleased to see you, and you seem to be very pleased to see me.' Another cheer broke out, and a rhythmic clapping and whistled version of 'The Stripper' filled the room. It was her cue.

She slowly unbuttoned two buttons of her blouse, then adopted a coy expression and held the material together for a few moments. Two more buttons followed, then the last two, and she pulled the blouse out of her skirt and held it closed for a second, looking around at the expectant faces, then took pity on them and opened it, revealing her silk bra and hardening nipples, already prominent under the soft, shimmering material. She handed it to Lee, who was rapidly assuming the role of coat hanger. She gained in confidence and walked around Simon like a model, one foot directly in front of the other, then offered her breasts up for inspection. He reached for them, but she smartly avoided his lunge, twisting like a matador away from the bull. The team cheered her on. Her excitement from arousal and alcohol was intense, as she vaguely remembered her skirt and the advice she had been given to 'put it in some water'. She walked slowly over to the bath, the crowd parting as she strode between the men, who hung on her every move as she unzipped the skirt, pushed it sensuously down her thighs and stepped out of it. She held it at arm's length over the water, and dropped it unceremoniously into the bath, feigning shock as a hand quickly grabbed it as a trophy. Her inhibitions gone, she relished the power she had over her audience, and began to revel in being the centre of attention for fifteen or so very horny men, in a way she had often imagined but never believed possible.

She posed in her heels and stockings, legs slightly akimbo, and ever so slowly bent over, her bottom facing the salivating Simon, and touched her toes. In the silence that followed, punctuated only by increasingly heavy breathing, she could have heard a pin drop. She held the position, allowing Simon and the rest to feast their eyes on her upturned bottom, the thin line of her panties bisecting her buttocks and broadening out as the material dampened and moulded itself against her blossoming pussy lips. She straightened up and pointed at Simon's straining jockstrap.

'What's that for? Moral support?' she asked, smiling lasciviously. Her question was comprehensively answered when she reached behind him and unclipped it, allowing his cock and balls to spring from a nest of dense ginger curls and harden still further as it reached its fullest size. She put on a theatrical gasp of surprise, and then brought laughter from his team-mates as she held her hand up, thumb and forefinger an inch apart, as if having just measured him. Any rumours that Dolly Part'em was a bit of a broiler and past her best were completely dispelled. Simon was having difficulty controlling himself, forgetting his wife and kids on the touchline.

For a minute or so Charlotte shimmied provocatively in her silk underwear, running her palms down the outsides of her stocking-clad thighs and bringing them slowly back up the inside until they brushed the V of her panties, all the while trying to avoid slipping on the wet tiled floor in her high heels. She glanced down at her perspiration-sheened breasts then selected another, younger player, tall and sinewy, probably a winger, and slid her outstretched arms around his neck, dragging her nails down his moist chest before finally pulling him against her, her hungry pussy nuzzling the erection concealed in his tight shorts. The noise and general clamour increased as he fought in vain to control his excitement, before embracing her with his powerful arms. She no longer cared about the filthy state she was getting into, but pushed him away anyway, watching his pleading expression as she continued to tease him, weighing her heavy breasts in each hand. He swallowed hard as she turned around rapidly, inviting him to unhook her bra.

Amidst more cheers, he did so, and the men feasted their eyes on her glistening, swinging breasts with their salmon-pink nipples, hard and prominent. She felt hot and intoxicated, knowing, without looking, that her moist, engorged pussy was by now also betraying her state of mind and body. Almost in a trance, she was leading the men like the Pied Piper. All of them were now naked, and all held enormous erections, some with long thick cocks, some short stubby ones, some ramrod straight, some arched upwards – but all excited to the point of spurting. She could feel her own wetness squelching in her pants, but was past caring.

Simon suddenly yelled in a voice distorted with excitement, 'Right, lads. A scrum down for our sexy lady!' She watched as they formed a circle, enveloping her as they linked arms, leaning forwards from the waist, so close that she found herself forced to sit on the floor, looking up at their happy faces. Charlotte lay back in the semi-darkness, breathing hard and wondering what to expect.

'Now, lads, the usual compliment!' boomed Simon. 'Hands on cocks, empty rocks!' She suddenly realised, as she saw each man take hold of his cock and begin to pump it slowly, then more urgently, exactly what was intended. Her fingers slipped inside her pants and sought out her clitoris as she sensed her predicament. She watched the men, mesmerised, her other hand caressing her heaving, greasy breasts. Some compliment, she thought, anticipating what or who was coming next, and instinctively shut her eyes, but then felt compelled to open them again to enjoy the spectacle to the fullest.

Virtually simultaneously, led by Simon, they each reached the point of no return and stood up, knees bending and hips heaving spasmodically, to ejaculate over her. Charlotte felt the first gentle impacts as globules of the milky come began to rain down upon her. Soon it was trailing off her breasts in a thick web, some running in silvery trails down her stockings whilst heavier showers smeared her face and hair. She watched, open-mouthed, as several long spurts erupted all over her, and was vaguely aware of thinking 'Willie Wanker's Chocolate Factory' and giggling at the mere ludicrousness of the comparison. The smell of their salute was strong and appetising, and she began to use her fingers to spread the cream over her breasts and between her legs, writhing in ecstasy on the floor, until her entire body was slick and glistening with their come. She stared up at the men, feeling like a freed wild animal, and the panting circle began to break up.

She had one more fantasy to be fulfilled and, recovering some of her composure and taking them by surprise, crawled quickly on all fours to the communal bath and slid in. With a whoop of approval, they all followed, and surrounded her again expectantly. 'Anyone seen the soap?' she asked menacingly, and some of the younger players moved smartly out of the way as she approached them. The older ones called her bluff, standing their ground. She caked her hands in soap and ran them over the players' glistening bodies, feeling their hardening cocks, exploring every nook and cranny. Soon there were a lot of very clean, contented men in the bath. She realised, with little concern, that she was no longer bursting to go to the loo, and her whole mind and body glowed and hummed.

She was breathless as she was helped out of the bath by the gallant Lee, who had, unbeknown to her, abstained from recent events, and was still sporting an unsatisfied erection of magnificent proportions. He gently towelled her down, his cock brushing her buttocks, and apologised profusely when he and she realised that her pants and bra had been pocketed as trophies. He retrieved her dripping skirt, which he wrung as dry as he could before she pulled it over her stained and laddered stockings, then covered her with her raincoat.

'Three cheers for Dolly!' yelled Simon as she left, and she returned their waves as she unsteadily retraced her steps along the corridor. Lee quickly wrapped a towel around himself and followed her, eventually pushing a wad of notes into her hand. 'If you ever need a recommendation, don't hesitate to give my name. And I'd like to see you again. For a drink, I mean. I really don't have a problem with your, er, job.'

She looked at his smiling, sincere face, completely ignoring the money, and rested her gaze on the prominent erection that was forcing a horizontal projection from his taut towel.

'I would like that very much,' she said, swallowing hard. 'And that.'

He glanced down, realising that she had had everything she wanted – except a cock where it mattered. He hesitated only briefly before firmly taking her hand. 'We've both got some unfinished business,' he muttered, half as a question, half as a statement of fact. She smiled and followed him as he opened a door off the narrow corridor and pulled her inside.

It was the Charlie the groundsman's store, dark,

windowless and smelling of petrol and grass. Lee flicked on a light switch to reveal a clutter of equipment dominated by a large seated mower. She looked around at the corner flags, the white-lining machine, the heavy roller and the drums of petrol and other liquids. Lee watched her eyes wandering around the room. 'I could see you pushing that around the pitch right now,' he said, looking at the white-lining machine. 'All the lines need redoing, so if you've got time . . .'

'It's me who needs doing,' Charlotte reminded him, as huskily as she could, before lifting a foot onto an oil drum and allowing her coat to fall away and reveal her still-hungry cunt.

She suddenly lunged towards him and grabbed the towel, leaving him standing there, tall, blond and muscular, with a hard, thick penis and an expression of pure lust. He looked like a dominant stag, the monarch of the glen.

'Well?' said Charlotte, shaking the towel playfully. Lee placed his hands on his hips.

'What's your real name?' he asked.

'I'm Charlotte,' she replied, confused and impatient. 'I've not got another one.'

'Whatever,' said Lee, unable to resist her any longer.

She removed her coat, and threw it onto the seat of the mower as he moved behind her, coming in so close that she felt his cock on the small of her back. He ran his powerful hands gently down her damp curves before cupping a breast in each one and pinching her puckered nipples into firm peaks. Then his hands grasped her hips and she felt herself being lifted into the air, as if she weighed nothing.

'All right?' he asked.

'Oh yes,' said Charlotte, feeling like a randy ballerina. She gasped, opened her thighs and then locked them around his waist, feeling his cock sliding between her buttocks until it suddenly found its home, filling her welcoming slit. Her body was comfortably supported as he held her breasts in his eager hands, and she pressed back onto his length, no longer needing to close her eyes to imagine her fantasy. He pumped into her, their juices making sexual music in the small room.

She wanted it, needed it, hard and fast, and he was of the same mind. His hips bucked as he climaxed, his cock threatening to slip out of grasping pussy, but she held him firmly within her and clenched every muscle she had as she squeezed and milked him, rubbing her clit like a brazen slut. She came herself, panting, then he lowered her to the ground and carefully supported her shaking body as she stood unsteadily on the dusty floor. She turned around and kissed him, burying her face against his neck and holding him tightly. She felt him return the emotion. 'Come with me,' he said, handing her her coat.

They slipped into the deserted referee's changing room and showered together, after which she left in a very cool interpretation of the 1st fifteen's away strip. 'Keep it as a souvenir,' he said, before escorting her to her car and getting her phone number. He couldn't understand how she could afford a sports coupé, but now hardly seemed the time to ask.

'Next Tuesday, then,' she said as she started the engine. He nodded, and watched as she drove out of the car park, his own mind filled with memories of a fantasy fulfilled. But how was he going to tell this racy lady that he was a boring accountant?

Later that evening, after a protracted apology to her Simon, who had seen her leave with Lee and was intent on telling everyone at the bank that the two-timing Ice Queen had thawed out, Charlotte contemplated her own action replay of the afternoon's events. She reached for her mobile and called Lee. As she heard his already reassuringly familiar voice she felt an equally familiar liquid warmth developing between her legs. Her fingers gingerly stroked the fabric of her pants and she smiled wickedly as she realised that she would never again be able to watch rugby on TV without needing a change of underwear – probably before the national anthem was even finished.

Beverly's Pastime Sage Vivant

Everybody needs a hobby. Mine is destroying marriages.

Like any lifelong pursuit, some practice is required to achieve any kind of commendable performance level. I did my practising as a teenager, using babysitting as my vehicle into couples' lives. I couldn't help but notice at the tender age of sixteen that my red hair, milky-white skin and burgeoning breasts were a powerful lure – I got babysitting gigs much more often than my plainer-looking friends did. I didn't realise the extent of my power, though, until I was eighteen, when Mr Rosenblum shot a sac full of come onto his wife's face at my bidding. Since then, I've known no greater power than that of eroding the very foundations of people's precious little holy matrimonies.

Fact: men want to bury their faces in my ass so badly that they'll forget years of marital commitments to get there. Exploiting this state of affairs is just plain fun. Millions of women do it every day. I am no different from them; merely more honest and certainly more memorable.

My distinction comes into play on a much deeper psychological level. Women, you see, have an instinctive urge to lay claim to men. Most of them believe marriage is the ultimate capture.

Women are fools. My goal is to drive this point home to them at every opportunity. Rarely, however, do they take my message well.

I own my own advertising agency in midtown Manhattan. Consequently, I meet hundreds of married couples every year. At 46, I've met all kinds, but few have cried out for abuse and ultimate destruction more loudly than Melissa and Christopher.

These two walked into the corporate cocktail party like they were at Disneyland. Certainly, Melissa could have worn that forgettably shapeless frock at any amusement park and been quite comfortable. Her husband, on the other hand, cut a more dashing figure. Well-groomed, handsome, dark hair greying gradually at the temples – his posture and grace told me he devoted time to his body.

Both of them seemed a bit shy, but she was downright clueless while he was simply reserved. I decided they were perfect.

I paused at the full-length mirror to smooth my navy-blue Armani suit. I'd bought it just yesterday, specially for the party. Elegant yet blatantly sexy, the jacket sported lapels that parted at my chest to reveal enough cleavage to distract anyone, male or female. It was sometimes difficult to find prêt-à-porter to accommodate my 36DDs, but this little number clung to me everywhere as if I'd been the model for its design. The short skirt hugged my round backside with such fetching aplomb, I wished I could kiss my own ass.

Heat permeated the space between my legs as moisture collected in my crotchless pantyhose. I smelled my own arousal at the thought of my impending conquest. As I sauntered over to the hapless couple, I was slick with anticipation.

I don't know if the shimmering waves of my flowing red hair or the jiggle of my corseted breasts caught his eye first, but I knew he was mine from halfway across the room. The frumpy wife turned her head to follow his enraptured gaze. Oh, the fear that galvanised that pudgy face.

'Hi,' I said decisively, extending my hand to him. 'I'm

Beverly Channing.' I put my other hand over his when he clasped mine. 'I'm certain I've met you before but I'm at a loss to remember where,' I continued. I fixed my green-eyed gaze on him while I parted my lips in a hungry smile. I held his hand too long for wifey's liking – in my peripheral vision, I saw her stiffen.

'Christopher Van Dyke,' he said, smiling. His hands were warm. He even smelled nice. Bvlgari pour homme, I believe. 'I'm afraid I've never met you before,' he added, stealing a darting glance at his wife to gauge her reaction.

We were off to a smashing start.

'No, I'm sure you're wrong. I never forget a good-looking man,' I teased and pressed my right breast into his arm. His color deepened.

He was taller than me but not by much. His wife, at a paltry five feet four inches or so, had the dimensions of a shopping bag. I still hadn't acknowledged her existence.

'Wasn't it Barry Goldman's party last spring?' I persisted. Everybody who was anybody attended Barry's parties. Odds were good that Dudley Dooright here had been on the guest list.

'Well, yes, I was there, but I don't remember meeting you,' he replied. His deep voice slid over my skin like a thousand little tongues.

'I was there, too. We never met you,' the little woman piped up.

I turned my head slowly but never quite made eye contact from beneath haughty eyelids. 'I have no recollection of meeting you. I was speaking to your husband.' I turned back to Christopher, who predictably then felt compelled to introduce his prickly little spouse.

'I'm sorry. This is my wife, Melissa.'

I nodded in her general direction, ignoring her

chubby hand tentatively extended towards me. She retracted it quickly and immediately reached for a passing canapé.

'Why don't you get us some drinks, Melissa?' I commanded as I continued staring into her husband's face. Christopher, confounded by my impertinence, met his wife's gaze imploringly: *Please do as this woman says. I'm sure this will be over soon.*

'Well, what would you like?' Melissa asked me, appropriately irritated to be serving me.

'Anything. Use your imagination. Surprise me,' I purred, still holding Christopher's hand. I had yet to look at her.

She stormed off, waddling towards the bar, unaware that drinks circulated through the party just like hors d'oeuvres.

He tugged his hand away from mine very gently. I found this clear yet lame attempt to assert his manhood rather charming. He was visibly disquieted by my presence but, once Melissa had disappeared, his eyes travelled down the length of my overheated body and back up again. He took this inventory surreptitiously, mind you, but he took it nonetheless.

'I didn't want to say so in front of your wife,' I lied, 'but I tried desperately to get your attention at Barry's party. I find you devastatingly attractive.'

Again, he blushed but recovered admirably. 'I wish I'd known.'

'Why?'

He cleared his throat and shifted his weight from one foot to the other. 'Maybe I could have given you a ride home.'

'Oh, that's not all I would have expected of you, Christopher.'

Have you ever had the satisfaction of watching a face work through an internal dilemma? The man parted his lips in involuntary protest and seemed to surprise himself when no words found their way past them.

'In fact,' I continued, 'why not let *me* take *you* home?'

He grinned and tilted his head to hide his sheepishness. 'But we just got here.'

'I know of a better party. The three of us could go together.'

'Three of us?'

'I assume you've got some kind of code against ditching your wife?'

He chuckled. 'Of course. I'm just not sure that she'd, you know, feel comfortable at another party.'

'Sweetheart, she doesn't look terribly at ease at this one,' I assured him, curious whether he was actually ready to leave his plodding dumpling at the party. Regardless of his desires, I wanted her along with us. Otherwise, what was the point?

I watched said dumpling make her way through the chic and chatty crowd as she tried to squeeze between bodies while balancing two champagne flutes. Horribly unsure of herself and eager not to offend, she disgusted me.

'Here she comes now,' I commented in my best monotone.

Christopher turned and satisfaction welled up inside me as I saw his face fall at the bumbling sight of her. He forced a smile to welcome her back.

'Champagne! Thank you, sweetheart,' he said to her in a fatherly way as he took a glass from her. He leaned forwards to give her an appreciative peck on her doughy cheek. As he did so, elbows jostled and the champagne in what was soon to be my glass poured onto my Walter Steiger pumps.

The bitch was starting to incense me.

'Oh! Honey! I think you spilled some champagne on your friend!' She exclaimed, mastering the obvious.

'He didn't spill it. You did,' I remarked coolly, surveying my soiled shoe as if it belonged to some street person.

She blushed furiously and looked from her husband to me and back to her husband, undoubtedly waiting for him to come to her defence.

'I saw it all quite clearly. You spilled champagne on my shoe. What I really can't fathom is why you're just standing there when you should be cleaning it up.'

Christopher froze, mute with disbelief. Tears welled up in Mrs Van Dyke's eyes during the pregnant pause before she crouched at my feet with a napkin. While she dabbed, I attempted to resume my conversation with her husband by taking yet another step closer to him. This movement caused me to squash Melissa's pinky. I heard her yelp and responded by discreetly placing my hand on the top of her head, to keep her crouching.

'Don't even think about getting up until that shoe is spotless,' I spat at her. At this moment, I also spread my legs so that if she were to look up, she would be treated to my glistening wet pooch.

'Now then, Christopher. Where were we? I was telling you about this other party I'd like to take you to. Who do you work for, by the way?'

'I'm with Bozell. I handle Bank of America.'

I flicked on my suitably impressed face, to which he responded like the egotist that most account executives are. He no longer seemed to care that his wife was on all fours at a posh cocktail party just to clean up a spill that he himself had made. He still didn't even know who I was or appear to be interested in finding out.

'Well, then. You need to go to this party more than you need to be here. All you'll find here are people moving up. I'll take you where the people have already made it and are enjoying the spoils.'

His face shone with excitement. When I cupped his basket in the hand I'd just removed from his wife's head, his eyes nearly bugged out of their sockets.

'Does that sound good to you?' I squeezed his ball sac ever so slightly.

He nodded, furtively trying to determine whether Melissa could see what I was doing. On her unbalanced way up, she did indeed catch the action and gasped in horror.

'Christopher!'

'Are my shoes clean?' I asked her, boldly staring her down.

She blurted something that has no English equivalent and I ignored it. Christopher's cock inflated in my hand. He blinked and blurted something equally unintelligible.

'Oh, the hell with the shoes. Are we ready to get to that party?' My face was close enough to his ear for him to feel my hot breath. My breast pressed into his arm and the memory of my hand at his crotch robbed him of the power of speech.

'Sure,' he finally uttered.

'What? Christopher! What's going on here?' She was a teapot ready to boil, a smoke-stack about to blow. Her phony suburban manners disintegrated and all of a sudden I noticed where I'd flattened her mousy, out-dated coiffure with my hand.

'Nothing's going on, honey. What's the matter?' he cooed to his wife. Unctuous bastard – how solicitous men could be when new pussy was at stake.

'Nothing's the matter,' I interrupted. 'Maybe you should just keep quiet while I'm trying to seduce your husband.'

Her whole face turned the colour of her acne splotches. Christopher laughed nervously in an attempt to make light of my comment. 'Don't be silly, Beverly,' he said with no discernible conviction. 'You're doing no such thing.'

'This discussion is getting tedious,' I announced. 'Let's get going.' I led the way to the door and out to my waiting limo. It didn't surprise me in the least when they both followed me.

'This is yours?' Melissa observed. Her naïve incredulity bored me so I decided to ignore her. She was probably used to people paying no attention to her.

I made her sit across from me in the limo so that I could be closer to Christopher. When I sat down, I made sure my skirt rode up indecently. I wore pantyhose constructed like stockings and garter belt – generous arcs of bare skin, including an unfettered crotch, characterise them. I nearly squealed with delight as Melissa's jaw dropped at the sight of my neatly trimmed but gaping crotch.

'Your wife seems to be disturbed by my lack of panties,' I purred into Christopher's ear. He was as close to me as I'd hoped and upon hearing my disclosure, he looked down at my lap. Reluctantly, he checked his wife's expression. Even Melissa's ample body could not contain her shock.

I led Christopher's hand to my slippery lips as Melissa watched. Once his fingers delved into my wetness, I grabbed a handful of his hair and brought his mouth to mine. Christopher's hand did not leave my gushing pussy. In fact, he was now spreading my juice over my growing clit. She leaned forwards and slapped his knee.

'Stop that, now!' She reprimanded.

At the sound of her slap, we stopped kissing and turned to face her ridiculous presence.

'What the hell was that?' I snapped at her.

'I want you to stop.'

I sat back in the rich leather seat and stared at her until she averted her eyes. '*You* want me to stop.'

'I want you both to stop,' the plump lady mumbled.

'Don't you like watching your husband play with my pussy?' I asked, slumping a bit so that Christopher could finger-fuck me. 'Tell you what, Melissa. You can play, too.'

'I don't want to play.' She pouted as Christopher buried his face in my neck. Under the erratic flashes of street-light through the limo's sun-roof, the shadows in her puffy face gave her a ghoulish quality. The poor cow didn't know who to be angry with, me or her amorous husband.

'Of course you do,' I insisted. 'Slide forwards on your seat, there, and get on your knees.'

'Why?'

'If you're going to ask questions, I'll have the driver let you out right here. We're only a few blocks from Harlem. Would you like that?'

'No.'

'Then do what I tell you. On your knees.'

Melissa heaved her unwieldy body forwards and landed with a thud onto her knees. The position put her much closer to my excitable crotch.

'Stick your face between my legs and tell your husband what I smell like.'

Horror crossed her face for a second time that evening. Or was it a third? In any event, she looked at her husband, who had long since put her out of his mind. His tongue played with my earlobe as his middle finger made squishing noises where I'd led it.

'Christopher!' she wailed, on the verge of tears. Her frustration made me wetter.

'Sniff my pussy, you pathetic whiner.'

Her face contorted into hideous expressions before the tears began to flow. I laughed, which disturbed Christopher from his ministrations at my neck.

'What's going on?' It was as if we'd awakened him from a pleasant dream.

'Your wife won't smell my pussy.'

'Come on, honey. Just play along. Everything's gonna be all right,' he said distractedly, now moving to kiss my mouth as two fingers pumped my hole. I subtly moved his face into my thick mass of wavy hair so that I could watch Melissa sniff down below. This was a show too good to miss.

She leaned forwards as if my muff were rotten meat. With her eyes closed, she ventured closer. I didn't know whether she just didn't want to see pussy up close and personal or didn't want to see her beloved's hands buried in happy juice. Either way, her extreme unease tickled me and I could only imagine that I was marring her psyche for life.

I loved disturbing her world, upsetting everything she thought was real. Seeing her pudgy form at my mercy while her husband indulged himself on me quickened my pulse. Who needed drugs or alcohol when a high like this was available?

She inhaled dramatically but briefly about six inches from my creamy centre, then backed up quickly.

'Are you afraid it'll bite or are you just expecting mine to be as rancid as yours?' I asked.

She stared at me, blustering yet wordless in her rage. Arms trembling, she struggled to hoist herself back into her seat. The violet atrocity she called a dress bunched up over her thick knees, making me crave something from Pillsbury.

'What do I smell like?'

'I don't know.'

'Christopher has to know what I smell like before he

eats me, don't you, baby?' I purred as I ran my fingers through his hair.

'Mmmm,' he replied, still breathing into my red locks. Suddenly he sat upright, and I giggled, realising he was finally aware of what had been going on around him.

'Tell him what he can expect to taste, Melissa, or the driver lets you off here.' Shouts from a passing car full of foul-mouthed youths reminded her where she was.

'She smells like perfume.'

'Is there anything about you that's even been *near* an imagination?' I wondered aloud.

'Let me eat you now, Beverly,' he pleaded. I liked his style – urgent yet refined. What was a class act like this doing with such a hausfrau? I couldn't wait for his tongue to lap up my juice. But first, some appreciation of the merchandise.

'Not so fast, loverboy. It's a little warm in here, don't you think? Help me with my jacket.'

He was barely able to restrain a grin as his suave hands dedicated themselves to working the buttons of my Armani jacket. He slid his palms over my ribcage to my sides, pushing the jacket open to reveal my blue corseted torso. The moonlight hit the upper hemisphere of my alabaster globes perfectly, highlighting their smooth, ripe roundness.

I helped him slide the sleeves down my arms until I sat there with the top half of me laced up in a corset and the bottom half's carefully trimmed pubic triangle barely covered with a skirt.

'Melissa, do you think it's right that I'm sitting here half naked with your husband?'

'No, I don't!' The woman sat upright, ready to concur with me, her adversary. What a stupendous fool.

'Then I insist that you match me, garment for garment.'

'What do you mean?' The fear returned to her face. Very gratifying.

'Strip, you idiot. Show me what passes for lingerie in the suburbs.'

'I most certainly will not, will I, Christopher?' She shot her spouse the most imploring look she'd probably ever mustered. And still it was a pitiful display of feminine wiles.

As for Christopher, he now sat erect, watching our banter like it was a tennis match. He'd never been in so ludicrous a situation before but was far more adaptable than his provincial wife.

'I don't see where it can hurt, honey. After all, she's half naked already. I'll even take my clothes off if it'll make you feel better.'

'I'll tell you when your clothes come off, sweetheart,' I informed him with gentle authority. 'For now, I want you to help Melissa slip out of that sweet little frock she's wearing.'

He moved towards his frightened wife. She squirmed to get away from him, as if there were somewhere she could go. He grabbed her by the shoulders to immobilise her and stared into her eyes.

'It's easier if you just co-operate, Mel.'

Mel. It sounded like a pudding flavour. Chill and serve. Watch it jiggle.

He unzipped her polyester sack and guided it over her head. She sat there, weeping, arms crossed over her beige Playtex bra. Even her seemingly inflatable arms weren't large enough to obscure the fullness of her bosom. I estimated that we were roughly the same age, yet this woman's flesh had deteriorated into a slack, overgrown wasteland some time ago.

I sat serenely, observing Christopher's face as he compared our bodies. Such a delicious moment, this silent epiphany in a man's mind when he considers running, screaming, from his sexless wife and into the arms of a beautiful, supple, willing woman.

During this moment of silence, I lowered the window. The purr of its motor went unnoticed but the rush of cool air did not. The Van Dykes turned to me, brows furrowed in confusion.

'Time to put out the trash,' I said, grabbing Melissa's dress and tossing it out into the mysterious metropolitan night.

'My dress! Christopher! She threw it out the window!' Just when I thought this woman could panic no further, she lapsed into new fits of fussing. I sent the window back up.

'Now then,' I sighed, stretching myself along the length of the limo's long back seat. Melissa sat whimpering as Christopher patted her knee in an attempt to comfort her.

'Come back to your seat, Christopher, and whip out that manhood I was fondling at the party.'

Melissa cried audibly now but her husband resumed his seat and immediately unzipped his fly. What he pulled out was a gloriously hard and thick cock. My mouth watered.

I paused, though, to consider what would humiliate this stupid woman more – my giving her husband head or her having to suck him off in front of me. I don't like second-guessing myself and I probably never would have hesitated if I hadn't wanted that cock so badly myself. I would have taken that fine piece of meat up any orifice, to be honest. Then I came up with the perfect solution.

'Melissa, I have another job for you.'

'No! No more! You're a sick woman.'

'Compliments will get you nowhere. I'm about to give your husband a fabulous blowjob and I'd like to include you somehow in the festivities. Slip your hand

into your pantyhose and play with yourself. Rub your
clit slowly if you don't like what I'm doing and frig
yourself like crazy if you do like it. Understand?'

More boo-hooing. I ignored her and extended my
stockinged legs across Christopher's lap. He stroked me
from my thighs to my toes, reverently and slowly. I
lifted my toes to his mouth, where he sprinkled each
toe with feathery kisses. I alternated feet and, with my
free one, caressed the smooth, purple head of his sur-
prisingly enormous rod. He moaned as the soles of my
feet skimmed across it.

A sniffle reminded me of Melissa's presence and I
turned to check that she was following orders. She was
not.

'Melissa! What's wrong? Can't find your clit in all
those folds?'

'Leave me alone!' She said with all the drama of a
made-for-TV movie.

'Play with yourself or you're out on the street. I think
you know better than to test me.'

The bawling chubette struggled valiantly to jam her
pudgy hand into the unforgiving spandex that encased
her belly. When she finally found what she was looking
for, I swung my legs around and sat on them, heading
for that delectable cock beside me.

'Now remember, fast if you're turned on, slow if
you're not.' I stifled a laugh – the very idea of this
woman having a sexual response was an outrageous
fiction.

Once my mouth engulfed the pure, hard heat of
Christopher's pulsating cock, my interest in Melissa's
degradation waned. I diddled myself as I sucked him,
primarily for my own pleasure but also to embarrass
her further. I knew she was watching. I could feel her
simpering gaze. How I wanted her to implode into her
own depleted womanhood.

My tongue circled his meat as my mouth travelled up his shaft. Up and down I happily went until the driver stopped at the door of my apartment building. I was careful to prevent Mr Van Dyke from spewing his gratitude. There was so much more to do yet.

Ben, my doorman, had seen me arrive home in various stages of undress and in a wide range of consciousness levels. He had never, however, seen me arrive with an overweight, half-naked housewife and her libidinous husband.

'Good evening, Ms Channing,' he said, nodding in that remarkably impassive style they must teach them at doorman school. As each passenger emerged, no sign of bemusement or disgust crossed Ben's face. He knew, as I did, that Sutton Place had its share of kink – it was simply more discreet about enjoying it than other neighbourhoods might have been. Ben had seen me corseted only once before, on a similar occasion, and let one side of his mouth turn up in a fleeting but appreciative grin.

Melissa wouldn't budge from the car, and Christopher had to yank her out by her stout little arms. She landed on the sidewalk like a bag of cement, her rolls of fat reverberating on impact. Her weeping had elevated into a whining drone, her face a smear of tears and unchecked rosacea.

She stood on the sidewalk in all her girdled glory, looking from her husband to me and then to Ben for signs that we, too, thought the situation untenable. She received no such confirmation. I was as poker-faced as Ben, and Christopher was so focused on his erection that he held it in his hand, watching me expectantly.

Ben let us into the building, where, to my great disappointment, we encountered no one in the lobby or the elevator. Melissa clung desperately to her husband throughout, despite his fixation on other matters nearer, uh, at hand.

The moment we entered my twelve-room condominium, I spun on my heel and faced the crying wench. I pulled a breast out of my corset and pointed it at her as if to shoot her with it.

'See this boobie, little Miss Crybaby? You're going to suck it if you don't *shut up*. Now follow me to the bedroom.' I walked backwards down the hall to keep an eye on her. Terror consumed her as adrenaline raced through my body. Christopher followed behind her, agog and short of breath.

Once in my bedroom, I positioned myself in front of the expanse of mirrored wall, standing like Wonder Woman.

'Christopher, sit on the floor between my legs. Eat me out.'

He moved quickly for a man in his fifties.

'Melissa, I'm going to feed you a breast as God intended it to be,' I told her, aiming a hard nipple at her. 'Come here and suck it while Christopher licks me.'

'No!' she sputtered.

'*Now!*'

As Christopher lapped away at what was now a completely drenched pussy, Melissa stepped forwards, apparently sapped of any further impulse to protest. She put her lips to my waiting nipple. I snatched it away instantly.

'You *are* a lesbian! I knew it! How dare you try to suck *my* beautiful breasts? Go sit in the corner and suck your own!'

She bawled louder and recoiled, speaking her husband's name to no avail. His face was smothered in juice and he showed no signs of coming up for air. I pointed to the upholstered Biedermeier chair across the room and she scurried over to it. I stared at her until she extracted one sagging breast from the Playtex brassière and tried to figure out how to get it to her mouth. For a moment, I feared the challenge might get the better of her, but eventually she stuffed a dark, useless nipple into her mouth.

'Don't let it sit there. Suck it.'

She obeyed. A more distasteful sight had never graced my bedroom.

'Remove my stockings, Christopher.'

He did so without a single pause from his tongue. Carefully, he rolled the waistband of my silk pantyhose down to my belly and over my hips, then down the length of my long, smooth legs. I watched as he savoured the contours of my thighs and the slopes of my calves. When they were off, I led him to the bed. I now wore only my corset.

'Unlace my corset now,' I instructed, standing before him as he knelt on the bed. I stared at Melissa menacingly to keep her suckling at her own teat. Christopher had his back to her. He unlaced me with that same wonderful reverence and attention to detail he'd demonstrated earlier. Some men were frightened by my dominance but this one knew that he was born to take orders. His wife had no idea that his strength lay in his submission and I hated her for her stupidity.

He removed my corset tenderly, as if both it and I were fragile. I altered the mood by pushing him onto his back and straddling his face while I dived into his manly goods. As we ate each other, Melissa whimpered softly. I would have reminded her to keep sucking but I didn't want to take Christopher's rock-hardness out of my mouth. I slapped my face with his cock, licked it wildly and sucked one ball and then the other into my hot mouth. When my mouth tired, I surrounded his prick with breast meat, smothering it, fucking it, and watching its raw head pop up intermittently between my soft mounds of flesh.

Between my legs, he tongue-fucked me with a skill I couldn't imagine him using on his sexless wife. He speared me expertly and rimmed my asshole like he'd been doing it for years. I dripped with delight.

I felt a surge in the base of his cock, signalling impending eruption. I put the action on pause to save him for the main event. Climbing off him, I looked at his pussy-smeared face and caressed it. The man possessed a certain undeniable charm. That charm, however, was not enough to deter me from my goal.

Melissa's breast hung forlornly over her distended belly. She sat there, numb, used up.

'Look at your wife, Christopher. She's the epitome of a sex goddess, isn't she?'

He turned to the corner where she sat, but offered no comment.

I got to my feet, watching my heavy breasts in the mirrored wall as they swayed and bounced with my movements. I enjoyed Christopher watching them, too. Melissa's eyes registered renewed fear as I approached her.

'Get up.'

She scrambled to her feet.

'I'm going to do something nice for you. You look like a woman who needs many things, not the least of which is a good diet, but for now, I'm willing to offer you a nice, hot bath. Follow me.'

I led her to the master bathroom, tiled in alternating squares of black and white marble. The large round bathtub, which could hold up to five people – and often had – sat atop a three-stair climb. She teetered her uncertain way upwards.

'Use whatever you want. Just get in the tub and stay out of our way.' I turned on the water for her, bounced one of her unsightly teats in my hand and walked out.

Christopher waited patiently for me on the bed where I'd left him. He was still fully dressed except for his exposed genitalia. A fetching sight, to be sure, but I wanted to see him fully naked, so I demanded that he strip for me.

As he undressed, his cock continued to point north-wards, an angle that one didn't often see in men his age. I was impressed but didn't tell him so. My pussy ached for his meat but I didn't tell him that, either.

We stood on opposite sides of the bed. As he dis-robed, removing each article of clothing as I told him, I turned my back to him and bent over so that his view was of my big round ass with slippery pussy lips virtually speaking his name. I slipped my hand between my legs and stroked myself.

'Christopher, what would you like to do to me?'

'I'd like to have sex with you,' he rasped.

'Of course you would, but what would that sex entail?'

He paused. Obviously, he'd never been encouraged to articulate his coital plans before.

I slipped a finger into my steamy hole, doing it slowly enough to let him hear the wetness.

'I'd like to fuck you, Beverly. I'd really like to fuck you.'

'How?' I increased the speed of my finger in my hungry hole.

'Can't we just do it?' He put a tentative hand on my hip. He was on the bed now.

I stood upright. 'Did I say you could touch me?' I shot fire at him through my eyes. He blinked but did not waver.

'No. I'm sorry.'

'When you see my fingers up my twat, what does it make you want to do?' I resumed the position.

'It makes me want to ram my cock up inside you and pump you until you scream.'

I smiled, because he couldn't see my face. Ah, the sweet thrill of victory.

'Then do it.'

Ram me he did. His thick manhood impaled my backside in one smooth movement, plunging so deeply I thought he might come up my throat. He pounded my ass hard as he held onto my hips to keep both of us grounded. I knew my ass cheeks shook provocatively with each thrust. I adored thinking about my ass.

He fucked me for several minutes before I felt him stiffen and prepare for orgasm. I turned to look at his face in the mirror and saw his sweet grimace just before he let loose into my now clenching cunt. He shouted as he spewed, which surprised and titillated me. As his shout subsided, I launched my own, quite without warning. The old man had screwed me into my own release and it took my body by storm. I nearly lost my balance in my delirium.

He collapsed on the bed when he was certain I was satisfied. I joined him seconds later. We said nothing as we caught our collective breath and spiralled to earth. When I gauged he had fully recovered, I took his hand and sat up.

'Let's go see how Melissa is doing.' Together, we headed for the bathroom.

There she sat, mired in suds. Our unannounced entrance jolted her and her eyes sprung open. Her Rotundness had taken advantage, it seemed, of my expensive bubble bath to pleasure herself. Such circumstances were enough to bring bile to my throat and yet my curiosity was piqued, for what could have prompted this overfed munchkin to reach that level of arousal? Was it my constant belittlement of her? Her husband's interest in me? My unadulterated beauty?

Whatever it was, I was more than willing to explore some new territory. Christopher glanced at me to gauge my mood. He was undoubtedly trying to anticipate what I might do next but, as we all know, that's not an undertaking for the faint of heart. I shot him a stern glance to ensure his silence.

'I see you've found your pussy, Melissa. I hope its rust doesn't leave a ring around my bathtub.'

She squinted at me as if she were wishing some unspoken curse on me. Her face pinched with revulsion and that just made me wetter. I knew I'd already done irreparable damage to their marriage but there's always room for more humiliation, especially for confused and insufferably bland females like this one. I climbed the steps to the bathtub, with no intention of sharing the same bath water but every intention of making her think I would.

I walked around the edge of the tub, still wearing my bustier but nothing else. Once I had found a spot I liked, directly in front of her of course, I unsnapped the garment and stood before her with nothing between us but suds. The trepidation in her eyes was positively invigorating.

'What are you going to do?' she asked me, voice quavering.

'If you're going to make me watch you jack off, you're going to have to watch me.'

I filled one hand with the enviably firm flesh of my left breast.

'Now grab yours,' I demanded.

She looked to her husband but I did not. My eyes stayed on her. I heard him say 'Grab your tit, Mel.'

Somewhere under my dense and fragrant bubble

bath, her pudgy hand took hold of a pancake with a nipple. I moved my right hand to my sex, where I spread my myself wide.

'Can you get a good look at this, Melissa? This is the sweet pussy your husband could have been screwing all these years instead of the musty hole that's now stinking up my bathtub. Look at me, you stupid bitch.'

She looked. Of course she looked. Who could look away? Nevertheless, I kept my eyes glued on her and ignored whatever sounds I heard coming from Christopher. I'd already conquered him and knew his allegiance was to me, not her – he wouldn't be stepping in to save her now.

I stroked the slippery folds of my pussy, creaming with every passing second that her gaze stayed on my hand.

'Play with yourself. Follow my lead. Maybe you can learn the timeless art of seduction.' I cackled. Her hands seemed busy. I certainly had no plans to check on her progress.

Something made me turn to look at Christopher, whose mood had palpably changed. He stood there smiling wryly, with his jacket open to reveal some tiny digital device. When he took it out of his pocket and held it to his eye, grinning, I understood that the man I'd just treated to the best sex of his life was photographing me with a high-tech camera. Too stunned to move or even hurl well-deserved invective, I tried to discern just what kind of foul play was afoot.

'You could get dressed, Beverly, but it wouldn't do much good. We've got what we need now. These cameras only hold a hundred images or so.'

'What the fuck are you talking about?' I finally spat.

He tossed me the terrycloth robe I had bought in Istanbul but most of it landed in the bath water. Mel grinned.

'It was funny that you mentioned Barry Goldman's party earlier tonight,' Christopher began. Fiddling with the device, he snapped another photo of me leaning against the Italian marble, breast in one hand, fire in my eyes.

'I was there the night you ruined Barry's marriage. And it was a damn good marriage, you evil slut. What you did destroyed Barry.'

'He didn't seem too distraught the night it happened. We screwed like rabbits.'

'I warned him about you,' he continued, completely ignoring my commentary. 'I knew the havoc you'd wreaked on others. He thought he was immune. Did I mention that Barry is my brother?'

'No, I believe you overlooked that. But please – give him my regards.'

'I'm going to give him more than that. These pictures are a start. They're likely to make him quite a bit of money, especially when he posts them on the Internet. The footage from the limousine should do well, too. Lots of different angles. Those webcams are really an innovation.'

'Bastard.'

'Oh, now I don't think you're in any position to be name-calling, Beverly. You outdid yourself with poor Melissa here tonight. By the way, she isn't my wife.'

'I find that reassuring,' I said, meaning it, though I didn't believe him for a second. Who would tote a frump like Mel around unless they were under some legal obligation to do so?

'Bitch,' Melissa said, throwing my words back at me, but she sounded so effete I didn't feel more than a sneer was due in reply.

'Melissa is my special partner. We play humiliation games often. She enjoys it. In fact, this night was as much for her as it was for me. I'm amazed that a champion player such as yourself didn't know you were being set up. But then, I knew you wouldn't be able to resist the easy target Mel presented. And I knew you and your delusional brain would try to break us up if you thought we were married. You're so predictable, Beverly. You put yourself right where we wanted you.'

I said nothing because I was trying to figure out how to drown Mel and have one more go at Christopher. I wanted to fuck him so thoroughly that he'd give me those damn pictures. But what about the webcam?

'Revenge is really quite sweet,' he continued. 'There's no telling what these pictures will do to your client base, Beverly. I wouldn't want to be you tomorrow.'

'Don't be silly. You wouldn't know *how* to be me.'

Mel climbed out of my tub with newfound grace. Though her body was still a repulsive sack of shapelessness, there was no mistaking the confidence that practically beamed from her. Damned submissives – they had wills of iron under their compliant flesh. It was a mindset I'd never understand or respect. Why submit when you could rule?

'I left you a little surprise in your tub,' Mel purred just before she yanked me from the ledge. The element of surprise worked in her favour and I found myself flailing about in her bath water. It didn't take me long to find my Armani suit, balled up and permanently ruined. And I thought the blue in the water had come from the Himalayan herbs in my exclusive blend of Eastern aromatherapy oils.

She'd stained my bathtub after all. But the stain to my reputation was the more indelible of the two. If I started packing now, I could make it to Canada in just a few hours. Advertising opportunities – and happy marriages – were in plentiful supply there, I'd heard. In fact, one of my former, and more attractive, colleagues had just moved there with his wife . . .

Handling Amanda Sasha White

Amanda Carrington set down the phone and listened once again to Emily – her secretary – giggling girlishly in the open-plan area of the office. It was the final straw. The girl's irritating simpering was grating in her ear so much that she could barely concentrate. Leaving her cushioned chair, Amanda walked around her large oak desk and made for the door. Enough was enough; this was an office, not a pick-up joint.

She pulled open her door and wasn't surprised to see that it was the young marketing executive, Jacob, who was perched on the edge of Emily's desk, distracting her from her work.

'Have you picked up my suit from the cleaners yet, Emily?' Amanda asked, making her voice sharp enough to cut through the young girl's romantic haze and bring her back down to earth – to work.

Emily jumped guiltily in her chair and turned to Amanda, a blush colouring her cheeks. 'No Miss Carrington. Not yet.'

Ignoring Jacob's gaze on her, Amanda arched an elegant eyebrow at her secretary. 'Then maybe you should do so, since I don't pay you to sit here and flirt, and you are still on the clock.'

'Yes, Miss Carrington.' She picked up her purse from the floor next to her desk and hurried off without another glance at the good-looking young man in a suit on the edge of her table.

'You were a bit hard on her there, Amanda,' he said. 'She was just entertaining me until you were done with your call.' Jacob straightened away from the desk and stepped towards her.

'I don't pay her to entertain you or anyone else, Jacob. I pay her to do her job.' She turned and walked back into her office, knowing he would follow.

'You don't pay her at all, Amanda; the firm pays her. Just like they pay you and me. And as your secretary you should appreciate her trying to make your clients more comfortable while you keep them waiting.'

Amanda sat behind her desk once more and looked Jacob in the eye. 'First off, you are not a client, so she needn't entertain you. Secondly, I don't keep clients waiting. And thirdly, what I appreciate is her doing what I tell her to do.'

Jacob opened his mouth but, before he could say anything, Amanda raised her hand to him. 'Enough, Jacob. I'm not going to argue with you about this.' She watched as he closed his mouth once more and stood in front of her desk, hands casually tucked into the pockets of his suit trousers. 'What is it you wanted, anyway?'

'I have a solution to our problem with the Williams proposal.' He grinned at her charmingly and started to detail his idea.

'You cancelled your own birthday dinner to work tonight?' The incredulous note in Jacob's voice grated on Amanda's already frayed nerves.

After Jacob had outlined his idea for the Williams proposal they'd moved into one of the conference rooms and begun making the necessary changes right away. Unfortunately the changes were taking longer than they had expected, but cancelling dinner plans wasn't a big deal. Not when landing the Williams account would cement her standing with the partners of the marketing firm.

They had already decided that Amanda would present the proposal the next morning, and there was no way she was going to leave the final touches of it to a playboy like Jacob, partner in the project or not.

It was already seven-thirty and the office was empty except for them. She didn't trust Jacob not to mix something small up, something that would make her stumble, make her look bad, but not bad enough to lose the account. Big Firm Marketing was cutthroat, and Amanda knew Jacob's easygoing personality was just a cover-up. There was something dark lurking just below his surface and she didn't trust him.

'This needs to get done. I can't just leave it to you.'

'Why not? I'm not your boyfriend. I don't need you to hold my hand and tell me how to do the job. We've already discussed what needs to get done.'

'What is that supposed to mean?'

'It means I can do it; go celebrate your birthday.'

'I meant the crack about Greg. What is it supposed to mean?'

'C'mon, Amanda, I've seen you with him. He's no match for you. You say jump and he asks how high. You cancelled on him after he'd planned a special night and all he says is 'Of course, dear, you do what you need to do. I'll be here when you're done.' Good-looking though he is, he doesn't have much of a backbone.'

'Greg is a mature, intelligent man. He supports my career and we have a very stimulating time together. It's not all beer, ball-games and boobs with him,' Amanda snapped back at him, telling herself it was enough.

'Hey! There's nothing wrong with beer, ball-games and boobs. If your man pulled his head out of his dusty old books and went to a ball-game with the boys he might learn how to handle you better.'

'Handle *me*?' Amanda worked to keep the anger from

her voice. 'I'm not one of your airhead bimbos, Jacob. Nobody "handles" me.'

'Maybe that's the problem.' The glint in Jacob's eye dared her to question that comment.

'There is no problem,' she stated firmly, ignoring the unaccustomed heat in her belly. 'How did we even get on this subject? I'm staying to finish this because I don't trust you not to screw it up, even with a step-by-step outline.'

Their eyes locked and the heat flared in her belly, then spread to the juncture of her thighs. Her nipples hardened and began to ache for attention. What was going on here?

'Enough!' Uncomfortable with the building tension, Amanda turned back to the conference table. 'Let's just get this done.' Pushing aside the confusing thoughts and emotions running through her, she shuffled some papers into order. Maybe it took more than a hot stare from Greg to get her body humming, but at least she respected and trusted him.

Amanda sensed Jacob's presence close behind her and fought the attraction she felt. The urge to turn to him, thrust her hands into his hair and pull his mouth to hers was strong, but she fought it. She didn't even like him; how could she want him?

'People always do what you tell them to, don't they?' Jacob leaned in and whispered in her ear, his breath warm and moist on her skin. As she tried to straighten up, her back hit the solid wall of his chest. He had her pinned close to the table; she couldn't straighten without asking him to move. And she wasn't about to give him the satisfaction of asking him for anything.

'Doesn't that bore you? Having people scared of you because they know you can make their life hell? Don't you ever just want to relax, let someone else take control?'

'No,' she answered.

'No? I think you're lying. I think you focus so much on work because the rest of your life bores you. No challenge.'

He stepped closer, pressing his chest against her back. She felt the nudge of his erection against her buttocks and repressed the shiver that ran through her. An uncontrollable urge to push him, to explore what was happening, took over.

'My life doesn't bore me,' she stated. 'You bore me.'

'Liar,' he whispered. 'I turn you on, and you don't even know why. I know you don't like me, but soon you'll crave me.'

What did that mean? Crave him?

With those cryptic comments he stepped back, walked to the other side of the table and began to talk about the proposal as if nothing unusual had happened.

Amanda struggled to get her mind back on the work, but her body wouldn't let her. Restless energy and burning heat swept through her veins, urging her towards something she couldn't, wouldn't, admit to wanting.

The next few hours passed with only work being discussed. Amanda did well, disguising her inner tension until they were closing the last of the folders, and then, unexpectedly, Jacob gripped her chin firmly in his hand and directed her gaze to his.

'I see passion in your work, Amanda, but none in your life. You order everybody about as if they were your personal lackeys. Even me – you treat me as if we weren't partners on this project, as if I didn't know how to put together a proposal. Well, I do, and you know what else I know? I know how to handle a woman like you.'

'I told you. Nobody "handles" me.'

'No?' he quirked an eyebrow at her. 'I'm going to.'

'Good luck,' she said with a laugh and pulled away from him, only to find herself spun around sharply and bent over the conference table. His erection pressed against her out-thrust ass while she struggled half-heartedly against the hands pulling her wrists behind her back. Holding them tightly in one hand, he quickly undid his belt with the other as he listened to her cursing him.

'Incredible vocabulary you have there, Amanda. However, not once have you used the word 'no' or told me to stop. Could it be that you enjoy being "handled"?' he taunted as he pressed against her and tightened his belt around her wrists.

His taunt hit home and stilled her struggles. She let her forehead rest on the table-top and gave in to the rioting sensations of her body.

Jacob's hand stroked down her back and ran smoothly over her buttocks. 'Fight me if you wish, but you can't fight yourself any longer.'

Amanda closed her eyes in shame at the knowledge that he was right. Her mind might be rebelling at what he was doing, but her body loved it. She could feel her pussy lips thickening and her juices beginning to pool. Her heart was pounding and her nipples shot bolts of pleasure to her warm sex every time she shifted against the hard table-top.

'Shhh,' he crooned as he lifted her skirt and bared her nylon-clad behind. 'I won't hurt you,' he promised. With one hand still on her back, pressing her into the table, the other quickly removed her panties. His hand was warm and rough on her skin as it smoothed over her bare buttocks, and she relaxed a little. 'Any more than you deserve, that is.'

A loud smack echoed in the room and Amanda felt the stinging pain as he brought his hand down sharply on her rounded cheeks. 'That is for Edward. The poor guy has enough confidence problems with women without your comments every day about his height.' Another loud smack echoed throughout the room. 'That is for Emily. She is your secretary, not your slave. Pick up your own dry-cleaning from now on.'

On and on Jacob went. Tears streamed silently down Amanda's cheeks as she lay bent over the table in submission. The tears weren't from the pain; Jacob's spanking wasn't really that hard. They flowed because Amanda was ashamed of the hunger she felt in her pussy. She unconsciously spread her thighs further apart and found herself hoping Jacob would stop spanking her and slide his hand between her thighs.

'Liking this, are you? I knew you would.' He stopped smacking her ass and she arched her back in invitation. 'You'll like this even better.'

Jacob efficiently unzipped his trousers and pulled out his cock. He rubbed it over her burning ass cheeks as he leaned forwards to speak into her ear again. 'Have you ever wanted to be filled so much that you've begged for it? I don't need to test you; I can smell your lust. I can see it running down your thighs. Oh, your thighs ... the way you spread them so wide for me without me even asking. I know you want this. Don't you?' He slid his penis between her thighs, then thrust it back and forth a few times so it rubbed up and down the length of her pussy.

'You want it? Take it!' He roughly shoved himself inside and started to fuck her. Strong hands gripped her waist he pumped hard and fast into her juicy hole. The sound of her muffled groans and his heavy breathing filled the air. Her insides tightened around him in spasms of pleasure as her body rejoiced in being used.

Jacob felt his balls tighten and knew that he was going to come soon. He lifted his hand and brought it down sharply onto her rump again. Her muffled squeal was just what he needed to hear to send him over the edge. Gripping her hips hard, he locked his knees and buried himself deeply into her as he felt his own juices flood from his body to hers.

After taking a moment to catch his breath, he pulled out of her and tucked himself back into his pants. He released the belt around her wrists then leaned close and kissed her damp cheek gently before strolling silently from the room. Amanda was left there, still bent over the table, looking used, exposed and strangely sated.

In the wee hours of the morning Amanda came to terms with the fact that she had enjoyed being disciplined by Jacob. She was a strong woman. Some said she was a bitch, but that didn't bother her; she'd had to be to get where she was in life. Raised to be self-reliant, Amanda always maintained her self-control. She didn't know how to be any other way. When Jacob took that control from her she had known, deep down, that she could've stopped him at any time with just a word, yet she hadn't. She'd been too turned on to stop him, or herself. More turned on than she had ever been before, so turned on that she had come just from his fucking her – a first for her.

As she lay in bed, remembering how he had felt inside her, her hands cupped her breasts and stroked her own soft skin. She imagined other scenarios involving his dominance. An image of her naked body tied spreadeagle on a king-size bed came into her mind and one hand travelled over her belly, past her trimmed patch of hair and between her pussy lips. Her fingers slid into her hole and she felt her inner muscles clench around herself. Pulling out, she spread her juices around before zeroing in on her clit.

The rigid little button was swollen and hard, begging

for attention. Flicking her finger back and forth over it, she brought herself close to the edge, but no matter how fast or how hard she played with herself she couldn't get off – until her other hand pinched her nipple harder, and twisted it just a little. The pleasure/pain from her nipple shot into her groin and she fell off the edge into the pleasurable abyss she'd craved.

As was typical of her personality, she decided as she drifted off to sleep that she would go after what she wanted. And what she wanted was to experience those intense feelings again.

Amanda awoke feeling ready to take on the world. She felt good about the proposal and her decision to seek out another experience with Jacob. She chuckled to herself; ironically she still didn't like Jacob, yet the thought of celebrating a new account with him after the presentation caused her knees to weaken and her nipples to harden.

The proposal went smoothly and the bigwig executives granted her company the account. A bottle of champagne was opened and the meeting turned celebratory.

'Good job, partner,' Jacob said as he refilled her glass.

'Thank you.' Strangely unsure of herself in his presence, she just stood there quietly.

'Why so quiet, Amanda? It's not like you.'

'I liked it,' she whispered.

'I'm sorry.' He leaned in closer. 'I didn't hear you.'

'I liked it,' she said in a firmer voice, looking into his eyes this time.

'I know you did. I knew you would. If you want more, you'll have to ask nicely.'

Amanda felt herself flush with anger as he strolled away. She watched as he chatted with the other businessmen and women, never once glancing in her direction again. The tension in her belly told her she was close to what she desired, but could she bring herself to ask him to treat her that way again? She had hoped that after she'd admitted her weakness he would just take control once again.

When he headed to his own office she took a deep breath, straightened her spine and followed him. As she stepped into his office, she closed the door behind her and leaned against it. He didn't even look up from the papers he was gathering.

'What do you want?'

'I want more.'

He still didn't look up, but just kept gathering his things.

'C'mon, Jacob, you know what I'm asking for.' Amanda fought to keep her voice calm. No way did she want him to figure out just how badly she really wanted this. 'You said you could "handle" me. Prove it.'

She knew that throwing out the challenge was a sure-fire way to get Jacob's full attention. They were the same that way, never able to resist a challenge, especially one issued so brazenly. Amanda stepped away from the door and started towards him. When Jacob looked up she was halfway across the room.

'Stop,' he commanded. Amanda's heart jumped at his tone. She watched as he locked up the files in his briefcase and set it aside. 'On your knees.'

She hesitated briefly before kneeling on the plush carpet. Her heart was pounding so hard she imagined he could see it thumping in her chest. 'How does this work? Am I supposed to call you master? I don't think I can go quite that far.' She tried to stop herself from babbling as he walked around the desk, undoing his trousers. Not sure what to expect when he stopped directly in front of her, she opened her mouth again.

'And I don't think I can handle much pain either. How do you know –'

'Shut up and suck my cock.'

Jacob's hands gripped her head and pulled her towards his dangling penis. She opened her mouth obediently and thrilled at the feel of his soft cock as it thickened and got stiff in her mouth. Greg didn't let her suck him off very often; he seemed to think it wasn't something a lady should do. But Amanda had always loved the feel of a hard cock thrusting in and out of her mouth, and this time was no different. She felt her own juices begin to flow and pressed her thighs together to ease the ache developing there.

'That's it, suck my cock. Tasty, isn't it? You like this, don't you? Doesn't matter if you don't, though, because I do,' he mocked. His laughter filled the office and he gripped her head harder.

Holding her still, he thrust himself deep into her throat at a slow deep pace for a few minutes. Amanda felt the head of his cock against the back of her throat and fought her gag reflex with every thrust.

'Oh yeah, take it deep. You're no good to me, Amanda, unless you can take it deep. Tilt your head back. That's it.' He sighed with pleasure and Amanda felt tears well behind her eyes. She also felt her nipples harden to a painful point and knew that it was happening again. It was as if every inch of her skin were itchy and aching to be scratched.

Jacob's fluids began to leak steadily from his cock. His hips, pumping faster, made it harder for her to breathe. She gripped his thighs tight, fighting the urge to push against him, to stop him from fucking her mouth. Warm goo oozed out from the side of her lips, slid down her chin and dripped onto her silk blouse. She tried desperately to drag breath into her lungs through her flaring nostrils and didn't give her expensive blouse another thought.

Jacob's breathing matched hers, harsh and loud, filling the room. She felt the sharp pain of his grip tightening in her hair as his cock hit the back of her throat hard and fast. She gagged but he didn't stop, just on fucking her mouth. She felt his cock swell and swell, then felt it throb as his come began to gush from the tip and spurt out. He held her face tight to his crotch, her nose buried in his pubic hair as his come overflowed from her mouth and trickled steadily down her chin.

He pulled back slightly and let her lick him clean before stepping back and zipping up his trousers. 'Very good, Amanda.' He strode to his desk and quickly wrote something down before picking up his briefcase and moving towards the door. He stopped next to where a dishevelled Amanda still knelt on the floor and dropped a business card in front of her.

'My address is on the back. You have half an hour to get there. If you're late, you'll be punished.' Then he was gone, once again leaving Amanda stunned at the intensity of her own response to him.

She parked her car outside his house and sat there for a moment, just looking at it and wondering what would happen when she entered it. There were still doubts floating around in her mind, and she couldn't shake the sense that she was on a precipice. Things were about to change for her forever. *Ridiculous*, she told herself. *It's only one night. What could one night possibly change?*

Pulling the door handle sharply open she exited the car and strode confidently towards the front door of the house. It was a nice house, beige siding with nondescript window treatments. It looked like a million other houses in the city. Nothing to be intimidated by.

Amanda pressed a manicured nail to the doorbell and waited. Impatience pushed at her consciousness and she reached for the doorbell again only to have the door swing open and reveal Jacob in the entranceway.

'Right on time, Amanda,' he said, gesturing her forwards. 'Too bad, I was looking forward to punishing you.' He laughed and bent over to kiss her gently on the mouth. 'Relax. I promise you'll enjoy everything that happens here tonight.'

There was a small fire burning in the grate, making the front room cosy. He offered her a drink and she accepted gratefully, palms sweaty and fingers trembling. Patience had never been her strong suit and this situation proved to be no different. Yet she stubbornly refused to let it show, not wanting Jacob to know how out of her element she truly felt.

'Nice house you have here. Very homey, not at all what I would have expected of you, Jacob.' Amanda strove to present a confident demeanour.

'No, it isn't, is it?' His glance swept over the room before it rested on her. 'Or maybe you just don't know me as well as you think you do?' He quirked an eyebrow at her.

'That could be true. You have managed to surprise me recently.' Amanda gave a small laugh. 'However, congratulations are in order for both of us. A job well done on the Williams proposal. Good work, Jacob.' She held out her wine-glass for a toast.

'Congratulations, Amanda.' He tapped her glass with his and sat himself comfortably on the sofa next to her before taking a sip.

Amanda couldn't hide the small tremor that whipped through her body at his closeness, and Jacob laughed softly. Running the back of his finger slowly down her cheek, he goaded her. 'Anxious, are you? Is that arousal causing you to shake? Or fear?'

'I have no fear of you, Jacob.' She met his gaze with a steady one of her own.

'Perhaps you should.' And with that he pulled a piece of black cloth from the back of the sofa and placed it over her eyes, tying it tightly behind her head. Taking her wine-glass out of her hands, he issued instructions in a firm voice. 'Stand up, turn right and walk slowly.'

She did as he said and stepped when he told her to. But walking up the stairs blindfolded was difficult. She wasn't aware of how much her sight affected her balance until it was gone.

At the top of the stairs she passed through a doorway and was told to stand still and strip off her clothes. Once she was naked she stood proudly, imagining him looking over her body. She felt a brief moment of insecurity over what she thought of as her too big hips only to be filled with lust as his hands drifted lightly over her body.

'You have a very womanly body, Amanda. It's a shame you hide it so well under your business suits. Soft in the right places –' a quick smack on her bare buttocks at this comment '– and firm in the right places.' This was followed by the whisper of a tongue over her stiff nipple.

'Hands above your head,' he commanded. She felt a soft cloth being wrapped around her wrists and then some tension pulling her arms higher as he let go of her hands. She felt something pressing against her lips and automatically parted them. Another cloth was inserted between her teeth and wrapped around her head, then tied tight.

She couldn't hide the violent shiver that ran over her body when she realised how helpless she was. Blindfolded, gagged, naked and tied with her hands above her head, Amanda felt the heat in her belly burn hotter and her pussy lips thicken as arousal overcame all other emotions.

'Now you are mine to use in any way I want. Let's see what secrets your body hides, even from you, Amanda.'

Jacob began to stroke his hands lightly over her body, brushing teasingly over her nipples and down her belly, then threading his fingers through her pubic hairs, fingering the split between her thighs. His other hand ran down her back, softly caressing her round derrière before dipping between her cheeks for a brief tease.

Amanda's body felt as if it were on fire, and only firm strokes from those hands could put it out. She clenched her teeth on the gag, trying not to let her whimpers escape.

'Want more?'

She felt his breath on the back of her neck, then the tip of his tongue slid around the shell of her ear. His hands gently cupped her breasts and she felt the wet heat of a mouth as he firmly nibbled across her breasts. A sigh of pleasure whispered out of her when his lips surrounded one nipple and sucked hungrily.

'Feel good, Amanda?'

Her body jolted in shock as her mind scrambled to make sense of things. How could Jacob whisper in her ear if he was sucking on her nipple? She felt another pair of hands brush over her waist and settle lightly on her hips as the mouth moved to her other breast.

There was another man in the room. Who was it? What was he doing there? She didn't know how she knew it was a man, but she did, and it only aroused her further, so much so that she gave up her thoughts and let her body rejoice in all the attention.

She felt an erection pressing against her buttocks as one pair of hands were removed from her breasts and slid down her body. One hand pressed against her belly, pulling her tight against the man while his other hand reached between her thighs and tested her wetness.

Then the warmth of his body was gone. Distracted by the sharp nip of teeth on her nipple, she didn't hear him rummaging nearby. Then the mouth was gone and her body screamed at the abandonment. Something pinched at her nipple and a shocked moan could be heard through her gag.

'It's a clothes-pin. Just like you use to hang your laundry.' He attached one to her other nipple and Amanda was surprised to feel the pain lessen and an intense arousal sweep over her. She hadn't known she could get more aroused than she already was.

He flicked the clothes-pins as one would flick a doorstop and jolts of intense pleasure shot through her body, straight to her groin. She squeezed her thighs together and felt how juicy she was getting.

As if reading her mind, Jacob told her to spread her thighs. Awkwardly she spread them as wide as she could while still keeping some semblance of balance.

'Not wide enough,' he commanded, and kicked her legs further apart, causing all of her weight to hang from her restraint. 'If your legs aren't wide enough, how is my friend supposed to eat your pussy?'

Amanda felt a tongue sweep over her pussy lips and jolted in pleasure. The tongue stopped licking her pussy and she groaned in delight as a mouth pressed into her, lips, tongue and teeth gently working her pussy over. A man – it was definitely a man's mouth that was eating her pussy. The roughness of a five-o'clock shadow chafed her thighs and his nose nudged her clit. She felt her muscles tighten as an orgasm began to take hold.

'STOP!'

The mouth was gone. Amanda's body screamed at the loss and she heard Jacob laugh softly. He flicked the clothes-pins again and a shudder went through her body.

'You are so responsive. Does your boyfriend never eat your pussy?'

When Amanda didn't respond to the question Jacob brought his hand down sharply across her ass.

'I want an answer. You must nod or shake your head when I ask you a question. Does your boyfriend ever eat your pussy?'

Amanda shook her head in answer.

'Does he ever spank you like this?' Another loud smack echoed through the room as he smacked her bottom again.

Amanda shook her head in denial once more.

'Do you want him to?'

No answer from Amanda this time.

Jacob brought his hand down three times in quick succession. 'Do you want him to, Amanda?'

She slowly made an affirmative gesture with her head.

'Very good, Amanda. I'm going to release your hands now. You are to drop to all fours like a good girl.'

Her hands were released and she took a minute to rub her wrists, trying to get the circulation back into them.

'Down, I said.' Jacob placed a hand in the middle of her back and shoved her roughly to the ground. 'Did I say you could stop to baby yourself? No. I told you to get on all fours.'

She quickly stabilised her position on her hands and knees. Hands gripped her by the hair and pulled her head up. Her gag was removed and a hard cock filled her mouth.

'You did well earlier tonight. I want to see if you can

make me come with your mouth again, while my helper punishes you for being so slow getting into position.'

Tears welled in Amanda's eyes and dampened the cloth covering them as she proceeded to suck Jacob's cock greedily while the other man steadily abused her bottom with the palm of his very large hand. The burning of her ass cheeks matched the burning in her belly as she felt her juices drip from her pussy down her thighs. She didn't think about anything, just rejoicing in the sensations swamping her body.

Her abuser stopped spanking her and inserted a finger into her hole. Her cunt clenched hungrily around the intruder. Then it was two fingers thrusting in and out of her. Her body started to rock back onto those fingers only to have them pull away, leaving her empty.

A muffled groan echoed around Jacob's cock and she heard both men chuckle.

'She's more than ready, Jacob.' The stranger's voice was deep and smooth, fanning the fire burning in her belly. 'May I?'

'Yes, you may,' Jacob answered him. 'He is going to fuck you now, Amanda. We're both going to fuck you.'

The unknown man gripped her hips and thrust his cock into her deeply. He began fucking her with steady strokes immediately; no preliminaries were needed. Her body rocked back and forth as she was filled with cock. Her breasts bounced with each thrust and her pinched nipples shot jolts of pleasure directly to her cunt.

The room became quiet then, all of them concentrating on sating their lust. The only sounds in the room were their groans and sighs of pleasure, and the wet sucking sounds coming from both Amanda's mouth and pussy as they were used.

Amanda felt all her muscles tense as Jacob's grip on her hair tightened, and she felt his cock hit the back of her throat at the same time as another cock was pounding deep inside her pussy. She felt hands briefly brush her breasts and then her nipples burned as if on fire when the clothes-pins were removed and blood rushed back into the hard tips.

Amanda was getting hammered from both ends and she couldn't hold back any more. She pulled her mouth roughly away from Jacob's cock and screamed as an orgasm ripped through her.

Slowly coming back to reality, she felt hot come land on her back and buttocks as both men shot their loads onto her naked back.

Heavy silence filled the room as everybody struggled to regain their composure. Amanda felt strong arms lift her and she was aware of going down a hallway. She felt gentle lips brush her cheek before she was helped to stand up and her blindfold removed. Jacob stood in front of her, looking into her eyes gently.

'You OK?'

She nodded quietly. They were in a bathroom.

'Take your time showering, and then let yourself out. Any questions before I leave you?'

Amanda knew what he was hinting at, but she didn't ask who the other man was. She wasn't sure she wanted to know. The only thing she was sure of was that she had been wrong: one night could change everything.

'When can I see you again?'

Till Eleven Louisa Temple

Tim stopped the car in the quiet suburban street, but didn't switch the engine off.

'OK. Number 16. I'll pick you up at eleven,' he said.

I got out and crossed the street to the illuminated front door, hearing the car pull away as I rang the bell. There was no going back now. It was time to do the dirty deed we had concocted the night before.

'Happy birthday, Mike,' I said when the door opened.

'Celia! Hi, thanks. Where's Tim?'

'He's going to pick me up at eleven,' I said. I had to advance onto the step, forcing Mike to move back into the house, or we'd have just stood there. I had to act now. I would bottle out if I procrastinated. He was peering down the road as if he expected Tim to walk up after parking the car. Well, he wasn't used to his brother's girlfriend coming to visit on her own.

'Eleven? Did you say he's picking you up at eleven?'

'Yes.' I was in the small hallway now. 'Shut the door, Mike. You are pleased to see me, aren't you?'

'Of course. But what . . .? Are you staying?'

I pulled a card from my coat pocket and held it out.

'Thanks.'

While he opened the envelope I took off my coat and hung it over the banister. Inside the card Tim had written: 'Happy birthday, mate. Enjoy!'

Mike looked up, the question he was starting to form dying to complete silence as he looked at me. I was wearing a tight black basque, lacy-topped sheer hold-up stockings and four inch black heels. My nipples were stained red with blusher and I had rubbed a little almond oil over them and depilated the hair on my pussy. There had been no need to oil myself between my legs because I had been wet ever since Tim had suggested this naughty idea the night before. Even so, just before we left our flat to embark on the mission, Tim had rubbed me gently and maddeningly slowly before buttoning up my coat. There was no doubt about it; I was horny as hell. The whole thing felt so ... naughty and wrong.

Mike stared at me, then looked again at the card. He glanced back at me and his eyes went to the closed front door – maybe he thought Tim was outside, choking back guffaws. Then he looked everywhere except at me.

I waited, wondering whether I should break the silence by taking his hand and leading him into the living room. Or upstairs. Or should I let him make the move? I decided to wait, and just stood there smiling invitingly. I could hear Mike's breathing and the gulp as he swallowed. My own heart was pounding. I'd always thought Mike was attractive, despite Tim's insistence that he was 'deadly dull' and 'well into old fartdom ahead of his time'.

He was taller than Tim, and big; muscular where Tim was lean; quiet, and slow to speak where Tim was quick and sharp as a whip.

'Celia, this is a joke, isn't it? Tim's going to burst in the back door with a camera and a load of his mates, isn't he? Catch us at it and have a laugh. Isn't he?'

Despite his worries, he couldn't stop himself from looking me over, reaching out and cupping my left breast. His big hand held it gently, then tightened, thumb and forefinger squeezing, slipping a little on my oiled nipple and sending a hugely unexpected lightning bolt of sensation down through my belly. His eyes glared intently into mine. They were more greeny-blue than I'd noticed before and the lashes were longer and thicker than a big bloke's had any right to be.

'No, Mike, really. He won't be back till eleven.'

'Well, I think I know my bastard of a little brother a bit better than you do.'

He dropped my breast and pushed me away, not hard but sharply, so I teetered after him in the ridiculous heels.

'Yeah. This is typical of his bad taste sense of humour. He knows I fancy you rotten.'

'Oh.' I looked at Mike then. Really looked at him. So Mike fancied me. I hadn't realised, the way he'd always been so cool and polite when talking to his kid brother's girl, who was too young and too silly to take much notice of. Well, Mike had to notice me now. Was this why I'd agreed so readily to the game, I wondered? Because I wanted the attention? 'Mike, it's eight-thirty. Tim's coming to pick me up at eleven. Until then we can do whatever you want.'

'What about you, Celia? What do you think, then? D'you think it's going to be a laugh? Will you tell him what I'm like? Compare us? Put me down? I've been compared to that flash fucker all my life. Now he's set me up for this.'

'No. I thought it'd be fun. I just wondered what you'd do, what it'd be like to confront someone with this, see what happens.'

He stood back then, leaning against my coat and looking me over carefully as if he was seeing me for the first time. His eyes, those really gorgeous eyes, stared into mine, no longer angry but with a question in them. As they dropped to my breasts I saw that question begin to be answered.

My tits were pushed up and squashed together by the tiny cups of the basque into curves that, I realised for the first time, were really rather luscious. My nipples hardened with a little shiver – excitement, fear, embarrassment – as Mike's eyes rested on them. The beginnings of a smile began to curve one corner of his mouth which, as I studied him in turn, I realised was quite a lovely, kissable mouth.

His eyes fell further now to take in my waist, narrower and curvier than I had ever imagined it could be, before Tim had pulled the hooks tightly together at my back. Mike was gazing at my naked mound. The soft triangle of flesh had looked so enticing and erotic in the mirror at home, exposed for the first time. With Tim's familiar arms around me, and Tim's familiar face smiling wickedly over my shoulder, we had both gazed at the new, erotic, wildly sexual woman staring back from the mirror. I remembered how I had pushed my buttocks against him and begged him to fuck me, excited by this strange new me. He had laughed shortly.

'Not now, baby. Got to deliver you. God, though, you make a gorgeous present.'

He'd gone to fetch my coat then, leaving me to admire myself some more, but also giving me time to wonder if he seemed a bit uncomfortable. Had my up-for-anything boyfriend gone too far this time?

But Mike, it seemed, couldn't tear his eyes away. His smile had grown to one of admiration. I had never shaved myself before, and nor had I ever been stared at quite so frankly and with such obvious appreciation. I looked back into those gorgeous eyes and attempted to move things on a bit. 'So, Mike, are we going to stand here all night?'

He gestured towards the door. My heels tapped across a wooden floor into a sparsely furnished room. A piece of pizza crust and a half-empty bottle of red wine were on the low table between the sofa and the TV.

Suddenly I felt sorry. Tim had said Mike would be

doing nothing for his birthday, but I hadn't realised nothing meant the TV and a take-away all on his own.

'Can I have glass of wine?' I asked.

'Sure.'

I sank down onto the sofa. The shock of cool leather against my naked thighs and hot wetness was a surprise. In the dim light I hadn't noticed at first, but it was enormous and covered in the softest buttery leather. The room stretched away into shadows, deceptively larger than one would think from outside in the quiet street. My heels were now sunk into the deep pile rug, which had a vaguely ethnic design in red and plum – colours that were echoed in a painting taking up a large part of the wall. The room was deliberately sparse, luxuriously so. Everything in it was big and quietly gorgeous. Mike's 'boring management job', 'something industrial to do with heaters', as Tim had described it, couldn't be going too badly.

Mike walked back in with a glass and I took a big gulp of the wine he poured, hoping it would turn this back into the laugh it was supposed to be. I'd read about wine having flavours of blackberry and chocolate but this was the first time I'd ever tasted them myself. I took another mouthful.

'This is really nice wine.'

He was looking at me quite coolly now.

'Yeah. I'm treating myself.'

Lovely as the drink was, it wasn't making our party swing. What had I expected Mike to do? Jump on me enthusiastically, I suppose. It's what Tim always did. I wasn't used to having to make much effort in the seduction process. Mike at least sat next to me, however, with one arm slung along the back of the sofa so he was half turned towards me.

'You're a beautiful girl, Celia. I always wondered

what Tim did to deserve you.' He lifted some strands of my hair and tucked them gently behind my ear.

His fingers, cool from the wine glass and gentle, moved down my neck to my shoulder and paused. I felt the warmth of his big hand as it rested on my skin and realised how much I wanted him to touch my breast again. Tim would've dived straight there, pulling, pinching and acting like a greedy teenager. Instead, Mike's hand came up to my face once again. Cupping my cheek, he turned my face to his and kissed me. His lips were as gentle as his fingers. He tasted faintly of the rich red wine and of himself, and this close I could catch an undertone of woody, citrusy aftershave. Nice. Expensive.

The kiss was continuing, slow, gentle and thorough – just our lips and his big warm hand holding my face. I felt myself begin to relax, sinking into the sofa and turning my body towards him. His lips pressed more firmly, pushing mine apart, and his tongue, warm, gentle and insistent, began to explore the whole of my mouth. His hand moved from my face and his arm wrapped around my shoulders, moving slowly and deliciously over my naked skin.

As our lips became wetter and my mouth opened wide to receive his kiss, I felt warmth begin to glow deep within myself. I parted my thighs, knowing I was becoming hot and wet and wanting to feel the naked lips of my cunt pressing against the soft leather of the sofa. I wanted that long deep kiss to go on forever but, I realised, I also wanted him to move down and lavish that gentle, insistent, thorough attention on my nipples.

As if he had read my mind, he sensuously grabbed one breast, our mouths continuing their exploration of each other. My breasts aren't small, I'm glad to say.

They're a nice firm handful, and a delight for any hot-blooded man to get a hold of. 'Not a bad pair of knockers', as Tim often said. But Mike's hand held the whole of one breast, warming it and making it tingle all over. With maddening slowness, he moved his thumb around the nipple area. I could feel it crinkling with longing and my nipple stood up, becoming ever more desperate to be explored by his fingers. The memory of the way he had squeezed it in the hall made the hard nut ache with longing.

I arched my back, desperate for more of him, and my thighs spread wider so that more of my pussy came into contact with the leather. I was mad for more of this man and all he'd done so far was kiss me. Suddenly even that was taken away. I moaned. I wanted him back. I'd just got going. But he held me away so he could look into my face.

'Celia, I've wanted to do that since I first saw you,' he said.

I was so flattered to think that I had caught this man's attention and that he really fancied me. I gasped his name, trying to push my body closer.

'Greedy girl!' he scolded. 'Did you get that from Tim? Ten-minute Tim, I'll bet. You're my present and I've got till eleven.'

His blue-green eyes were looking into mine. My lips were swollen with his kiss. His thorough stimulation of my breast was sending arrows of fire straight to my clitoris and now he was smiling at me. I didn't know what to say. On the three or four brief times we'd met, he had just been Tim's stuffy, slightly superior older brother. How could I tell him of our childish idea for the prank I was playing? How could I say, 'Mike, I thought you were a big, dull, early middle-aged bore? I thought it would be fun to tease you?' How could I have been so stupid? I was confused as well as aroused.

He wasn't dull at all; he was maddeningly sexy. He knew just how to excite me and he wasn't going to be rushed. So how come he was all alone on his birthday, with nothing but a take-away and the TV? At least I could ask him that.

He shrugged and grinned.

'What should I be doing?' he said. 'Getting rat-arsed down the pub? That's not my style. Not any more. Anyway, a person should play with their presents on their birthday, don't you think?'

His fingers, still around my breast, resumed their slow circling of my nipple. Gently easing and exciting the hard bud, he began to kiss me again. His lips explored my face, kissing and nibbling every inch of it. I reached out for his body, feeling solid muscle and the strong male neck where short dark hair curved into the magically soft skin just behind his ear.

He eased me back until I was lying full-length on the sofa. It was easily big enough for us to lie side by side. He held me close and I gasped as, for the first time, I felt the rock hard length of his erection against my thigh. I reached down to touch him and ran my nails along its length through the tight fabric of his jeans. It was his turn to gasp. Good. He wasn't so in control after all.

God, he was big. I wanted to explore him now, to feel the heft of his big cock in my hand and my mouth – my cunt. I undid the button on his Levi's, but he took my hand away and carried it to his lips, kissing my fingers so that what could have been a rejection turned into a luscious new excitement. His lips warmed my palm, and I was able to cup his face for a while before he moved slowly along my arm. I felt as if he were uncovering skin I never knew I had. The inside of my upper arm and then my armpit tingled with a life they had never known before, sending darts of fire to my nipple then straight down between my legs. I arched my back, desperate for my aching nipple to be in his mouth. He gave the side of my breast one long loving lick, circling the nipple with a tongue like fire. Then he pulled my arm over my head, rolling on top of me so the great length of his cock pressed against the centre of my body, making contact with my pussy for the first time. I pushed upwards to rub against the rough denim.

'What's the matter, my lovely? You're getting very excited,' he whispered. 'Doesn't Tim keep you happy?'

The bitter edge to his voice whenever he mentioned Tim cut like a knife now that I was so tender and aroused for him. I wanted to make Mike happy, I realised. I wanted to explore his body and make him moan in pleasure. I wanted him to enjoy me and not work me over in some battle with his brother.

What could I say: 'Mike, I'm ... sorry we met like this?' But I wasn't – this was the best sex I'd ever had and he hadn't even got to my waist, let alone below it.

'No.' I settled for a straightforward answer to his question. 'Tim doesn't make love like this.'

I think he was surprised that I admitted it, for he bent his head to pay the attention to my breasts that I had been longing for. He swirled his tongue in long slow circles around my nipples, his hot breath teasing them into rock-hard buds. Then, closing his lovely wet mouth around one, he began to suck, tonguing it softly as he did so. If he hadn't been lying on top of me, I'd have shot like a rocket to the ceiling and stayed there. Instead, I bucked and moaned underneath him, holding him to me, my fingers in his dark hair.

He sucked on me, moving from one nipples to the other, gradually increasing the intensity until both nubs were huge and red as raspberries. Then he lifted his head, squeezed my breasts together and admired his work. I was so full of pleasure, I laughed at him.

'What?' He grinned back, his mouth wet and gorgeous. His cock must be straining like a wild beast encased in those jeans. He hadn't even attempted to get it out. It was driving me wild.

'Mike, you're lovely,' I said, gyrating myself against him, rubbing my hands up and down his muscular thighs.

'You're not so bad yourself, Birthday Present. Glad you came with batteries included.'

The ugly tension was broken, Tim forgotten. We were here for ourselves alone now and as if he realised it too, he kissed me long and deeply. Then he stood up. Bereft of his weight and warmth, I just lay there, looking up at him.

'Come on.' He took my hand and pulled me up, his eyes never leaving my body. Part of me wanted to lie there and be looked at by him forever. But I was led to the foot of the stairs and sent up them with a little push that ended with his fingers trailing between my buttocks and down to slip electrically up inside me. My pussy was swollen and dripping with anticipation and I could feel his eyes all over my arse cheeks. I knew their roundness was accentuated by the tight waist of the basque, and I forced myself to sway slowly up the stairs although I wanted to drag him down onto them right there, or race up three at a time to the nearest bed.

At the top I stopped, unsure which way to go. He put his arm round me and led the way. The ridiculous fuck-me shoes sank into the velvety carpet and I was glad of his solid strength to steady me; glad in more ways than one. This mad prank had become much more than I had expected, and all my bearings were lost except the flaming heat between my legs that was aimed at this man's touch like a compass searching for True North.

Inside the bedroom he left me, crossing the room to switch on the light beside the bed, then sat down and watched me, kicking off his trainers and leaning back on his elbows. From the long bulge that was still in his jeans it was obvious he was enjoying the sight. I circled the room, enjoying his gaze and, to be honest, looking for clues that told me more about him than simply that he had good taste, could afford to indulge it and, somewhere, had learned to make the kind of love I had only dreamed about.

His smile had an echo of Tim's cruel beauty, I thought as I walked to the vast bed, then began to crawl across it towards him. The plump duvet sank softly beneath my hands and knees. My breasts swung, golden in the dim light, their painted, swollen tips dark against the snowy billow of the bedclothes. His eyes glittered darkly and all his attention was on me. With my heightened senses I could smell him before I touched him, the musky male heat of his skin like no other and already dear and familiar. He lay back as I approached and it was my turn to kiss him.

Then I teased his mouth with my breasts as I moved down his neck to his shirt, kissing each new inch of skin as I slowly eased the pearly buttons from their snug holes. He shuddered as I lapped my tongue sensuously over each tight pink nipple. I traced a snail's trail with the tip of my tongue down the silky drift of dark hair that led enticingly beneath his jeans.

By now, my sex was poised above his head and it felt at once both vulnerable and illicit. Mike put his hands up to hold my waist and ran them down over the corset to the naked skin of my hips. I felt his thumbs slide down to caress my shaven pubis and heard the sharp intake of his breath as they reached the soft swollen notch directly above my clit.

Me? I'd forgotten how to breathe. All my senses were

on him, knowing he was smelling me, feeling me and would soon be tasting me; knowing my fingers were only millimetres and a denim's thickness from his cock, with my mouth coming up fast and ready to taste him.

His thumbs parted me, pushing the skin up and exposing my clitoris directly above his mouth, my inner lips glistening and pink.

I undid the second button on the jeans, revealing the thick blunt tip of the cock that I had been longing for since he'd first laid his hands on me. As I licked my first taste of him he sighed and, pushing my outer lips far apart, buried his face in my exposed pussy, sucking the wet swollen folds into his mouth, his tongue lapping and circling my clit like it was coming home.

I ripped the remaining bronze studs out of the button-holes and his great cock reared out at me, heading straight into my open mouth like it, too, was coming home. I snaked my tongue round the thick, ridged knob, circling and circling, sucking and sucking.

I could feel his hands gripping my hips, holding me in a vice-like grip exactly where he wanted me. My mouth and throat opened wider than I had ever known, greedy to take him right down to the hilt, lips, nose and chin grinding deep into the hot crisp heaven of pubic hair as his groin arched up to meet me.

My cunt felt huge, as if it could have swallowed both of us up. Great warm waves of delight were sweeping out from his tongue and taking over all my senses. I was impaled by him from both ends and lost in the hot soaring plunge of his mouth and cock. But, held firm in his hands, I knew I could soar, swoop and plunge but not fall. As I shuddered and bucked I felt him grip harder, holding himself back as I came all over his face. Although this climax soon peaked, I was far from finished and wanted to feel him lost inside me, the way I had just been lost and full of him.

He pulled out of my gasping mouth, kissed my thighs and then swung me round to lie beside him. My smell was all over his mouth and I lay against his shoulder, my breath still fast and ragged as I stroked his wonderful face.

He smiled at me, and in the dim light his face looked more like Tim's than it had before.

'Birthday baby, was that good? We haven't finished yet.'

I nodded against his chest, thinking how expertly he was spinning out the pleasure. At this rate we'd be fucking solidly till eleven. This thought couldn't be spoken, though, because I didn't want this to end at eleven. I leaned up on my elbow, wanting to say something about how good this was.

'So,' I began, 'you said you fancied me.'

He grunted, a bit wary now.

'I had no idea,' I said. 'I wish I had known. How come Tim knows?'

He looked at me suspiciously. 'You really don't know?'

'No. Course not.'

'So why the hell did you turn up here, tonight of all nights, dressed like this?'

'I know it must seem mad, but honestly, I thought it would be a laugh. Maybe – I dunno – I wanted to see what you'd be like. I thought it would be fun. I've always wanted to dress up like this and take it to the limit, but I've never dared, and you, well ... I suppose you seemed really safe,' I trailed away lamely.

'And dull. What did you think I'd do? You didn't think I'd be any good at it, did you?'

His face was hard. I knew I had to be totally honest if I wanted this thing to go on beyond tonight.

'No. I thought you'd maybe leap on me and it would all be over in half an hour.'

'And then what? We'd make polite small talk for two hours?'

'Tim told me nothing this wild had ever happened to you before.'

He snorted. 'So I was supposed to cream my jeans at the sight of you. Then just after nine you call Tim, everyone pisses themselves laughing and you all go to the pub. Who's the bet with?'

'What?'

'He's my brother, remember – I know what he's like. His idea of a joke would be to set someone up then bet how big a fool they'd make of themselves.'

'Has he done it to you before? Is that why you're so bitter about him?'

There was a long silence before he answered.

'Yeah. But it wasn't me he set up; it was a girlfriend of mine. He made her look a fool. It was years ago, we were quite young. She didn't believe the joke had nothing to do with me. Nothing I could say would make her believe any different. Even after I forced Tim to apologise and swear it was all his stupid idea. But she finished with me over it.'

'Did you really care about her?' I asked. He made that non-committal snorting sound that men do if you try and make them talk about feelings. 'What was the joke?'

'He sent her an outfit like the one you're wearing, as if it was from me, asking her to dress up like you, shaved cunt and all, and come and be my birthday present. So she turned up on my birthday, but everyone was there – my mum and dad, even my gran, and all my mates. The parents were going to take Gran out for a meal after they'd wished me happy birthday but, of course, she wasn't to know that.'

'Christ. Poor girl. What did she do?'

'Oh, kept her coat on. Looked daggers at me while

she made some small talk with my mum. Then stormed out soon as the parents had left. Sent the ring back.'

'Oh shit.'

'So you didn't know anything about this?' he asked, not believing I could be so naïve.

'No, Mike, honestly.'

'You just thought you were rescuing a pathetic saddo by providing some sizzling birthday sex?'

'The solitary pizza did seem to point that way,' I conceded.

'Hmmph.' He did that man thing again, but there was more of a laugh in it this time.

'Well, for your information, tomorrow night I'll be drinking rum punch or banana daiquiris, or whatever it is you drink in Barbados, sitting in my private chalet in the Caribbean.'

'Oh yes?'

'I've always wanted to scuba-dive,' said Mike. 'Now I've got the time and the money to learn. I'm flying out to Barbados at five tomorrow morning. That's when my birthday's really gonna start and that's why I was having a take-away, not getting pissed, and planning an early night. Until you turned up, of course. You're an unexpected bonus, Birthday Present.'

And no doubt some girl was cramming her bikini wardrobe into a suitcase even as we spoke, I thought, bitterly and stupidly disappointed. If that was it, then, I decided to make sure he'd be too wiped out for any passionate holiday lovemaking, at least for the first couple of nights. I was determined to get a go of that juicy fat cock of his.

As if he'd read my mind, he turned to me and, running a hand along my thigh, said, 'It's a long flight. I'm leaving the laptop at home and I don't have anything to do but sleep.' His fingers parted me, stroking my wetness luxuriously and then pushing deep inside to begin thrusting rhythmically, as if I were being stroked from the inside out and back again, over and over. His mouth echoed the same rhythm on mine, long and luxurious. I was getting ready again, and the sight of his growing cock was making me even wetter.

I wanted all of him, or as much as I could get. If there was just this final hour, then I would make the most of it, and so I pushed his jeans over his hips, revelling in the firm smooth skin of his back as it swelled to satisfyingly muscled buttocks.

'This is a stupid thing,' he said suddenly, stopping and rolling me over onto my stomach. 'I'm fed up with it digging into me.'

And he began to unhook the basque, then flung it to the floor and started stroking my buttocks, waist and back. I had thought the control of the corset sexy, but this was delicious freedom, to feel him with the whole of my skin, no armour between us.

He lifted my hips and I pushed my buttocks up, spreading my legs, wanting him to see how wet and swollen he had made me, wanting him to finally push that great penis of his all the way in. But maddeningly he continued to stroke me, sliding one hand between my legs, his thumb circling gently around the tight muscle of my arse and the rest of his hand sliding up to stroke my clit and send hot fire to my breasts, hanging just above the bedcover.

'Mmm, I like you like this,' he murmured, nuzzling my buttocks.

All I could do was moan his name over and over. I had never wanted any man inside me so badly. It seemed he could turn me on with an understanding of my body and its needs that I had never dreamed possible before. He took his time. He wasn't like Tim, all brash and bluster and no finesse. I thought to myself of the satisfaction and pleasure I had been missing out on.

He increased the pressure of his fingers, all the while nibbling and making patterns of soft little bites all over my buttocks and the tops of my thighs above the hold-ups.

The pleasure built and built. My face was crushed against the pillow, my mouth open to draw in great gasping breaths and my body completely open to him.

'Do you like this?' he asked.

'Yes, yes, oh yes,' I replied. I liked being asked questions when I was having sex.

'Go on, say you want it,' said Mike. 'Tell me,' he urged.

He rolled me over and, at last, pushed hard and thick inside me up to the hilt. I was crying out by now, sobbing and shrieking my delight and his name, and he was thundering into me in a huge thudding rhythm. Dull Mike. Mike the heating engineer with nothing much going for him. Mike the saddo. Yeah, right. He came quite quickly, and that wasn't surprising with all the build-up we'd had. He pumped into me with thrusts that rocked the great bed and had me shouting my triumph, taking everything he had to give.

Our rhythm slowed and changed to the gasping and heaving relief of survivors flung out of the surf and onto the beach, delight at being alive in every tingling cell of our bodies.

But the pounding continued. It was the door. Someone – Tim! – was banging on the door. Now I knew what people meant when they talked about post-coital sadness. I was left bleak and washed-up, the smell of sex thick in the room. Mike rolled off me.

'Yeah?' He leaned against the window he'd opened, looking down – naked, male, arrogant.

I heard Tim's voice, then Mike walked to the crumpled jeans, fished keys out of the pocket and tossed them down. He turned to look at me. In ten minutes I'd be out of his life – nothing but a memory. A bad-taste birthday prank, a party game where the forfeit was my heart and there was nothing I could do about it. I'd gone into this strutting, stupid and ignorant in my daft fuck-me shoes. I would damn well prance out, though, head high.

I smiled up at him.

'That was everything I ever dreamed sex with you could be,' he said.

'It was beyond my wildest dreams,' I replied.

Tim was climbing the stairs.

'Come with me,' he said.

'What?'

'Come with me to Barbados.' He sat down beside me and the smile that spread like sunshine across his face was the reflection of my own.

I heard myself say the reply before I'd thought about it. 'Yes.'

'Hey, bro.' Tim appeared. 'Didn't I tell you she was my best girl? I said I'd make it up to you one day.'

His face looked white and stricken as he stared at us from the bedroom door. I lay still, beached on the bed, Mike sitting beside me, his hand over my pussy like it belonged there.

Signal Failure Jan Bolton

Dave Ashton couldn't finish the washing up, tidy the house, see to the dog and still be at work on time. The way things had turned out over the past year, he couldn't care less if he was late again; punctuality was the least of his problems. He'd grown to loathe the smarmy boss and his perfect life. All the concessions he'd made to the railway company's management and their corporate rebranding initiatives. 'Got to smarten up, Dave,' they'd told him. What did they know about the things normal men had to deal with? After Margaret had left him, trying to make ends meet was enough to drive a saint up the wall. He still owed twenty years of fixed interest rate payments on the semi, and there hadn't been the spare money to bring the place up to modern décor standards. And these days it was as if every other TV programme was rubbing his nose in it. Some manicured ponce would be sounding forth about cracked hessian drapes and patio spotlighting for your alfresco evening dining. Yeah, right. If he paid the gas bill on time it was a cause for celebration. Mood-enhancing colour co-ordinates would have to wait.

The mortgage payments were sucking him dry as a biscuit. But although his finances were going through a crisis, there was a silver lining. The sense of freedom he felt at being shot of Margaret and her constant nagging had rekindled his interest in other women. After the first six months of her going, the shame of being left for a richer man had passed, and recently he'd begun to feel pretty happy about his lot. He could meet his mates down the pub when he liked. He could loaf about and please himself and not have to worry about minding his language when the mother-in-law came round, 'cos she didn't come round any more. And, best of all, he was able to build up a collection of adult videos that he indulged in with a guilty relish that kept him hornier these days than he'd ever been. He was 45 years old – an age most men would say their desire had been on the wane for at least ten years – but, unlike the blokes who had to keep getting it up for their flabby wives, Dave was rediscovering his perkiness and playing the field. And no need for Viagra. Wasn't he just the lad.

Dave got himself ready for work. Stripped to the waist and whistling along with the insurance ad theme tune from the TV, he pulled a freshly washed shirt from the laundry basket. He'd had no time to iron it, and it was still a bit damp and smelt of fabric conditioner as he put it on over his broad and hairy chest and tucked it into his briefs. Then on went the uniform – a little scratchy and too thick for his liking, but he didn't have a choice. It was the rules that you had to wear the uniform. He stuffed his sandwiches into a small sports bag and patted them down over his new copy of *Young and Horny*. It had been burning a hole on the living room table, but he was saving it for his break later on, when he'd get an hour off to please himself. It was usually in the afternoon that he got the horn something rotten. The job didn't demand too much imagination, just alertness, and he often found himself drifting into the X-rated zones of his mind – the furtive places where cunts and cocks were king; where women were dirty and men were brutal and life centred around the honest pursuit of the voluptuous abyss. Maybe he'd take the magazine into the loos and have a lovely slow wank, then spurt all over the pictures. But maybe he'd get lucky and get the real thing. Maybe Kelly would be good to her word and keep her promise to visit him.

Kelly. 22 and a gob on her like a builder's mate. Brash and ballsy and shameless, she had let Dave do her round the back of Cheekie's nightclub in Gloucester two weeks back. He'd had her up against the wall and banged her sweet little cunt for only five minutes before losing it in a spasm of molten panic. He'd been a bit embarrassed that he hadn't been able to last very long, but her behaviour had done for him. He hadn't expected a young girl like that to be so dirty. All those years with Margaret, he'd got used to female orgasms being silent. But this little vixen had let it rip out into the night air, telling him, 'I'm coming, I'm coming.' What a lovely little performer. With Margaret, he had never known whether she had or she hadn't half the time; confusing business for a bloke, all that. This one, though ... Blimey. He'd started rubbing her, only through her knickers as well, and she'd instantly been right up for it. She'd let forth a stream of filth in his ear, telling him she wanted to cream all over his hand, taking over his movements and making him rub her harder. Then he'd eased his fingers into her knickers and felt how hot and sticky she was. He'd started rubbing himself mindlessly against her leg, his cock huge in his pants as he pushed his fingers over her clit. If she hadn't come so quickly and he hadn't got his cock out right away he'd have probably shot a load into his trousers. She'd barely finished the throes of her climax than he had whipped it out and was inside her like a randy cur in the pedigree pen. No preliminaries – it was straight in there, arse pumping like a good'un.

Seeing a young girl come like that had made him shoot so hard and so fast he had changed his opinion about the type of women he liked. He didn't want all that coy nonsense any more. After doing Kelly he realised it was the sluttish girls that were the most fun – and the most honest. Since then, he'd got a bit of a reputation among his mates for being a young pussy hound. But they were just jealous 'cos they had to keep it in their pants for their wives. The irony was, the wives were always too tired, what with the kids, and school and shopping and everything. They might as well have had their dicks chopped off for all the fun they got out of being married. This made Dave feel incredibly chipper. He was a free man, all right.

He'd run into Kelly again the following week, but she had been out with her girlfriends and hadn't wanted to break up the party by going off with someone else – girls' night out and all that. She was looking great. She was a big girl, a size 16, she'd said, but she filled out the sparkly dress she was wearing a treat. Her skin was scrubbed and buffed, her cheeks glowing and her lips coated with a slick sheen of gloss that seemed to be in vogue these days. Lips: moist, juicy, parted. The way women's fashion had changed in the past couple of years, it seemed to Dave as if all young girls had been styled for porno. Maybe he was imagining it, maybe he was just looking harder at the available goods, but females these days certainly seemed to have men where they wanted them. They were so confident, swaggering around and swearing with slogans striped across their tracksuit pants saying things like: 'gorgeous'; 'princess'; 'bling bling'. They all wanted money and jewellery and designer stuff and flash cars – something Dave couldn't give them. Yet get them pissed and it soon became evident that what they wanted most of all was male attention. They wanted to be told they were really pretty and sexy and that they were driving you wild. Flatter them enough and buy them a few drinks, and you could have your hand up their tops in no time and get into their little thongs before nine o'clock on a good night and still leave yourself enough time to have a few drinks before last orders. Oh yes, the girls were behaving more like lads every day, roaming around in packs, drinking themselves into a stupor and causing a racket in the town centre at the weekends. Still, Dave wasn't complaining. That was what being young was all about.

Dave ran a spot of gel through his thick black hair, patted some aftershave around his chops and was ready to leave the house. Hopefully, old misery guts Wallace would be up in the control room and wouldn't notice him sneaking in a few minutes late ... maybe it would be his lucky day. He threw some doggy treats in the bowl for Rascal and was off out the door – an honest man on his way to an honest day's toil.

'Kel, you going to meet that bloke, then?' said Alysha as she and Kelly and their other mate Angela sat outside the McDonald's in Gloucester's main shopping precinct, doing nothing in particular.

'Dunno. I'm thinking about it.'

'He was that one who come up to us last week, yeah?'

'Yeah. He's all right, isn't he? Fit for a middle-aged bloke.' She picked at her trainers. 'I'm fed up with those skinny bastards with no money.'

'D'you think he's got any money?'

'Dunno. Can't imagine he earns that much 'cos he works for the bloody railways.'

'More than you earn, though, eh?' said Alysha. 'You've only got your Saturday job.'

'Yeah, Kel,' piped up Angela, her tightly pulled-back dirty blonde hair gelled into a ball at the back of her head. She lit up a cigarette and looked at her mobile.

'You never know ... remember that bloke who took me up to Scotland last year? He was older and everything but it was great to have someone look after you, you know. They pay for everything. Put you up in hotels and drive you about and that. And they're never gonna be mouthy about what you do with them. Not like Craig and his lot.'

'He wants me to go up to Beverston station for one o'clock.'

'Bit of a way, isn't it?' said Alysha.

'Got nothing else to do, have I?' said Kelly. 'I'm going to text him now, actually, see if he's still around.'

The girls crowded round Kelly as she sent a minimal message through to Dave.

'I wish I could afford some decent gear. Can't go and see a bloke wearing Primark, can I?' she whined.

'I'm so sick of having no money,' said Alysha, throwing her long black hair across her shoulder. 'Still, it'll get better when we leave school next year. Imagine how good we would all look if we could afford the kind of stuff those fucking posh cows in Cheltenham prance about in.'

The girls all sat quietly for a second, minds drifting into reveries of designer elegance: buttery leather jackets by Valentino, pink Burberry for the new season and strappy Manolos. They saw pictures of all this and more every month in the magazines they pored over. But their reality was Primark and What She Wants and dreaming on.

'Yeah,' moaned Kelly, aware that most designers did not make clothes for a girl of her size. 'I might have lost a bit of weight by then.'

'Oh, shut up,' said Alysha. 'Don't you worry about it. You know all the blokes like you. It doesn't matter that you're bigger. Look at your tits compared to mine!'

It was true that Alysha was somewhat flat compared to Kelly. And it was true that men seemed to gravitate towards Kelly when they were out.

Then her mobile went off – she had a text message from Dave: 'Wear something sexy. C U @ 1.' All the girls squeaked with excitement at the intrigue.

'Oh, go on, Kel. You gotta go. Go on. He sounds nice. He was quite good-looking, wasn't he?'

Kelly already knew she was going to go. She didn't let on to her mates, but she had been reading a lot about sex and thought about it all the time. Alysha looked very grown-up but she was still quite immature about men, really. And when she'd tried to talk to Angela about what she did with the bloke she went to Scotland with, she'd told Kelly it was 'private'. Boring. The thing was, she couldn't stop thinking about the time at Cheekie's the other week when he'd seemed so grateful, so enthusiastic. And the feel of him, oh my God – he felt like a real man! He was so built and horny. Christ, that's what she'd been waiting for. Maybe she'd been a bit naughty to tell him she was 22, but he might have grassed her up if she'd said she was only 17 'cos Cheekie's had an over-21s licence. She wished she was 22; she might have a bit more money by then. And a proper sex life with a real man. She felt like she had really been able to let go with Dave. She hadn't had to worry that he'd blab around her mates. It was really different and exciting.

She remembered she had bought a low-cut top last week, and she could wear her shiny satin skirt with the split up the side. It was cheap, but he'd like that. Not exactly day wear, but it would do the trick for what Kelly was planning. And that was spending an afternoon being worshipped and having sex with a fit grown-up bloke!

* * *

Since he'd got the text from Kelly, Dave had been hard in his uniform at the promise of pounding into that sweet little hole again. At least, he hoped that's what would happen. She'd been quite pissed the last time, and now they were going to meet in the cold light of day, who could predict how things would turn out? Girls were particular about where and when they let you at the goods. Maybe he was wrong to have invited her to such a boring location, especially one where he worked. He kicked himself for that. He should have asked her out to a restaurant or something, but it was too late now. And she hadn't balked at his suggestion of her wearing sexy clothes. Maybe that was a bit cheeky. Maybe he'd been reading too much porn. Still, she hadn't complained.

He was like a cat on hot bricks for the next hour, and when one o'clock came he couldn't believe his luck as she presented herself at the station ticket office. The little tart had come through. There she was in a tight satin skirt stretched across her fleshy arse, bare legs with knee-high boots thrusting her figure into a lovely shape. A see-through flimsy top set everything else off to a tee. She flashed him a smile as she walked across the concourse and up to the ticket window. He could feel himself already getting hot in the uniform.

'I'd like a cheap day return to Cheltenham, please,' she said in an affected parody of an upper-class accent.

Dave laughed animatedly. 'All right, Kelly. Fancy getting a bite to eat?' he asked as casually as he could, inside punching the air in blokeish triumph as his colleagues threw him a look of curiosity tinged with confusion. He knew they would be too timid to ask questions, but they would all be nosy as hell later as to who she was. He caught a glimpse of old Wallace the station manager out of the corner of his eye. He could hear him thinking aloud: 'A niece or a friend's daughter, or who, exactly, Dave Ashton? And where are you going with her? And why can't I come along?'

''Cos you're a miserable fucking wanker, Wallace, that's why!' Dave, cheery as a dog with two dicks, pinched a grape from a bunch lying in a bowl on the counter and flicked it high into the air before catching it effortlessly in his mouth. Hey hey. Jack the lad at 45.

'OK, let's go down Billy's,' she replied, reverting back to her Gloucester brogue as Dave emerged and flung open the door of the ticket room. They walked out of the station hall and along the road to the small row of shops that served the local area with newspapers and good old British grease in the form of egg, bacon and chips.

'What you been doing today, then?' asked Dave. 'Been shopping?'

'Yeah,' she said. 'Been down the precinct with some friends.'

There was an awkward silence between them for a few moments until she stopped dead and turned to him.

'Look, Dave. You didn't ask me up here to go and eat a late lunch, did you?'

'No, love. To be honest I had something else on my mind.' Dave smiled, amused by her brazenness. 'I wasn't sure that you'd be up for anything else, though,' he said. 'A bloke can be too optimistic. I've been down that road before and been disappointed.'

Kelly opened her rucksack and showed Dave the cans of beer she'd pilfered from the bar in her mum and dad's living room.

'Good girl!' said Dave, reaching for a can.

'I like your uniform,' she cracked.

'And I like your skirt. Oi! Are you taking the piss out of me?' he asked, cracking open the beer. 'This is Great

Western Trains property, you know. Mind if I rub my hands all over your arse?'

Kelly giggled and coquettishly flicked her dead-straight long brown hair around herself.

'I'll take that as a yes, then,' said Dave and, encountering no resistance, cupped his hand under her curvy buttocks.

'Hey! Shouldn't we go somewhere private?' she hissed, a little scared at being felt up in the street in case anyone she knew was passing by, not least her mum.

'Only place I know isn't exactly a girl's dream date location.'

'Where's that, then? Round the back of the station?'

'Not quite that bad. It's up the tracks a little, halfway to Kemble. No one will be up there today, though. They only do engineering work on Sundays. There's a special hideaway up there where the track blokes keep their clobber.'

Kelly grabbed the can from his hand and took a swig of lager.

'So what are we waiting for?' she asked.

Cassie was running dangerously late. It was just conceivable that she would make it to Tetbury by two. It was now half-one. The wedding was at three and she knew she would have to change right there on the train rather than risk checking into the hotel and then putting on her outfit. For God's sake, she had to do her hair and make-up in the bloody train toilets, nasty limescale sink and smeary mirror and everything! To hell with Giles and his promise of a ride up; it just didn't bloody happen, did it? He'd let her down at the last minute. What a cock. And he knew that her car was in the garage. She just couldn't bear the disappointment.

Couldn't he see what he was missing? Why had he
chased after her all year when, now that they had the
chance to really show all the other lot how good they
could be together, he'd bloody lamed out? He'd been
giving off the right signals; she hadn't imagined it.
When they'd drunk champagne at Randall and Aubins
only two weeks ago, he'd ordered oysters and Cassie
had felt like he'd really wanted her. Giles was the right
one, and why wasn't he here? Everyone in Chelsea
would think it peculiar; they would think he had found
something out about her and had cancelled at the last
minute. She couldn't bear it! She hated Giles for doing
that. Still, she was going to be the best-dressed at the
wedding, Giles or no Giles, whatever that horrible bitch
Emma had spent on her outfit, Cassie had Prada and
lingerie to die for. The ensemble was ready in her
suitcase, beautiful, ready to slide over her perfectly
toned tanned frame. She wanted to give off the right
signals.

Heavenly, heavenly beauty – shimmering pampered
darling in the British Rail loos. She pulled out her
Guerlain Red Pastel travel compact and brushed her
cheeks with translucent stardust. It sat upon a smooth
coating of Ultima II Diamond Crème and Armani's Fluid
Sheer No 2. Lashes coated with Sculpte Cils Longeur
Extrème by Chanel gave an instant smoky eye above St
Laurent's Radiant Touch. With every coating she was a
cover girl supreme. And the Dior frosted pink lip-gloss
was *the* final touch for the reflection she wanted; the
one she'd been eager to bask in. Cassandra, lovely
beauty, you are the one that Giles will cry over; the one
the other girls will loathe because you are the most
beautiful. No one can touch you now.

But, she realised as she put the finishing touches to
her outfit, the train had not moved for about fifteen

minutes. What exactly was going on? She could hear the carriage doors banging, and some commotion. Flinging the door of the toilet open, magic lip-marker in hand, she stood poised and petulant, and listened to the nasal announcement. Signal failure five miles outside Kemble. Passengers would have to wait 30 minutes before they set off again. For fuck's sake! She fumed; she returned to her first-class seat; she called everyone she knew would be at the wedding. They all had their mobiles switched off. Cassandra sulked, but there was no audience this time to see how pretty she looked when she was angry. There was no Daddy to stroke his little girl's hair and make it better with a nice pressie from South Molton St. What was most infuriating was the realisation that she was going to have to do something under her own steam to rectify the situation. Maybe if she walked for a while up the track she could get somewhere to call a cab. For God's sake, it just wasn't good enough. Emma Hope heels in great lumps of gravel would not propel her along very fast. And she had loads to carry. Oh God, Giles would never forgive himself for letting her down. She would make sure of that.

Kelly and Dave made their way along the railway track, sipping beers, swapping anecdotes about good nights out and sharing local gossip. Kelly was getting bolder with every sip of beer she took, and she had taken to teasing Dave something rotten, enjoying the power of watching his discomfort. His arousal was so keen that Kelly could smell the male pheromones coming off him. She knew it was taking all the willpower in the world for him not to shove his hand into her knickers straight off and start feeling for the prize.

'You're a filthy sod, Dave Ashton, you know that,'

she said. There was no mistaking that both of them had met up for sex but still she passed the onus for their assignation onto him. Female prerogative.

'I've never had any complaints,' he said, knowing full well that Margaret had always complained whenever he'd got his cock out. There was always something wrong. He was too crude. It was too late. The flowers needed watering. She had a chicken in the oven. Anything to stop him having a good time. Still, that was all behind him now.

'I ain't complaining,' she said. 'In fact, I like it that you're so upfront about things. I can relax more than if I was with someone my own age. I kind of like it that you're taking liberties with me.'

'I can take worse liberties with you than I'm doing now, girl,' he said, making a grab for her breasts.

'I'm going to make you beg for it, then,' she said, moving herself away from him a metre or two. 'Where's that private shack you told me about?'

'It's just there,' he said, pointing to a rundown wooden hut about 50 metres up the track.

'Well, you follow me and I'll make it worth your while,' teased Kelly, sauntering off in front of Dave, her hips swaying slightly. She walked in an exaggerated fashion in front of him, then slowly lifted her skirt up over the twin mounds of her backside so she was showing all her arse flesh, bisected, Dave could just make out, by a thong. By this time Dave had a hard-on so fierce he was aching. He just wanted to get his cock into her warm juicy cunt and spurt a load out. Fuck, it was torture.

They reached the hut and Dave went to unlock it from a bunch of keys that he pulled from his bag. As he did so, one of the keys caught the edge of his copy of *Young and Horny* and it fell out of his bag and onto the track, spilling open at an unmistakably lewd spread. Wet pussies were peeping though tight young legs and girls of all sizes were ramming brightly coloured dildos into themselves with exaggerated expressions. That's torn it, thought Dave. Now she'll think I'm a real pervert. Kelly was onto the magazine faster than a dog at a rabbit, shrieking with laughter as she turned the pages. She had always wanted to get a good look at a magazine like this and was fascinated. Dave was relieved that she seemed entertained rather than offended. Yes, girls these days were certainly unshockable, it seemed.

'Ooh, look at this,' she teased. 'What you gonna tell me, it ain't yours?'

'S'right. It's old Wallace's, innit?'

'Who's he, then?'

'The miserable cunt back at the station who makes my life purgatory,' said Dave.

'Yeah, right. Of course it is,' she joked. 'I bet you're talking about the one who was leering at my tits.'

'That'll be him,' said Dave, laughing. 'And guess who's the lucky one and who's the loser.'

They both laughed as Dave unlocked the door to the storehouse and they entered, Kelly still glued to the porn mag with the enthusiasm of a teenage boy. The hut smelt of creosote and old metal – a totally masculine aroma of grandfathers' sheds and manly building things. Kelly found a table and went and sat on top of it, hitching her skirt up and leaning her legs on a chair so Dave could see right up her skirt as she continued to look at the magazine. He helped himself to another beer from her bag and started to rub himself through his uniform trousers at the sight of the living spectacle before him. Kelly was transfixed, unable to tear her eyes away from what she had found. She was entering a world of adult fun and she liked it. She liked the effect she was having on Dave and men in general. It didn't matter that she was bigger than the size fashion decreed was the limit of sexual attractiveness. It seemed irrelevant when she acted the slut. Contrary to all that was gossiped about in school, when a hot-blooded male was raring to go it didn't matter what size you were.

She leaned back on the table and, emboldened by the drink, began to display herself to the very aroused Dave, pulling the thong between her sex-lips, the juice darkening the material.

'You're driving me mad, girl, looking at that,' he said, his voice losing its light-hearted edge and sounding all of a sudden more serious. 'You know you can only tease a bloke so long before he snaps.'

'Before he goes off at the deep end,' she added, still playful and saucy. 'Here, Dave,' she began. 'Why don't you pump my sopping hole full of your spurting come?'

Dave spluttered his drink as he laughed through a mouthful of lager.

'You what!' he said.

Kelly was reading directly from the small-ads in the magazine, shrieking with mirth and giving full vent to her broad Gloucestershire accent as she said things like: 'Ram it up my dirty arse, spunky boy' and 'Double-D tit-wank with sex-starved housewife'.

She was actually crying with laughter, bent double on the dusty old table as Dave stood in the middle of the room with a huge boner, shaking his head and smiling broadly.

'What am I going to do with you, eh, girl?' he said. 'I can't shag while you're making me laugh so much.'

'Oh, go on,' she answered. 'Give us a go.' And then breathlessly, tears streaming down her face: 'Get your pumping man-meat out and stuff it up my twat!'

Slowly Dave unzipped his trousers and hooked his

cock out from its constricting home. It was a beauty and stopped Kelly in her tracks. Eight inches of thick gristly sex-bone pointed at her from inside the roll of his fist. Then he began working it, bringing the pleasure to bear in the time-honoured fashion that has been the way of male masturbation since time immemorial.

'Why don't you do yourself while you read that magazine,' he said. 'No funny stuff, though. Go on. Be serious for a minute so I can concentrate. I've always wanted to see a girl bring herself off to dirty pictures. I'd love to show you my video collection.'

Kelly laughed. 'You sound like a right old perve,' she said. 'Why do you need that when you can have the real thing?'

'You don't understand. Porn is a man's prerogative.'

Dave moved closer to the table as Kelly lay back on it, only for her to let forth another stream of obscenities.

'Fuck me, what's going on here?' she cried, looking out of the window. 'We've got a right one here, Dave. Have a look!'

'Oh, Christ, what now?'

'Look. Out the window. She saw me with my tits out and everything.'

'Who?'

Dave craned his neck and saw, coming down the tracks, a well-groomed young woman struggling with a load of designer shopping bags and looking extremely flustered heading for the hut. Suddenly she disappeared from view and Kelly and Dave looked at each other, both wondering where she had come from.

'Oh, for crying out loud, can't I have a few minutes?' he said, exasperated, as he shoved his clean shirt into his pants for the second time that day. It still reeked of fabric conditioner. He reminded himself not to use as much next time as he strode over to open the door and find out what was up. They were a bloody long way from Harrods. What on earth was she doing on the tracks?

Cassie was furious. Her feet were sore from walking along the gravel and her case and bags had cut into her hands. The wind that had been blowing along the corridor of the railway line had mussed her hair and she was now so late for the church that only an immediate cab could save the day. Curse Giles! And had she just seen some girl with her top off? The day was turning out to be decidedly odd. As she headed for the wooden hut, a railway official came out to meet her, zipping up his flies, no less!

'What's up, love?' he asked. It was obvious to Cassie what had been going on. Her eyes flew to his groin, where a bulge was evident in his uniform pants. He noticed her looking at him, and gave her a cheeky wink.

Cassie was curious to see what kind of woman would allow herself to be mauled during the afternoon by such an oaf and, without further ado, she barged into the hut, complaining of her awful ordeal. She strode into the middle of the room, her heels clacking loudly across the floorboards, her designer apparel immediately catching the attention of Kelly.

'I need a cab. Now,' she spat. 'I don't have a local number but I presume one of you will.'

She raised her head haughtily and waited for Dave to jump to her assistance, but he simply strolled in behind her and ran his hands through his hair and rubbed the back of his neck.

'Sorry, love. I can't say I have.'

Kelly sat on the corner of the table, nonchalantly swinging one leg and regarding Cassie with the air of insolence that is afforded to adolescence. She shrugged her shoulders.

Their indifference was infuriating. The train failure was probably the fault of this lunkhead, whiling away the time with his sluttish friend when he should be checking the trains were running on time.

'Do you know what is going on up there?' she continued with unconcealed venom, pointing in a vaguely easterly direction. 'Do you realise that one of your bloody trains is stuck for half an hour on the tracks while someone sorts out signal failure or something. I have a wedding to go to!'

'Ooh, that's nice,' Kelly said cheekily. 'Got a nice day for it.'

'Happens all the time,' said Dave.

'What? Signal failure?'

'No. Weddings. Isn't worth it, love. Stay single and have more fun. That's my advice.'

It was then that Cassie spotted the porn mag lying open on the table. She darted her eyes away from it, but, without meaning to, her gaze once more flew to Dave's crotch and she realised he was still hard. This railway oaf hadn't even lost his erection, even though she had been shouting at him. It was becoming more difficult for Cassie to concentrate on complaining. She'd always had a thing about men in suits with big hard-ons; that's what she'd noticed about Giles the first time they'd dated. Shame he'd never put it to good use. Now here was one in a uniform with a hard-on, which was even better. And, actually, he was rather attractive in a rough sort of way. Suddenly, the atmosphere in the room began to change. Cassie was becoming aroused despite herself, and this softened her anger. She tried another approach.

'Look, I'm not bothered by what you people are

doing. Really, I don't care. I just need to get to this wedding and I need a cab. I don't have any local numbers. Please –' Cassie looked at Kelly, '– you must have a number logged in your mobile or something?'

'Oh, I guess I might.' Kelly sighed, and searched through her directory. 'Where do you want to go?' she asked.

'Tetbury. The main church.'

Kelly gave the cab office directions to the street that ran beside the railway hut and asked them to stop by the slip road.

'Twenty minutes,' said Kelly, hanging up, swinging her legs and looking at Cassie with a wicked gleam in her eye. 'What are you going to do till then?'

Cassie sensed that if she stayed where she was then something very unusual was going to happen with this couple. But her alternative was to continue walking along the tracks in her Emma Hope shoes. There was no conest.

'Is it OK if I wait here?' she asked.

Maybe it was the drink; maybe it was an insouciant disregard for privileged young women with more money than sense, but at that moment both Dave and Kelly were seized with a sudden wickedness to involve this spoilt young creature into their games. They were both still incredibly horny.

'Here, love,' Kelly said suddenly, sliding herself off the table and holding open the magazine at a page featuring some oiled guy with a huge cock. 'This'll pass a few minutes. I bet you've never seen one as big as that? Mind you, Dave's is not far off!' She laughed, becoming bolder. 'I bet you don't have a copy of this under your bed, do you?'

To their surprise, the immaculately presented stranger calmly placed her bags in the corner and quipped: 'In answer to your first question, no, I haven't seen one as big as that. Not in real life anyway. And no, I'm not in the habit of buying porn mags. I don't read that sort of thing.'

Kelly looked at Dave and cooed, 'Ooooh, get her!' She walked over to him, her skirt riding high up her legs, and began rubbing his crotch, brazenly looking Cassie in the eye.

'What's the matter, girlie? Magazine not real enough for you? Like it a little bit more down to earth than your posh boyfriends give you?'

Cassie didn't know what to say. It was true. Giles was such a prig. She always expected him to be more fun than he actually was. She often went home unsatisfied. Maybe she could have some fun here, with this couple. They were both quite attractive, after all.

'So...' she began tentatively. 'Were you two about to have sex?'

Dave was having a great time. It was as if he had been waiting for this moment all his adult life: two horny young women about to fight over his cock and a couple of cold beers with his name on it afterwards. Result. Well, there was no holding back now. Might as well finish what he started. He slowly unzipped himself, looking from Kelly to Cassie and back again to check that this was really happening. Kelly had snuck her hand into his shirt and was rubbing his chest. As soon as Dave pulled his pride and joy from his uniform, Cassie sunk to her knees hungry to get her lips around it. Then, bliss, as his entire length was eased into the warm and moist cavern of the stranger's mouth.

'Are you getting wet down there?' Dave asked her.

He need not have worried as Kelly interrupted, 'She's got her mouth full at the moment, Dave. Shall I check for you?'

No one spoke as Kelly squatted down and slipped a hand under the woman's dress and went for her clit. Dave was already worried that this scene would test his endurance; that he'd lose it too soon. The unexpected lesbian action was almost too much.

'She's slippery as an eel, Dave. I think she wants a right seeing-to.'

Kelly then grabbed Cassie and pulled her to her feet, handling her as if she was their prisoner. She didn't seem to mind. Dave watched as she responded to the rather rough treatment with a look of rapture. Then she whispered to them: 'I really like it. You can do what you want to me, actually. But I want him to fuck me.'

'Oh, you do, do you? Well, if you're going to get what *I* came here for, then I'm going to have some fun as well. Kelly sprung into action and grasped Cassie from behind in a half-nelson, dragging her back to the table.

'I'll hold her while you do her, Dave', she said, taking the opportunity to rub her hands all over the girl's tits.

Dave's cock was aching by this point and fit to burst. As Kelly pulled the woman's dress up from behind, she exposed a set of panties so flimsy and soaked they could have won first prize at an obscenity contest. Kelly slid a finger into what served for a gusset and tugged downwards.

'She's gagging for it, this one,' Kelly said. 'I've heard about you posh birds; orgies and whatever in those big country houses.'

'Oh, I wish,' said Cassie. 'More like boring dinner parties.'

'Hold her, Kelly,' said Dave, preparing himself for the thrill of a lifetime. Then he was in and fucking her. She was tight and moist and panting. He loved doing it like this, still fully clothed and ready to run anytime. Twenty years of Margaret and quiet naked oozing under the duvet was a death sentence compared to this. Oh, God, this was so good. He felt like a king. And as he was inside her, this little piece was rubbing her clit as Kelly was mauling her tits and running her hands all over the girl's body.

'Oh, you girls. I'm going to shoot my load in a second,' cried Dave as he forced himself into her cunt.

'Over my face, please,' said Cassie as she pulled away from him and sank to the floor once more, looking up in awe at the magnificent sight of his penis about to spurt.

Then Dave had his cock in his hand and was pumping it with Cassie underneath.

'I'm gonna shoot all over your face,' he said, his neck and throat tightening as could feel his spunk rising in his balls. 'I can't resist a woman who asks nicely.'

In a couple of seconds it was white lightening fever as he ejaculated all over her face and Kelly was working her hand faster and faster until she, too, cried her orgasm into the air.

Dave and Kelly hurried back along the tracks, giggling with each other. He was twenty minutes over his lunch hour and he knew he would get a bollocking from old Wallace. Still, no man could have turned down the opportunity for that little sojourn. The cab had arrived and taken Cassie to her wedding, albeit after they'd scrambled up the grass verge to the road, Cassie looking decidedly ungroomed after her session in the hut, and having the gall to complain about getting her shoes muddy.

'I never knew you had those kinds of tendencies,' he said to Kelly, referring to her lesbian antics.

'Well, it seemed like the right thing to do at the time,' she replied. 'And anyway. I'm not complaining.

We're going out to Cheekie's tonight, and I'm going to be showing off my new designer gear; showing my mates what my fancy older man has bought me.'

Dave looked worried for a second. 'What do you mean, "what I've bought you?"' he asked.

Kelly said nothing, but pulled from her rucksack a Burberry handbag and Hermès scarf. Dave looked astonished.

'Well ... she can afford it,' Kelly said. 'Helped myself while she was helping herself, so to speak.'

'You light-fingered little tyke!' exclaimed Dave as they ran laughing down the tracks on their way back to the station. When they got there, sure enough, Wallace was waiting with a face like a bulldog chewing as wasp, checking his watch.

They made a point of having a snog right in front of him before they parted.

'See you later then,' Kelly cried out to Dave, as she sashayed off down the road. 'Nine o'clock outside Cheekie's. And remember ... you owe me one!'

Yep, life had certainly taken a turn for the better, thought Dave, as he whistled his way back into the station, winking at Wallace on his way.

Smooth Hands, Soft Lips, Sharp Teeth
Francesca Brouillard

I lean over the balcony into a night fragrant with honeysuckle and breathe in the sweet air, trying to drown the feeling of nausea. I shouldn't have drunk so much. It was a mistake. Like coming here, to Lucy's wedding, to France at all. It was a mistake. I don't know anyone, don't speak the language, don't even have much in common with Lucy any more. It was ridiculous to have imagined that the wine would make my French more fluent; I've barely understood a word all evening.

The splintery wood of the balustrade scratches my hips through my new dress. I should be more careful with it but I really can't be bothered. Behind me, exotic voices rich with drink and high spirits drift onto the balcony as a door is opened.

The sounds of partying fade abruptly as that same door is closed. Footsteps come slowly in my direction, then stop. A lighter is snapped and a waft of rich woody tobacco drifts across the balcony, mingling with the heady perfume from the garden below. Giant trees absorb the moonlight, leaving a darkness that clings warmly to my skin. I feel hidden by the night.

After a few minutes the silence, disturbed only by the chirping of cicadas, is broken by a foot grinding out a cigarette. More footsteps. Instead of going back, though, they come in my direction and stop behind me.

I am aware of a presence so close I can almost feel breath in my hair. I don't look round. The last thing I want is someone trying to strike up a conversation.

Suddenly two hands touch me lightly on the hips and a mouth begins nuzzling the back of my neck, brushing me with soft damp lips. I freeze.

Surely it's a mistake; someone must have made a rendezvous and taken me for their waiting lover. What should I do?

The caresses on my neck turn to kisses, trace the line of my vertebrae to the V where my shoulder-blades disappear into my dress. I shiver as the sensation sends goose-pimples down my back and turns my nipples to hard buds. Now the tongue runs swiftly up the side of my neck to my ear. I close my eyes and breathe out slowly. It seems too late to point out the mistake now; I should have done something the moment he laid hands on me. Besides, I have no idea what I'd say.

The hands encircle my waist, trace the gentle slopes of my belly, then slide up my ribs to the sensitive hollows of my armpits, where they slip under the straps of my dress and, presumptuously, into my bra. For a moment the stranger's palms cup me in their warmth, supporting the weight of my breasts. Then they begin massaging. Unfamiliar fingers seek out my nipples and press them firmly into my flesh in an odd yet strangely erotic gesture. I close my eyes and lean back.

The pressure inverting my nipples is soon released and the teasing fingers coax the soft sunken cones back to hardness. I blush, embarrassed by my nipples responding so eagerly; embarrassed by my body's response to a stranger's touch. Still I say nothing. And I somehow know that he won't, either.

Skilful hands carefully extricate my breasts from my bra. There's no attempt to unfasten it or slip the straps from my shoulders. They are prised from their lacy cups

SMOOTH HANDS, SOFT LIPS, SHARP TEETH **277**

and rested on the taut under-wired fabric. The bra digs in, pushing my breasts together and thrusting them up like an offering. It feels slightly uncomfortable, yet exciting, as if they are being made more accessible, more pert to his touch. He knows what he likes.

As the anonymous hands and mouth begin to map the intimate parts of my body, I can no longer maintain the illusion of mistaken identity. No one as attentive as this would mistake another woman's body for his lover's – even after too much to drink. He has the intuitive and confident touch of a man who knows instantly what a woman desires and how to arouse her passions.

Pulling me back so I am leaning against him, he raises my skirt and begins stroking my thighs, moving his hands gradually upwards until they slip under the thin lace of my knickers. Then his fingers slide into the dark slick of my cunt and prise my secret lips apart.

Wet with anticipation and brazen in my anonymity, I press against his hand, desperate to rub the hard nub of my clit against him. He slips a finger into my opening but barely enters me. I wriggle, hungry to feel him deep inside me but he makes no attempt to push further. A second finger slides in and my sex contracts, trying to suck them deeper, but instead they curl behind my pubic bone.

Biting my lip, I strain against him, trying to make those tantalising hands reach up and fill me, yet he refuses to give me more than his dabbling fingertips. Is he merely squeamish or is he sadistic?

Suddenly the gentle probing behind my pubic bone triggers an electric surge. A zinging current shoots from the nerve endings in my clitoris right up to my nipples, which seem to spark with static. My cunt explodes in a rush of hot lava that threatens to melt my thighs and dissolve me altogether. I shudder convulsively and, if it weren't for his arm round my waist, would collapse to the floor.

Any awareness of the fingers inside me, or the stranger himself, are lost in the sheer force of my orgasm. For those few climactic moments I am oblivious to anything beyond the sensations which consume my body, but as I return bit by bit to reality I am overcome with embarrassment. I feel vulnerable and exposed in this unbalanced encounter. There has been no give and take; no mutual loss of control. I haven't even seen the face of my anonymous 'lover'.

I try to turn my head but he stops me, pushing me gently forwards till I am again leaning against the balcony. After kissing the top of my head, he moves away and I feel the sultry night air caress my back.

A lighter flicks as he walks off and the faint scent of his cherrywood tobacco reaches my nostrils. I don't look round.

The following morning, when I go down to breakfast, Mme Fleuret, who runs the small family hotel in which I am staying, hands me an envelope.

'Mademoiselle, this has come for you,' she says. The writing is bold and confident – most definitely not Lucy's – and I can feel a small packet inside. I go up to my room to open it.

A short, curious note invites me to dinner at the Chat D'Or restaurant at 8.30 this evening and requests that I wear the same dress as last night. It is signed in a flamboyant scrawl that is, I suspect, deliberately illegible. My anonymous lover obviously liked what he felt.

I don't think I can face it – dining with this man who has had such intimate knowledge of my body. It would be excruciatingly embarrassing, especially if, in the cold light of sobriety, we found a lack of attraction for each other. Besides, what impression must he have of me, so drunk that I just opened my legs and let him do what he did? It's not the sort of profile one would want to set out with for an evening in a high-class restaurant.

I tear open the enclosed packet, expecting some *petit cadeau*. Disappointed, I find only a disposable razor. I wonder briefly if he'd found my armpits too stubbly but, since I'd depilated them before the party, it seems unlikely. A quick inventory of body parts brings me to only one conclusion, and it is one I find shocking. He wants me to shave downstairs.

I slump on the bed, appalled that this complete stranger should have the cheek to try and get me to shave myself to go out to dinner with him. What does he think I am? Some cheap tart who gets off on doing it with strangers? He's obviously a pervert.

Suddenly I'm furious with myself, and feel not just indignation but shame at how I behaved last night. Whether it was due to drink or my body's craving I don't know, but the fact remains: I never made a single move to resist this man's advances, yet now I'm getting all uppity when he wants to take things further. I'm confused. It's eight months since I last had sex and I've not had a dinner date for even longer. I'd be stupid to turn this invitation down. Especially to Le Chat d'Or. And, after all, I fly home tomorrow, so any embarrassing incidents can be left behind.

As for the razor – well, he can just go and jump if he thinks I'm going to do that for him!

I squat awkwardly in the shower, squinting into the propped-up mirror and reflecting on my total mental U-turn since this morning. Dipping the razor in the basin of warm water once more, I shave the remaining hair from my mound.

It's not for him, I assure myself. It's just curiosity to see what I look like. I put down the razor and wash off the suds. The inside bits of my cunt peep pinkly through the shorn lips, and the crinkly folds, normally hidden by the nest of hair, are now quite visible. I'm shocked by how much is revealed and how unfamiliar my cunt now looks, yet find there is something decidedly erotic about this flaunted nakedness.

My newly discovered confidence carries me majestically to the doors of the restaurant then deserts me. It is only the arrival of a group of diners holding the door expectantly open that cuts off my escape.

An immaculate waiter greets me and seems to know immediately where to seat me when I give my name. The small table is set for two with a spotless white cloth and heavy old cutlery. The restaurant manages, in a way seldom achieved in England, to combine spaciousness and intimacy. The tables are carefully positioned in cosy alcoves and booths, while the clever use of mirrors creates a feeling of space.

Once he has helped me to my seat, the waiter bows slightly and leaves, only to return almost instantly with a bottle of Sauternes. With great deference he pours me a drop to sample then fills the glass when I nod my approval, placing the bottle in a cooler beside me.

Then, in very slow English, as if reciting parrot-fashion, he informs me that Monsieur is terribly sorry but will not be able to join me. Monsieur has taken the liberty however of ordering for me, and hopes I will stay to enjoy the most excellent food. I feel a rush of relief followed by a twinge of disappointment. Maybe I should just leave. As I waver the waiter reappears, bearing a platter of artichokes in a sea of golden butter. My mouth waters. Pointless to go before eating, I decide, watching him slide the succulent globes onto my plate.

The wine soon dulls the awkwardness I feel at dining alone, and by the time the waiter returns to remove the remains of the main course I am quite mellow. He passes me an envelope addressed in a familiar hand, then retires. I open it, expecting to find a note of apology, and am instead shocked by the content. It requests that I take advantage of the interval before dessert to visit the ladies' room and remove my panties.

The audacity of the request is immediately overshadowed by the realisation that my absent dinner companion must in fact be present and observing me. Why else the bizarre instruction, if not for his entertainment? I look around quickly, trying to spot a lone man or someone who appears to be watching, but the other diners, all families or couples, seem either too wholesome or too engrossed in their food or conversation to be aware of me.

The back of my neck begins to prickle; it is uncomfortable to feel you are being watched. A tremor runs down my body, leaving a rash of goose bumps on my arms and pursing my nipples. I swig back a large mouthful of wine and top my glass up from the near-empty bottle. Does this stranger think I'm going to go along with all his kinky requests? Maybe I should get up and walk out. I cradle the glass in my hands and lean back in an attempt to look composed. After all, the choice is entirely my own. I don't have to obey anyone's instructions. The thing is, a part of me, fuelled by the wine no doubt, is egged on. I've gone along with everything else he's done or suggested so far, so why stop now?

In the toilet cubicle I stuff my knickers into my handbag then have a sudden panic that they will drop out when I open it to get my purse or keys. I take them out again. What else can I do with them?

The washroom door opens and someone comes in.

Maybe I should just put them back on and return to the table. It's unlikely the stranger – wherever he is – will be able to tell. Hurry ... people will wonder what I'm doing in here. I spot the paper sanitary bags hanging on the back of the door and, in a burst of inspiration, drop my knickers into one and chuck it in the disposal unit.

There's no changing my mind now.

When I come out of the ladies' room I notice a 'no entry' sign on the door I came through from the restaurant and an arrow pointing towards another door. It seems odd but I assume it is to avoid congestion. As I open the exit door and step through, the lights suddenly go out and I am grabbed from behind. One arm snatches me round the waist and another crushes my chest. A large hand closes over my mouth to stem my scream.

Shock and terror leave me unable to breathe and my heart begins to pound against my ribs as I hyperventilate. I feel myself pulled backwards, presumably so my assailant can lean against the door, then his breath comes hot on my ear as he shushes me. For some unaccountable reason this reassures me, somehow, and I begin to wonder whether I'm being rescued from something rather than abducted.

The man's hold on me is neither rough nor threatening, and peculiarly, has the sensation more of an embrace than a constraint. My initial fear and panic ebb a little and, as I relax, the hand is removed from my mouth and laid instead across my shoulders. I become aware of other people in the room. Then soft footsteps and a whiff of cologne indicate a presence approaching me. I stiffen. A hand touches my chest, feels for the strap of my dress, and carefully slips it off my shoulder. My captor shifts his grip slightly and I feel my breast shudder as the strap drops, releasing it. Then two hands begin to squeeze and caressing it.

I breathe in sharply, about to shout for help, then feel the warmth of a mouth on my nipple. I hesitate; my brain tells me I should be alarmed at the situation, but the peculiar events of the past two days have disrupted my sense of reality. As I feel my nipple being teased to a hard cone of arousal, I submit.

There is something about being constrained that heightens pleasure. There is no point struggling or fighting my captors. I can only give myself up to whatever they choose to do to me and I find this helplessness arousing.

Another body approaches me and rough hands touch me on the arm then move impatiently up to my shoulder. They follow the dress down to my other breast and seek the hard pebble of my nipple. These hands, more urgent than the others, do not bother removing my strap. Instead they tug the dress to one side and pull my breast free. There is no gentle squeezing this time but the sharp unexpected shock of teeth biting my nipple. I yelp and my body recoils, but the teeth continue to grip and a tongue begins to flick.

The arms around my waist and shoulders tighten their grip but the sadistic treatment of my nipple is not something I wish to pull away from. I force my body to relax and let the sensation transcend pain into that sweet pleasure that can only be reached by crossing a certain threshold.

I swap my focus between the gentle sucking of one breast and the savage biting of the other – between the sensual and the sexual. The warm arousal in my belly from the one complements that darker pleasure from the other that causes my cunt to flash-flood.

I gasp and feel my pelvis tilt back in response. This

brings a stifled moan from my captor, whose erection I now detect in the small of my back. The arm around my waist loosens its grip and moves across to my belly. He starts tugging at my dress till he can grasp the hem and tuck it up, baring my thighs and hips. His hand now slips down between my legs, squeezes the plump folds of my sex and slides into my slit. A finger, slick with my wetness, begins circling my clitoris.

The rough-handed man has begun sucking my nipple through the sharp space between his teeth, and the exquisite spasms of pain have a new raw edge that makes me contract inside. My captor pushes all his fingers into my wetness, and although he can't reach my opening from this angle, I can tell he is desperate to.

Deep in my chest I feel the groaning start. My hips are now thrusting in time to the sucking and biting on my nipples. As my breathing becomes faster my captor removes his hand from my denuded sex and pushes it between us, down into the crevice between my buttocks. I tense, tightening the muscle ring of my anus as a finger probes the opening. Sensing resistance, the finger buries itself deeper in my crack till it can slide, unobstructed, into the hungry heat of my vagina. As I strain to feel it deep inside, my orgasm begins to erupt.

I bite my lip to control the rising moan, but realise it will not be contained. My captor clamps his free hand firmly over my mouth and shoves hard into me with the other. I feel shock and release as his fingers simultaneously enter deep into my vagina and rectum. The scream that curdles in my throat, a cocktail of pain and pleasure, is caught in my captor's hand and echoed by a suffocated grunt as he climaxes against me.

As I come to my senses I realise that the other men have moved away and I am slumped back against my captor. He gently pushes me upright, releases my skirt and smooths it down over my thighs, his hands lingering momentarily over my hips and belly. He then pulls up the strap of my dress and, with great delicacy, eases my breasts back inside. I wince as his hand brushes the chewed nipple and notice that he takes extra care when arranging my dress on that side.

He opens the door and ushers me out.

I am once again outside the ladies' room. Going in, I lock myself in a cubicle and take stock of my state, dabbing the stickiness from my thighs and peeping at my breasts. One has a lovebite haloing the nipple and the other still bears the deep imprint of teeth.

Walking back to my table I am conscious of my dishevelled appearance but don't care. My nipples remain rudely erect from the chafing of my dress. They would normally make me fold my arms in embarrassment, but right now I feel like flaunting my sexuality. As the dress swishes electrically across my nude mound with each step it sends a delicious tingling up my cunt, and I wonder how many years of pleasure I've wasted covered by panties and pubic hair.

While eating my dessert I wonder if the incident in the dark room was what my anonymous lover had planned for me; it would explain the note instructing me to remove my panties – a simple ruse to lure me to the ladies. But why the shaving? And which one was my anonymous lover? The one who had bitten my nipple to such exquisite pain was too rough and the other, who had caressed my breast so tenderly, too safe.

I want it to be my captor – the one who restrained me in an embrace that kept me helpless while the others toyed with me; the one who dabbled indulgently in my juices then pierced me doubly with his fingers;

the one who orgasmed with me then, with such care, adjusted my clothing.

Needless to say I'm unlikely to find out now. The meal is almost finished and I'm flying home in the morning. He must remain anonymous, merely a sensual memory that will end up feeling like a dream.

At the end of the meal the waiter informs me that a taxi is waiting for me. I'm surprised and, in truth, relieved not to have to walk back to the hotel.

The waiter escorts me out and opens the rear door of the large old-fashioned car that is parked outside. It has tinted windows and a glass grille separating the passenger from the driver. The interior light isn't working but, as I step in, I detect the reassuring, masculine smell of leather seats. I sink back luxuriously into the deep upholstery and stretch my legs out into the vast space in front. We pull away and I let my imagination play back the events of the evening.

When we hit an occasional pothole my breasts jiggle, loose inside my dress, and the pain, like an electrical wire connecting nipple to cunt, triggers a contraction deep inside me.

We're soon back at the hotel but, instead of pulling up at the front, the taxi goes round the back of the building and parks in the dark car park. The driver gets out and opens my door. As I try to clamber out of the sunken embrace of the seat, I find him gently pushing me back. He gets in and closes the door, filling the car with the sweet cherrywood smell of tobacco I remember from the balcony, which seems like a long time ago.

His lips find my mouth and he begins kissing me. I let him fill me with his taste of tobacco and desire. His kisses follow the curve of my throat to the hollow of my collarbone, then down to the rise of my breast – light, damp and exciting.

Pausing, he slips the straps off my shoulders and pushes my dress down. I wince as he brushes my raw nipple and put my hand on his head to push him away. He removes it gently while circling my nipple delicately with his tongue. I wonder if the teeth marks are still there, and if he can feel them. He licks my other nipple, then trails his lips down the shallow valley of my cleavage.

There is no awkward undressing; he raises my hips and slides the dress deftly over my thighs and off. His kisses then proceed swiftly to the hard angles of my hip bones, where he runs his tongue down the dip of my pelvis and explores the crease between my swollen lips and my thighs. I can feel the roughness of his stubbled cheek grazing my mound, and sense his arousal at the naked flesh.

One of his hands slides under my thigh and starts fingering my slit. With unexpected abruptness he thrusts his fingers inside me, squelching in the juices that betray my desire and, on withdrawing his fingers, proceeds to rub the wetness into the bald folds of my labia. I feel the skin tighten as it dries, then the heat of his tongue as he begins to lick my juices off.

He pushes my knees apart so he can get his head right between my thighs and press his tongue up into my cunt. My body shudders; he wedges his arm between my legs, forcing them apart so I am completely opened up to him. His teeth tease my clitoris, hard as a pebble, till I begin to moan, then he laps at my cunt again with his tongue.

Moments later I feel something hard and cold push against my opening. I clench in response, unable to work out what it is. His fingers massage the wetness of my slit till I relax, then he forces the tip of the unyielding object into me. I wriggle, perturbed at its size. It is stretching me wide, too wide for comfort and I am alarmed, fearing it will split me. I try to push him away but am powerless against his bulk and the subtle lapping of his tongue on my clitoris. Eventually his persistent fingers gently work the object inside me, the slickness of my traitorous juices assisting him.

It feels huge. Soft fingers begin stroking my clitoris in light circles, making my cunt contract so that, despite myself, the strange rod is drawn even more deeply inside me. Once it is inserted, my lover carefully folds my knees together and lays me on my side. I am trembling.

His fingers touch my lips and push into my mouth, making me taste the coppery saltiness of my own juices. He slips them out and I feel the silky tip of his cock pressing against my mouth. I part my lips and let him push it in till it rubs against the back of my throat, flooding my mouth with saliva. His cock is short but thick and fills my mouth satisfyingly without threatening to make me gag. He gasps as I run my tongue along the shaft and tease him with my teeth.

Deep inside I can feel my muscles squeezing the monstrous object; my lover rocks it to and fro in a way that seems to stimulate every nerve between my knees and navel and draws jagged gasps from me. My mouth matches the contractions and his cock swells, forcing my jaw wide. I am being stretched to splitting at both ends yet my nerve endings are begging for more. I push my head hard into his groin and arch my back, embracing the solid rod inside me and relishing the sensation of being so totally invaded. I feel like I want him to push so deeply into me that his cock and the rod meet inside me.

My lover's breathing becomes faster as he thrusts against me and twists the object inside me. I explode suddenly, convulsing in waves that bang my head against his belly and send his juices flooding down my throat.

Finally the rod, twitching between my thighs, destroys my last vestiges of control. My climax spasms over and over as if the muscles were trying to crush the rod inside me.

With a sound that is more animal than human, my orgasm subsides and I slump, exhausted, with his cock still in my mouth.

He helps me dress then holds the car door for me. We stand for a few moments in the soft darkness of the car park, not touching, unsure what to say. In the end I break the silence.

'I'm flying back in the morning.' It seems an inadequate note on which to finish such an intimate encounter.

'*D'accord. C'est au revoir maintenant.*' His husky brown voice sends a surge of regret through me.

He takes my fingers in his hand and raises them to his lips in a quaintly old-fashioned gesture but, instead of kissing them, he places the first two fingers in his mouth and rolls his tongue around them. It is so intensely sexual it makes my belly clench again in desire.

He sucks them one by one then draws them slowly from his mouth and kisses the tips chastely before lowering my hand and taking a step back. I take this to be a signal that the evening is at an end. I turn and walk back through the car park to the front of the hotel. He remains standing, just as I left him, and I can tell he is watching me till I round the corner out of sight.

Tears press at the back of my eyes but I refuse to submit till I reach the privacy of my room, where I weep myself to sleep. My outpouring of emotion is not one of regret. These are the tears of release; of knowing something so intense, and so rare.

A week after I got home a parcel arrived – a heavy cardboard tube with a French postmark. A frisson went through me as I recognised the handwriting. My brother was staying at the time and, playfully bullying as he is, insisted I open it there and then.

It contained a beautifully carved wooden totem pole about a foot long. It was slightly bent, presumably warped, and exquisitely worked. Closer examination revealed the carvings to depict a series of imaginative sexual acts and it was only while studying these weird and gymnastic couplings that a most embarrassing thought occurred to me.

'Let me see,' Mark said, and snatched it from me. He laughed. 'Wow, it's wonderful! Look at the work that's gone into that ... the detail ... the craftsmanship.' He looked up at me. 'Someone must think a lot of you – this must be worth a small fortune!'

I couldn't think what to say.

'You know what it is, don't you?'

I didn't dare voice my suspicions but Mark went on regardless.

'It's an antique dildo – that's why it's got this curve in it. It's from the Far East, I should imagine. Who sent you this?'

'Erm . . .' I could feel myself blushing furiously. If my brother suspected where that wooden rod he was stroking so sensuously had been! He tested its weight appreciatively in his hand. 'It's a formidable size. Awesome, in fact.'

I got up sharply from the table and started gathering the torn packaging up to hide my discomfort. As I went to drop it in the bin I noticed a label. It was the sender's name and address.

The Watcher Bontine Taylor

Clare was not expecting anything out of the ordinary to happen that morning. The faculty building was almost deserted so early in the day; students usually put in an appearance just before lunch, unless forced to attend, and only Pat, the cleaner, was about, vigorously twisting a mop in her steel bucket. Clare passed and nodded to her before letting herself in to the humanities department.

'He's in already,' was Pat's enigmatic comment as the cleaner raised her eyebrows. Clare guessed she was referring to her new colleague, Andy.

'He starts early. Is that a problem?' she asked.

Pat shrugged. Clare deduced that Pat didn't care much for her colleague, although she was at a loss to fathom why. Peeking through the door, Clare could see that Andy was already seated at his computer. He turned around when he heard her come in and Clare immediately noticed that his gaze was rather lascivious, taking in her body from top to toe. It was a bold look that missed nothing and appraised everything. 'Bedroom eyes', her mother would have said.

Andy was a newcomer in the department, and Clare was his senior, yet he appeared unaware of status or rank. His bold hazel eyes continued to study her. Maybe Pat was right to be wary of him. Clare felt slightly intimidated by his interest, but something about it also made her feel excited. For a brief moment, she felt confused.

'Good morning. You're in early,' she said, breaking his gaze.

He smiled at her. 'I always feel more able to concentrate early in the day.' He stretched, letting her see his sinewy shoulders through his thin shirt. Clare busied herself, collected her lecture notes and went off to the library to do some further reading before class began. She was relieved to have an excuse not to stay in the room with him; he definitely had some agenda.

Returning at lunchtime to check her emails, she sat down, trying not to look at Andy, who was still there, and logged on. She had high-priority messages in her in-box. Andy stood up and yawned, facing her, his crotch at the same level as her eyes. She realised this was deliberate and found herself gazing, mesmerised, at the bulge in his trousers while willing herself to turn away. The guy definitely had a hard-on. His face, with its knowing half-smile, turned slightly away from her.

'Time for some lunch,' he said casually. 'See you later.'

Clare murmured something appropriate as she watched him depart. He thinks I fancy him, she thought, irritated. The cheek of it! How can he be so bold as to parade himself like that in front of another member of staff? She tried to push his antics out of her mind, but the thought of his bulging crotch stayed with her throughout the rest of the day and even as she went home in the evening. The image of Andy appraising her body kept flashing into her mind in a most unnerving fashion. Maybe she had been mistaken. Or maybe it was a one-off incident. Time would tell.

The next day Pat was waiting for Clare in the lobby when she arrived for work. Her hoarse whisper made Clare move closer to her.

'He's in. Queer chap, if you ask me. Just say if you

want me to come in at any time. I could always find something to do. Gives me the creeps, he does. You be careful, love.' Clare's response was to smile reassuringly. She knew Pat would have liked to gossip about Andy, but it didn't seem appropriate. After all, he hadn't actually done anything; at least not yet. And Pat was a bit of a gossip.

'It's good to know you're looking out for me, Pat,' she said, 'but I'll be OK. Thanks, though.'

The corridor outside Clare's office was empty and she approached her room with a little more care than before. She didn't really know anything about Andy and since the previous day she was now a little apprehensive of him.

The door to the office was just ajar. Clare paused to look before she pushed it open. Andy had his back to her. He was sitting at his computer terminal and his right elbow was juddering with movement, close to his body. What was he doing? Her amazement grew. There was no doubt about it; he was definitely playing with himself. Unable to turn away, mesmerised, she watched him wank himself. The picture on the screen was too far away for her to see clearly, but it appeared to be two figures closely entwined. It was definitely Internet porn.

Before she knew how to react, Clare was becoming aroused, and that was uncomfortable. Suddenly she cleared her throat. Without looking round, and as if he had all the time in the world, Andy zipped himself up and placed his hands on the keyboard, disconnecting from the website. Should she stay or leave? This was her office, Clare told herself, and he was the one who should leave if anyone did. She decided to act as though she hadn't seen a thing. Bright and breezy would do it, she thought.

'Morning,' she sang, hanging her coat on the door

hook. Andy looked at her, saying nothing. There was no guilt in his gaze, only an unspoken question. He was smiling.

Then Clare considered the notion that he had wanted her to see him. They both knew the rules: any member of staff found to be downloading porn or behaving with sexual impropriety could be dismissed. It had happened before, and the university board would stand no nonsense in that respect. Yet he was willing to take that risk.

Andy excused himself and went to the loo, where, Clare assumed, he was taking care of his still large erection. She felt more aroused than she had for a long time, and while he was out of the room her fingers slid down the front of her skirt and into her panties, until she was fingering herself. A little rub on her clitoris and she could feel herself shudder with anticipatory pleasure. It would be hard to hold on until the evening, and her partner, Lawrence, might not be in the mood.

Andy came back and began searching for something in a drawer. Clare observed his slender shoulders, small tight buttocks and curly hair. She felt an urge to stroke the back of his neck but then realised that she would really like him to do that to her. A hand on the back of her neck always made her shiver in a way that was deliciously exciting. He turned round and looked straight at her. She realised she was blushing. Did he know that she had been touching herself? Uncomfortable now with the dynamic that had been set up between them, and unsure how to use it, Clare left the office to turn on the photocopier in the main area and put the phones through. It was not really part of her job, but Clare needed something to busy herself with.

Other members of the department began to arrive, and Clare went about the normal tasks of the day, preparing her lecture notes for the afternoon and trying to spend time on her PhD. Her work was important to her; she was researching the role of the family in caring for the elderly in Asian communities, and she taught keen young trainee social workers. It could be demanding and exhausting work, as the number of students had increased in the last two years, but she was good at it. She was usually tired when she got home. Today she was both excited *and* tired – a curious mixture of feelings.

That evening, Lawrence announced that he had a bad cold coming on and was going to bed early. Clare tried to hide her disappointment, but Lawrence full of a cold was not a sexy object, so she sat alone downstairs curled up on the deep-green settee and watched *Eurotrash*. It was mildly titillating, but the excitement of the morning had dissipated, and the sight of some rather overweight Belgians dressed in pony-girl clothes did not restore it. Clare's body felt restless and unsatisfied. She craved a more subtle sensuality and allowed her mind and fingers to wander, letting her imagination work on a mental image of Andy, his cock now visible in her mind's eye in all its rude hardness.

Her fingers rubbed and stroked and drew back, delaying her orgasm to heighten her pleasure. She couldn't get Andy out of her thoughts. He wasn't her usual type, being far too slim – Clare had always preferred brawnier guys. But there was something about the energy that had sparked between them, and the fact that their attraction for each other was so inappropriate, that she found the thought of sex with him incredibly arousing. She recalled the image of him masturbating at his desk, and this did the trick as she succumbed to her lascivious thoughts, gasping with the intensity of her climax. Lawrence looked at her curiously when she went to bed later. He, it seemed, had not been able to sleep.

'You were making some strange noises down there,' he said accusingly.

'Was I?' replied Clare innocently, before changing the subject. 'Would you like a hot drink, a Lemsip or something, before you go to sleep?' Grumbling, he accepted the offer. Clare slid out of bed and, with an inaudible sigh, went down to the kitchen and thought about the next day at work. Somehow she knew that the frisson between her and Andy was not finished with. He had sensed her arousal, and she felt anxious and excited about the prospect of seeing him again.

The email arrived the next morning. Clare came into the office and, with a mixture of relief and disappointment, noted Andy was not there. She logged on, expecting the usual notices and queries about coursework.

There was one email of a different kind – from Andy – and she went into it last of all. It contained a website address accompanied by the words: 'Someone to watch over me – don't stop. Andy.'

Andy was out. So was Jo, the other part-time colleague who sometimes put in an appearance in the office, but suffered from a nervous complaint and was frequently off sick.

Clare looked in the diary. Andy would be out most of the day, involved in seminars at the sister college. She approached his computer terminal and logged on using his name and password, which he hadn't bothered to hide from her. She wasn't going to risk her career by being found logging into a porn site from her own machine. It was all right for Andy; his area of research led him legitimately into some strange highways and byways. But here, in the university, Big

Brother was watching, and staff had suffered the consequences in the past. She shivered at the thought, tapping in the site address he'd left her, and clicked on the search icon.

It was a site devoted to voyeurs. She spent a few minutes guiltily and furtively browsing its content. There were a number of first-hand accounts of watching or being watched, and several images appeared with shocking abruptness on the screen. Most were designed to cater for male tastes, and especially gay men. She found the small, slightly fuzzy pictures on the screen titillating but unsatisfactory, and was rather shocked by the other categories she was being invited to view – bestiality and teenage boys, for example. Were there any limits to this strange world she had stumbled upon? On the screen appeared a picture of a man sucking another man's dick, and at that point she moved away from the site, afraid that someone might come in. It was the most explicit image so far, and she'd barely started looking. She forced herself to log off and get on with her work.

Later in the day, Andy came back. He glanced at her without saying much, seeming aloof, then sat down and quite deliberately ran both hands up and down his thighs. He turned his computer on and sent her another email: 'Tomorrow morning. Eight thirty. Watch me.'

She did not reply. Already she could feel herself becoming moist and wanting to make her fantasy a reality. She would be there; she would be anywhere, for him.

She spent a restless night. Lawrence still felt unwell and grumbled about her tossing and turning.

'What's the matter with you?' he demanded.

'Oh, nothing. Just a lot going on at work.'

'Well, I can't sleep with you moving about all the time. I'll go next door.' Clare protested, but not too much, and Lawrence wrapped an old duvet around himself before, with a long-suffering air, moving into the spare bedroom. Finally Clare got some rest. How curious to have such secrets from her own boyfriend, she thought. How strange to be entering this twilight world of Internet porn and voyeurism – Lawrence would not have the faintest idea what his respectable girlfriend was up to.

The next morning she felt light-headed and excited. She left Lawrence still asleep and crept out of the house early and quietly.

The campus was quiet when she arrived, and she looked to see where Pat had got to, but she was noisily cleaning in the next office along. The Hoover masked all other sounds.

Clare approached the office, her heart thumping, and stood at the door, peeping through the gap, unsure exactly what she was waiting for. He was in there. He was sitting where he had sat yesterday, with his back turned towards her, and he was stroking himself, slowly and sensuously. She went hot and cold at the same time, and realised she was in the power of this slender, compelling man.

He swivelled round smoothly and slowly on his chair, his hand still on his cock, and this time she could see it, standing proud and erect in his lap, as he ran his hand up and down, faster and faster, not looking at her at all. Clare's skin was hot and her knees trembled. He slowed down, taking his time stroking himself so that she could see his cock's size and fullness. Suddenly he lifted his eyes and fixed her with a direct gaze of recognition, just in the split second before he ejaculated. Then his eyes closed, keeping the moment to himself. Clare's face had turned scarlet and her breath was coming in shallow gasps as she watched him. She was aching with longing – longing for him to enter her and extinguish her unbearable need. But Andy acted as if nothing had happened. He wiped himself off, got up, made some coffee, offered her one and, after collecting his lecture notes from a file, went off to deliver a lecture on 'Censorship and the Law' to a group of uninterested first-year students.

Clare was in turmoil. She had never, until that fateful morning, thought of Andy as sexually attractive. He had been in the post about three months, and had seemed reserved and hardworking, keeping himself to himself, though he did have a strangely compelling quality that had led Jo, the part-timer, to comment that he made her uneasy. Clearly there was more to him than they knew, and he had somehow managed with the most minimal communication to involve her, to get her to collude with him in an activity that could have both of them dismissed. What should she do? It was intoxicating stuff, and she knew she couldn't let it go. She was far too excited by him – by his distance, his lack of inhibition, his ability to take control over her sexual arousal – to stop now.

Another email awaited her at the end of the day: 'Your turn. Eight thirty.'

Now she was panic-stricken. She had agreed to be a voyeur for him; now he was asking her to reverse roles. She crept home that night to Lawrence, who was feeling a bit better and talking about football, but all the time her mind was on Andy.

Early the next morning, Clare dressed with care, wearing a skirt that unzipped at the side and her sexiest underwear. Could she go through with this? No – it was impossible. But she had seen him in intimate detail;

why should he not see her? She was terrified, yet drawn like a moth to a flame. She arrived at eight twenty and noticed him in the car park, waiting for her. She went into the office and sat down, spreading her legs slightly. Pat was nowhere to be seen. She half closed the door and undid the zip of her skirt. She was not wearing tights or stockings, as the weather was still warm. She slid her hand down her flat belly, into her underwear, and closed her eyes. She let her fingers rub along the edges of her sex lips, moistening them, then rotated her hand on her pubic hair and over her clitoris, feeling a familiar warmth growing in her body. She worked her fingers slowly at first, then faster. The door creaked slightly. He was there; he was there, watching her. She was beyond stopping. She inserted one finger and kept it there while she used the palm of her hand to rub herself. She felt light-headed with desire. It was amazing, like nothing she had experienced before – and it was all to do with him watching. Suddenly she came, her orgasm causing her to double up and exhale sharply. She looked over her shoulder towards the door. He was standing there, watching her most intimate moment. He nodded slowly, smiling, and Clare felt both vulnerable and wanton. What on earth would happen next in this curious relationship?

All the rest of the day she was in turmoil. What had she done? This was dangerous territory. She – who had always been so careful, so faithful, so fastidious about her body – had done something dirty, forbidden, but oh, so exciting. It was as if a door had been opened and a world of secret pleasures lay within, hers to enjoy.

Lawrence would never know. She hadn't slept with Andy, and she wasn't in love with him, so from that point of view she was innocent. This was fantasyland, nothing more. But a little voice told her that it was a great deal more. The thrill of the forbidden excited her more than Lawrence ever had.

Work took her mind away from the episode. Next day she read her email with anticipation and fear, but there was nothing. Andy sat at his desk, sorted out his notes, chatted about this and that to other members of staff and, for most of the time, was involved with students. She realised that like two illicit lovers, they were colluding in not talking about what had happened.

There was no email that day, or the next. Clare was bewildered. Was that it?

Was that all there was? Amazed at her own bravery, she took the initiative. She sent an email: *'I await further instructions.'*

When Andy received it he did not look at her; he gazed at the screen and smiled to himself. She left before he did that day, and there had been no reply by five-thirty. It was tantalising; he was really leading her on and, the more he did so, the more she tried to follow.

The next day, Friday, Clare found an envelope in her pigeonhole. Andy was already in. Could this be from him? Clare stayed outside their office to open it, her heart thumping. In the envelope was a map of the town, with a warehouse along the wharf outlined in red. The words 'Fourth floor, 2.30 tomorrow' were written in Andy's spidery hand. She knew the wharf area well. The old warehouses were rundown and some of them were empty. There were projects afoot to turn them into fancy apartments, but it hadn't happened yet. Clare shivered. No way, she thought, no way. I'm not putting myself at risk like that. It's asking for the worst kind of trouble to take this out into a public area.

She did not reply to the letter, and nor did Andy approach her. She was both glad and sorry that Lawrence had recovered from his cold and was intending to watch a football match on Saturday afternoon. She wanted Lawrence to protect her from herself, yet knew she would have rebelled if he had tried to stop her. She also knew there was no way she could confess to him what she had become involved in. He'd go mad. That evening, already having accepted that she might go, she wrote a letter saying that she had gone to meet a friend at the warehouse, and planned to leave it on their bed to cover herself, just in case anything happened to her. Hopefully she would get back before Lawrence did.

Saturday morning was filled with the usual chores of shopping, doing the washing and tidying up, and Lawrence, who had been off work with his cold, helped her a bit, guiltily, before asking whether she minded him going to the football without her. She assured him she didn't. She said goodbye to him at one-thirty and then turned her attention to herself. No, she wouldn't go. It was too weird, too creepy. What could happen in such a place? And the answer came back – 'anything'.

How should she dress? What should she wear under her clothes? She decided to dress casually, in her tracksuit and trainers, which made her look younger than she was but gave a freedom of movement she would not have in her more formal get-up. Underneath she wore a thong and a flimsy transparent bra. She would look very different from when Andy had last watched her. She realised she was highly excited but also scared stiff. While she was thinking, still dithering, her mobile phone rang. She picked it up as if it were red hot. 'Come on, you know you want to,' said the voice, commanding her. Then the caller hung up. It was two-fifteen.

* * *

She walked in a daze along the riverside until she came to the wharf area. Stone-built, five or six storeys high, these buildings had gantries and loading bays where ships had unloaded their cargo before the river had silted up and become unnavigable. The river was glistening this morning between two glossy mud banks, and assorted seabirds were scavenging for food along the water-line.

Halfway along, Clare came to the block of warehouses marked on the map. The names were carved in stone over the entrance at the side: Prospect Warehouse, India Warehouse, Deacon's Wharf. She turned down a lane between two high buildings and turned right. Here was the entrance to Shaftesbury Warehouse.

She took a deep breath and went through the side entrance. The huge scarred wooden door was already open. Her feet rang on the stone flags as she turned the corner and began the long ascent up the stone stairs.

Landing one. The door was locked with a brass padlock. There was a sign saying 'Steadfield Water Sculptures', but aside from the damp cement under the door there were no clues about what else might lie inside. She went on up to the second floor. 'Catlow and Son Electronic Components', said the sign. The door was open on this landing and she could hear someone whistling and a machine whirring. A radio was playing somewhere, at low volume. She walked up to the next landing. The third floor – she only had to go up one more flight. The third floor was shut up. Huge spiders had made their nests in the corners of the windows. They must have been there for generations, they were so thickly spread, Clare thought. The webs were like funnels, and the spiders' legs were just visible at their ends as they poked out of the centres. Clare shuddered.

Her feet were dragging now. On up to the fourth floor. There was a breeze on her face, no doubt from a hole in the roof or a broken window. It was quiet up here. Who would be waiting for her? Her heart was pounding. Finally she reached the fourth floor. The heavy wooden door was closed, and she slowly pushed it open. Beyond was a bare-boarded room, vast in its proportions and, as far as she could see, empty.

She stood in the doorway, waiting. There appeared to be no one there. She was scared now; scared in case someone suddenly appeared and frightened her. She tiptoed into the ballroom-like space and looked around. There was nothing here except a few owl feathers and a hole in the ceiling, allowing her to look up and see the roof, collapsed in one place where the rain had got in. She walked to the window and looked out. Opposite was another warehouse, and another window. It was about twenty feet away from her and, as she peered across, she suddenly became aware of movement behind the glass. She tried to make sense of what she was seeing.

Suddenly the whole scene became sharply focused. There was a man – not Andy – wearing a black mask over the upper part of his face, and a thin woman, also masked; both of them turned to look towards her. The man grinned at Clare, licking his lips and sneering suggestively. She saw he was naked except for a black harness around his genitals, which held a black leather penis sheath in place. His cock was erect, and Clare started when he pressed himself close to the glass and began to rub himself up and down. His partner ran her fingers across his body in a grotesque parody of love-making, while he grinned and looked at Clare. As she stood there, transfixed, the man turned to the woman, took off his leather sheath and entered her, standing up. They were perfectly matched for height. As if they were in a performance piece, they assumed another position with exaggerated gestures, the woman bending over with her legs straight while the man entered her from behind, slowly pulling out of her before pushing forcefully again and again into her cunt. And all the while the man was grinning at Clare.

She was faint with excitement and fear. She was so wrapped up in watching the couple perform their double act that she never heard the footsteps coming behind her.

Ah! A hand was over her mouth. The other held her firmly.

'Shh. Watch.'

She ceased to struggle, realising it was useless. The hand over her mouth moved away and gently began to stroke her hair, her neck and her sides. One hand slipped into her tracksuit bottoms and the other slid inside her top, undoing her bra. Clare wanted it, wanted it badly. She continued to watch the couple gyrating. She did not want to see the person who was touching her; she could continue to look at the other two and at the same time be aware of the person behind her, touching her with such expertise. The hands moved down to her thong and tweaked it playfully up into her bottom-crack. Then fingers brushed her pubic hair; and she shivered with arousal. The couple had stopped their activity and were now watching Clare and the person with her. They were smiling and encouraging her.

The person behind her – whom she imagined was Andy – indicated that she should bend over. His strong hands put pressure on her back then eased her tracksuit bottoms down her legs. She stood there, bent over in her thong, her firm rounded breasts with their erect pink nipples bobbing slightly as she panted with excitement. She obeyed the will of the man, and was glad she was supple from her yoga training. Would he fuck her? She felt disappointment mixed with relief when a smooth plastic object entered her then turned on, vibrating. The person behind her knew just how to use it, varying the strokes – fast, slow, gentle, thrusting – then returning it slowly over her clitoris. She could hold on no longer. She pulled the vibrator towards her clit and rubbed it against herself before collapsing in a heap on the floor, gyrating as her body spasmed in orgasm. Her eyes were shut for several moments as she recovered from her post-orgasmic haze. When she opened them, there was no sign of her partner, and the couple in the other building had gone too. All that was left was her tracksuit and her trainers, lying forlornly in a dusty pile near the window. Quickly and guiltily she got dressed and, in a strangely detached, dreamlike state, made her way home.

Lawrence noticed how odd she was when he returned from the match. She wouldn't talk to him and kept avoiding his eyes. He became worried and then angry, demanding to know what the hell was wrong. She couldn't tell him, of course, but pleaded she had a cold coming on and went to bed. He could hardly complain. Clare was quiet on Sunday, and all Lawrence could get out of her was that she had caught his cold – and indeed she did feel very unwell.

On Monday morning Clare was not fit to work and phoned in sick, praying it would not be Andy who answered. But it was. He was correct, formal and matter of fact. He would inform the office and her students. She should come back when she felt better. He made no mention of Saturday. She felt frightened at the thought of what she had done and her body still remembered the touch of his hands and the vibrator between her legs. She felt unclean, suddenly, and had a long hot bath to restore her equilibrium.

She made it into work on Wednesday, pink-nosed and watery-eyed. Andy was out, but there was a message waiting for her. It said: 'Are you still in the game?'

She replied: 'I don't know what the game is.'

The next day there was a reply: 'The game is watching. Do you wish to play?'

How do I say 'No'? Clare wondered. She emailed back: 'Do I have a choice?'

The reply came swiftly: 'You have a choice.'

She did not reply. There were no more emails that week. He was waiting for her to make up her mind, and he seemed in no hurry about it.

The weekend seemed without excitement, and she viewed the prospect of work again the following week with something approaching eagerness.

Early on Monday morning, Pat stopped her as she was about to enter the suite of offices. With a furtiveness Clare had not seen in her before, the cleaner drew her to one side.

'You know him in there?'

Clare nodded, fearful of what was coming next.

'You want to be careful. I went into the room to water the plants just now, and he –' Pat lowered her voice to a hushed whisper '– was, you know, looking at something strange on his computer. Porn, I call it. So you be careful. You won't tell him I spoke to you, will you?'

Clare promised she wouldn't, adding that Andy sometimes looked at explicit images in the course of his work. She could tell Pat didn't believe her.

When she went in, however, Andy was innocently filing notes and greeted her with his usual 'Morning'.

Clare decided the next move should come from him. Suddenly she felt less afraid of him and actually rather amused.

There was an email waiting for her: 'Further delights await you. Open the attachment if you wish to know more.'

As soon as he was out of the room she opened the attached document. It was in the form of a letter from a woman called Charlotte, who spoke of how much she enjoyed being watched having sex with her partner, Charles. Underneath was an address on the outskirts of town with a time given as nine-thirty the following Thursday.

When Thursday came, Clare had a meal with Lawrence and told him in all innocence that she was slipping out later to visit a friend. Lawrence as usual did not ask questions. He was trusting; too trusting, Clare thought. Already she was damp with anticipation.

The venue turned out to be a small semi-detached house, respectable and neatly kept with an entry phone by the door. At nine-thirty exactly, heart pounding, Clare pressed the doorbell. There was a buzz as the door catch was released. She stepped inside. The hall was painted a rich red and lit with antique lamps that rested on two small mahogany tables. A gilt-edged mirror hung on the wall. Clare waited for further instructions. A woman's voice from a hidden speaker said: 'Come in to the room on your left.' She did as she was told and entered the room.

It was very different from anything she had imagined – far more opulent. The walls were dark, and the bay window was hung with expensive and heavy plum-coloured drapes. There was also a double water-bed there, covered by a silky Oriental quilt. Bolsters and pillows were stacked up at one end: comfort was paramount, it seemed. Two huge candles in wall sconces gave a flickering light to the room. There were no chairs, so Clare perched on the end of the bed, feeling the ripples beneath her as she did so. A delicious tingle ran through her thighs and between her legs. She felt quite overcome with anticipation and excitement, a heady mix. She studied the room more closely. A large mirror hung from the wall facing the bed. She walked across to it and considered looking behind it to find what she was sure would be there, a viewing window. However, she decided against doing this to preserve the mystery. She just had to assume she was being watched. The thought unnerved her, but again she felt the rush of excitement. A voice came from the speaker.

'You are right, the mirror is for viewing. We are glad you did not decide to investigate more fully. Under the cushions on the bed you will find some clothing. Please put it on.'

Clare reached under the cushions and drew out a shiny black plastic catsuit. She held it up to inspect it. Never had she worn anything so clinging and reveal- ing, or anything that would cover her so tightly and completely. Lawrence wasn't into dressing up, and she had never been bold enough to buy such things for her own pleasure. Now, in this strange house of delights, was her first opportunity to explore fetishism as well as voyeurism. She was embarrassed taking off her clothes at first, but when she slid her naked body into the strange, slinky garment, she felt very different and instantly more confident. She stood erect in front of the mirror, hands on her hips, surveying her trim figure clad in the clinging black PVC. The ring at the top of the zip under her chin glinted in the candlelight. She looked fantastic.

'The boots are by the bed,' the voice intoned. 'Put them on.'

Four-inch heels! Clare had never worn anything so high. She teetered a bit, trying to get her balance. The boots were soft PVC and they zipped up reassuringly to complete the outfit.

'You may wish to wear a mask,' said the voice. 'There is one under the pillow where you found the body suit.'

Clare found a neat little mask, which covered the top of her face. She thought there was probably a whip somewhere, too, but decided not to search for it. She felt amazingly alive and excited, naked inside her suit, which fitted snugly across her bottom and between her legs. She lay back on the bed and shut her eyes, revelling in the feel of the plastic material and wondering what her observers would think of her. Would they be getting as aroused as she was? Would Andy be there, wanking a huge erection? The door opened quietly, and Clare was immediately alert.

It was a woman – tall, full bosomed and dressed in an elaborate and ornate robe, with a dark purple turban over her hair. She reminded Clare of an opera star about to perform in *Aida*. She watched as the woman approached her, noticing how her heavily made-up eyes sparkled as they scrutinised her. Her fingers were covered in diamond rings, and Clare watched in fascination as the woman's blood-red nails and jewel-encrusted fingers moved up and down her catsuited body, appraising her. She spoke in a deep husky voice that had an East European accent.

'You are new to this, yes?'

Clare nodded.

'Very nice.'

What was going to happen? Clare hadn't thought that such a woman might be involved. But she didn't mind.

'Stand up and unzip the suit.' It was an order. She swung her legs over the edge of the bed and stood up, swaying a little in the high heels. The woman stood back and surveyed her. Clare felt for the fastener at her neck and pulled it down slowly, teasingly, then stood with her legs apart, spike heels digging into the floor, her firm body ready to obey this woman. Her breasts bulged either side of the opening, firm mounds only partly revealed, and as the zip moved down a little patch of dark pubic hair showed at the base. Clare tucked her hand into the opening, the woman watching her closely.

Clare was enjoying herself, and her curious companion made no move to get close to her, or to take off her own clothes.

'Excite yourself, please,' came the order. 'This is what I want to see.' The woman sat on the edge of the bed and moved Clare a little with her hand so that she was standing in front of the mirror, sideways on. Clare knew others were watching, which excited her even more. She imagined what Lawrence would say if he saw her. He certainly wouldn't recognise her now!

Clare let her fingers take over. She caressed her breasts through the PVC then slid her hands down her body to the lips of her sex. The woman watched intently.

'I think we will let the others join us,' she said. Clare paused, uncertain how to respond, as the woman left the room. She could not reach a climax standing in such a position, and the zip was starting to hurt her hand. She lay down on the bed to get more comfortable. Then the door opened quietly as a dark-haired man and a blonde woman entered, masked, dressed in dark silk sarongs and looking very exotic. Clare closed her eyes and gave herself over to the peculiar experience. So, she was to be the only one dressed in fetish clothes. Perhaps that was their thing.

The man approached Clare and, without delay,

reached into the suit and began stroking her breasts. He was certainly very forward! It was a deliciously exciting feeling and the anonymity of the masks allowed her to feel more confident about what was happening. It was slightly impersonal but all the more exciting for it. Then the blonde climbed onto the bed and immediately went for Clare's bottom half, easing her hand into the catsuit and finding her soft pubic hair. Clare squirmed, suddenly wanting closer contact with them and more freedom from her constricting outfit.

'Shall I help you?' she asked, reaching forwards and easing the garment off Clare's shoulders a little. 'There, that's better.'

'Thank you.' Clare still felt constrained, but she was free enough to be able to get the couple's hands where she wanted them. The woman reached into a fold in her sarong.

'You may like to use this –' she handed Clare a small vibrating egg '– for inside.' Breathless, Clare nodded, reaching into the suit and tucking the small, smooth egg into the folds of her pussy. It was an incredible sensation. She realised they were being careful with her, and noting her responses. The man especially was studying her closely. Clare closed her eyes, wallowing in the sensation.

The man gently ran his finger around Clare's lips, tracing their outline. She knew what was coming as he reached underneath his garment. She opened her mouth to receive his cock, which she was pleased to see was meaty and hard. She writhed with pleasure, licking the man's cock a little, then paused.

'Please continue,' he said. The voice was deep and sexy. Clare, intensely excited, obeyed at once, and found herself trembling as the intensity of her arousal from the vibrating egg made her feel weak. The man rubbed his cock over her face then withdrew, and Clare lay back on the bed, gasping as the couple began to pleasure each another. Were they the couple she had seen at the warehouse? She thought they were, and hoped they would let her join in with their games. Clare watched, fascinated, as the man entered his partner and thrust hard. The woman moaned her delight and encouraged him, rubbing her hands all over his body. It was obvious that performing was their thing. Clare was squirming again now, rubbing the vibrating egg harder against her clit. The man then turned to her, his dark eyes glittering behind the mask in the half-light of the room.

'Do you want to join in?' he asked. Clare nodded. Before she knew what was happening, he withdrew from his partner and fished the vibrating egg out of Clare's suit, denying her the orgasm she was about to have. He passed it to the woman, who then reached out and placed it back in Clare's hand before gripping her wrist and directed it towards her own cunt as she lay on her back. Overcoming all inhibitions, Clare parted the woman's thighs and gently played the egg up and down over her clit in the rhythm she liked herself. Breathless with desire, she stroked the insides of the woman's thighs and pressed the egg right into the folds of her pussy. The man, hugely erect, positioned himself behind Clare, then grasped her buttocks and began to knead them. Slowly he drew the PVC suit down over her shoulders and back, skilfully stripping her.

Again Clare bent forwards over the woman, keen to see her come, all the time aware of the tantalising view she herself was presenting to the stranger behind her. Then she felt him pull the suit over her buttocks and slide his hand into her pussy. After a moment's hesitation he entered her from behind without difficulty.

Clare had got so wet that she was more than ready for sex. She gasped in delight and shock, but didn't stop what she was doing to the blonde woman. She realised that, for the first time, she was being unfaithful to Lawrence, but she was beyond caring. There was no way she could turn away from this intensely sexual activity. It was too delicious.

Suddenly, at the sight of her partner fucking this newcomer to their games, the blonde woman cried out in delight and pulled Clare's hands tightly between her legs. Clare was amazed at what she had done: she had made another woman come, albeit with the help of the egg. The sight of this beautiful stranger in the throes of her orgasm threw Clare into a frenzy of desire. Without delay she began frantically rubbing at her own clit, her face mashed in between the legs of the blonde woman as the man pounded her from behind. She breathed in the woman's scent, overcome with the sense of how wanton she was being. Then, with a shuddering climax, Clare fell forwards onto the woman. The sight of the two women sprawled before him triggered the man's own violent orgasm, and he gripped Clare tightly around the hips as he pumped his final, exquisite strokes.

They all lay still for a few moments, then the man slowly rose to his feet, put on his sarong and kissed Clare's hand with a small bow. His partner kissed her on the lips.

'A debut to be proud of,' he said, before leaving the room with his partner. Once alone, Clare sat up, uncertain whether she was free to go. She looked for her clothes and began to dress. The door opened and the older woman came in.

'This is enough for today,' she said. 'You may get dressed. Do you want to see who has been watching you?' She didn't, not really, but the woman took no notice. She removed the mirror, and behind it a screen appeared showing three masked figures. One had a familiar build and hair. Could it be Andy? At that moment he grinned, and she knew she was caught up in something she could not escape. But she had no wish to. She couldn't be absolutely certain from this distance that the masked, smiling man was Andy. She would say nothing and see what happened. Better not to know. It would be a mystery. 'You can play again,' said the woman, noting Clare's response to the man on the screen, 'if you wish to.' The woman flicked the screen off and left the room, and Clare finished dressing again before letting herself out of the unassuming suburban house. Life was going to be very different from now on.

LOOK OUT FOR THE ALL-NEW BLACK LACE BOOKS – AVAILABLE NOW!

THE AMULET
Lisette Allen
ISBN 0 352 33019 8

Roman Britain, near the end of the second century. Catarina, an orphan adopted by the pagan Celts, has grown into a beautiful young woman with the gift of second sight. When her tribe captures a Roman garrison, she falls in love with their hunky leader, Alexius. Yet he betrays her, stealing her precious amulet. Vowing revenge, Catarina follows Alexius to Rome, but the salacious pagan rituals and endless orgies prove to be a formidable distraction. **Wonderfully decadent fiction from a pioneer of female erotica.**

Coming in February

COMING ROUND THE MOUNTAIN
Tabitha Flyte
ISBN 0 352 33873 3

Flighty Lauren is on the top of the world, literally, travelling in the Himalayas to 'find herself'. But while enjoying the rugged landscape she runs into Callum, her first ever boyfriend, and soon *everything* turns rocky. Lauren still loves Callum, Callum still loves Lauren; the problem is that he is on his honeymoon. Then, while trekking, Callum gets altitude sickness. Lauren wants to take care of him and tend to his every need, but what will happen if his new wife finds out? **A jaunty sex comedy for the backpack generation.**

FEMININE WILES
Karina Moore
ISBN O 352 33874 1

Young American art student Kelly Aslett is spending the summer in Paris
before flying back to California to claim her inheritance when she falls in
lust and love with gorgeous French painter, Luc Duras. But her
stepmother – the scheming and hedonistic Marissa – is determined to
claim the luxury house for herself. Still in love with Luc, Kelly is horrified
to find herself sexually entranced by the enigmatic figure of Johnny
Casigelli, a ruthless but very sexy villain Marissa has enlisted in her
scheme to wrestle the inheritance away from Kelly. Will she succumb to
his masculine charms, or can she use her feminine wiles to gain what is
rightfully hers? **A high-octane tale of erotic obsession and sexual rivalry.**

Coming in March

GOING DEEP
Kimberley Dean
ISBN O 352 33876 8

Sporty Brynn Montgomery returns to teach at the college where she
used to be a cheerleader but, to her horror, finds that football player
Cody Jones, who scandalised her name ten years previously, is now the
coach. Soon Brynn is caught up in a clash of pads, a shimmer of pom-
poms and the lust of healthy athletes. However, Cody is still a wolfish
predator and neither he nor his buddies are going to let Brynn forget
what she did that fateful night back in high school. **Rip-roaring,
testosterone-fuelled fun set among the jocks and babes of the Ivy
League.**

UNHALLOWED RITES
Martine Marquand
ISBN 0 352 33222 0

Twenty-year-old Allegra is bored with life in her guardian's Venetian palazzo – until temptation draws her to look at the curious pictures he keeps in his private chamber. Physically awakened to womanhood, she tries to deny her new passion by submitting to life as a nun. But the strange order of the Convent of Santa Clesira provides new tests and temptations, forcing her to perform ritual acts with men and women who inhabit her sheltered world. **A brooding story of art and lust in the cloisters.**

Black Lace Booklist

Information is correct at time of printing. To avoid disappointment check availability before ordering. Go to www.blacklace-books.co.uk. All books are priced £6.99 unless another price is given.

BLACK LACE BOOKS WITH A CONTEMPORARY SETTING

☐ IN THE FLESH Emma Holly	ISBN 0 352 33498 3	£5.99
☐ SHAMELESS Stella Black	ISBN 0 352 33485 1	£5.99
☐ INTENSE BLUE Lyn Wood	ISBN 0 352 33496 7	£5.99
☐ THE NAKED TRUTH Natasha Rostova	ISBN 0 352 33497 5	£5.99
☐ A SPORTING CHANCE Susie Raymond	ISBN 0 352 33501 7	£5.99
☐ TAKING LIBERTIES Susie Raymond	ISBN 0 352 33357 X	£5.99
☐ A SCANDALOUS AFFAIR Holly Graham	ISBN 0 352 33523 8	£5.99
☐ THE NAKED FLAME Crystalle Valentino	ISBN 0 352 33528 9	£5.99
☐ ON THE EDGE Laura Hamilton	ISBN 0 352 33534 3	£5.99
☐ LURED BY LUST Tania Picarda	ISBN 0 352 33533 5	£5.99
☐ THE HOTTEST PLACE Tabitha Flyte	ISBN 0 352 33536 X	£5.99
☐ THE NINETY DAYS OF GENEVIEVE Lucinda Carrington	ISBN 0 352 33070 8	£5.99
☐ DREAMING SPIRES Juliet Hastings	ISBN 0 352 33584 X	
☐ THE TRANSFORMATION Natasha Rostova	ISBN 0 352 33311 1	
☐ SIN.NET Helena Ravenscroft	ISBN 0 352 33598 X	
☐ TWO WEEKS IN TANGIER Annabel Lee	ISBN 0 352 33599 8	
☐ HIGHLAND FLING Jane Justine	ISBN 0 352 33616 1	
☐ PLAYING HARD Tina Troy	ISBN 0 352 33617 X	
☐ SYMPHONY X Jasmine Stone	ISBN 0 352 33629 3	
☐ SUMMER FEVER Anna Ricci	ISBN 0 352 33625 0	
☐ CONTINUUM Portia Da Costa	ISBN 0 352 33120 8	
☐ OPENING ACTS Suki Cunningham	ISBN 0 352 33630 7	
☐ FULL STEAM AHEAD Tabitha Flyte	ISBN 0 352 33637 4	
☐ A SECRET PLACE Ella Broussard	ISBN 0 352 33307 3	
☐ GAME FOR ANYTHING Lyn Wood	ISBN 0 352 33639 0	
☐ CHEAP TRICK Astrid Fox	ISBN 0 352 33640 4	
☐ ALL THE TRIMMINGS Tesni Morgan	ISBN 0 352 33641 3	

☐ ARIA APPASSIONATA Juliet Hastings   ISBN 0 352 33056 2
☐ THE RELUCTANT PRINCESS Patty Glenn   ISBN 0 352 33809 1
☐ WILD IN THE COUNTRY Monica Belle   ISBN 0 352 33824 5
☐ THE TUTOR Portia Da Costa   ISBN 0 352 32946 7
☐ SEXUAL STRATEGY Felice de Vere   ISBN 0 352 33843 1
☐ HARD BLUE MIDNIGHT Alaine Hood   ISBNO 352 33851 2

BLACK LACE BOOKS WITH AN HISTORICAL SETTING

☐ PRIMAL SKIN Leona Benkt Rhys   ISBN 0 352 33500 9   £5.99
☐ DEVIL'S FIRE Melissa MacNeal   ISBN 0 352 33527 0   £5.99
☐ DARKER THAN LOVE Kristina Lloyd   ISBN 0 352 33279 4
☐ THE CAPTIVATION Natasha Rostova   ISBN 0 352 33234 4
☐ MINX Megan Blythe   ISBN 0 352 33638 2
☐ JULIET RISING Cleo Cordell   ISBN 0 352 32938 6
☐ DEMON'S DARE Melissa MacNeal   ISBN 0 352 33683 8
☐ DIVINE TORMENT Janine Ashbless   ISBN 0 352 33719 2
☐ SATAN'S ANGEL Melissa MacNeal   ISBN 0 352 33726 5
☐ THE INTIMATE EYE Georgia Angelis   ISBN 0 352 33004 X
☐ OPAL DARKNESS Cleo Cordell   ISBN 0 352 33033 3
☐ SILKEN CHAINS Jodi Nicol   ISBN 0 352 33143 7
☐ EVIL'S NIECE Melissa MacNeal   ISBN 0 352 33781 8
☐ ACE OF HEARTS Lisette Allen   ISBN 0 352 33059 7
☐ A GENTLEMAN'S WAGER Madelynne Ellis   ISBN 0 352 33800 8
☐ THE LION LOVER Mercedes Kelly   ISBN 0 352 33162 3
☐ ARTISTIC LICENCE Vivienne La Fay   ISBN 0 352 33210 7

BLACK LACE ANTHOLOGIES

☐ WICKED WORDS 6 Various   ISBN 0 352 33590 0
☐ WICKED WORDS 8 Various   ISBN 0 352 33787 7
☐ THE BEST OF BLACK LACE 2 Various   ISBN 0 352 33718 4

BLACK LACE NON-FICTION

☐ THE BLACK LACE BOOK OF WOMEN'S SEXUAL   ISBN 0 352 33793 1   £6.99
   FANTASIES Ed. Kerri Sharp

To find out the latest information about Black Lace titles, check out the website: www.blacklace-books.co.uk or send for a booklist with complete synopses by writing to:

Black Lace Booklist, Virgin Books Ltd
Thames Wharf Studios
Rainville Road
London W6 9HA

Please include an SAE of decent size. Please note only British stamps are valid.

Our privacy policy
We will not disclose information you supply us to any other parties. We will not disclose any information which identifies you personally to any person without your express consent.

From time to time we may send out information about Black Lace books and special offers. Please tick here if you do not wish to receive Black Lace information. ❏

Please send me the books I have ticked above.

Name ....

Address ....

....

....

....

Post Code ....

Send to: Cash Sales, Black Lace Books, Thames Wharf Studios, Rainville Road, London W6 9HA.

US customers: for prices and details of how to order books for delivery by mail, call 1-800-343-4499.

Please enclose a cheque or postal order, made payable to Virgin Books Ltd, to the value of the books you have ordered plus postage and packing costs as follows:

UK and BFPO – £1.00 for the first book, 50p for each subsequent book.

Overseas (including Republic of Ireland) – £2.00 for the first book, £1.00 for each subsequent book.

If you would prefer to pay by VISA, ACCESS/MASTERCARD, DINERS CLUB, AMEX or SWITCH, please write your card number and expiry date here:

....

Signature ....

Please allow up to 28 days for delivery.